A MARRIAGE OF CONVENIEN(

If You GIVE A

Billionaire

A BRIDE

ANN EINERSON

Paperback ISBN: 978-1-960325-08-2

Cover Design by Sarah, Okay Creations

Dev Edited by Tabitha Overby; Bryanna, @bryannareads, Kaity, @bookswithkaity

Edited by Paula Dawn, LilyPad Lit

Proofread by Britt Taylor, Paperback Proofreader

Formatted by Jovana Shirley, Unforeseen Editing

*To those who feel unworthy—you are seen,
and you are valued beyond measure.*

PLAYLIST

Marry You - Bruno Mars
Make You Mine - Madison Beer
we can't be friends (wait for your love) - Ariana Grande
Dear Future Husband - Meghan Trainor
Paper Rings - Taylor Swift
Until I Found You - Stephen Sanchez
Love Of My Life - Harry Styles
i like the way you kiss me - Artemas
Can't Help Falling in Love - Haley Reinhart
All of Me - John Legend
Kiss Me - Ed Sheeran
Unconditionally - Katy Perry
Wanted - Hunter Hayes
I Guess I'm In Love - Clinton Kane
Surround You - Echosmith

AUTHOR'S NOTE

Hey, Reader!

Thank you for picking up *If You Give a Billionaire a Bride*. This is an interconnected standalone in the Aspen Grove series and can be read on its own.

If You Give a Billionaire a Bride is a marriage of convenience that starts with a Vegas wedding between a reformed playboy and his best friend's sister in a banter-filled, spicy billionaire romance. It's a low drama, light and fluffy romance meant to tug at your heartstrings and have you swooning over Cash and Everly's chaotic love story. It's a slow burn, but when the spice hits, it hits hard.

If You Give a Billionaire a Bride contains explicit sexual content, profanity, mention of an absentee parent, mention of bullying (past, off page), mention of car accident (past, off page), facial scar resulting from accident, emotional/verbal parental abuse.

Reading is meant to be your happy place—choose yourself, your needs, and your happiness first!

Xoxo,

Ann Einerson

If you give a billionaire a bride, he may be tempted to marry her in Vegas after one too many drinks. And if he marries her in Vegas, he'll convince her to move in with him. He'll make sure they share a room, buy her nice things and constantly call her "wifey," because he plans to keep her forever…

PROLOGUE

CASH

"WE SHOULD BREAK UP," WHITNEY announces on our way out of algebra class.

Her unfeeling declaration shouldn't surprise me since I knew this was inevitable, but I didn't expect her to dump me a few hours before prom.

I stop in the middle of the hallway, not caring that I'm blocking traffic. "Why now?" I ask, tightening my grip on my backpack straps.

She looks down at her pink painted nails, refusing to make eye contact with me.

"Things have been different since the accident. You're different." *Translation: Now that your face is fucked up, I can barely stand to look at you.* "Graduation is right around the corner, and with me leaving for Princeton at the beginning of the summer, it only makes sense for us to part ways now." *Translation: I want a clean break so I can date someone I'm not embarrassed to be seen with.*

Now that I'm no longer the "ruggedly handsome lacrosse player," as she so fondly used to call me, she's eager to replace me with someone who won't ruin pictures with a jagged scar marring half his face.

"Cash, are you listening to me?" She waves her hand in front of me to grab my attention when I don't respond.

"My face may be fucked up but my ears work just fine, Whit," I say through gritted teeth.

"What did I say?" she challenges, hands on her hips.

"That you're embarrassed to be seen with me, and you want to date other people. Does that sum it up?" Okay, so those weren't her exact words, but we both know that's what she's thinking.

"You're twisting what I said," she retorts, raising her voice and taking a defensive stance, arms folded tightly across her chest.

The sound of someone snickering catches my attention. That's when I notice the sizable crowd of students lingering in the hall, interested to hear how this argument unfolds.

"You're right. We have grown apart," I say, keeping my voice steady.

Whitney's eyes widen in shock at hearing me agree. That's when *she* notices our audience, causing a sudden shift in her blasé attitude. She gets fidgety and twirls a piece of hair around her finger, shifting from foot to foot.

"What are you saying?" she demands, glancing back at her friends who have joined the group of spectators.

From her reaction, one would assume she's the one being dumped in front of an audience, not the other way around.

"We should break up," I say, echoing her earlier declaration.

"Just like that?" she demands. "You're not even going to try to convince me to change my mind? How could you humiliate me in front of—"

"Cut the theatrics, Whitney," Theo interrupts her rant, standing beside me in a silent show of support. "You said it yourself. It's over. Don't embarrass yourself more than you already have."

He must have been in the crowd watching things play out. We've been best friends since preschool, and he's one of the few people I can count on always to have my back.

"Mind your own business, Theo," Whitney spits out. "This is a private conversation between me and my boyfriend."

"Ex-boyfriend," I interject. "You were just telling me you wanted to break up, remember?"

"And from where I'm standing, this is as far from private as you can get," Theo adds. "Now, why don't you and your friends get lost?" He shoos her like a dog.

Whitney's cheeks turn bright red when the hallway fills with laughter. "Are you really going to just stand there and let him disrespect me?" she whines.

"Theo's right. It's best if you leave," I say calmly.

"You'll be sorry," she fumes. "Don't come begging to win me back when you see me with my new prom date tonight. He's a freshman in college," she throws in my face before storming away.

Her entourage hurries after her, and the crowd quickly disperses now that the spectacle is over.

3

It shouldn't surprise me that she has another date lined up. She would never risk the humiliation of going alone.

"Good riddance," Theo mumbles under his breath. "Remind me again why you dated her. She is such a diva."

"I don't know." I shrug. "She was nice when we first met. Plus, all the guys on the lacrosse team kept saying we'd be good together, so I figured, why not?"

In truth, I can't be with the girl I've always wanted, and Whitney was a welcome distraction. She is attractive and popular and made me feel important—until my accident.

"College chicks are going to fucking love your scar. It makes you look badass." Theo pats me on the back.

"Thanks, man," I say, ready to move on from this topic. "Where's Everly?" I scan the hall as the group disperses, but she's nowhere to be seen.

Everly, Theo's twin sister, tags along most of the time, making her one of my closest friends.

The smug expression on Theo's face turns serious. "You're not the only one who was stood up for prom. Jacob broke things off with Everly right before eighth period." His voice drips with fury. "He left her crying alone in the school parking lot."

I clench my fists at my side, the urge to kick Jacob's ass building inside me. Everly is the sweetest, most beautiful girl in school, and frankly Jacob never deserved her.

"What a scumbag," I spit out in disgust. "He needs to be put in his place." No one disrespects Everly and gets away with it.

"Get in line," he snickers.

"Where is she now?"

4

"I'm not sure. She said she wanted to be alone and took off on her bike," Theo says with a worried frown. "I should skip prom and go look for her. I'm sure Cara will understand if I have to cancel our date."

I shake my head. "There's no reason for you to spend the night wallowing in misery like the rest of us. Go home and get ready to pick up Cara. Don't worry, I'll find Everly." There's only one place she would go if she wanted to be alone without dealing with unwanted visitors.

Except for me, that is.

"Are you sure?" Theo asks, concern etched on his face.

"Absolutely. We'll make a night of it," I assure him.

If I could convince Everly to attend prom with me, I'd do it, but knowing her as I do, she'll want to stay as far away from Jacob and the dance as possible.

Theo nudges me with a mischievous glint in his eye. "Look, there's Jacob now." I glance over to him walking toward the school entrance with his friends. "Are you thinking what I'm thinking?" Theo questions.

"That it's time for payback?" I smirk, cracking my knuckles as I stalk toward Jacob.

Theo cracks. "You read my mind."

First, I'm going to make Jacob Barlow pay for hurting Everly, and then I'm going to find her so I can mend her broken heart.

As I pull up to the old Miller place, a smile crosses my lips when I spot Everly's robin-blue bike parked against the house.

The place has been abandoned for over twenty years, but it's become the hangout spot for my siblings and friends. Ev, in particular, has taken a liking to it and comes here when she needs peace and quiet.

I make my way through the overgrown lawn to the backyard, where I find Everly. She's stretched out on a flannel blanket, her sanctuary under the shade of the giant oak tree, lost in a book. Her black hair falls in waves down her back, a sight that always takes my breath away. I smile when I see she's wearing her favorite pair of Doc Martens.

Seeing her like this takes me back to the day in our tenth-grade English class when she came in wearing a white V-neck top, light-wash jeans, and those same Docs. Even though we've known each other our whole lives, that was the first time I saw her in a new light and I swear my heart skipped a beat when she waved at me with her signature megawatt smile. I couldn't take my eyes off her during class.

When the bell rang, Theo grabbed me by the collar and dragged me out into the hall, shoving me against the closest set of lockers. He noticed me watching Everly and warned me she was off-limits.

I couldn't jeopardize our friendship because of a crush on his sister, so I did my best to suppress my feelings for Everly. It wasn't easy. Something about her called to me, and it kept drawing me in like a gravitational pull, despite my best efforts.

Like she can sense that I'm thinking about her, she looks up at me with tear-stained cheeks as I approach. My chest tightens at seeing her sad. I would do anything to take away her pain and bring a smile to her face.

"Mind if I join you? I brought dinner." I hold up a bag of takeout from Willow Creek Café—Her favorite restaurant in Aspen Grove.

"Did Theo send you?" She eyes the food warily.

"No. He told me what happened with Jacob, and I figured this is where you'd be," I answer truthfully.

Without waiting for an invitation, I sit on the blanket and set the bag in front of me. Everly watches with interest as I take out two bacon cheeseburgers, fries, and a chocolate shake topped with extra whipped cream and a cherry—all her favorites.

"Why come if you knew I wanted to be alone?" There's a hint of sass in her voice.

She's not afraid to go head-to-head with me and doesn't hesitate to set me straight when I'm out of line.

"My mom always says chocolate is the best cure for a broken heart." I hold out the shake, a smile tugging at my lips when she takes it.

"She's absolutely right." Everly grins as she takes a sip. "Want to tell me why you're here with me instead of at prom?"

"Whitney dumped me after school," I state flatly.

"Oh, Cash, I'm sorry." Everly places her hand on my arm. "I hate that bitch," she says with conviction.

Her touch sends a jolt of electricity down my spine, and it takes every ounce of willpower to maintain a poker face. She has no idea how I really feel about her, and it has to stay that way.

A few weeks after Theo told me Everly was off-limits, Whitney showed interest in me, and I threw all my energy into our budding relationship. She was the perfect distraction, helping me temporarily forget about my attraction to Everly, those feelings simmering below the surface.

"It's for the best." I shrug, reaching across Everly to grab a fry.

"Oh my god, Stafford," she gasps when she spots the swollen knuckles on my left hand.

"What happened?"

I grin at her use of my last name. She's called me that since ninth grade when I started playing lacrosse. *Stafford* was stitched across the back of my jersey, and the nickname stuck. Whitney has always resented that Everly calls me that, but I couldn't care less what she thinks now.

I like it when Everly uses it. I love it.

"Tell me what you did," she presses when I don't answer her question right away.

"Jacob Barlow said something that pissed me off, so I punched him in the face," I tell her with a grin.

She gasps, her eyes wide with shock. "Oh, Cash, please don't tell me you did it because of me."

"Do you want me to lie?"

She shakes her head. "I want the truth."

"I did it because he hurt you," I confess simply. "He deserved it." When he called Everly a frigid bitch after Theo and I confronted him for dumping her, I let my temper take over. I have zero regrets.

"You shouldn't have done that," she scolds me, a worried look on her face. "What if he had hit you back? You could have been hurt."

I laugh, pointing to the scar on my face. "As long as he aimed for the left side, we wouldn't be able to tell the difference."

"That's not funny, Cash." Everly scolds me. "Jacob was provoking you. His dad is the president of the school board, you know this. What if you get suspended?"

God, her protective side is so adorable.

I've been sent to the office so often that I'm on a first-name basis with the principal. I have a habit of letting my fists do the talking when someone is being a bully and am late more often than not. One more offense won't make a difference.

In the grand scheme of things, it doesn't matter anyway. Graduation is only a month away, and I don't think I want to go to college. Not that I've had the courage to break the news to my parents yet.

"It was worth it," I promise Everly. "Now eat before the food gets cold."

"You don't have to tell me twice." She grabs a burger and unwraps it before taking a large bite. A subtle moan escapes her lips as she chews.

"Good?"

"Mm-hmm," she acknowledges around her mouthful of food.

I'm entranced as I watch juice dribble down her chin. Without thinking, I gently wipe it away with my finger, freezing when I realize what I've done.

"Sorry," I say as I yank my hand back.

Her brown eyes meet mine as she traces her mouth where my finger grazed.

"Don't be." She offers me a reassuring smile. "You know I'm a messy eater, so I appreciate it."

I clear my throat. "Yeah, I'm happy I could help." I brush the sauce off on a napkin before I do something out of line like lick it from my finger.

Thankfully, Everly isn't paying attention. She's chewing methodically, lost in thought. "Why are boys so stupid?" she mumbles under her breath.

"I could ask the same question about girls," I tease.

"Hey." She playfully slugs me on the shoulder. "We're not all self-absorbed snobs like Whitney. Honestly, I'm not sure what you ever saw in her."

She was a distraction.

What stings the most about what happened with Whitney is the fear that other people will react the same to my scar. I used to be comfortable in my own skin, but since the accident, I'm not so sure anymore.

"Hey, Stafford," Everly says, her sing-song voice snapping me out of my pity party.

"Yeah, Ev," I reply.

"Do you believe in soulmates?"

"I'm not sure," I answer honestly.

"Is it weird that I do?" She watches me, anticipating my reaction. "I like to think there's one person out there that I'll grow old with and who will love me unconditionally, no matter what." She chews on her lower lip as she considers her next words. "What if I'm destined to date losers for the rest of my life?"

Everly is a dreamer who sees the world with a glass-half-full mentality. Which is why I don't have it in me to tell her that Jacob most likely won't be the last man who breaks her heart.

Relationships are messy and tangled up with so many emotions, and I, for one, plan to avoid them in the future. They're nothing but complicated, inevitably leading to pain. Why anyone would want to subject themselves to that brutality is beyond me.

"Ev, you're only seventeen," I remind her. "You've got plenty of time to find your *one*."

"But what if he never comes?" She leans back, looking up at me with those innocent brown eyes.

God, why does she have to be so pretty?

"I'll tell you what." I give in to temptation and play with a strand of her hair. "If you can't find him, and we're both still single when we're thirty, we'll get married."

Everly bursts out laughing. "You can't be serious."

I've never been more serious in my life.

In an alternate universe, I like to think that I could be her *one*. The person to make her laugh every day, her Prince Charming, and the one she couldn't live without.

In this reality, I'm just the court jester she tolerates because of my sense of humor and upbeat attitude. I'm not the prince who sweeps her off her feet, or the knight in shining armor she rides off into the sunset with.

"I may not be your first choice, but I promise you I'd be an excellent substitute," I tease.

Everly raises a brow in a silent challenge. "Oh, really?"

"Absolutely. I would make you laugh every day, make sure you had an endless supply of takeout from Willow Creek Café, and build you a dedicated room for your shoe collection."

She bats her eyelashes. "How could I ever refuse such an offer?"

"Do you have a pen in your backpack?"

An idea strikes me, and I decide to run with it, fully committed to this ludicrous, yet oddly inevitable agreement.

"Yeah, sure." She nods, grabbing her bag from the other side of the blanket. She pulls out a black ballpoint pen and hands it to me.

"Thanks." I take a napkin from the pile that came with our food order, set it on the discarded fry box, and hunch over to write.

"What are you doing?" Everly cranes her neck to get a better view.

"You'll see." I cover the napkin with my hand so she can't see what I'm writing.

Midway through, I look up to find her gaze locked on mine. It's as if time stands still and we're the only two people in the universe sharing a connection deeper than words. A silent agreement, connecting us in the moment.

She's the first to look away, and I quickly return my attention to the note.

"There, that should do it," I announce triumphantly when I've finished.

"I don't know if a napkin would hold up in court." Everly giggles when I hold it out for her to read.

Cash Stafford & Everly Townstead promise to marry each other if they're both single when they turn thirty. This agreement is legally binding.

"Well, we better sign it then." I scribble my name at the bottom and pass it to her along with the pen.

She uses her book as a hard surface beneath the napkin, sticking the tip of her tongue out in concentration as she signs her name neatly next to mine. I'm mesmerized by the details of her heart-shaped face, the smattering of freckles across her nose, her long eyelashes still damp with tears.

What was Jacob thinking, letting her go? She's so damn beautiful.

And off-limits, I remind myself. Theo has made that crystal clear.

"There, all done," Everly declares with her signature smile.

Someday a lucky son of a bitch will give Everly everything she deserves—but it won't be me. The consolation prize is knowing that I did something today to ease her heartache, even if just a little, and her smile makes it well worth the effort.

1

EVERLY

FOURTEEN YEARS LATER

I SWIRL THE TOOTHPICK IN my cocktail, frowning at the lone green olive floating in the watered-down vodka and vermouth. With a resigned sigh, I pluck the olive from the glass and pop it into my mouth, the briny taste doing little to improve my mood.

I expected to be served a top-shelf liquor and a more generous garnish, considering the exorbitant cost of a drink. But I suppose that's the price you pay for hiding out in a hotel bar on the Strip.

If my father were here, he would demand a refund and bring every bartender and server in the place to tears on his way out the door. He's a ruthless businessman, willing to do whatever it takes to come out on top, even at the expense of those closest to him.

My phone buzzes, interrupting my pity party for one. A small smile tugs at my lips when I see who's calling.

"Hey, August," I answer.

"Aren't you supposed to be schmoozing with clients right now?" he asks with a hint of amusement.

"Aren't *you* supposed to be in bed? It's past midnight in London," I quip.

He chuckles. "It's the weekend. I just left the club, and was hoping my call would go straight to voicemail so I could leave you a message about how lucky I am that Dick sent you to Vegas instead of me."

My lips curve into a sly grin at his comment. My father's name is Richard, but August has a bad habit of calling him Dick, especially when he's in one of his moods, which is almost always. It would be a disaster if August ever slipped up and called him that to his face. Thank god my dad moved back to New York a few years ago and spends most of his time in the States, so we don't have to see him in person very often.

"My last meeting ended early, so I stopped by the hotel bar for a quick drink." I frown at my unimpressive cocktail. "At least I stuck around until the end. If I remember correctly, you skipped out a full day early the last time my dad sent you to meet with a client."

"What did he expect, sending me to Louisiana during Mardi Gras? My clients wanted to party, and who was I to deny them? I closed the deal, so he has nothing to complain about," he grumbles. "You're the responsible one, which is why he sent you this time."

"That's not true. He would have sent Liam if he wasn't busy running the European division. I swear he sends me to these things just to torment me." I cringe, knowing there's more truth to that than I care to admit.

Dad walked out on us at the end of my and Theo's senior year.

It nearly destroyed my mom when, only a month after they finalized their divorce, he announced he married a European socialite with ties to the royal family. August and Liam, her two sons, were both in their early twenties. They went to work for my dad and have been with Townstead International since.

I had no interest in meeting them at first, but after college, I reluctantly agreed to join the company and had to work with them since I requested to be assigned to the London office. August and I bonded over our dislike of my dad and became fast friends. Liam is laser-focused on the business, so we don't spend time together outside of work, but we have a great rapport.

Despite my best efforts, Theo refuses to have anything to do with our dad and won't meet August and Liam, even though he lives in London. As far as he's concerned, they're strangers and should stay that way.

"You should be out partying and getting laid, not spending your last night in Sin City in a stuffy hotel bar, surrounded by balding middle-aged men looking to make the most out of their trip before going back to their wives and kids in the suburbs," August says.

We may be step-siblings by definition, but he is my closest friend, which means we talk about almost everything.

I glance around the room, surveying the other patrons. Most of them fit his description to a tee—older men with receding hairlines and ill-fitted suits.

"I'm going to have to pass on the partying and getting laid." I take a long sip of my martini. "As soon as I finish my drink, I'm ordering room service and taking a nice, long bath." Given the choice, I much prefer a night of solitude over being in a crowded room with people I have no interest in associating with.

August lets out an exasperated sigh. "Everly, it's been two years since you broke things off with Landon. Isn't it time you started dating again?"

I bristle at his comment. "I have moved on," I state firmly.

I swore off dating the day I caught Landon, my ex-fiancé, cheating on me with his assistant. It had been a typical Tuesday afternoon until I walked in on them doing it doggy style in Landon's apartment.

Men are far more trouble than they're worth. My collection of handy rabbit vibrators gets me off more times in a week than Landon did in the whole of our five-year relationship.

I've learned the hard way that getting emotionally attached to someone only leads to heartache, and I don't plan to put myself through that again.

"You're in Las Vegas," August declares with gusto. "One night of making bad decisions, like getting drunk and having filthy, hot sex with a stranger, can't hurt." I wrinkle my nose in disgust. "Haven't you heard the saying, what happens in Vegas stays in Vegas? This is the perfect opportunity to let loose and have a good time. Then you can return to London and be your boring old self again," he jokes.

"Gee, thanks for the self-esteem boost," I mumble as I take another sip of my drink.

He's not wrong, but his words still sting.

Apparently, the handful of times I've joined him for a night out or met Theo for dinner doesn't count as a social life. I can see why he finds it unhealthy that, aside from my demanding work schedule, I prefer to spend my limited free time alone.

"Everly, I care about you and want you to be happy. You deserve to settle down someday and find someone who worships the ground you walk on."

I used to want that, too, but things have changed.

"I don't have any interest in…" My voice trails off when movement in the corner of my eye catches my attention. I glance up just in time to watch a newcomer enter the bar area. From my vantage point, I can only see his profile, but there's something strangely familiar about him.

The stranger has dark-blonde shaggy hair that falls to his chin and stubble covering his chiseled jawline. While everyone else in the hotel bar is dressed in business attire, he's wearing dark-wash jeans, a white long-sleeve dress shirt with the top two buttons undone, and leather loafers. Even without seeing his face, I can sense he's trouble.

He's captured the attention of every woman in the room, their gazes locked on him as if he's the ultimate prize. As for me, I have no interest in him whatsoever.

Then why can't I stop staring?

"Everly, are you still there?" August's voice breaks through my trance.

It's a good thing we're not video chatting, or he might notice the blush spreading across my cheeks when I realize I've been checking out a stranger. I'm usually indifferent to men, and this one shouldn't be any different.

"Yeah, I'm here," I reply, keeping my gaze fixed on my drink.

"When are you coming home?" August asks.

"My flight leaves for London in the morning."

"You could always spend the weekend in Vegas," he persists, like a dog with a bone.

"I'd much rather sleep in my bed tomorrow night."

"Fine," he says with a defeated sigh. "But if you change your mind and need a day to recuperate, let me know."

"I'll see you bright and early on Monday, August," I tell him.

"Travel safe."

As soon as I hang up, a middle-aged man sits next to me, despite plenty of other seats at the bar. My guess is he was waiting for me to finish my conversation before he approached.

I ignore him in favor of pretending to read an email. The last thing I want is to be pulled into a conversation with someone I'm not interested in talking to. I'm scolding myself for not leaving the bar while I was still talking with August. I blame the devilishly handsome stranger for distracting me.

"Excuse me." The guy next to me taps me on the shoulder.

I look over and meet his beady black eyes. Sweat drips down his temples, highlighting his receding hairline. He pulls out a grimy handkerchief from his pinstripe suit, which is too small around the middle, and wipes his brow.

I grimace when he sets the used handkerchief on the counter between us.

"Can I help you?" I ask, trying my best to hide my repulsion.

"I'm Larry. I'd like to buy you a drink." A grin spreads across his face, exposing a poorly done set of veneers, which makes it more unsettling than friendly.

"I appreciate the offer, but I already have one." I lift my glass for emphasis.

"You definitely need something stronger." His nasally voice grates against my ears.

"No, thank you."

"Come on, baby. From the moment I saw you, I wanted to tell you that if beauty were a crime, you'd be serving a life sentence."

I let out a choked noise. "I'm sorry if I gave the wrong impression, but I'm not interested."

Being direct tends to be the most effective approach when turning down someone's advances. It leaves no room for misinterpretation or for leading someone on for the sake of being nice, which never ends well.

Larry's eyes narrow. "Is this how you treat someone who compliments you?"

"It's how I treat men who don't know how to take no for an answer." I grab my purse, ready to hightail it out of here. I'm startled when his meaty hand clamps around my upper arm.

"Sit. Back. Down," he hisses sharply.

"Let me go," I say through gritted teeth. This guy has another thing coming if he thinks I'll comply with his harassment. "I said I'm not interested." I place my hand over his and dig my fingernails into his skin, causing him to loosen his grip.

"Why you little bit—"

"Don't even think about finishing that sentence." The deep voice sends a thrill down my spine.

Curiosity gets the better of me, and I find the stranger I was ogling earlier hovering over my unwanted guest. A sharp exhale passes my lips when I realize he's not a stranger at all—it's Cash Stafford. It's no wonder he felt familiar. He's been my brother's best friend since we were kids, although I haven't seen him in almost fifteen years.

The unwanted sensation of butterflies in my stomach when his eyes soften and he flashes me a smirk before turning his attention back to Larry.

"Leave now, or I'll call security," Cash threatens calmly.

Larry gives him a wary glance, not daring to question his order. He has enough sense to shove his handkerchief in his pocket and scurry out of his chair, and rush toward the exit. His compliance may have something to do with the jagged scar on Cash's face, spanning from his left eyebrow, carving a winding path across his cheek down to the corner of his mouth. The pronounced pinkish color gives him a menacing appearance.

My memory takes me back to after his accident when he expressed how much he hated the scar because it served as a constant reminder that his outward appearance was different from everyone else. It didn't help that Whitney, his high school girlfriend, never shied away from complaining about how it looked whenever she got the chance. In my opinion, it's sexy as hell. A reminder of Cash's willingness to help someone in need—consequences be damned.

My hands tremble as Cash gives me a wicked grin. He may be devastatingly handsome, but from what Theo's told me about him over the years, I was right to think he was dangerous—just not in the conventional sense.

Something tells me he won't be as easy to get rid of as Larry was.

2

CASH

I BLINK RAPIDLY, MAKING SURE that Everly isn't a mirage.

My meeting with the Stafford Holdings board of directors just wrapped up, and I stopped by the hotel bar for a drink before meeting up with some friends to party. I don't get to come to Vegas often, so I take full advantage of its nightlife when I do. The last thing I expected was to see Everly Townstead being accosted at the bar by some creep.

I'm distracted when my phone buzzes with a text, coincidentally, from her twin brother.

Theo: Don't play too hard while you're in Vegas.

Cash: I can't make any promises.

Evidently, he didn't deem it relevant to tell me Everly was going to be in Vegas the same week as me.

Theo and I have remained close since high school, staying connected through calls and texts when he moved to London ten years ago after graduating from culinary school. However, I haven't seen Everly since the summer after high school. We fell out of touch when she moved away to college, and our paths never crossed over the years.

I slip my phone into my pocket to avoid any more distractions.

"Hello, Ev." Her childhood nickname passes my lips like it was only yesterday when we were hanging out in the backyard of the old Miller house.

"Stafford." She gives me a curt nod but averts her gaze.

Despite her cold greeting, warmth floods my chest at her use of my nickname. It almost makes up for her mask of indifference and her refusal to make eye contact. The Everly I grew up with was friendly and affectionate. In contrast, this version is distant and guarded.

"Theo didn't tell me you'd be in Vegas," I say, sliding into the seat on her left, avoiding the chair her unwanted guest just vacated. The creep may think he got away with how he treated Everly, but he's mistaken.

Everly finally meets my gaze, fixing me with a scowl. "Do you and my brother make a habit of discussing my whereabouts?"

"No, not usually," I answer with a hint of amusement.

"He told me you're living in London and heading up the European division of Townstead International. That's impressive," I commend her.

My conversations with Theo usually revolve around sports, business, and our one-night stands. His family is a sensitive subject, and he doesn't talk about his parents, or share much with me about Everly's personal life.

Everly tugs her lower lip between her teeth, a habit that hints something is bothering her—at least it did when she was younger.

"He exaggerated the truth," she says with a hint of cynicism. "My dad put my step-brothers in charge of the European division when he shifted his focus to global expansion, and I report directly to them." There's bitterness in her tone, but I'm unsure if it's directed at her dad or step-siblings.

"You're a senior executive at an international real estate firm. That's something to be proud of." I rest my arms on the sticky bar counter.

"It's fine, I guess," Everly replies curtly. "August and Liam give me full autonomy, which I appreciate," she adds in a softer tone.

I'm captivated when she picks up her martini, tilting her head back to finish her drink in one gulp. Her impeccably manicured nails are painted crimson red, matching the lipstick stain she's left on the glass.

"My mom says that if someone tells you they're fine, it means they're anything but," I muse, shifting my focus from her mouth back to her eyes.

"That sounds like something Johanna would say," Everly replies with a faint smile.

She turns her attention away from me as she tries to flag down the bartender. He's preoccupied with two flirtatious women at the other end of the bar, lining up a row of shots in front of them. While Everly is momentarily distracted, I take the opportunity to observe her more closely.

She's dressed in a pristine ivory suit with a white lace camisole peeking out from under her jacket, complementing her smooth, olive-toned skin. Her jet-black hair is tied up into a flawless high ponytail. Her chocolate-brown eyes are dull, like the spark inside her has been diminished, and she has a stern expression etched on her face, begging the question, what happened to make her so jaded?"

Is there a reason you're still here?" Everly's exasperated tone jolts me back to the present. "Don't you have business to attend to or something?" She waves toward the exit, her voice betraying a trace of uncertainty.

"Are you that eager to get rid of me, Ev?" I lean in closer, inhaling the scent of her perfume—a mix of jasmine, lavender, and vanilla.

God, she smells incredible.

I have the compelling desire to close the distance between us and draw her close. But, considering her indifferent reaction to seeing me, I doubt she would appreciate it.

As I look around, I'm aware that every other man in the hotel lobby is watching her, waiting for their chance to approach her. They're shit out of luck because if I have anything to say about it, she'll be leaving with me. I'm certain Theo would prefer Everly go with me than stay alone at the hotel bar surrounded by men she doesn't know.

Looking down to regain my composure, I notice she's traded in her Docs for designer bold red heels.

"Of course not." Her voice drips with sarcasm. "What are you doing in Vegas on a Friday night?"

"Why do you think I'm here?" I challenge her.

She tilts her head to examine me, tapping her lips with a red fingernail, a thoughtful expression crossing her face. "I've heard you're quite the ladies' man and that you travel a lot for work. So I assume you're wrapping up a business trip or here for a weekend of debauchery. From the stories Theo has shared with me, I'd guess the latter."

I furrow my brow. What the hell has he told her? Sure, I avoid committed relationships like the plague, but that doesn't make me a womanizer.

"Which is it, Stafford?" Everly taunts me. "And remember, I'm on a first-name basis with your mother, so you should think twice before lying."

I press my lips together to suppress a chuckle. It's nice to see her sassy side shining through the guarded mask she's hiding behind.

"I'm here for both," I admit casually. "Stafford Holdings had an emergency board meeting this afternoon. Harrison had a conflict in his schedule, so I flew in from London to attend on his behalf."

I leave out the fact that the urgent meeting was to discuss a business deal with her father.

My family owns Stafford Holdings, the largest real estate firm in the country. When my dad retired three years ago, my oldest brother Harrison stepped in as CEO of Stafford Holdings. He made my other brother Dylan Chief Financial Officer, and I was shocked when he named me Chief Operating Officer.

Nine months ago I volunteered to head up the new Stafford Holdings office in London, which means I've spent the majority of my time there. Despite Theo's hectic travel schedule, we meet up at a bar or club a handful of times a month now that we live in the same city. Coincidentally, I haven't crossed paths with Everly since I've been there.

"If you're here for business, how does pleasure factor into that equation?" Everly asks with a raised brow.

I swivel my chair to face her. "I'm an opportunist. I never pass up the chance to sprinkle in a little pleasure." I wink.

Everly shakes her head with disappointment. "What happened to you, Stafford? I don't recognize this version of you."

She's right. It's apparent that we've both undergone significant changes since high school.

Before my accident I was a confident person. After, I remained unfazed on the outside, putting on a front for my family and friends. In truth, it was a crushing blow every time I was with someone who couldn't see past my physical flaws. First with Whitney, followed by a string of unsuccessful first dates during the summer after graduation. Even now it's a hit to my self-esteem whenever a person treats me differently when they get a close look at my face.

I learned early on that I'm not the kind of guy a woman takes home to meet her parents.

From experience, I've learned that most women can't resist elusive men. They abandon their instincts and repulsion when drawn to a charming playboy who has no interest in commitment. My scar works in my favor. It garners sympathy and allows me to portray the detached flirt who will give a woman a night she'll never forget, with no unwanted strings attached.

"I could ask the same thing about you," I fire back. "The Everly I knew would never be so quick to judge and would have greeted me like an old friend, not like a stranger."

"At least I'm not a Casanova, bragging about my conquests like they're trophies," she retorts sharply, like I've struck a nerve.

Damn, that was harsh, but true.

I'm used to snide remarks about my playboy lifestyle, but it bothers me that Everly thinks of me that way.

I pick at her abandoned cork coaster, my hands itching for something to do.

"Sorry to disappoint you, Ev, but what you see is what you get. The same can't be said for yourself," I say bluntly.

"What the hell is that supposed to mean?" she snaps, her eyes blazing with defiance.

I lean in toward her so only she can hear me. "Where's the optimistic, cheerful girl who viewed the world through rose-tinted glasses I grew up with?"

Ironically, we're both concealing our true selves, just in different ways.

Everly narrows her gaze at me. "Stop pretending like you know me." I don't miss the hint of sadness in her voice.

I drum my fingers against the bar top, considering my next move.

"You're right, Ev. We're practically strangers," I admit. "But I want to change that if you'll let me."

"What do you mean?" Her voice betrays her curiosity.

"Spend the night with me," I state boldly.

3

EVERLY

I CAN'T BELIEVE THE AUDACITY of this man. We've only spent five minutes together, and he's already trying to get me to have sex with him—unbelievable. I've heard the rumors about him, but I didn't think he'd be this brazen, and with me no less.

"That line may have worked on the roster of women you've been with in the past, but it will absolutely not work on me." I scowl, lifting my chin to meet his gaze. "If Theo heard that you just tried to proposition me in a hotel bar, he would be appalled."

Cash presses his lips together, attempting to hold back from laughing. "Ev, if I were asking you to sleep with me, I'd come right out and say it."

I sigh in relief, but a part of me feels dejected at his apparent indifference.

"You're not?" I ask, giving him side-eye.

"Don't think for a second that it means I'm not interested," he says, his hazel eyes twinkling with mischief. "A friend of mine owns a nightclub next to Premiere, and I always stop by when I'm in town. They serve top-shelf alcohol, which is loads better than the watered-down shit they serve here." He gestures toward the liquor display behind the bar. "What do you say? Get a real drink with me?"

He thinks that's more convincing.

"No thank you," I say without hesitation.

Men spell trouble, and I can't forget it. Although August's notion of embracing one night of making bad decisions plays in my mind. Getting a drink with Cash would undeniably qualify as a bad decision.

"Why not? It's just one drink," he urges.

I rub my temples, trying to keep calm despite his persistence. "Because I have a hunch one drink would turn into two with you," I say bluntly.

The adult version of Cash exudes sex appeal and confidence and cannot be trusted. He's the type of man I avoid like the plague. They lure you in with pretty words, lavish gifts, and empty promises—leaving you to pick up the broken pieces once they're gone.

"Ev, it's only a drink with a friend," he assures me like he can read my mind. "It sounds like you've had a long week and could use a night out."

"I have no interest in watching you get plastered and gyrate against every woman in the club. Now, why don't you take a hint and disappear like Larry?" I regret my comment when a brief flash of hurt flashes across his face.

"Whoever caused you to become so distrusting deserves to suffer for what they did." Cash places his hand on mine. "Word of advice. Don't judge a book by its cover. Just because I haven't had a serious girlfriend since high school and like to have a good time doesn't mean I'm a bad guy."

He leans in so his mouth brushes against my ear. "For the record, I was going to take you to a piano bar on the club's second floor. You're the only woman I have any interest in spending time with tonight," he murmurs as he lifts his hand off mine.

I feel a pang of loss when he moves back, takes out his wallet, and places a crisp hundred-dollar bill on the counter. He didn't order anything, so I assume it's to cover my martini and leave a generous tip.

A sense of unease washes over me when he slides off his barstool without a word.

I'd let him walk out the door if I knew what was good for me. However, despite my pretense of indifference, the thought of not seeing him again for an undetermined amount of time doesn't sit well with me.

What happens in Vegas stays in Vegas.

August's advice from our earlier conversation pops into my head.

One drink with Cash Stafford can't hurt, right? Like he said, it's just a harmless night catching up between two childhood friends.

I must be a masochist because I have a habit of putting myself in situations with men who I think I can trust, only to end up hurt and alone. I shake my head in disgust. That line of thinking is exactly what Cash called me out for. I'm so cynical and quick to make assumptions. He has done nothing to deserve that.

When I look up, he's halfway across the lobby. I toss my phone into my purse and chase after him.

"Stafford, wait," I shout, disregarding the questioning looks from the other guests.

He spins around, searching my face for a moment, a grin lighting up his features when it seems he's found whatever it was he was looking for.

His reaction sends another uncontrollable flutter through my stomach.

"Yes, Ev?" he asks, tapping his foot while he waits.

"I want to go to the piano bar with you if the invitation still stands." I hold my hand up when he opens his mouth. "But I'm holding you to your promise about it only being one drink. We'll catch up, and then I'll be on my way."

August would be so proud.

"If that's what you want." He opens the door before I can question him further, placing his hand on my lower back as we step out onto the street.

That was too easy.

So much for just one drink. I'm buzzed enough to feel more like the Everly that Cash used to know than I have in years.

When we arrived at the piano bar, the line to get in was wrapped around the block, but we were ushered inside and taken to the best seats in the place, offering the perfect view of the stage.

We've been here for over an hour and I'm still awestruck by the charm of the place.

Crystal chandeliers cast a warm glow over the plush velvet couches and polished marble flows. The massive space is filled with the notes of a grand piano playing a lively jazz piece as servers hurry from table to table.

Our waitress appears and shoots Cash a flirtatious smile while checking him out. She set her sights on him as soon as we were seated at our table. The noticeable gap between us speaks volumes, indicating we're not a couple. "Can I get you anything else, sir?"

"Yeah. Can we get another shot of tequila and another whiskey on the rocks?" he says as he taps his empty glass.

"Certainly," the waitress coos, her voice dripping with honey.

I roll my eyes at her obvious display of interest. She couldn't be more transparent if she tried.

"Thank you." Cash gives her a grin before she walks away.

Our waitress isn't the only one who has noticed him. Every woman in the piano bar steals glances in our direction, blatantly eye-fucking Cash every chance they get.

His wavy hair falls around his face, concealing most of his scar, except for a small section near his chin, adding a touch of mystery to his appeal. The top two buttons of his shirt are undone, and his muscular forearms are visible with his rolled-up sleeves, making him irresistible eye candy.

I appear to be the only one immune to his charm.

At least that's what I'm telling myself.

"You were glaring at the waitress again," Cash observes. "Did you want something other than tequila?"

"I was guessing how long it'll take you to invite her back to your room tonight. Just say the word, and I'm happy to make my exit so you two can have your privacy."

"Somebody's jealous." He scoots closer and throws his arm over my shoulders.

"What are you doing?" I hiss.

I attempt to move away, but he gently pulls me back into his embrace. "I'm making sure there's no question that I'm here with you," he says softly.

His words cause me to melt into his arms, reminiscent of our high school days when he would comfort me in the same way… I forgot how much I missed it.

The waitress reappears at our table with our drinks in hand. "Here you are—" She stops short when she notices Cash's arm around me.

"Is there a problem?" Cash raises a brow.

"No, not at all," she says as she collects our empty glasses.

"That'll be all, thanks," he says, effectively dismissing her.

I don't miss her crestfallen expression at being rejected.

Cash has a way with women that draws them in. He has always been kind, genuine, and straightforward, qualities women appreciate. In contrast, my frosty demeanor turns most men off, but it hasn't fazed Cash. Even when I told him off, he brushed it off like it never happened.

"Cheers." He holds up his glass of whiskey, bringing it close to the shot of tequila I have in my hand.

"Cheers," I echo as our glasses clink together, downing the shot in one swallow.

This is my fourth shot since we arrived. I'm not sure how I've allowed myself to get so tipsy. After my watered-down martini at the hotel bar, the tequila was a welcome improvement.

This has to be my last drink, or I'll end up doing something I'll regret, like kissing my brother's insanely attractive best friend.

As Cash lifts his drink to his lips, I notice a flash of color on his wrist.

That can't be what I think it is.

I grab his wrist to examine it closely, a splash of whiskey spilling onto my arm from jostling his glass. He's wearing a blue and white corded bracelet on his right wrist that looks identical to the one I gave him when he was in the hospital recovering from his accident.

"Is this—"

"The bracelet you made?" He pauses, looking me in the eye. "Yeah, it is."

In high school, I went through a phase where I learned to make macrame friendship bracelets. I made one for Theo and our friends. I had planned to give Cash the one I made for him at school, but he was hit by a car the night before.

When Theo and I went to visit him in the hospital after his accident, I brought the bracelet with me.

"Why do you still have it?" I ask breathlessly.

"It's… special," he states matter-of-factly. "When I was in the hospital, everyone who came to see me looked at me with pity. Even Theo treated me differently. But not you. When you stepped into the room, you cracked jokes about how pale I was and how you were convinced I had been turned into a vampire." He stares into the distance as if he's being drawn back into the memory. "I told you I was worried about what everyone would think of me when they removed the bandages on my face, and that's when you gave me this." He rubs the faded string between his fingers. "You told me whenever I felt discouraged, the bracelet would serve as a physical reminder to have courage and to remember that I'm stronger than I think. And you were right; it's been my lucky charm ever since."

I gaze at the visible part of his scar. It's clear he views it in a negative light—a physical reminder that he's different. I wish he could see it the way I do.

When I lock eyes with him, I confirm his sincerity.

The bracelet's colors have faded, and the edges have frayed, and yet he's continued to wear it all these years.

My breath hitches when he reaches out to tuck a stray piece of hair behind my ear. If I were sober, I would swat his hand away and remind him that this is just drinks between friends. Tipsy me seems to have forgotten about boundaries, leaning into his hand like a kitten being stroked on the head.

Maybe I'm not so immune to his charms after all.

"I have a confession," he murmurs so softly I have to strain to hear him. "There's something else I kept."

"What is it?" I don't bother hiding my curiosity.

"The napkin that we used to sign our marriage pact on. Do you remember?"

I stare at him wide eyed. "I do."

How could I forget the worst day of my life up to that point being turned around because of Cash's thoughtfulness?

My boyfriend dumped me just hours before our senior prom. I was humiliated that I was naïve enough to think that we were going to be together forever.

When Cash found me reading behind the old Miller house, he listened to me ramble on about soulmates and how worried I was that I'd never find mine. The joke is on me because I learned the hard way that there isn't such a thing. Relationships never last, no matter how much you want them to.

Most friends would have laughed off my silly notions, but not Cash. He came up with the idea for us to sign a marriage pact as a backup plan, and despite my new perspective on love being a myth, I never forgot the sweet gesture.

"I figured you threw it away."

"Never." He gazes at me, and up close I can see the golden flecks in his hazel eyes. "I liked the idea that in an alternate reality you'd be mine." I feel lightheaded when he caresses my cheek with the back of his hand, his knuckles rubbing against my jaw.

The sober me would tell him he's full of shit and remind him that a woman can't be owned. Too bad the tipsy me is relishing the fact that Cash Stafford just confessed in a roundabout way that he kept the marriage pact we made in high school because he likes me... or at least he did.

"I have an important question to ask you," he says.

"Which is?" I ask, my curiosity piqued.

He leans in closer, like he has a secret to share, and trails his fingers along my arm, sending a course of electricity through me at the touch. "Please tell me you're single," he murmurs.

"That's not a question," I quip playfully.

"I can't ask you to marry me if you're with someone else," he says with a mischievous, boyish grin.

An uncharacteristic giggle escapes my lips. "That's the most ridiculous thing I've ever heard."

"It makes perfect sense." He removes his arm from around my shoulder and clasps my hands in his. "We're both single, in our thirties, and there's a chapel right down the street. Marry me, Ev."

I stare at him, trying to process his words. "We haven't seen each other in fourteen years," I remind him.

Thanks to the alcohol, it's like my brain is on a coffee break, leaving me unable to come up with a better retort.

"So?" Cash murmurs. "They say absence makes the heart grow fonder, don't they? Some connections can't be ignored, no matter how long you've been apart."

I knit my eyebrows in confusion. "What are you saying?"

"Marry me," he repeats, sidestepping my question. "Our pact still means something to me, just like this bracelet does," he says, nodding to his wrist. "*You* mean something to me." Cash cradles my face, sending a shiver down my spine. "Haven't you heard the best things in life are worth waiting for? Now that you're finally here with me, I don't ever want to let you go."

I briefly close my eyes, wishing he'd stop saying all the right things.

After being engaged to a cheater with average looks, tying the knot with Cash would be a major upgrade. He's devastatingly handsome and charismatic. Not to mention I've known him since we were kids.

"You're serious about this?"

He nods his head. "I promise I'll make you happy. You just have to give me a chance to prove it, Ev." My heart skips a beat when he presses a kiss to my forehead. "Make me the luckiest man alive, and agree to be my wife."

Nibbling on my lower lip, I feel the weight of his gaze.

Maybe this isn't such a terrible idea after all. He has worn my bracelet for all these years and admitted that our silly marriage pact meant something to him. Plus, he punched Jacob Barlow in the face when he stood me up at our senior prom. That's true loyalty.

Wait. Am I really considering this?

Warning bells ring loudly in the back of my mind, reminding me those aren't valid reasons to marry someone, but one too many shots of tequila have drowned out my logical thinking.

"When was the last time you did something just because you wanted to? Be brave, Ev, and take this leap with me," Cash urges.

"Stafford, are you daring me to marry you?"

"Maybe," he murmurs. "Is it working?"

"Yes," I say, a grin spreading across my face, reflecting his contagious excitement. "I think it is."

4

CASH

I GROAN WHEN I OPEN my eyes to the sun streaming through the window.

My head is pounding with a splitting headache from drinking too much whiskey last night. I used to party until dawn, catch a few hours of sleep, and wake up feeling good as new. Now, anytime I have a few drinks, it feels like I've been hit by a dump truck, the effects lingering for hours.

As I shift in bed, I'm aware of a warm body curled up behind me, which is strange since I never invite anyone back to my apartment or hotel room. The women I've slept with know my terms—one night, no strings attached, and no misconceptions of a long-term commitment. And I always leave before they wake up.

When I glance over, my breath catches when I see Everly lying next to me. Dark tresses fan out across her pillow, her full lips slightly parted while she sleeps soundly.

The last time I saw her before last night was a few weeks after high school graduation. Her parents had just gotten divorced, and she left for college early. Theo and I took her to the airport, and as much as I hated seeing her go, I told her she would have the adventure of a lifetime.

"Fuck," I mutter.

I'm in the same bed as my best friend's sister, and I can't remember what happened after we left the piano bar last night. *This is bad. Very bad.*

I disentangle myself from her, easing her arm from my hip so I can get up. I pause when she stirs, letting out a soft moan, but within seconds her breathing evens out.

I'm relieved to find my phone on the nightstand and unlock it. A cold sweat breaks out across my forehead when I see my screen saver has changed to a photo of Everly and me sitting in the back of a bright pink Cadillac.

In front of a wedding chapel.

She's wearing a fitted white wedding dress, completed with a short veil and high heels. A small bouquet of daffodils rests on her lap, and she is smiling into the camera. My arms are banded around her waist as I look down at her with affection.

Holy fucking shit.

I wipe my hand across my face, pausing when a cool piece of metal brushes against my skin. The weight on my ring finger registers, and my gaze shifts to the nightstand where the marriage certificate confirms my suspicions—Everly and I got married.

Memories from last night begin to flash back into my mind. Everly laughing while browsing a rack of wedding dresses at a boutique located in the Shoppes at Premiere. An officiant dressed as Elvis reading us our vows. Me carrying Everly across the threshold of our hotel room.

I vaguely remember ordering room service. After our dinner of cheeseburgers, fries, and milkshakes, we watched several reruns of *Big Bang Theory* in bed, and fell asleep cuddling.

I'm still wearing last night's white button-up shirt and boxer briefs, and I breathe a sigh of relief when I glance over at Everly and see she's in her bra and panties. The only piece of clothing on the floor appears to be her dress.

The only thing that could have made this situation worse is if we had sex.

I run my fingers through my hair and consider the mess we're in. I've done a lot of stupid shit, but this takes the cake.

Theo is going to kill me when he finds out, and I don't even want to imagine how Everly is going to react when she wakes up and realizes she's married to the guy she called a Casanova. I could wake her up to talk about what happened, but I figure it's best to let her sleep.

In the meantime, I'm going to take advantage of Premiere's world-class room service and order some food for us. Hopefully, her favorite breakfast will help ease the shock when she wakes up to this unexpected situation.

"Cash Stafford, where are you?" Everly's furious voice carries down the hall.

I don't respond, taking another bite of my acai bowl. There's no predicting what will happen when she finds me, so I might as well enjoy what could very well be my last meal.

The sound of her bare feet against the hardwood floor fills the living room as she storms in. Her hair is gathered on the top of her head in a loose bun, and she's dressed in the same white dress she wore last night.

"Good morning, Ev. How did you sleep?" I pop a piece of banana into my mouth.

"Cut the shit, Stafford. Care to explain this?" She sticks out her hand, thrusting the massive diamond on her finger into my face.

"It's a ring." Another memory surfaces of me calling in a favor to have the manager of the upscale jewelry store on the second floor of Premiere show us the exclusive collection of rings they keep under lock and key—one of the many perks of my family owning the hotel.

The five-carat pear-shaped diamond set me back two hundred thousand dollars, yet it felt like it was meant to be since it fits her finger perfectly.

I may have gone overboard, but in my buzzed state, I loved the idea of Everly walking around with a giant rock on her finger, so there was no question who she belonged to. It's not like I can't afford it. Even sober, I find it oddly satisfying.

"Why are you acting so calm?" She throws her hands in the air in frustration. "We got married last night. How could you let that happen?"

"Me?" I point at my chest. "You were happy to go along with it. I recall you were adamant that we—and I quote—*find the perfect dress for the best night of my life*. That detail must have slipped your mind," I taunt her. "I appreciated the ego boost. It's not every day a pretty woman says getting married to me is the best thing to happen to her."

In fact, it's the last thing I expected to hear in my lifetime, considering I swore I'd never settle down.

"The four tequila shots might have impaired my decision-making skills, but unfortunately, not my memory." She grumbles. "I have a low tolerance for alcohol."

"That would have been helpful information to have last night." On the bright side, she remembers what happened.

She bites down on her lower lip as she paces the room.

I rise from the couch and move in front of her.

"Take a deep breath," I say, placing my hands on her shoulders. "It's going to be okay."

I'm intrigued by the enigmatic woman before me, curious about what brought about her transformation. Above all, I want a glimpse of my Everly because I'm sure she's still in there somewhere.

"How can you say that?" she protests. "We're practically strangers, and now we're legally bound together. I don't even know what kind of car you drive, your favorite food, or if you were lying about your relationship status. Those are all things I should know about a person before I agree to date them, let alone marry them."

God, she's adorable when she overthinks.

"I own a Jeep Wrangler YJ Rio Grande that I store in my parents' garage. When I'm in London, I walk to work since my apartment is close to the office. My favorite meal is my mom's homemade lasagna and garlic bread, but I'm a fan of everything she cooks," I say, ticking each item off on my fingers. "And I didn't lie about my relationship status. I'm as single as a person can get."

At least I was until last night.

She sighs. "Thank god. The last thing I need is to be the other woman this time."

This time?

I decide against asking her to elaborate, given the predicament we're in.

"Why don't you have some breakfast before it gets cold?" I usher her over to the couch and gesture to the dining cart. "I ordered French toast topped with whipped cream, sliced banana, and extra syrup—just the way you like it."

She blinks back at me. "Let me get this straight." She puts her hands on her hips. "You woke up to find out that we were married, and instead of coming up with a solution, you ordered breakfast?"

"You could just say thank-you."

"Why would I do that?" she retorts.

"Just in case your tastes have changed, I also ordered scrambled eggs, Belgian waffles, and an acai bowl with berries. I've never had a wife, so hopefully you'll cut me some slack if I do this all wrong," I joke, hoping to lighten the mood.

She stares ahead with a vacant expression, and after several seconds, she shakes her head like she's coming out of a trance.

"We. Got. Married. How can you be concerned about food right now?" She waves frantically at the food cart. "You should be finding the quickest way to get out of this, not concerned about what kind of fruit I like with my French toast."

I've done a lot of reckless things in my adult life. Like when I decided on a whim to spend a month off the grid in India.

Or when I spent a night partying in Los Angeles with the Sovereign Kings, a world-famous rock band, and woke up the next morning in Japan. Before yesterday, my most impulsive decision was buying a private jet because I hated asking Harrison for permission to use the shared Stafford Holdings' plane. Those things pale in comparison to getting hitched to my best friend's sister.

"You're right, I'm sorry." I gesture for her to sit. This time, she gives in, sinking into the couch. "What do you think we should do?" I ask, hoping she has a plan because I haven't thought that far ahead yet.

"We'll go back to London and have our lawyers draw up the paperwork for an annulment. It should be straightforward, and this will be a distant memory by next week," Everly exclaims as she claps her hands together.

She's a little too enthusiastic for my liking. My stomach churns at the idea of pretending this never happened. Suddenly, the few hours we spent together feels insufficient.

"Sounds like a great plan, but we have a big problem," I tell her.

"Bigger than marrying someone in Vegas who you haven't seen in fourteen years?" she challenges.

I chuckle at her seriousness. "If you were to ask my mom, the answer would be yes. I'm supposed to be in Aspen Grove for family photos this afternoon, and she'll never forgive me if I'm not there."

My mom has been looking forward to having new family photos taken for a while. She doesn't think she sees me and my siblings enough and will find any excuse to get us together.

51

Dylan is the only one who lives in Aspen Grove, preferring to give his daughter, Lola, a sense of normalcy. Harrison and I have apartments in the city, located on the top floors of the Stafford Holdings headquarters we renovated three years ago. However, I've spent most of my time in London for the past nine months.

My sister Presley, and her boyfriend, Jack, have a massive apartment in New York that spans the entire ninetieth floor of a skyscraper and offers a breathtaking view of Central Park.

"What do your family photos have to do with me?" Everly asks.

"We're married. I'm not letting you out of my sight until we figure this out."

"You cannot be serious," Everly huffs in annoyance. "Go to Aspen Grove, and when you get back to London, we'll take care of this."

"I don't think so, wifey." The new term of endearment rolls off my tongue. "We're sticking together until we get the annulment."

Her dark eyes widen. "Don't call me that."

"Why not? According to the state of Nevada, you're my wife until we dissolve this marriage." I can't help but egg her on. "Is there a reason you don't want to go to Aspen Grove?"

"No." Her gaze shifts to the ground. "I just haven't been there in a while."

"It'll only be for a few hours, and then we can go back to London," I promise.

She gives me a skeptical look. "Fine, but we fly back tonight. I have to catch up on a lot of work before Monday morning."

I'm still baffled that she's working for Richard. He never passed up the chance to tell her and Theo how disappointed he was in them when we were kids.

I had the displeasure of meeting with him in New York last week, and it solidified my opinion that he's a vindictive son of a bitch. My brothers and I spent three hours with him, and he didn't bring up Everly once, which is odd since she plays a significant role in his business.

"That shouldn't be a problem. Family photos shouldn't take more than a couple of hours. Plenty of time for the pilot to refuel before we take off."

Unless my mom decides to intervene when she learns the truth about our marriage. Given her track record of meddling in my siblings' personal lives I wouldn't put it past her.

My phone buzzes again, likely the hundredth text I've gotten in the past ten minutes.

With a brisk pace, I move up the walkway to my parents' modest two-story Cape-style home.

I'm halfway up the steps when Everly places her hand on my arm to stop me.

"Is everything okay?" I ask.

"I just got an urgent email from an important client dealing with a crisis. I need to call him," she says.

"Yeah, sure." I do my best to conceal my disappointment. "Just come inside when you're finished."

"You're going to tell your family the truth about what happened between us, right?"

"Yeah, of course."

I was hoping she'd be there when I broke the news about our impromptu marriage and annulment. My mom has always considered Everly part of our family. I can only imagine her reaction when she finds out that Everly is her daughter-in-law and in the same conversation that we're dissolving our marriage.

My pulse is racing when I step inside the house. I'm not expecting to find my mom and siblings hovering in the entryway, all wearing looks of sheer panic. I'm bombarded with questions from all directions as soon as they see me.

"Where have you been?" Presley demands, pointing at the clock on the wall. "We've tried calling you a dozen times, but it kept going to voicemail."

"You're late," my mom says, echoing my sister's frustrations. She places her hands on her hips like she used to do when she would scold me as a kid. "You know how important this photoshoot is. I was worried sick when we couldn't reach you."

"You were supposed to fly back last night," Harrison says, studying me suspiciously.

Nothing gets past him. Luckily, he doesn't bring up the fact that I was supposed to call him after my meeting with the board. I completely forgot about it when I ran into Everly. He must have called the chairman for an update. I'm not looking forward to him losing his shit when he finds out what I've done.

"Yeah, well, something held me up in Vegas… or should I say, someone." I keep my reply vague because it's hard to find the right words to explain that I got married in Las Vegas to Everly Townstead, of all people.

"What are you talking—" Presley cuts herself off as she points to the ring on my finger. "What is that?" she asks with a gasp.

Oh shit.

"My wedding ring," I answer truthfully. In the mad dash to make our flight, I forgot to take it off.

"I'm sorry, your what?" Presley screeches.

"I got married." I do my best to downplay the announcement. "My wife is on a call but she'll come inside as soon as she's finished. Is it alright if we wait for her, Mom?"

She gapes at me in shock, clearly taken aback by my announcement.

"Your *wife?*" Presley laughs. "Very funny, Cash. Who put you up to this?" She turns her glacier stare on Jack. "Was it you?"

He holds his hands up in defense. "I know better than to play practical jokes on you, little vixen."

"What about you two?" She glares at Harrison and Dylan. "Because this joke is even less funny than the time you had Jack arrested."

When Presley brought Jack to Aspen Grove for the first time and pretended they were dating, Harrison was suspicious. After some recon, we found out that Jack was Presley's boss who had been tormenting her for years. We decided to prank him to teach him a lesson for messing with our sister. It's the best practical joke we've ever pulled off, although I don't think Jack would agree.

Dylan holds up his hands in defense. "It wasn't me."

Harrison shakes his head. "I had nothing to do with this."

I make the mistake of stealing another glance at my mom. Her expression radiates pure happiness, and I can't bring myself to tell her the full truth, at least not yet.

"I'm serious, Presley," I say with a straight face. "We got hitched in Vegas last night and came straight to Aspen Grove to share the good news with our families."

It occurs to me that Everly hasn't asked to see her mom while we're in town. Theo doesn't have contact with her, but according to him, Everly does. So I wonder why she doesn't come to visit.

"You got married and didn't invite your own mother? Shame on you," my mom interjects, smacking me upside the head.

"I'm sorry," I say with a sheepish grin.

She seems more upset that I didn't tell her than at hearing the news that I got hitched. She's probably just grateful that she didn't have to play matchmaker like she did for Presley and Dylan, which explains why she looks so happy right now.

Mom might deny it, but she's made it her mission to intervene with my siblings' love lives, and Presley and Dylan have both found their better halves thanks to her. I can work with this reaction—that is until I have to break the news about the annulment.

Everyone's attention goes to the front door when it creaks open, and Everly steps inside.

"Oh, speaking of my wife," I say, a smile spreading across my face.

I don't think I'll ever get over how much I like calling her that.

Harrison and Dylan exchange a confused glance when they see Everly and take in the giant diamond on her ring finger. I mentally pat myself on the back for choosing that one—no chance anyone will miss it, even if this whole thing is over by Monday.

"Oh, Everly," my mother exclaims. "Welcome to the family, sweetie." She pulls her into a hug, and Everly shoots me a glare.

I smirk back at her, giving her a thumbs-up.

She's going to make me pay for this stunt later, but I might as well enjoy the ride while I can.

5

EVERLY

"THANKS, JOHANNA." I MUSTER A genuine smile as my eyes dart between Cash and his mom.

I was prepared for the Staffords to give me the cold shoulder when I walked in, angry that Cash and I recklessly got married and were rushing to get it dissolved. Instead, I'm being welcomed as if I were part of the family because Cash led them to believe that I am.

Letting him handle it alone was a huge mistake; now we're in an even bigger mess.

"This is the best news." Johanna pulls back, giving my hand an affectionate squeeze.

Her kindness tugs at my heartstrings, reminding me how much I used to love spending time here.

The Staffords are as close to a perfect family as they can get. They love each other unconditionally and have always stood together. As a kid, I envied Cash's relationship with his parents; they were so caring and attentive. In contrast, my dad was cruel and vindictive, and my mom was more interested in escaping reality and indulging in a lavish lifestyle than taking care of Theo and me.

"You weren't this excited when Marlow and I announced our engagement or when Presley told us she and Jack are getting a summer home in Aspen Grove," Dylan chimes in.

"He has a point, Mom," Presley adds. "We shouldn't be surprised, considering Cash has always been your favorite."

"You're just jealous." Cash sticks his tongue out.

"That's enough," Johanna scolds. "I love you all equally and won't have you argue otherwise. I'm just delighted to have Everly as a daughter-in-law. It's a dream come true." Tears trickle down her cheeks, and she quickly wipes them away.

My chest tightens at her response. She had a soft spot for me when I was a kid, which meant a lot to me since I've never been close to my own mom.

Cash gives me a warning look, silently urging me not to break the news that this isn't real. Nervously tapping my fingers against my thigh, I weigh my options. Based on her initial reaction, Johanna will be crushed if we come clean, but my guilty conscience tells me that deceiving her isn't right.

This is all Cash's fault. How dare he make this situation more complicated? We wouldn't be in this situation if he had told his family the truth. I should have stood my ground back in Vegas, returned to London alone, and let our lawyers deal with the fallout.

Damn that tequila.

"Why is your mother crying?" Cash's dad emerges from the hallway, his voice filled with concern.

He runs his fingers through his short black hair as his gaze sweeps over his kids, pausing when he notices me standing on the other side of Johanna. A puzzled expression crosses his face; I'm probably the last person he expected to see standing in his entryway.

"Don't worry, Mike, they're happy tears," Johanna assures him between hiccups. "Cash and Everly got married yesterday. Isn't that wonderful?"

Mike pushes his tortoiseshell glasses up on his nose, giving Cash and me cautionary glances. "Yeah, that's great news," he says, sounding unsure as he tries to appease his wife.

My conscience won't let this go on any longer, and my inner voice shouts at me to end this charade.

"Would it be alright if I talk to Cash outside?" I ask.

His face pales at my request.

"Of course, sweetie." Johanna smiles at me. "Just don't take too long. The photographer is out back, and we don't want to keep her waiting."

"This will be quick," I promise as I tug Cash's arm, dragging him onto the porch. He closes the door behind us, and as soon as we're out of his family's sight, I yank my hand away.

"What the hell was that?" I whisper-shout. "You were supposed to tell them the truth, not make your mom think this marriage is legitimate. She's going to be devastated when she finds out that not only did we lie to her, but this"—I gesture between us—"isn't real."

I'm wary when he flashes me a playful grin.

"What?" I ask with my hands on my hips.

"Oh, come on, you can't deny our chemistry," he says, taking a step closer to me.

I shake my head in denial. "You're imagining things."

My visceral reaction when he walked into the hotel bar was a fluke. I'm chalking it up to an instinctual reaction caused by sexual tension that's been building up for the past two years. It has nothing to do with Cash.

If I say it enough times, I'll believe it.

"If that's the case, care to explain why you stared daggers at every woman who dared to look my way? Or better yet, why you couldn't stop eye-fucking me last night?"

"Apparently whiskey makes you delusional because I was not eye-fucking you last night, Stafford," I retort.

"Sure you weren't." He cradles my face, gliding his thumbs against my skin. For a moment, I forget my reservations and lean into the comforting warmth of his hand.

He can get me to drop my guard without even trying. I think it's because he's familiar, evoking memories of our childhood friendship when I trusted him implicitly. My instincts tell me I can do the same now, but my mind isn't so sure.

I take a step back, causing him to let go of my face. "I told your mom we wouldn't be long. Is there a reason your family thinks we're happily married?"

Cash runs his fingers through his hair, which seems to be a family habit. "I was going to tell them what happened, but Presley noticed my ring before I could, and when I saw how happy my mom looked, there was no way I would disappoint her. It's not that big of a deal." He tries to brush me off.

"Not a big deal?" I raise my voice. "Cash, we got married. Even if it was an accident, we have to take responsibility for our error and fix it. Lying to your family isn't going to make this situation better. We have to go back in there right this minute and come clean. That's the only option."

The last thing I want is to cause a rift between Cash and his family. From what I've seen in the past twenty-four hours, he has a laid-back approach to life. He loves his family, and has a big heart, but he doesn't take things seriously, including himself. Everything is a game, and he doesn't consider the consequences when he acts rashly.

In some ways, I envy his carefree attitude. He's not afraid to take risks and doesn't share my inability to roll with the punches.

"I didn't lie, I just omitted some details," he offers.

"That's literally the definition of lying." I let out a frustrated sigh. "If you're unwilling to rectify this, I will." I try walking past him, but he holds out his arm to stop me.

"Everly, it's not that simp—"

We're interrupted by the door creaking open and find Harrison and Dylan standing in the doorway with suspicious expressions.

They join us on the porch, and Harrison closes the door behind them. He folds his arms across his chest, studying us both with the intensity of a detective.

His black hair is styled in a tapered fade, and his muscular arms fill out the sleeves of his short-sleeve polo. The scowl on his face strikes me as odd, given that he was the approachable-teddy-bear big brother when we were kids. It appears we've all changed to some degree since then.

"You've got some explaining to do, Cash," Harrison boldly states with a raised eyebrow. "Last week, you told Dylan and me on a conference call that you never wanted to settle down. Now, suddenly, you're waltzing into Mom and Dad's, announcing that you're married—to Everly Townstead. It doesn't add up."

"Her name is Everly Stafford now," Cash states with a confidence that makes me want to shake some sense into him.

"It's still Townstead," I correct him, not caring that I'm lecturing him in front of his brothers.

"Seriously, what is going on?" Dylan interjects. "The optics won't look good if this marriage is fake and it gets out to the board of directors," he says as he adjusts his glasses.

He's sporting black slacks paired with a light blue polo shirt, and his black hair is cut short. With his thick-rimmed glasses, he reminds me of a modern-day Clark Kent.

The Stafford brothers have all aged like fine wine, all incredibly attractive, but admittedly, Cash is the only one who makes me weak in the knees when he looks in my direction.

Harrison pinches the bridge of his nose. "Dylan's right. If the media or the board finds out, this could tank the acquisition."

My heart sinks as I get the sense that I should know what they're talking about, but I don't.

"What acquisition?" I voice my confusion.

"She doesn't know?" Harrison asks, alarmed.

Dylan snickers as he leans against one of the porch pillars. "Oh, this is going to be good."

"What are they talking about?" I demand, turning to Cash.

One thing I cannot tolerate is being the last to know something, which happens often when my father is involved.

His eyes widen as he studies me. "You really don't know?"

"If you would tell me what you were talking about, I could answer your question," I retort.

He fiddles with his bracelet, avoiding eye contact.

"Stafford Holdings is in the process of buying out Townstead International," he says reluctantly. "I was in Vegas to meet with our board of directors since Harrison and Dylan both had conflicts."

I blink at him in confusion. "Come again?"

"Your dad approached me a few months ago with a lucrative proposal for us to buy Townstead International," Harrison explains, trying to diffuse the tension. "Dylan's team gave the deal a tentative green light, so we're moving ahead with the acquisition."

I balk at the realization that my dad withheld this from me. Although I shouldn't be surprised since he does it all the time. If August and Liam had been aware of this, there's no question they would have told me. I can only imagine they won't take the news well.

"Wait a second." I glance over at Cash, who looks ready to bolt. "If you knew, why wouldn't you tell me?"

"I assumed your dad already had, and figured you didn't mention it because of the legal restrictions in place on what can be talked about between companies until Stafford Holdings takes ownership of Townstead International."

"What about this morning when you woke up with a ring on your finger? That would have been the perfect opportunity to broach the subject. Were you lying when you said we'd fly back to London and get an annulment?"

My pulse quickens at the idea that he could be playing me. That this was a sick joke to guarantee the deal goes through. Or this is just another scenario where Cash flies by the seat of his pants with no concern for repercussions, and I'll be left paying for it.

"No, of course not," he says quickly. "I promise we'll get in touch with our lawyers as soon as we leave and will have this resolved by Monday, just like you want."

"I wouldn't advise getting an annulment," Harrison interrupts.

I jerk my head in his direction, having forgotten for a minute that he and Dylan were here.

"Harrison is right," Dylan adds. "This would cause a shitstorm if the media caught wind of a fake marriage in the middle of a merger. Not to mention, our board would have a field day."

I place my hands on my head, attempting to regulate my breathing. This cannot be happening. Any second now, I'm going to wake up in my bed, and this will all have been a bad dream.

"Why should it matter what Everly and I do?" Cash asks Harrison. "Our marriage doesn't financially benefit anyone, so who cares if we get it dissolved?"

I glance at Harrison and Dylan, who both have serious expressions on their faces, confirming that Cash is the only one who fails to grasp the severity of the situation.

"How do you think the board of directors will react when they find out you met up with the daughter of Townstead

International's CEO right after you left a pivotal board meeting discussing the acquisition? I can spin the story of you marrying your childhood friend, but it's going to be damn near impossible to convince them if your attorneys file for an annulment come Monday morning. They'll assume you only got married to disclose sensitive information that could impact stock prices or shape market perceptions. If that happens, the deal will go up in smoke." He snaps his fingers for emphasis.

When Harrison puts it that way, it makes the situation even more dire. My hands shake as reality sets in. He's right. If Cash and I get an annulment now, we'll jeopardize our jobs, the acquisition, and both companies' reputations.

I let the tequila and Cash's charm cloud my judgment. Now there's a possibility I could be stuck married to him for an undetermined amount of time. I swear I'm never taking tequila shots ever again.

"What do you suggest we do?" I direct my question to Harrison. He's the most level-headed person here, and I can trust that he'll give it to me straight.

"I would prefer that you stay married and pretend that you're in love. That includes in front of our parents and Presley. I don't trust her not to spill the beans to Mom." I stare wide eyed at Harrison while he speaks. "It works in your favor that you grew up together and both live in London. If anyone asks, we'll tell them you reconnected at a local pub, fell in love, and got married on a whim while you were both in Vegas for work."

Even anticipating his advice doesn't make it any less of a bitter pill to swallow.

"It won't be that bad," Cash offers when he notices me wringing my hands.

"Not *that* bad? Stafford, we haven't seen each other in fourteen years. Now, suddenly, you think I want to live with you? Harrison just told us this could upset the merger. When my dad finds out what I did, he won't be as understanding as your brothers." I gesture toward Harrison and Dylan, who are observing our tense exchange.

My dad won't let this lapse in judgment go unpunished.

Dylan steps between Cash and me. "Woah there, lovebirds." He chuckles nervously. "Why don't you talk this through in private before determining how you want to move forward? We're not going to force either of you to do anything you don't want to." He looks me in the eye. "Whatever you decide, we'll support you both. Right, Harrison?"

"As the CEO of Stafford Holdings, I recommend you stay married for the sake of the companies." Harrison gives me a rare smile. "But as an older brother, I would never abandon either of you, regardless of how you want to move forward."

I'm taken aback by their loyalty. Harrison and Dylan could easily disregard me to fend for myself and direct all their energy on helping Cash clean up the mess we've made. Instead, they treat me like I'm a valued addition to their family, which is far more than I can say for my father.

"You're right." Cash sighs. "Ev and I—" He stops when Johanna opens the door and steps outside with a perplexed expression.

"What on earth are you all still doing out here?" she scolds. "The photographer is getting impatient."

"Is it alright if I wait in the kitchen for Cash?" I ask.

"Absolutely not," Johanna says firmly. "They wouldn't be family photos without you in them, sweetie. Now come along." She places her hand on my back, guiding me inside.

Her sentiment is touching, but it's overshadowed by the knowledge that this illusion will shatter once the truth comes out. I'll be left alone on the sideline, picking up the pieces.

I look back to glare at Cash, paying no mind to Dylan and Harrison, who are struggling to stifle their laughter.

It's official—this day is shaping up to be a complete disaster.

6

CASH

EVERLY FOLLOWS MY MOM INTO the backyard while giving me the cold shoulder.

She has plenty of reasons to be upset with me, starting with putting her in this predicament. I have a tendency to dive into situations without evaluating the potential repercussions of my actions, and I suspect I'll face the fallout when we're alone later.

The last thing she wants is to pose for photos with my family and pretend we're in love, especially when she's upset about me not bringing up the acquisition sooner. As soon as I suspected she might not be aware of it, I should have addressed it. To hell with the merger's confidentiality rules. I should have put Everly first. I won't make that mistake again.

Once we get to the back deck, Mom and Harrison leave us to help Mike and the photographer with arranging a couple of wooden benches in front of an ivy arch on the property's edge.

Everly and I stand side by side as Marlow comes out of the house dressed in a bright blue summer dress and silver sneakers. Her golden-blonde hair falls in waves to her waist, framing her distinct, mismatched eyes—one blue, the other green.

She moved in next door to Dylan a year and a half ago, and he didn't exactly roll out the welcome mat. Everything changed when his long-term nanny quit, and Marlow stepped in to help care for Lola. It didn't take Dylan long to fall for Marlow, and after three months where she lived abroad, they moved in together and recently got engaged.

"Look who finally showed up," Marlow teases me.

"It's good to see you, Mar." I wrap my arm around her shoulder in a side hug.

"You must be Everly." Marlow extends her hand to Everly, who accepts it with a small smile. "I'm Marlow, Dylan's fiancée, and that's our daughter, Lola." She motions out into the yard, where Lola is running, chasing after their dog, Waffles.

"Waffles stole my headband again," Lola shouts in our direction.

Marlow adopted the Australian Shepherd/Corgi mix with comically large ears from an animal shelter before she moved to Aspen Grove. She felt an instant connection because he also has mismatched eyes—a combination of one brown and one blue.

I laugh when I spot the three tiny furballs with floppy ears trotting closely behind Lola, yipping with excitement.

Dylan slings his arm around Marlow's shoulders and tugs her close.

"I can't believe you're keeping the whole litter," I say with a hint of amusement.

Marlow recently started volunteering at the local animal shelter, and a couple weeks ago, someone brought in three Aussie-Corgi mix puppies they found on the side of the road. Instantly reminded of Waffles, she knew she had to take them home with her. What started as an offer to foster them quickly led to her adopting all three.

"Yeah," Dylan grumbles, but his tone changes when he glances down at his fiancée with affection. "Marlow doesn't want to separate them."

"They're part of our family, and I won't abandon them," she declares. "Who else would love them like we will?"

"I'm sure Cash and Everly would." Dylan smiles at us. "What do you say, lovebirds? Do you want an adorable puppy as a wedding present? Consider it therapy to bring you closer when the honeymoon stage is over." He winks at me.

Everly fixes him with an icy stare. At least we can agree that Dylan's joke isn't funny. The last thing we need is to add an untrained puppy to the mix.

"Dylan, tell me you did not just try to pawn off one of our dogs." Marlow swats him on the chest.

"I'm sorry, sunshine." He places a kiss on her forehead. "I was just messing around. They're not going anywhere," he promises.

Dylan might not be enthusiastic about sharing his home with three more furballs, but he's smitten with Marlow. He would do anything to make her happy, even if it means being the owner of four energetic dogs.

"Let's hope you have better luck training them than you did with Waffles," I taunt, shooting him a playful smirk.

"Hilarious," Dylan responds dryly.

"I thought so." I grin triumphantly, squaring my shoulders.

Everly glances between us with a confused look.

"Waffles wasn't trained when I adopted him," Marlow explains to Everly. "Dylan made it his mission to whip him into shape, but Waffles gave him a run for his money."

"Hey, now," Dylan playfully chides, his voice filled with amusement.

"I'm just messing around," Marlow quips, using his own words against him.

Dylan chuckles. "Touché." He takes Marlow's hand, lacing his fingers with hers. She gives him a soft smile, and he looks at her like she's his entire world. When Marlow came along, Dylan was a grumpy cynic whose primary focus was raising Lola and growing Stafford Holdings. She has brought light into his life and taught him how to smile again.

Even as a carefree, unattached bachelor, I often wonder what it would be like to look at someone the way Dylan looks at Marlow. My gaze drifts to Everly, who's watching Marlow and Dylan's interaction closely, chewing on her lip. Despite our less-than-ideal circumstances, I'm glad she's here. It didn't occur to me how much I missed her until I saw her sitting at that hotel bar in Vegas.

"Dylan, Cash, why are you all just standing around?" Harrison shouts from the yard. "The photographer is waiting." He motions for us to get a move on.

"We're coming," Dylan hollers back.

"You ready for this?" I whisper in Everly's ear.

"Do I have a choice?" she mutters.

"Nope." I grin, taking her hand in mine as we follow Dylan and Marlow to join the rest of my family.

Two hours later, my cheeks hurt from smiling so much. Lani, the photographer my mom hired, isn't messing around. She must have taken hundreds of photos by now, and I'm hoping she'll wrap things up soon.

Everly has kept her distance despite Lani and my mother constantly encouraging us to stand closer together. She talked with my dad and siblings in between poses and tolerated my mom's never-ending questions.

From my shameless eavesdropping, I've learned that Everly depends on coffee as her lifeline, works long hours, and is a décor enthusiast.

I'm the type to go with the flow and never sweat the small stuff, but even I'm left wondering how we can pull off a fake marriage. We couldn't be more opposite if we tried.

I don't own a coffee maker—I prefer protein shakes and smoothies. I'm usually the last one to arrive at the office in the morning. And let's just say the décor in my London apartment is somewhat lacking.

"Cash, Everly, you're up next," my mom announces, breaking me out of my thoughts.

What is she talking about?

"For what?" Everly questions, mirroring my confusion.

"Couple photos," my mom states like it's obvious. "I have no pictures of your wedding, so this is the next best thing." She clasps her hands together with anticipation.

"Come sit over here." Lani motions toward a blanket she's laid out, with several fruit trees and the barn in the background. "Everly, I'm going to have you take off your shoes, if that's alright."

"Okay," Everly says, her voice filled with uncertainty.

She's wearing a light blue spaghetti-strap dress. Her hair is styled in loose waves, and she has on a pair of open-toed heels. Even without advanced warning, she came ready to crush family photos.

She's a goddamn vision. I can barely contain my fingers itching to reach out and draw her close to me, to feel the warmth of her skin against mine.

"I'm going inside to make dinner," my mom announces. She turns to Marlow and my brothers, sitting on a nearby bench. "I could use some help."

"Sure thing," Marlow jumps up, pulling Dylan along with her.

"Have fun, you two," Dylan calls out as they walk toward the house.

Harrison gives Everly a sympathetic look before he follows behind.

Presley and Jack disappeared inside thirty minutes ago, right after their photos. I don't even want to guess what they're doing.

My dad is playing with Lola, Waffles, and the puppies on the deck, and when my mom reaches the patio, she gestures for him and Lola to go inside too.

With everyone out of view, Everly exhales and her tense shoulders drop. I offer her my hand to help her down onto the blanket, but she shakes her head.

"I can do it on my own," she says curtly.

"I know, but I want to help," I reply, my hand cradling her elbow as she lowers herself to the ground.

She glances up at me, her eyes softening for a moment. "Thanks," she murmurs.

Everly settles on the blanket and I take a step back as she slips off her shoes. Once she's finished, she shifts to the middle and smooths out her dress, waiting for further instructions.

"Cash, sit behind her, please," Lani directs me. "You're going to spread your legs with your knees slightly bent and once you're in place, Everly will lean against you," she instructs.

Once I'm seated, Everly reluctantly leans into me, her back pressed against my chest as her thigh brushes against my leg. She fidgets with her hands and I can feel her breathing quicken as she leans into me.

"Cash, wrap your arms around her and kiss her forehead. Everly, hold his hand and place your other hand on his calf to show off that gorgeous ring of yours," Lani instructs.

Everly's eyes widen in alarm, but luckily, I'm the only one who notices. Lani is too busy checking the settings on her camera, and my family is all inside.

It was convenient that my mom required every member of our family to help with dinner except Everly and me. I don't buy it; she always has an ulterior motive. She probably figured she'd get better photos of us without an audience, and I'll do my very best to make sure Everly is as comfortable as possible.

Everly lets out a nervous laugh as she awkwardly rests her head on my shoulder. Her hands tremble as she places one on my knee and the other on my lower leg.

Lani moves positions, and the angle of her camera focuses on my left side. My hair is pushed back from my face, which means my scar is visible. My body freezes up, and my breathing becomes shallow. I was so focused on making sure Everly was okay that it didn't cross my mind that couple photos would include close-ups of our faces. There's a reason I don't like to look in the mirror. I'm not under any illusions that I'm physically attractive, and prefer to avoid daily reminders of that.

Group shots are easy to manage since I can stay in the back and angle my face away from the camera. However, I steer clear of close-up photos whenever I can.

Everly tilts her head back, worry etched on her face. "Are you alright?"

"Let's try another pose," I suggest. "I'd prefer my good side showing." I gesture to my face.

"If you'd like, I can edit out your scar," Lani offers.

"Absolutely not," Everly interjects sharply, glaring at Lani before looking back at me. "You're beautiful. Your scar is part of you." Lowering her voice so only I can hear, she adds, "This situation isn't easy for me either, but we'll get through it together, okay?" She gives me a soft smile as she brushes her hand across my scar.

I blink down at her, rendered speechless. I'm well aware that most women don't find me attractive. They tolerate my looks because they have to, but no one has ever called me beautiful. Part of me wants to dismiss her words as mere pity, but I know that's not accurate. If it were anyone besides Everly, I wouldn't believe it, but she's not one to mince her words.

"Whatever you say, boss," I choke out, overcome with unexpected emotion.

"Everything okay?" Lani asks.

"Yes," Everly says, turning back to face her. "We're all set to continue."

"Perfect. Cash, wrap your arms around her," Lani says when I don't move.

If she finds it strange that Everly and I are uncomfortable with each other, she keeps it to herself. Thank god Dylan and Harrison are inside, or they'd be teasing us without mercy.

I band my arm around Everly and pull her tight against me. My racing heart reverberates in my ears, its steady rhythm grounding my senses. Everly's shallow breaths are a dead giveaway that I'm not the only one affected by our proximity.

She feigns indifference, but now and then, I catch her mask slipping. Like when she couldn't stop sneaking glances at me when I walked into the hotel bar. Or when I woke up with her clinging to me like a baby koala.

"Everly, scoot a little closer to Cash, please," Lani calls out from behind her camera. "Pretend I'm not here, and you're just sharing a special moment as newlyweds."

Joke's on her because Everly would rather watch me get struck by lightning than be my wife. Unfortunately for her, she's stuck with me—at least for now.

The sooner we cooperate, the sooner this will be over.

I take the opportunity to enjoy this fleeting moment as I bury my face in her hair and inhale the scent of jasmine, lavender, and vanilla. She smells like heaven, and I'm forced to push aside any thoughts of her writhing against me in pleasure.

Fuck me.

Maybe taking photos together was a bad idea. This woman is toying with my mind. One minute, I'm agreeing that getting an annulment is a good idea, and the next, I'm consumed by an overwhelming desire to explore every inch of her.

My instincts take over as I grip her hair in my fist and push it over her shoulder. A part of me can't help but wonder what it would feel like if I peppered kisses along her neck, holding her hair like this. Would she hum in delight or cry out in pleasure as I played with her breasts, alternating between pinching and twisting them with my fingers, my tongue slipping inside her mouth.

That's not an appropriate thought to have during a family photo session.

That doesn't stop my cock from pulsating with excitement. I use my newfound daydream to keep me in the present as I caress Everly's hand in a hypnotic fashion—back and forth, back and forth, back and forth. She sits still as a statue but grips my calf tightly, proof that my touch is affecting her—no acting necessary.

Her reaction pushes me forward, and I drag a finger along her arm, leaving goosebumps in my wake. I pause for effect, and as she lets out her next breath, I plant several kisses along her shoulder as my hands tug her closer to me. The tension crackles between us.

"Why don't you kiss her on the mouth, Cash," Lani suggests as she snaps another picture.

That's a terrible idea.

Common sense doesn't stop me from fixing on Everly's plump red lips, practically begging to be kissed. Technically, our first kiss was at the chapel after we exchanged vows, but we were both buzzed, and I didn't get to enjoy it the way I wanted to. There's no chance I'm passing up the opportunity to taste her now that we're sober.

One little kiss can't hurt, right?

I'm sure that thought will come back to haunt me later, but I can't find it in me to care.

My dick is doing the thinking when I lightly grasp Everly's chin and tip her head back, coming face-to-face with her wanton expression, her chocolate-brown eyes ablaze with desire. Our intermingled panting is music to my ears as I slant my mouth across hers.

"Can I kiss you, Ev?" I murmur.

"You'll smear my lipstick," she whispers teasingly.

"Fuck it, I'm kissing you anyway." I brush my lips against hers in a teasing stroke, and I'm both shocked and pleased when a soft moan escapes her mouth. As I deepen the kiss, the tension between us becomes an inferno.

Our lips are interlocked as I cup her cheek with my hand. She shifts position—her ass pressed against my rock-hard cock.

Kissing her is like tasting forbidden fruit. Every touch is electric; every breath is charged with anticipation, making it all the more sweet.

I'm lost in the moment when Lani's high-pitched voice jolts me back to reality. "That was perfect," she exclaims. "I got so many incredible shots. I'm all set."

I jerk my head up to find her retrieving her equipment bag from one of the benches nearby. Everly and I were so caught up in the intensity, I briefly forgot Lani was here.

My gaze pings back to Everly. She stares at me, cheeks flushed, like she can't believe what just happened. She finally snaps out of it, scrambling out of my arms, pausing when she sees my face.

"Uh, you should take care of that," she says as she motions to my lips.

I swipe at my mouth with the back of my hand, grinning when I glance down at my hand, now marked with red lipstick.

"I'm going inside," she announces, refusing to make eye contact.

She puts her shoes back on in record time before hustling toward the house.

"I'm right behind you."

Holy shit, I just kissed Everly… again.

Now is not the time to panic; it won't do me any good.

When I look at the house, I spot Harrison and Dylan watching out the window with smug expressions on their faces.

Even I'm starting to see that our dilemma has gotten out of hand. The sooner we leave for London, the better.

Something tells me that our kiss just complicated things, especially since now I want to do it again… and *again.*

7

EVERLY

"BYE, GIGI. BYE, PAPA," LOLA yells from the window as Dylan pulls out of the driveway, the headlights cutting through the dark. "Bye, Presley and Jack! Bye, Cash and Everly!"

"See you tomorrow, ladybug," Johanna calls out as we all wave goodbye from the front porch. I hear Waffles and the puppies barking in the back seat as they drive away.

Dinner with the Staffords felt like old times. It was a loud, chaotic, and lively affair. The Stafford siblings still tease each other mercilessly, but the love they share is unmistakable.

Harrison pulled me aside before leaving to return to the city and told me he'd call Cash tomorrow once we've discussed how we'll move forward. He wanted to make sure I knew I could come to him directly if I needed someone to talk to. It means a lot that he didn't demand Cash and I stay together, but didn't miss the subtle warning in his tone that one solution would be far less complicated than the other.

"Well, we better get going," Cash announces. "It's getting late and the pilot wants to get a move on if we're going to leave for London tonight."

"Don't be silly." Johanna waves him off. "It's late. You and Everly are spending the night. You can fly back tomorrow once you've had a good night's rest."

I have a sneaking suspicion she has an ulterior motive for suggesting we stay, considering the private jet we took here is the definition of luxurious.

"Thanks for the offer, Mom, but we really need to get back," Cash tells her.

I'm glad to see him stand his ground—unlike earlier when he couldn't tell her the truth about our relationship. Not that I'm bitter about it or anything.

"Nonsense," Johanna pushes back. "You've had a long day, and it would be best if you stayed here. Don't you agree, Mike?"

He glances between his wife and son. "You kids are welcome to spend the night," he answers diplomatically.

"I don't think—"

"I insist," Johanna interrupts. "You're staying with us, and that's final."

Cash lets out a loud sigh as he glances in my direction. "Fine, Mom, you win. We'll stay."

This cannot be happening.

My eyes widen. I'm ready to confront him and demand that we leave tonight, but one look at Johanna stops me. She has a warm smile on her face, but there's a determined glint in her eye. She's made up her mind.

So, I'm staying at the Staffords' tonight.

But Cash and I are definitely talking about this once I get him alone.

"Doesn't this remind you of when you stayed here for the first time?" Presley smirks at Jack.

"It does." He tugs her close to his side and places a kiss on her temple.

"We fell in love here," Presley explains when she notices my quizzical expression. "I was living in New York, working as Jack's assistant. He's the CEO of Sinclair Group, a large investment firm. After three years of sidestepping our mutual attraction, a disastrous work trip to Aspen Grove ended up with us pretending to date because my family despised my boss."

I stiffen at her mention of them fake dating. It's eerily similar to the situation Cash and I are in, except we took it a step too far and got hitched.

"The night we arrived," she continues, "my mom insisted we stay here in my childhood room with only one bed since we told her we were a couple."

"Little did we know that Johanna knew all along that we were pretending and that I was Presley's boss," Jack chimes in.

Wait, did Presley just say one bed?

I let out a nervous laugh, unsure how else to respond. My mind flashes to memories of Cash's childhood bedroom, and I panic.

"At least tonight won't be awkward since you're married and all." Presley beams at me.

She has no idea.

"Good night, sweetheart." Johanna pats Cash on the shoulder. "I'm so glad you're here, Everly." She gives me a passing kiss on the cheek.

"Me too," Presley adds. "I've always wanted sisters-in-laws, and I'm so happy I now have you and Marlow. Although we're still waiting for her and Dylan to make it official."

Guilt washes over me, worried about disappointing her when she finds out the truth.

Before I can respond, Cash ushers me inside and upstairs to the second floor. I tense as he pushes open the door to his childhood room.

"After you," he says, his hazel eyes lingering on me as I brush past him. My pulse quickens at the touch, and I suppress the urge to glance back.

His room hasn't changed much since high school. The full-sized bed has a navy-blue bedspread and pillows, with a nightstand and lamp on each side. A black dresser beside the closet is topped with several lacrosse trophies and two photos from before his accident—one of his family and the other of him, Theo, and me sitting on his parent's porch on our first day of high school.

The space is much smaller than I remember. This isn't going to work.

I take a step back, bumping into Cash before I can attempt to make a break for it.

He closes the door and must recognize the irritation etched on my face.

"Are you okay?" he asks, gently touching my arm.

"You did not just ask me that." I shrug his hand off, but the warmth from it lingers on my skin. "Your brothers are more concerned about the gravity of the matter than you are, and they're not the ones who woke up married this morning," I remind him. "There's nothing wrong with rolling with the punches, but this is a marriage we're talking about. I need you to take this seriously."

"Ev, relax," he says in a soothing tone. "We'll get this all sorted out, I promise. Let's take my mom's advice and get some rest. I'm sure things will seem less daunting tomorrow."

I inhale a long breath through my nose and count to five before exhaling. The last thing we need is for Johanna to come upstairs to check on us, wondering why we're fighting on our first day as newlyweds.

"Delaying this conversation will not make it go away," I mutter, folding my arms across my chest.

"Is there something you want to get off your chest?" Cash prompts.

"Yes, several things, actually," I answer honestly. "For starters, you should have told me about the acquisition while we were at the hotel. Even if I knew, we should have discussed it beforehand. You and your brothers blindsiding me this afternoon was humiliating."

From a logical standpoint, I understand Cash didn't deliberately withhold information. He assumed I knew about the business deal, but it doesn't stop me from expressing my annoyance.

"And it wasn't fair of you to put me in this position—the family photos and spending the night here." I gesture around the room. "I understand you're close to your family, but they deserve the truth. I don't like the idea of keeping secrets from them."

He's not the one his parents and Presley will hate once the truth comes out. Plus, it's not like his brothers will fire him if this all goes south. I have so much more to lose.

"Is that all?" he retorts. "Don't hold back. I can handle honesty."

"That's debatable," I mumble under my breath. "You've been acting like this isn't a serious predicament."

"At least I have a sense of humor," he says. "You're plenty serious for the both of us."

"Oh my god, you're absolutely insufferable," I say loudly, throwing my hands in the air in frustration.

Cash's eyes soften at my reaction. "I'm sorry, Ev. I'm not intentionally trying to make things more complicated." His tone is apologetic.

He has always used humor to navigate difficult situations he's unsure how to confront. While it's not my preferred approach, I recognize the importance of being understanding and supportive. We're in this together, for better or worse.

"We're both doing the best we can." I give him a wry smile. "There's not exactly a handbook on how to navigate waking up accidentally married to your brother's best friend."

Cash's eyes light up with amusement. "She *does* have a funny side."

"You bring out the worst in me," I tease, and he gives me a broad smile. "Listen, the most pressing issue right now is that we don't have our suitcases. What am I supposed to sleep in?"

We left our luggage on the plane since we were supposed to only be here for a few hours.

"You can wear one of my T-shirts," Cash says, going over to the dresser in the corner. He pulls out a gray T-shirt and tosses it in my direction.

"I can't wear this," I tell him as I catch it.

On closer inspection, I see that it's the Linkin Park T-shirt he let me borrow back in high school. He and Theo had been obsessed with the band when we were in eleventh grade. When they came to Maine during their tour, Cash and Theo got tickets, and I tagged along. One of the many perks of having a twin is you have built-in friends. Someone standing next to us spilled a drink on my shirt, and Cash saved the day, letting me wear the band tee he'd bought as a souvenir.

We got back to Aspen Grove late, and Johanna insisted we stay at their place. Theo and I ended up sleeping on the floor in Cash's room. I can't remember the last time I had as much fun as I did that night.

"It's either that or sleep in your underwear. I don't mind either way." Cash smirks.

I take deep breaths to maintain my composure. He's only lightening the mood, and I should appreciate his effort. It would be far worse if he were grumpier than I am.

"You remember where the bathroom is?" He nods toward the connecting door.

"Yup."

I clutch the shirt close to my chest as I make a mad dash to the bathroom, locking the door behind me. Once I'm alone, I set the band tee on the counter and look into the mirror. My reflection portrays a polished, put-together businesswoman, but inside, I'm a hot mess.

"God, this is such a disaster," I mutter as I fight back tears.

How could I have let a routine business trip to Vegas end with a spontaneous marriage, and potentially face a reality where I can't get out of it for the foreseeable future because of a deal between our family businesses that I knew nothing about?

"What am I going to do?" I ask my reflection.

The silence is deafening. I consider calling August, but it's the middle of the night in London. Besides, there's nothing he can do to help. Who am I kidding? He'd commend me for my irresponsible behavior.

I hate to say it, but maybe Cash is right. Tomorrow is a new day; hopefully, things won't seem so bleak come morning.

The soles of my feet throb, and I grip the counter to keep steady as I slip my heels off, sighing in relief when my feet touch the cool tile. They're my favorite heels, but they're not the most practical when standing for hours.

I check the top drawer to find several toothbrushes still in the packaging. It looks like Johanna hasn't changed much around the house in the past fourteen years.

After brushing my teeth and washing my face, I change into Cash's T-shirt. Even after being in a drawer for years, it holds the faint scent of his cologne—citrus, musk, and sandalwood. The shirt hits my mid-thighs, and I curse myself for not asking for a pair of sweats.

For a moment, I consider sleeping on the bathroom floor, but quickly decide against it. Minutes ago, I was scolding Cash for being immature, and now I'm hiding out, which is just as bad.

After giving the bottom of the T-shirt a firm tug, I ease the door open and peek my head into the bedroom. Cash is sitting in bed, back against the headboard, with the covers pulled up to his waist as he reads something on his phone. He must have used the bathroom down the hall to get ready.

His bare chest is on display, and I catch a glimpse of his sculpted stomach. My gaze peruses the defined contours while he's preoccupied.

Thankfully, I come to my senses before he catches me ogling him… again. I have a bad habit where he's concerned, but it's not my fault he's so damn sexy.

I straighten my spine and cross the room. I'm halfway to the bed when he looks up, his gaze shamelessly trailing down my bare legs.

"You're staring," I snap, not caring that I'm being hypocritical. It's not like he saw me checking him out, so it's irrelevant.

"I remember the night I bought that shirt," he says, gesturing at me with a lazy grin.

My stomach flips as a rush of warmth flows through me, knowing he remembers that night with the same fondness as I do.

I clear my throat. "Speaking of T-shirts, where's yours?" I nod to his bare chest.

"I sleep naked," he ribs me, his eyes twinkling when he notices my jaw drop. "Don't worry, just from the waist up. Besides, given your ogling when you came out of the bathroom, I don't think you mind."

A blush spreads across my cheeks. "Sure, from a distance you're easy on the eyes, but the second you open your mouth, all bets are off," I taunt.

"And yet you still married me," he says as his gaze drifts back to my legs.

"Why do you have to be so infuriating?" I hold my hand up when he opens his mouth. "Don't answer that; it was a rhetorical question."

I gingerly climb into bed next to him. Unfortunately, there aren't enough pillows or space to build a barrier between us, so I slide as close to the edge as possible.

Before I can turn off the lamp on my side of the bed, my phone buzzes, and several texts appear on the screen.

Landon: I had a meeting with your dad yesterday.

Landon: I'll be in London in a few weeks and want to take you to dinner.

Landon: I miss you, babe.

Even after two years, he won't leave me alone. He cheated on me but thinks I should forgive him. Usually, when he's had too much to drink, he reaches out, begging me to take him back, and other times, he's vindictive and bitter because I called off our engagement. The first time he texted me after our broken engagement I blocked his number, but the next week he texted me from a new one.

It doesn't help that he does business with Townstead International and that my dad thinks we should be together.

Another reason Cash and I shouldn't be getting involved. I don't mix business and pleasure anymore.

"Who's texting you this late?" Cash leans over, trying to get a glimpse of my phone screen.

"Nobody," I reply too quickly, turning the screen away from him.

"Uh-huh." His tone is skeptical. "Make sure to tell whoever he is that you're in bed with your husband. That should shut him up."

I raise a brow. "How do you know it's a guy?"

"Only an ex, a lover, or a previous hookup would text you at this hour on the weekend."

He's spot-on, but I'm not about to admit it.

"Good night, Stafford," I say, sidestepping his remark. "You better stay on your side of the bed," I warn him as I turn off the lamp.

"You weren't concerned about designated sides of the bed last night," he mocks in a playful tone.

I fluff my pillow and settle into it, facing him. "That was the tequila, not me."

"Oh, so now we're playing the blame game?" He grins from ear to ear. "In that case, I'll do what I can to stay on my side, but this mattress has a habit of pushing me to the middle of the bed."

"You're unbelievable," I scoff.

"I try my best." He winks before he turns, his back facing me.

Why does it irk me he had the final word? No matter how many insults I toss at him, he remains unfazed.

I flip over to face away from him as he turns off his bedside lamp, plunging the room into darkness, and I squeeze my eyes shut. I'm not a fan of the dark. A few seconds go by, and Cash shifts around to get comfortable.

His back touches mine, but he doesn't move away. I refrain from saying anything, deciding it will only encourage him. Instead, I remain still, concentrating on my controlled breaths.

While I wait for sleep to take me, my mind drifts to our unexpected kiss this afternoon.

When the photographer told Cash to kiss me, I should have protested, but there was a part of me desperate to feel his mouth on mine—the brief moment we shared at the chapel had me longing for more. As I met his gaze, I felt the gentle whisper of his breath on my skin. When our mouths met, it sparked a wildfire of affection I never wanted to end. The desire to keep him close outweighed all logical reasoning.

I press my thighs together, determined to banish the unwanted thoughts from my mind. But it's difficult when the man haunting my dreams is lying next to me. Unable to fall asleep, my mind wanders to our night in Vegas.

Cash throws a hundred-dollar bill on the table and takes my hand.

"Where are we going?" I ask as he weaves through the piano bar, tugging me along.

"You just agreed to marry me. There's no way in hell that I'm waiting another second to officially make you Everly Stafford."

He opens the door to the club, and makes his way down the street.

"Stafford, wait," I grab his arm and force him to stop in the middle of the sidewalk. "What do you mean you don't want to wait another second? You literally just asked me."

Cash's expression softens, a smile forming on his lips. He cups my cheek with his hand, and traces my jaw with his fingertips. "I've wanted you since the tenth grade, Ev. There's no way I'm letting the chance to call you mine slip through my fingers now."

My mouth falls open, and my eyes widen at his declaration.

"You're joking."

He shakes his head. "I've had a crush on you since you walked into our tenth-grade English class with your hair falling down your back in waves and wearing your favorite Doc Martens. You gave me one of your signature smiles, and I was a goner."

I tilt my head and nibble on my lower lip. "Why didn't you tell me?"

"Theo caught me staring and confronted me after class. He made it clear that you were off-limits if I wanted to stay his friend, and I couldn't risk losing you both."

"What's changed?

"Now I know what it's like to live a life without you in it."

I blink up at him, unable to speak. This is madness. I should ask Cash to take me back to my hotel, but the hopeless romantic inside me that's been dormant for years has resurfaced and refuses to miss her chance at the happily ever after she used to dream of. No matter how fleeting it may be.

I'm pulled from the memory, when Cash shifts in bed. A reminder that the hopeless romantic won out and I'm now in bed with my husband.

I still can't believe we got married.

There's something intoxicating about his confession that he's had feelings for me since high school, and my heart races, recalling the warmth of being held in his arms last night. It makes it so much harder to resist the temptation to move to his side of the bed to be close to him again.

It's going to be a long night.

8

CASH

I WAKE UP WITH EVERLY DRAPED across my chest. Her head is nestled in the crook of my shoulder, her leg hitched over my thigh, and her arm wrapped securely around my waist. In sleep, her features appear softer, the creases around her eyes ease, giving way to a peaceful expression. The weight of the world has been lifted from her shoulders as she relaxes into the security of my arms.

As I shift beneath her, my rigid cock presses against her stomach, straining against my boxers.

Fuck.

I carefully maneuver out from under her, avoiding waking her up. The last thing I want is for her to panic and blame me for invading her space. Although, technically, she was on my side of the bed.

The last two mornings, I've woken up way earlier than usual. I'm a night owl, and I sleep in every chance I get. When

Harrison first took over Stafford Holdings, he held early morning meetings with Dylan and me. However, after I missed half a dozen in the first month, he stopped scheduling any with me before 10:00 a.m. He'd be shocked if he could see me now.

While I'm close to my siblings, I often feel like an outsider.

From an early age, Harrison was primed to take over Stafford Holdings. He graduated college with a business degree and went on to complete his MBA. Aside from a rebellious stint playing professional hockey for a year, he's the perfect son.

Dylan is a financial whiz and graduated at the top of his class. After his long-time girlfriend stepped out on him and Lola when she was just six weeks old, he was a single dad until Marlow came into his life.

And then there's Presley. She's the long-awaited daughter who can do no wrong in my parents' eyes. After high school, she ventured out on her own, determined to be recognized for her own accomplishments, not the Stafford legacy. Now she's thriving as a marketing associate at Sinclair Group.

Unlike my siblings, I've never had ambitious goals or the drive to achieve tangible success. I have more straightforward aspirations. Making people laugh, caring for my family and friends, and living life to the fullest makes me happy. Most people mistake those qualities for laziness, lack of motivation, and unproductivity. My accident taught me to embrace each day as it comes and not to worry about what tomorrow might bring.

My mind is wide awake, so I decide to go for a run.

I check my phone and find that I have multiple texts all from Theo.

Theo: How was your Friday night in Vegas?

Theo: Say hi to your family for me.

Guilt gnaws at me when I glance over at a sleeping Everly. I can only imagine what Theo will do when he finds out I married his sister. He explicitly said she was off-limits and won't care that it was fourteen years ago. I decide to hold off on texting him back until Everly and I decide how we want to move forward.

I send my pilot a text, requesting that one of the crew members deliver the suitcases we left on the plane to my parents' house. They stayed at the Coastal Haven Inn last night, a local bed-and-breakfast, so they should be well rested.

As quietly as possible, I dress in a pair of running shorts and shoes I left here during my last visit. I'm in the habit of keeping clothes here since my mom prefers her kids to stay at her house when we come to Aspen Grove.

Since it's the middle of the summer—and will be scorching once the sun rises—I don't bother with a shirt and walk softly toward the door. I steal one more glance at Everly, loving how she looks in my bed before I slip out of the bedroom and sneak down the stairs.

As I step onto the porch, I'm greeted by a chorus of birds chirping and the golden light of the sun coming over the horizon. I close my eyes and breathe in deeply, savoring the fresh air.

After my accident, I spent a month confined to the hospital and another two stuck at home, so when I finally got the green light from the doctor to exercise, I started running. It gave me the chance to get outside and release all the pent-up energy I had bottled up. It's become my lifeline—a way to clear my head and stay fit. Even with the gym in my London apartment I prefer to exercise outdoors as much as possible.

Today, of all days, I'm glad to have the chance to get out and calm my mind.

After a grueling eight-mile run, I return to my parents' house to find our suitcases on the porch. Someone from the crew must have dropped them off while I was gone. Now Everly will have all her things so she can get ready before we leave.

I was gone longer than I planned, taking a spontaneous detour from my usual route.

Curiosity led me to the old Miller House. After all this time, the place remains abandoned, yet I couldn't help but notice the 'for sale' sign in the neglected front yard.

When I go inside my parents' house, it's still quiet, so I head straight to my bedroom to take a shower. After setting the suitcases near the doorway, I notice that the bed is empty. The bathroom door is ajar and I can hear the sink running.

I cross the room and steal a glance inside to find Everly standing at the vanity, washing her face. She's still dressed in my T-shirt, her golden, toned legs on full display. When she leans forward to splash water over her face, the T-shirt rises, giving me a glimpse of her lacy white panties that hug her ass just right.

Fuck me, she's a goddamn vision.

Her phone rings on the countertop, and she flinches when she checks the screen before answering on speakerphone.

"Hi, Dad." She grabs a hand towel, patting her face dry.

"Where are you?" Richard barks. "You were supposed to call me after your last meeting on Friday."

Everly shuts her eyes as she exhales slowly. "Why didn't you tell me Stafford Holdings was buying out Townstead International?" she asks, ignoring his question. "Have you told August and Liam?"

I don't miss her voice wavering. She puts on a strong front to conceal her emotions, but in the past twenty-four hours, I've witnessed several instances where her facade of indifference has cracked before she refortifies her walls. I wish she didn't feel like she had to conceal herself from me. Everyone deserves to have a person they can confide in.

Guilt washes over me for not putting in more effort to stay in direct contact with her over the years. She became withdrawn after her dad walked out on her family, and after she left for college, I figured she wanted a clean slate. I shouldn't have made that assumption.

"Who told you about that?" Richard demands.

Everly folds the hand towel and hangs it on the rack. "I ran into Cash Stafford on Friday. He was in Vegas for a board meeting and assumed I knew about the deal."

"That's unacceptable," Richard seethes, his voice raised. "Harrison said he was meeting with the board. They're not taking this deal seriously if they sent Cash to present the proposal. My company deserves more respect than that."

I don't give a damn what Richard thinks, but I hate that he's right. The board wasn't pleased that I went in Harrison's place, and they insisted Dylan call in for the meeting. It was humiliating that they didn't trust me to handle it alone.

Where Harrison is considered a powerhouse in the industry and Dylan the level-headed genius, I'm the irresponsible brother who likes to party. I can't change how people view me, so I stopped caring a long time ago. But moments like this serve as a reminder of how I'm perceived by most, and I can't stop the negative thoughts that creep in.

"Don't insult my husband that way," Everly snaps, slapping her hand across her mouth as soon as the words come out.

A smile tugs at my lips. For someone who doesn't want to be married, she's sure quick to jump to my defense. It doesn't matter that her calling me her husband was a slip of the tongue—she still said it.

"Your *husband?*" Richard barks. "The last time I checked, you weren't dating anyone. What did you do, Everly?" His tone is condescending.

"I was hoping Cash and I would have everything figured out before I talked to you," Everly says softly as she bites her lower lip.

"Spit it out already," Richard shouts into the phone, causing Everly to shrink back.

"Cash and I sort of got married Friday night." She winces, bracing for his reaction.

"What the hell do you mean, you *sort of* got married?" Richard hisses.

"It… it was an accident," she stammers. "I had too much tequila, and it clouded my judgment. One thing led to another, and we ended up at a wedding chapel on the Strip." If she chews on her lip any harder, she's going to draw blood. "I'll fix this, Dad, I promise. We'll get the marriage annulled as soon as—"

"You stupid girl," Richard says, not giving her a chance to finish explaining. Everly flinches at his harsh insult. "Do you realize what you've done? You could sabotage the chances of Stafford Holdings buying my company because of your incompetence."

A growl escapes my lips. If Richard were here in person, I would give him a piece of my mind. He has no right to disrespect Everly like this. She wasn't aware of the deal until yesterday, so she's not to blame.

I knew about the deal, and my brothers were far more understanding. Harrison might disapprove of my actions, but he would never prioritize business over family. If I called him right now and told him that Everly and I don't want to go through with this charade, he wouldn't be ecstatic, but he'd accept it. Even when I've been an irresponsible dumbass, he's always there for me.

"I'm sorry," Everly murmurs despondently.

"Under no circumstance will you get this marriage annulled. Do you understand?" Richard states, leaving no room to argue. "You've made your bed—now it's time to face the consequences of your actions."

I clench my hands at my side, forcing myself not to intervene. Despite Richard's disrespect toward her, I don't think Everly would welcome my interference. Richard's primary concern should be his daughter. Yet, all he cares about is himself and a tentative business deal. He's a selfish bastard, and I wish I could knock some sense into him.

"Okay," Everly says in a meek voice.

This isn't the sexy, confident woman I've spent the past day with. Right now, she's a daughter desperately craving her father's love, but it's nowhere to be found.

"I don't care what you have to do to make it work, but you're going to be a good little wife and stay married until the deal is finalized," he orders. "If you mess this up for me you can kiss your career goodbye. I'll make sure no one else in the industry will hire you." Richard's harsh tone sounds more like he's threatening a business rival than having a conversation with his daughter.

Everly stands with slumped shoulders, her entire body seeming to shrink inward as tears stream down her face.

I fucking hate Richard.

I swear to god, the bastard will pay for how he has treated Everly. It might not be today, but he'll get what's coming to him, and I'll find satisfaction in watching him suffer when he does.

9

EVERLY

"I HAVE TO GO. I'M pulling into the country club and can't be late for my tee time. Do not disappoint me, Everly Rae," Dad says sharply before ending the call, leaving me alone with my racing thoughts.

I hold on to the bathroom counter for support as I inhale deeply through my nose and count to five before exhaling, fighting to keep the tears at bay.

Growing up, I was taught that crying is a sign of weakness. It's ironic how my dad told me that, yet he's the reason I'm feeling this way.

He's always valued power and success over building relationships with his family. And when I agreed to work for him, my desire for financial security and independence outweighed his negative treatment.

Movement near the doorway has me spinning around to find Cash leaning against the wall, his hands clenched into fists at his sides, a scowl on his otherwise relaxed face.

"How long have you been standing there?" I ask with trepidation.

"Long enough to affirm my overwhelming disdain for your dad." He strides across the bathroom and hops up on the countertop like we're two pals having a casual conversation. "Why do you let him talk to you that way? You deserve better."

"It's complicated," I reply vaguely, hoping he'll drop it.

"Why don't you uncomplicate it for me?" he suggests, using my response from yesterday.

How do I explain that my need for security and stability outweighs my father's mistreatment when I don't think he would understand? Cash may have the perfect family, but mine is far from it.

"How much has Theo told you?" I ask, curious about what my brother has shared with him.

"Not much," Cash answers. "I know he doesn't have contact with either of your parents and changes the subject if they're brought up in a conversation."

I lean against the vanity next to where he's sitting, emotionally drained from my conversation with my dad.

Cash doesn't rush me to speak, waiting patiently as I collect my thoughts. I tap my fingers against my thigh as my mind races.

"There's no pressure to talk about it if you'd rather not. I'll be here when you're ready," he says, offering comfort.

"No, you should know. Just please don't judge me." I inwardly cringe at how vulnerable I sound.

"Never," he vows as he holds my gaze, studying my expression.

"My mom has always had unpredictable mood swings. Some days she was energetic, and others she could barely get out of bed. It didn't help that my dad was indifferent. He spent most of his time at the office and traveling for work, not wanting to deal with his home life."

Theo tried getting our mom help, but she refused, and he was angry at my dad for leaving. After graduation, he moved to New York, cutting off all contact with our parents. He thrived, especially after Cash dropped out of college and joined him in the city.

On the other hand, I was alone, attending college on the west coast. It was sink or swim, and I was determined to prove that I could succeed on my own, even though it was more challenging than I expected.

"I had no idea you and Theo were dealing with so much," Cash admits. "I knew your parents had problems, but I didn't realize how bad it was."

I'm caught off guard when he winds his arm around my waist and pulls me into the space between his legs.

"No one did. Our parents' broken marriage wasn't exactly something we wanted to talk about with anyone. My dad definitely didn't want it becoming town gossip." It must be the intoxicating mix of his scent, sweat and raw masculinity, that has me leaning my head against Cash's bare shoulder. "Mom blew through the money she got from her divorce settlement within a few years—designer clothes, expensive jewelry, spa days in the city. By the time I graduated from college, all her money was gone."

Cash strokes my arm with his hand, soothing the turmoil within me.

"Shortly after, Dad reached out with a job opportunity that I couldn't pass up. It paid enough—more than enough—to provide a comfortable life for myself and pay my mom's bills. Despite our strained relationship, I couldn't bring myself to abandon her. And I thought having a career would guarantee I'd never have to rely on anyone." I let out a humorless chuckle. "Which is ironic since my dad holds all the control now."

I leave out the part that, no matter how illogical it sounds, I cling to this twisted hope that someday, my dad will finally see my value and treat me the way I deserve. The chance of that happening is slim, but I'm not ready to give up a career that has made it possible to create a life that I wouldn't have otherwise.

"Damn, Ev, I'm sorry," Cash murmurs sadly, his lips brushing against my ear as he speaks.

His familiar presence makes it difficult to keep my emotional barriers intact, and I worry that if I'm not careful, I could end up hurt again.

"No one knows the full truth." I pull away from his comforting embrace and meet his gaze. "I've shared some things with Theo and my step-brothers, but I don't want to get them involved. It's my burden to bear."

Theo has made a name for himself in the restaurant industry. He owns several restaurants, co-hosts multiple cooking shows, and teaches at a prestigious culinary school in the heart of London. The last thing he needs is for the media to catch wind of his family drama, and getting him involved in my issues would do just that. And he would be disappointed in me if he found out I was giving our mom money.

"He wouldn't see it that way. You're the most important thing in his life."

"If that's the case, you're in so much trouble when he finds out you married me," I taunt, lightening the mood. "You might want to keep those running shoes close by when you tell him." I nod to his feet.

"Gee, thanks for that." Cash chuckles as he runs his hands through his hair.

"My pleasure," I tease.

Maybe I shouldn't make light of it. There's no chance Theo will let Cash off the hook when he finds out what's happened. I'm not looking forward to that conversation.

"Have breakfast with me at Brew Haven?" Cash asks, his eyes pleading. "Like you said last night, we have a lot to talk about. We're meeting the pilot at the airfield in two hours, so we have plenty of time."

"Won't your mom be offended if we don't eat here?" When we were kids, she would make a big breakfast on the weekends, which is one reason Theo and I liked to sleep over.

"Nah, she'll be fine with it," Cash insists, then hesitates, second-guessing himself. "But she's still in bed, so if we leave soon, we won't have to risk it. I just need to take a quick shower, and then we can go."

My face heats at the idea of him standing naked under the cascade of water. His handsome face and well-defined chest leads me to believe the rest of his body is equally as impressive.

I blink rapidly, banishing the thought. "I could go for coffee and French toast."

"That's my girl," Cash praises, kissing my forehead before getting off the counter.

My stomach flutters at him calling me *his* girl, but I push the feeling aside, desperately trying to fortify the walls around my heart, and yet somehow, he's managed to knock down another brick.

"Why is everyone staring?" I whisper as we wait for our breakfast to arrive.

The aroma of ground coffee and fresh-baked pastries fills the air of Brew Haven. The coffee shop hosts a weekly Sunday brunch, so the place is buzzing with activity and packed with patrons eager for their caffeine fix and a hearty meal.

We're seated in a booth toward the back, but that doesn't deter the other patrons from craning their necks to get a better look at us.

"They have nothing better to do. Have you forgotten that's how it is in a small town?" He gives me a sly smirk. "How long has it been since you've been back?"

"Christmas break my freshman year of college," I admit hesitantly.

"That was the year my family went to Paris for Christmas," he says.

"Yeah." I lower my gaze as I fidget with my napkin. "Your mom told Theo to invite me, but I declined because I didn't want my mom alone for the holidays. When I got to her place, she was packing for a trip to Cabo. Apparently, she met an accountant online who paid for them to go to an exclusive resort."

"What did you do after she left?"

"I went back to school in California."

I don't tell him that all my friends had gone to visit their families, so I spent Christmas alone in my dorm. It was also the first time Theo and I spent a holiday apart, which made it even harder. But knowing that he was celebrating with the Staffords brought me peace of mind.

"Where is your mom now?" Cash asks.

"Out of town," I say, keeping my answer vague.

She called last week to tell me she found her soulmate in Bali and he's taking her on a spiritual retreat. If I had a dollar for every time she's claimed she's found *the one*, I'd be a millionaire.

My mom's unhealthy relationships with men is one of the reasons I stopped believing in true love. She tarnished my belief in soulmates by claiming every man she's been with is hers. Combined with my personal experience, I've concluded that love either festers, fades, or ends in a bitter divorce, leaving both parties broken beyond repair.

This is why Cash and I have to resolve our current dilemma before we become like my parents. I shudder at the thought.

I'm about to tell him how I think we should move forward when our server, Kelsey, arrives with our food order.

"Here you are." My mouth waters as she sets a steaming cup of coffee and a plate of French toast, topped with banana and extra whipped cream, in front of me.

She hands Cash his protein breakfast bowl filled with scrambled eggs, sausage, slow-roasted tomatoes, spinach, and scallions. From what I've noticed, he's very selective about what he eats and leans toward healthier choices. Spinach and kale are fine, but I'll never sacrifice my French toast and whipped cream.

"Thanks, Kelsey. This looks incredible," Cash says as she sets his side of artisan sourdough toast on the table.

I suddenly lose my appetite when she shoots him a flirtatious smile and unashamedly checks him out.

"Yes, thank you so much. My husband and I can't wait to dig in," I say, reaching for my fork.

Kelsey's smile drops when she notices my ring. "Oh, of course. I'll let you get to it," she says before she hurries off to the front of the shop.

Satisfied, I cut into my meal. "This French toast looks even better than I remember."

When I glance at Cash, he hasn't touched his food. Instead, he's staring at me like I've grown an extra head.

"Is there something wrong with your order?" I say as I take a big bite, savoring the crispy edges and soft center.

"Nope," he says smugly. "I was just wondering if you're going to get jealous of every woman who serves us when we go out. If that's the case, we should consider sticking with takeout." He flashes me a cheeky grin.

"What's wrong with what I said?" I ask, my tone defensive. "She was practically drooling all over you, even though I was right here. It doesn't help that you flirt back." I shake my head in mock disappointment.

"Trust me, you'll know when I'm flirting," he says with a wink.

I sip my coffee, hiding my smile behind the cup. I'm not ready to admit that our friendly banter is growing on me.

"How would you like it if we had a male server and I was just being nice by placing my hand on his arm and telling him how big and strong he was?" I reach across the booth and place my hand on his upper arm, unable to resist needling him.

"I'd tell him to step away from my wife," he growls playfully. "Like you did when you called me your husband."

"You're a smartass," I quip, holding up my left hand and flashing the massive ring on my finger. "You've reminded me nonstop since I woke up with this thing, so I figure why not use it to my advantage?" I plop a piece of banana in my mouth.

He leans across the table, his voice low enough so only I can hear him. "Ev, let me make something clear," he says earnestly. "I may joke around a lot, but I mean it when I say that I'll support whatever you decide. If you want to take that ring off right now, say the word, and I'll call my lawyer to draw up the annulment paperwork. Our short-lived marriage will be nothing but a distant memory when we land in London."

He pauses, giving me a chance to process what he said. "But, if that's what you want," he says, his infectious, cheerful energy back in full force, "you'll have to tolerate me for a few more hours since we're flying back together."

"What about my dad?" I voice my biggest concern. "He means it when he says he'll fire me. And what about Harrison and Dylan? The deal could fall apart if we break things off," I remind him.

"I don't give a damn about Richard," he growls. "Your happiness comes first, and I'd gladly step down as Chief Operations Officer at Stafford Holdings if it would appease the board. Hell, I could live in the jet for a while. Now, that would be an adventure." He gives my hand a squeeze before leaning back in his seat.

I stare at him in stunned silence as he takes a drink of water. He has a gift for making everything seem so simple. No matter how bad things get, he always has a smile on his face and finds the silver lining. It's a sharp contrast to my bleak outlook.

Would it be so bad to stay married to him for a brief period? The acquisition is underway and should be complete within a few months, most likely sooner. I take another bite of my French toast and consider the pros and cons.

Pros—Cash Stafford is easy on the eyes. Just because I have no plans to sleep with him doesn't mean I can't appreciate him from a distance. There will never be a dull moment with him around, and I won't lose my job.

Cons—That damn kiss in his parents' backyard still lingers in the back of my mind. If I'm subjected to his hotness for too long, there's no telling what I'll do… but is that really a con?

"You're staring," Cash taunts.

"I'm thinking."

"A little too hard, it seems." He nods to my furrowed brow.

"We should stay married," I announce.

"You think so?" His fork pauses on the way to his mouth.

"Yes. Logically, it makes the most sense. There's no reason either of us should lose our jobs. We can go about our lives as normal, and nothing has to change," I state confidently.

I mentally pat myself on the back as I cut another piece of my breakfast.

"So… you're moving in with me," Cash says, disregarding my statement entirely.

My fork slips from my hand and clatters on the table, drawing attention in the coffee shop. "What did you say? I think I heard you wrong. There's no way you just suggested that we move in together."

I've lived alone since I graduated from college. The closest I came to moving in with someone was when Landon and I were a couple. He slept over at my place a lot but wanted to wait until after the wedding to live together, which, in hindsight, should have been a major red flag.

"You heard me correctly. Newlyweds live together, and for all intents and purposes, that's what we are." He flashes his wedding band at me.

"Okay, you can move into my place," I say, but regret the words as soon as they pass my lips.

My apartment is my safe haven—the one place I feel at ease and can let my guard down. I'm not sure I want to share my personal space with a stranger. Technically, Cash isn't a stranger, but he might as well be.

He shakes his head. "Your apartment is a forty-minute drive from the city. Mine is only fifteen minutes from both our offices, albeit in opposite directions," he declares with a self-satisfied grin.

I narrow my eyes at him. "How do you know where I live?"

"Theo told me when he helped you move into your new place last year. I was supposed to help, but Harrison needed me in Maine that weekend."

I wonder if we'd still be in this predicament if we had crossed paths sooner.

"Fine, I'll stay at your place, but I'm keeping my apartment so I have a place to go when this is over." I point at him with my napkin in hand. "Oh, and I get my own room."

It's important I lay the rules down early to establish boundaries.

"Okay," he replies before taking a bite of his eggs.

That was easy… too easy.

I watch him polish off the last of his breakfast, mesmerized by the way his lips close around the fork.

"You're not going to argue with me?"

"Nope," he says.

"As long as we're living together, I would prefer you didn't bring other women over."

Cash lets out a low growl. "I'm only going to say this once, Ev. As long as we're married, there won't be anyone else. For either of us."

"You can't be serious."

"I mean it. Regardless of how we feel about this marriage, we made vows, and I'm committed to mine," he states with conviction.

His sentiment sends butterflies through my stomach, but I have to remember they're empty words wrapped in a pretty package. This arrangement is just a means to an end for both of us.

"Are you sure, Stafford? There's no telling how long this acquisition will take to finalize." I lean in and whisper, "Can you go months without sex?"

He raises a brow as he takes a drink of water. "Can you?"

"That's what my toys are for." I give him a satisfied smirk. "They've gotten me through the last two years. A few more months will be a piece of cake."

His eyes widen in surprise, and he chokes on his water, sputtering as he sets his glass on the table.

After pausing to collect himself his hazel gaze holds mine hostage as he says in a low voice, "You wouldn't need toys if you were with the right man."

Is it getting hot in here?

My pulse races as I lift my napkin from my lap and wipe my mouth, trying to appear unaffected by his statement. "Thanks for the unsolicited advice."

"Anytime." Thankfully, he breaks our eye contact when Kelsey drops the check off at the table. "We should get going if we want to make it back to London tonight."

"Wait." I reach to grab his arm. "Under no circumstance can we tell Theo that our marriage isn't real. He would lose his shit."

Cash's eyes widen at my request. "Ev, you can't be serious. He's my best friend and we run in the same social circle. He's going to find out one way or another."

"I didn't say to keep it from him that we're married, just not that we're staying married because of the acquisition." I give him a pleading look.

My brother has always been my fierce protector, and I never want to disappoint him.

Admitting that I made a reckless decision to get married in Vegas is one thing. But it'll be worse if Theo knows how bad things have gotten with Dad. If he finds out that Dad demanded I stay married because of a business deal, he'll feel compelled to intervene, even though it's not his responsibility to fix my problems.

Cash lets out a heavy sigh. "Let me get this straight. You're suggesting that we not tell Theo that Stafford Holdings is buying out your father's business. Which means when we break the news to him, he'll think our feelings for each other are real and that we got married in Vegas on a whim because we want to be together?"

I nod. "Exactly. The same as what we told Presley and your parents. The only people who will know the truth are Harrison and Dylan."

"What about your step-brothers? I think you have to tell them. They have a right to know about the acquisition and how it'll affect them."

I rub my temples, warding off an impending headache. Our situation is getting more complicated by the minute.

"At this rate, we're going to need a chart to keep this all straight," I say with a hint of amusement. "Are you sure you just don't want to get an annulment? It seems like the easier option."

Cash chuckles. "Where's the fun in that?" He reaches across the table, taking my hands in his. "I'm all in if you are."

"Yeah, Stafford, I'm in."

My heart hammers in my chest as his eyes hold mine. I'm entranced as he traces circles on my palms with his thumbs, sending an electric current spark through my veins. His touch is quickly becoming addictive, and I almost let out a sigh of disappointment when he lets go.

He stands and tosses a hundred-dollar bill on the table as a tip. "We should head out. We're supposed to meet the pilot in a half hour, and my mom will never forgive me if we don't say goodbye first.

Once he has paid the bill at the cash register near the front, he holds the glass door open for me, and we exit the coffee shop. I almost run into him when he suddenly stops by the newspaper dispenser.

"Is everything okay?" I ask.

He takes out a copy of the *Aspen Grove Gazette*, holding it up for me to see. On the front page are photos of us from high school, accompanied by a wedding announcement congratulating us on our marriage.

The curious glances from the other patrons in Brew Haven make more sense now.

"How did the newspaper get wind of this? Only your family knows about our marriage."

Cash chuckles. "That explains why my mom slept in this morning. She was probably up half the night sharing the news with all her friends."

Sounds like something Johanna would do. She tends to overshare when she's excited about something. Another pang of guilt strikes me as I consider how she'll react to the truth that none of this is real.

"You're lucky Theo doesn't still live here, or you'd be in serious trouble," I taunt.

"That's not funny," Cash mutters.

"It really is." I laugh as I walk away.

The past twenty-four hours have been a whirlwind, and I can't help but question how difficult things will be once Cash and I are thrown back into reality as roommates posing as newlyweds.

10

CASH

I watch as Everly climbs the steps of my private jet, refusing my offer to help with her luggage.

Even though it's Sunday, she's dressed in business attire—flare-legged black slacks, an ivory tank top, and open-toed black stiletto heels. Because of the sweltering heat, she ditched her suit jacket in the car. Her hair, coiled into a low bun and secured with a multitude of bobby pins, tempts my imagination. I can't resist picturing those silky black locks cascading down her back if I were to free them. I imagine sinking my fingers into her hair as I tenderly kiss her lips, and my mind runs wild, taking me back to our kiss at the wedding chapel in Vegas.

"Do you, Everly Townstead, take Cash Stafford to be your lawfully wedded husband, to have and to hold, from this day forward, for better or worse, for richer or for poorer, in sickness and in health, to love and to cherish, until death do you part?"

"I do." Everly *giggles as she gazes at me with those big, beautiful brown eyes.*

"And do you, Cash Stafford, take Everly Townstead to be your lawfully wedded wife, to have and to hold, from this day forward, for better or worse, for richer or for poorer, in sickness and in health, to love and to cherish, until death do you part?"

"Hell yes, I do." I caress Everly's cheek with my thumb. *"I promise, Ev, I'll make you laugh every day and spoil you endlessly."*

"By the power vested in me by the state of Nevada, I now pronounce you husband and wife." The officiant glances at me. *"You may kiss the bride."*

Fueled by the alcohol buzzing through my veins and not giving a damn that we have an audience, I trace Everly's jawline with my thumb. She melts into my touch, and I take the opportunity to claim her as mine. I wrap my hand around her waist and dip her backward. She winds her arms around my neck to keep her balance.

My tongue dances along the seam of her lips in teasing strokes, and I groan with satisfaction when she opens her mouth to welcome me inside. Her invitation sends a coursing need flowing through my veins.

I've never felt this way from a kiss before—all-consuming, ravenous, passionate. It feels right having her secured in my arms as I fuck her mouth with my tongue. I'm never letting her go.

"Cash, are you coming?" I'm brought back to the present by Everly waving her hand in front of me. "Are you okay? You spaced out for a minute there." A concerned expression crosses her face.

My gaze narrows in on her lips, the memory from our night in Vegas lingering in the back of my mind. "I'm great," I say as I lock eyes with her, determined to win her over.

Her eyebrows knit together, forming a slight furrow. "If you say so," she replies with a hint of doubt.

The last thing she wants to hear is that I was daydreaming about the kiss at our wedding ceremony. Or that I've been fantasizing about the one we shared at my parents' house. Given that she's as cuddly as a porcupine, the odds of me getting a third kiss are slim to none.

Everly spins away from me to climb the last few steps of the plane, and I take advantage of her being distracted to adjust the hard-on in my pants. The mere memory of having her lips on mine sends an electric pulse through my body. She evokes a primal response from me like I've never felt before, and I'm struggling to rein it in.

The flight attendant stands inside the plane's entrance and greets us with glasses of champagne. "Welcome," she says to Everly. She flashes me a broad smile and brushes her hand against my arm as I pass by. "It's good to see you again, Cash."

"Thanks, Lily," I say, focusing my attention ahead as I pass past her into the cabin.

Unsurprisingly, Everly and I both pass on the champagne.

The jet's interior is furnished with eight leather seats to the left, two long couches to the right, and a large flat-screen TV built into the far wall. The cabin is relatively compact, making space for the bedroom at the rear of the plane.

Everly moves to the row in the back, and I follow, taking the seat next to hers.

"There are plenty of other places to sit. Why don't you take one of those?" she suggests, giving me a pointed look.

"I want to sit next to my wife, if you don't mind," I tease as I nudge her shoulder.

She rolls her eyes. "You're insufferable."

"Thank you." I stretch my legs and lean against the headrest to get comfortable.

"That's not a compliment," she grumbles as she stashes her purse in the compartment in front of her seat. "I couldn't help but notice the flight attendant was overly friendly with you."

"She's getting a big bonus because of our delay. Of course she's going to be nice." Everly nods, staring straight ahead. "There's only one person who has my attention, and it's not her." I absentmindedly run my finger along a stray piece of her hair, tucking it behind her ear. She shivers slightly at my touch, her gaze locking onto mine with a flicker of interest before it vanishes as suddenly as it appeared.

Everly might have heard about my reputation from Theo, but it unsettles me that she only sees me as a charmer who's looking for my next conquest. I'm determined to prove that she's the only woman I have eyes for now.

"Don't say things like that."

I raise a brow. "Why not?"

"Because they're just empty words," she says, like it's an undeniable fact.

"I meant every single one, wifey," I murmur in her ear, giving her hand a gentle squeeze.

She stiffens at the touch, her fingernails digging into the leather armrests. I feel a rush of adrenaline, seeing my effect on her.

"Stop calling me that," she says, but her voice lacks conviction.

"Not a chance. You're my wife, and I plan to remind you of that every chance I get."

"Are you sure you can survive indefinitely without sex?" she taunts.

"Can you?" I quip.

"I have my toys, remember? I'll be just fine." She tilts her head toward me, a smirk playing on her lips.

"Well, I have my hand, so we're on an even playing field." I wink.

There's no chance in hell I'll be able to stop fantasizing about her lying beneath me on the bed, as I tease her breasts with my hands, and sink inside her warm heat.

Everly may come across as reserved and closed off, but she's also a confident, alluring woman. I'm venturing to guess her sexual desires have been neglected because of her past experiences.

She's tightly coiled like a twisted rope, waiting for the right person who is patient enough to unravel her complexities— someone who views every flaw and imperfection as intricately woven threads in her story.

The problem is I don't stand a chance at being that person for her when all she can see is the sum of my playboy reputation.

Truthfully, I'm tired of being perceived as a manwhore who is selfish and uncaring—they're wrong. Being upfront with the women I've slept with has made things far less complicated.

For a guy who keeps women at arm's length, I'm acting like a lovesick puppy where Everly is concerned. She's shot every rule I have to hell, and oddly enough, it doesn't bother me.

I would have thought after fourteen years, I'd be over my one-sided interest in her. I was wrong. It's like I've reverted to a teenager, and all the suppressed feelings I've kept hidden are fighting to rise to the surface every chance they get. She's captivated me with her quick wit and sharp tongue, and my fascination grew to adoration when she called me beautiful yesterday while I tried to hide my scar.

Now that Everly and I are bound together, I'm committed to keeping my promise to make her smile every day. She was willing to confide in me about her rocky relationship with her mom and deserves to have someone in her corner who knows the truth. Someone who's determined to give her a chance to spread her wings and break free from her dad's control once and for all—she shouldn't settle for anything less.

The rest of the flight back to London is uneventful. Everly used the time to catch up on work, and I spent mine watching her—incognito, of course. The car ride is the same. She's busy reviewing documents, only looking up occasionally.

"We're here," I say when the driver pulls up to my apartment building.

Everly doesn't respond, too absorbed in the pile of papers on her lap. She's hunched over reading as she chews the pen cap in her mouth. I gently tap her on the shoulder to get her attention.

She snaps her head in my direction. "I'm sorry. What did you say?"

"We're here," I repeat, motioning to the apartment building outside the car window.

The driver is already waiting on the sidewalk when I get out of the backseat. I hand him a fifty-pound note and direct him to the doorman, who will make sure our suitcases are delivered to my apartment.

I stick my head back into the SUV. "Ready, wifey?"

Everly shoots me a disapproving scowl as she finishes putting the documents inside her purse.

"What will it take for you to stop calling me that?" she clips, ignoring my hand in favor of stepping out of the vehicle by herself.

"Already changing your mind about staying married?" I ask, a smile tugging at one corner of my mouth.

"No, but I..." She trails off when she sees the towering building above us. "Wait. You live here?"

"*We* live here."

There's no telling how long we'll be staying together, so she should get accustomed to the idea of the apartment being ours.

"This is where the city's wealthiest residents live. I know Stafford Holdings is a billion-dollar company, but I'm surprised you'd choose this place, given your modest upbringing."

I shrug. "I like extravagant things when they pique my interest. This building has all the amenities I could want, plus it's close to the office, so it seemed like the most sensible option."

The majority of my wealth comes from investments Dylan makes on my behalf. I've never been good at that kind of thing, and since he's a number whiz and enjoys playing the markets, I've let him have at it. And it's paid off big time.

My base salary goes toward giving substantial bonuses to my direct reports each year. Dedicated employees are what makes a company great, and by prioritizing my staff's needs, they're happier and more willing to put extra effort into their jobs.

I've never brought up these additional bonuses with Harrison or Dylan. I'm sure they'd consider my decision foolhardy and imprudent.

The way I see it, I have more financial resources than I could ever use in my lifetime, and I want to share the wealth with those who've earned it.

Max, my doorman, nods in our direction as he opens the door for us to enter the building.

Standing tall with a neatly trimmed beard and salt-and-pepper hair, he never fails to offer a warm, welcoming smile when I walk by.

"Thanks, Max." I shake his hand.

"My pleasure. And who is the lovely lady?" He grins at Everly.

The only other woman I've ever brought back to my apartment was Presley when she and Jack came to visit last month.

"This is my wife, Everly," I say proudly, wrapping my arm around her waist.

"Congratulations." Max beams with approval. "Welcome to the High Rise, Mrs. Stafford. If you ever need anything at all, don't hesitate to ask."

She smiles back at him. "Thank you, I appreciate it."

If Max wasn't in his sixties and happily married to his high school sweetheart, I might be jealous of Everly's genuine reaction to him. As it is, I'm glad she'll have someone other than me to look after her while she's staying here.

We head inside, and Everly takes in her surroundings. The lobby is the definition of timeless luxury and elegance—the building manager's words, not mine. A massive crystal chandelier complements the intricate white molding, and on the walls, modern art pieces depict famous sites in England.

Everly's heels click against the marble floors as we walk to the elevator that goes straight to the penthouse. When the door opens, I motion for her to step inside first before following behind. I press my thumb against the biometric fingerprint scanner and the elevator begins its ascent.

She clamps her eyes shut and holds the handrail with a death grip.

My brow furrows with worry. "What's wrong?"

"I don't like elevators," she admits.

"Fuck," I utter under my breath.

I rush to her side, wrapping my arm around her in a show of comfort. "I'm right here, Ev. I promise it'll be over soon."

She lets out a shuddered breath as she rests her head against my shoulder. Her rapid breathing mirrors the unsteady rise and fall of her chest. I lean in to whisper soothing words in her ear as I hold her close. I'm careful not to press her for more information about why she's scared. She'll tell me when she's ready.

In the meantime, I'll do what I can to make her comfortable while she's living here. I mentally remind myself to add her thumbprint to the private stairwell, giving her direct access from the lobby to the penthouse so she doesn't have to take the elevator.

When we finally reach the top and the elevator stops, she peeks open one eye to make sure the coast is clear. Once she deems it safe, she slips away from my embrace and steps around me, hurrying into the entryway of my apartment.

I immediately miss the warmth of her in my arms, but am quick to set those feelings aside. When she looks back at me, I offer her a cheerful smile.

"Welcome home, Ev." I motion around the massive space.

"For now," she states.

I hold my tongue to avoid adding fuel to the fire. I have a hunch she'll have plenty to be angry about once she's finished her tour. I might have left out an important detail about our sleeping arrangement during our conversation at the coffee shop.

"I still want you to feel comfortable while you're here. Can I get you a glass of water, or do you want to sit for a minute?"

Everly shakes her head. "Thanks for offering, but I'm feeling fine now," she says, her eyes drifting to the floor-to-ceiling windows in the living room that provide a panoramic view of the city. Moonlight streams through the glass, bathing the modern penthouse in soft, natural glow.

"This place is incredible." She slowly spins in a circle as she takes in her surroundings. "Did you just move in?"

I shake my head. "Nope. I bought the place nine months ago."

"Where's all your furniture?" She waves to the living room that's completely bare aside from a TV mounted to the wall and a beige loveseat.

"Last year, when Harrison announced the opening of an office in London, I volunteered. I've been splitting my time between here and our headquarters in Maine, so I didn't see the point in setting up the place."

She heads into the spacious kitchen that boasts white high-gloss cabinets, stainless steel appliances, and marble countertops. The only furniture in this room are two bar stools pushed up against the island.

"Oh, thank god you have a coffee maker," she exclaims when she spots the all-in-one coffee and expresso machine on the counter. "This thing is high-tech," she says with a low whistle. "You'll have to teach me how it works."

I rub the back of my neck sheepishly. "I've actually never used it. I prefer a protein shake or smoothie and rarely drink coffee."

"So why do you have this fancy gadget?" She waves toward the stainless steel appliance.

"I overheard you tell my mom that you start your day with coffee and wanted to make sure you had your morning fix while you're living here."

Her eyes widen in surprise. "You bought me a coffee maker?"

"Yeah," I shrug. "It's the least I could do to make the transition easier for you. I also had the cupboard stocked with a selection of coffee and mugs."

"Thank you, I appreciate it." Everly murmurs. "I can't wait to give it a try. I'm going to take a look around the rest of the house now."

Before I can tell her I only gave Marcus, my friend who's an interior designer, the go-ahead to fully furnish and decorate my bedroom, she zips away to explore the rest of the apartment. Her heels echo against the custom-made hardwood flooring, and then—

"Cash Stafford, you have some serious explaining to do," she shouts from the primary bedroom.

Right on cue.

I don't bother postponing the inevitable. As soon as I step through the door, she tosses a pillow at my head. I duck to avoid it, only for her to pelt another one that clips my shoulder. Thank god I refused to let Marcus add any decorative pillows to my bed, or I would be facing a full-scale pillow assault.

"You lied to me," Everly accuses, storming toward me and jabbing me in the chest with her finger.

I hold up my hands in defense. "Woah. I never lied."

"Yes, you did," she counters. "You promised I would have my own room. I've checked every one, and this is the only one with a bed or any furniture whatsoever. Which means you were expecting me to share this bedroom the entire time," she shouts, the sound reverberating against the walls.

"You can sleep anywhere you like. Although, if you choose one of the other bedrooms, I suggest you lay down several blankets, or the wood floor might get uncomfortable." I shouldn't provoke her when she's this angry, but I can't help myself.

She glowers at me, her hands on her hips. "If that's the case, explain why all my things from my apartment are in *your* bedroom. Thanks for asking permission to have strangers go into my home and move my things, by the way." Her tone drips with sarcasm. "How did they get in?"

I smirk. "I can't reveal my trade secrets."

It's remarkable what a quick call to the building superintendent and an offer to replace all the kitchen appliances in the building can do.

"If you had someone pack up my things, why wouldn't they have brought my furniture too? And don't you dare tell me they conveniently brought every single item I own except for my bed and dresser," she threatens.

I don't plan to.

"My team couldn't get a moving truck on such short notice, and could only fit so much in the SUV. You're lucky they could fit all your shoes."

It's half the truth. After spending the last couple of nights in the same bed as Everly, I've decided I don't like the idea of us sleeping in separate bedrooms. It's just a happy coincidence that I only have one bed.

"And what's your excuse for moving all my things into *your* bedroom?"

"I told them you were my wife. In case you didn't know, it's common for couples to share a bed."

She paces the floor in front of me. "This arrangement will not work. I'll call a moving company first thing in the morning and schedule my bed set to be delivered at their earliest convenience."

I frown at her suggestion, not liking that idea one bit. I'm not above calling whichever company she hires and bribing them to cancel the delivery.

"That's not a good idea," I state in a serious tone.

She crosses her arm. "Why not? It's the perfect solution."

"Eventually you'll return to your apartment, and it'll be a hassle to move everything back. My friend Marcus is an interior designer. He wasn't happy when I rejected his proposal to decorate the full apartment. I'll call him and have him furnish one of the other rooms for you."

"You promise?"

"Absolutely."

I will reach out to Marcus eventually, but I never said when. Everly is as stubborn as they come, and I have to use every loophole to my advantage to keep her here with me while I can.

"Let me guess. You expect to share a bed until then?"

"Sure, why not?" I play it casually. "We've slept in the same bed the last two nights. Mine is a California King, so you won't even notice I'm there." I have a feeling that won't stop her from rolling over to my side in her sleep. She can't get enough of me—in her sleep, anyway.

Everly eyes me with pursed lips. After a few moments, she says, "Fine, we'll do it your way, Stafford. But remember, this is a temporary arrangement. I'm moving out of this room as soon as I have my own space."

I can't contain my smug smile. "Whatever you say, wifey."

"Stop calling me that," she huffs in frustration.

"According to the notarized marriage certificate in my bag and that diamond on your finger, you belong to me. And like I've said before, I'm not going to let anyone forget it—including you."

"You won't make my time here easy, will you, Stafford?" she asks with an eye roll.

"Not a chance, Ev, but only in the best way possible," I reply with a grin.

11

CASH

LAST NIGHT WAS PURE TORTURE. Everly paraded around the primary bedroom wearing nothing but a lace tank top and booty shorts while she unpacked. Her long legs and generous curves were on full display, and it took all my willpower to keep my hands to myself. I swear she did it to mess with me as payback for not having another room ready for her.

This morning, I woke up to her clinging to me like a second skin, resulting in a raging hard-on. I resorted to taking a cold shower and another long run. The time change must be messing with my head. Plus, it's difficult to sleep when the woman next to me plays the starring role in my fantasies but is off-limits.

If the past two days have been any indication of how the rest of this arrangement is going to go, I may need to reconsider my stance on sharing a bedroom.

Everly left for work before I finished my run, and after a second cold shower, I walked to the office, wanting more time to clear my head.

I've been so distracted with thoughts of her that I haven't been able to get much done, and it's already mid-afternoon.

My inbox is overflowing. I have a backlog of projects due this week, and several calls have been scheduled with Harrison and Dylan. Not to mention the massive stack of résumés Harrison sent via courier for several open associate positions in our London office.

Fortunately, I have Carol to help me sort through them all. She's a retired real estate manager in her late sixties who re-entered the workforce when she found my job posting for a temporary assistant position. Her industry knowledge is impressive, and she doesn't miss a thing.

I've been staring at the same cover letter for ten minutes when my phone pings with a text.

Mom's Favorites Group Chat

Mom: Did you and Everly make it back to London?

Presley: More importantly, has Everly had enough of you yet?

Cash: Yes, we made it back.

Presley: You ignored my question.

Cash: It was a lame question.

Mom: Cash, apologize to your sister this instant.

Presley: Yeah, Cash, listen to Mom.

Cash: At least now we know who Mom's favorite really is.

Mom: I don't have favorites.

Cash: That's not what the name of our group chat says.

Mom: Presley, I thought you changed that. I told you before that Harrison and Dylan will be upset if they see it.

Presley: They're big boys, they'll get over it. It's their fault for not wanting to be a part of our conversations.

Last year Presley started a group chat for our siblings and parents. My dad didn't join because he never checks his phone. Harrison left the group after his phone went off one too many times during a board meeting, and Dylan followed suit after we teased him about his nonexistent dating life before he and Marlow got together. Now, I'm the only one Mom and Presley have to pick on.

Cash: I'm happy to trade places with one of them if they've changed their minds.

Presley: Very funny.

Mom: Cash, when are you and Everly coming back to visit?

Cash: We were just there two days ago.

Mom: Yes, and? I miss you and want to get reacquainted with my new daughter-in-law.

Presley: What about Jack and me??

Mom: I miss you both too, sweetheart.

Cash: I should get back to work.

Presley: Funny, I've never heard you say that before.

Mom: Presley, be nice to your brother.

Presley: Oh, now who's your favorite?

Cash: Have fun, you two.

I put my phone down on my desk and lean back in my chair. No one has ever doubted my family's strong bond. We may be a tad overbearing, particularly my mom, but her unwavering love for her kids is heartwarming—Everly included.

I sit up straight when I hear Carol's voice from outside my office.

"You can go right in," she says brightly. "I'm sure he will welcome the interruption."

There's only one person she would let into my office without checking with me first, and if I'm right, this conversion will not end well.

I am seriously considering hiding under the desk when Theo steps inside my office. He's dressed casually in jeans and a white T-shirt, but his murderous expression is all business. The vein in his forehead looks ready to burst.

I should have made myself scarce while I still had the chance.

"Tell me this is one of your Stafford pranks and that you did not marry my sister." He slams a photocopy of the *Aspen Grove Gazette* on my desk, staring at me accusingly with deep brown eyes the same shade as Everly's.

"Where did you get that?" I ask calmly, maintaining my composure. Not my best response, but I'm caught off guard by the bitterness in his voice.

Theo has every right to be furious, and I figured Everly and I would break the news to him together to ease the tension. Why is it that she's conveniently absent whenever I tell another person that we got married in Vegas?

"Dylan forwarded it to me this morning with the subject line *Welcome to the family*," Theo fumes, running a hand through his dark hair.

Shit.

This reeks of one of Dylan and Harrison's practical jokes, and the timing couldn't be worse.

We've pulled a lot of incredible pranks on each other, our family, and our friends. Like when Presley brought Jack back to Aspen Grove, and we had him arrested for trespassing. Or when Dylan was training Waffles, and Harrison and I tied a treat to his tail so he wouldn't obey when Dylan gave him a command. However, I don't find this particular prank very funny when my life is on the line.

"Is this why I haven't heard from you or Everly since last week? I should have known something was up when you didn't text me back," Theo says.

He's my best friend and I'm afraid of how this will affect our relationship. He's privy to every detail of my checkered past and has been my wingman since we were eighteen. There's no way he will let me off easy for marrying his sister, and that's why I ghosted him over the weekend. Everly is the most important person in his life, and he'll see it as a betrayal, especially since he made it clear she was off-limits years ago.

"We should wait to have this discussion when Everly can join us," I hedge, subtly sliding my chair away from where he's standing.

As kids, Everly was the only one who could reason with Theo when he lost his temper.

"Oh, now you're dependent on my sister to fight your battles?" he growls. "You better tell me what the hell is going on before I lose my patience," he demands.

I think we've moved past that already.

I may be in good shape, but my workouts focus on cardio and moderate weightlifting whereas Theo prefers heavy lifting and boxing. I wouldn't stand a chance against him in a ring, let alone here in my office.

I'm totally screwed.

"Four months ago, you fucked a model you met in France, and the month before that, an actress in LA." He sneers in disgust. "And now, out of the blue, you're married to my sweet and fragile sister?"

Everly sweet and fragile? Try fierce and unyielding.

"For the record, I haven't slept with anyone since the model in France. Including Everly," I add before he can make assumptions. "I'm not claiming to have changed overnight, but she makes me want to be a better man."

That's the truth. Every minute I spend with her ignites the longing to be her knight in shining armor. She deserves someone who will stand beside her, ready to help her conquer her dragons.

"When are you going to get to the part where you *married* my sister without telling me?" Theo jabs his finger at the news article on my desk, then recoils. "Have you been seeing her behind my back?"

I vehemently shake my head. "No. We ran into each other in Vegas. Funny how you conveniently never mentioned she'd be there."

"You haven't seen her in years. I didn't think you'd care."

"Of course I would. It's a good thing I was there because a guy with wandering hands was accosting her." I frown at the memory of his meaty paw digging into Everly's smooth skin.

Theo's anger morphs into unadulterated rage. "Tell me you roughed him up."

"I would have, but I figured Everly wouldn't want me to make a scene, so I took a different route with better results."

I explain how I bribed the hotel security manager to send me the surveillance footage—which I sent to Van, a friend who works on the IT team at Stafford Holdings headquarters. He tracked down the man who harassed Everly. It turns out Larry Hansen is a mid-level manager at an accounting firm in Atlanta. Or should I say he was? My family's network is pretty damn impressive if I do say so myself.

"And what, that gives you an excuse to take advantage of Everly?" Theo spits his question.

"I would never hurt her, and you damn well know that," I state. "I took her to a piano bar to catch up and reminisce about the good ole days." I rake my hand through my hair. "Remember the night of senior prom when Everly and I hung out alone?"

"Yeah," he says with apprehension.

"She was upset about her breakup with Jacob, and I wanted to comfort her however I could. We made a marriage pact on a Willow Creek Café napkin and agreed that if we were both single in our thirties, we'd marry each other." I realize how silly it sounds when I say it out loud. "After one too many drinks, it came up and one thing led to another…" I trail off, reluctant to say the rest.

"Spit it out," Theo demands, frustrated at how long it's taking me to get the point.

I might deserve his anger, but if Everly were here, I doubt this conversation would be spiraling out of control.

"We got married at a chapel on the Strip."

"So the announcement in the *Gazette* was real?" Theo's voice is deadly, his dark eyes narrowing into slits.

"Yeah, Everly and I got hitched."

Before I can process what's happening, he grabs me by the collar and slams me against the nearest wall.

"You son of a bitch," he snarls in my face. "How the fuck could you do this to Everly? She's not a disposable plaything for you to use and discard. Don't you think she's been through enough after what Landon did to her?"

"Why does that name sound familiar?"

"He was Everly's douchebag fiancé." Theo's voice drips with disdain.

Everly was engaged?

Now that I think about it, I recall him mentioning Everly's snooty boyfriend a few years ago, but he left out the part about them taking their relationship to the next level.

"What did he do to her?"

Now that Theo has had some time to release his anger, I push his hand off me and step to the side, putting some space between us.

"She caught him banging his assistant at his apartment when she stopped by unannounced. Now it makes sense why he didn't want to live with her until after the wedding. He was using his place to hook up with other women," Theo says.

Everly's distrusting behavior makes so much more sense now. The barriers she has in place are to protect herself from getting hurt, because the person she should have been able to trust above anyone else betrayed her. I can't imagine what she went through in the aftermath and the strength it took to build herself back up.

No wonder she's been so wary of me. She assumed I was a playboy who toys with women's hearts, just like her lowlife ex-fiancé.

"Damn, I wish I knew sooner," I say.

In the past, Theo and I didn't talk much about Everly, but now I wish we had.

"She asked me not to tell anyone, and didn't want to be pitied."

That tracks, but it must make for a lonely existence without a support system she can confide in.

"I have something to say, and you're going to let me finish before you try slamming me against the wall again. Got it?" I raise a brow, waiting for Theo to respond.

"Fine, but make it quick," he snaps.

He's never been one for patience.

"My crush on Everly started in the tenth grade. Hell, you threw me up against a set of lockers just for looking at her the wrong way, so your reaction now doesn't surprise me." I massage my sore shoulder. "I would never intentionally do anything to hurt either of you." I hold his gaze and say with conviction, "Everly and I are both adults, and I'm not forcing her to stay married to me. So you can either get on board or explain to her why her brother isn't willing to support her decision. After everything she's been through, the least you can do is trust her judgment."

"Damnit, Cash." Theo blows out a breath as he sits on my desk. "You're not playing fair."

"This isn't a game, and Everly isn't a pawn," I state as I perch next to him.

"At least we can agree on something," he says as he glances over at me. "I'm just having trouble wrapping my head around how she could be okay with this. She's a workaholic, keeps to herself, and hasn't been on a proper date since she ended things with Landon. Now she's married to you? You have nothing in common."

"We balance each other out," I answer truthfully.

"Fuck." He rises from the desk and scrutinizes me as if searching for any sign of deception. "I was really looking forward to punching that pretty-boy face of yours."

I burst out laughing. "Aim for the left side the next time you have the urge. Everly might tolerate half my face being fucked up, but I don't think she'd like it if I didn't have a pretty side."

He scoffs. "You're joking, right? She's always had a thing for your scar. I heard her tell Whitney it was sexy as hell after she caught her talking shit on you in the hallway the week after you two broke up."

Warmth spreads through my chest. "Everly said that?"

"Yeah, she did," he assures me. "I'm not happy about this new development, but I'm going to give you the benefit of the doubt. However, if you do anything to hurt her, I won't hesitate to punch you next time."

A twinge of guilt prickles at my senses.

I wish I could come clean about the buyout—the real reason Everly is staying married to me. Theo won't be so forgiving once he finds out I withheld important information, but I can't betray Everly's trust.

"Now that Everly and I are married, I can call you *brother*, right?" I rib him.

Theo shakes his head, smirking. "Not a chance."

Not only do I have to win Everly over, but now I've got to prove to Theo that I'll always be there for him too. No matter what it takes.

12

EVERLY

"You're staring again," I say to August without looking up from my computer.

"I'm processing," he says.

I was the first to work this morning, but when he arrived, he stopped by my office for an update on my weekend and got far more than he bargained for. After I dropped the bombshell about Cash and I getting married, he made himself right at home on the upholstered couch in the corner.

I glance over at him, reclined back with his hands laced behind his neck. He's wearing a tailored navy-blue suit, a light blue dress shirt with the first button undone, and white sneakers.

His jet-black hair is styled with the top in curls and the sides trimmed into a tapered fade. And that British accent has both men and women falling for him instantly, drawn in by his classic good looks.

"Don't be so dramatic," I scold him with a hint of a smile. His electric blue gaze meets mine. "Oh, I'm sorry. How should I react to you getting back to town two days late and announcing that you're married?" He sits up straight. "Not to mention the bomb you dropped about Townstead International being acquired. I'm not looking forward to sharing the news with Liam."

I was right to assume my dad hadn't told anyone else about the deal. He's been going behind our backs for months, and if he were working with anyone other than the Stafford brothers, I'd be worried about the outcome.

After hitting send on the email I've been working on, I give August my full attention.

"I'll have you know this whole mess is your fault," I goad him. "If you hadn't encouraged me to let loose while I was in Vegas, I never would have entertained the idea of getting a drink with Cash. Or several." I mutter the last part under my breath.

August chuckles. "It's about damn time you were spontaneous and let loose a little. I was concerned you forgot how to have fun."

"I don't think getting married to someone I haven't seen in fourteen years qualifies as *a little loose*. It was downright reckless. Which brings me to my complaint." I rest my elbow on my desk and prop my chin on my hand.

"Oh, I can't wait to hear this." August leans forward in his seat.

"You were wrong. What happens in Vegas most certainly does not stay in Vegas." I hold out my ring finger for emphasis.

He lets out a low whistle as he gets up from the couch. "It's even bigger up close. It must have cost a fortune," he observes, grabbing my hand to examine the ring.

August isn't wrong. The five-carat pear-shaped ring is surrounded by smaller diamonds that sparkle in the light. It's both stunning and elegant, and yet despite its size, it doesn't feel overwhelming.

I can't help comparing it to the flashy emerald-cut diamond Landon gave me when he proposed. The thing got caught on everything because it was so bulky, and I didn't like the way it looked.

To Landon, I was merely an accessory, valued more for my connection to my dad than for who I am. In contrast, even after all these years, Cash sees through my facade and makes me feel truly seen.

"The ring is stunning. You're one lucky woman," August says.

"Yeah, it's nice," I hedge, refusing to admit I secretly love it. I can't get attached since I'll have to return it once this is all said and done.

My time with Cash has been brief, but that doesn't stop the pricking sense of unease that persists when I'm reminded our arrangement has an expiration date.

"Where are you living?" August questions.

"Cash's place."

"But you love your apartment."

"I do, but he lives at the High Rise, which is only fifteen minutes from our offices. Plus, his place has amazing perks. I talked to his doorman on my way out this morning, and he told me that Cash has a private gym on the floor below us, and he

also has access to a full-service sauna and spa in the building."
I clasp my hands together with excitement.

"You're living at the High Rise? Damn, you didn't tell me
your man was *that* loaded. Lucky you, living a life of luxury."
August gives a nod of approval. "Please tell me the sex is
amazing. It wouldn't be a proper wedding night without a good
fuck," he remarks unabashedly.

"Seriously?" I scold him while a flush warms my cheeks.
"He's not *my man*, and for your information, no, I haven't had
sex with Cash. Sleeping in the same bed is enough for—"

His jaw drops. "Woah, hold up." He lowers himself onto
my desk as if my admission has rendered him unable to stand.
"You're telling me you're sharing a bed and haven't gotten laid
yet? This is the perfect opportunity to have some of the best
sex of your life with no strings attached." He pauses when I
give him a pointed look. "Okay, fine, there are loads of strings,
but they'll all be severed once this arrangement is over, so
you've got nothing to lose, right?"

He makes it sound so simple, but experience has taught me
otherwise.

If Cash and I aren't careful, there's no hope of coming out
of this unscathed. Wrestling with my attraction is proving
difficult, and it's jeopardizing the boundaries I've set to protect
my heart.

"How do you think Liam will take the news about the
acquisition?" I ask, deflecting his question.

"Oh, he's going to be furious, just like I am. I guarantee
Dick had no intention of telling us until Stafford Holdings
signed on the dotted line. He always keeps us in the dark when
it suits him, and this situation is no different." August clenches

his jaw. "We've worked our asses off for years, and this is how he repays us? It's despicable."

Liam and August joined my dad's company to avoid conflict with their mom. She was adamant they support the family business for the sake of her reputation. The financial incentive was lucrative, but my father's dictatorial management style overshadowed it.

We could all benefit from a class that teaches adult children ways to stand up to their toxic parents.

"Don't worry. I'm confident the Stafford brothers have done their due diligence and recognize the value you and Liam bring to the company." I offer him an encouraging smile. "I saw them over the weekend, and it's obvious they're juggling a lot of responsibilities right now. They don't have the capacity to take over the day-to-day operations of Townstead International while managing their billionaire-dollar enterprise."

His furrowed brow doesn't give me confidence that I've eased his concerns.

"Fantastic." August rolls his eyes. "It'll be like working for Dick, but now there will be three of them to boss us around and pocket all our profits." His voice drips with sarcasm.

"You've got it all wrong. Cash and his brothers aren't like that. You may not know them yet, but I do, and I know they'll be fair."

The Stafford family may be billionaires, but they don't act like it. Johanna and Mike were adamant about raising their kids to be humble and hardworking. That's why they raised them in Aspen Grove, in a modest house well below their means.

"For someone who says your marriage is strictly for convenience, you sure seem smitten with your husband," August says with a smirk.

"I am not," I insist a little too quickly.

"You keep telling yourself that." August's eyes twinkle with amusement. "If I were married to a hot billionaire, I'd be having the best sex of my life. And no, those toys of yours are not comparable to a well-endowed man who knows how to please a woman."

"Oh my god, please stop," I beg him. "While I appreciate the unsolicited advice, I am sure I won't be sleeping with Cash."

Maybe if I repeat it enough, I'll believe it.

My mind wanders to the kiss we shared during our photoshoot. The way it felt to be wrapped in his arms as he leaned in, a gentle whisper of breath on my skin. The temptation to feel his lips on mine was too strong to resist, goading him to close the distance between us.

I was lost in the moment and when Cash pulled back, I panicked when I saw my lipstick on his mouth. It didn't help that there was a photographer there capturing what should have been a private moment.

Last week, being in a relationship was the furthest thing from my mind. Now, I'm fighting off feelings for a man who has irresistible humor, a seductive smile, and a touch that sends a shiver down my spine.

"Our marriage exists only on paper and once this is all over, we'll go our separate ways. I tell August, brushing my hands together in a wiping motion.

"I'll believe it when I see it." He snickers.

Why does his comment have me questioning my declaration?

"I have to get back to work," I announce as I check my computer screen to find that thirty new emails have hit my inbox since we started chatting. "Unless you want to do my work for me?"

"No, thank you." August quickly retreats toward the door. "I've got to go break the news to Liam. Wish me luck," he grumbles.

"Good luck," I holler after him.

I'm just relieved I'm not the one who has to tell him about the acquisition.

I'm exhausted when I get back to Cash's apartment. It was a long day at the office, and I hadn't eaten since August shared his chicken club sandwich with me earlier this afternoon. My stomach growls just thinking about the juicy grilled chicken and crispy bacon served on sourdough bread with tangy mayo. I should have grabbed dinner on my way back to the apartment.

When I enter the penthouse, there's an upholstered bench in the entryway that wasn't there this morning. I sit and experience immediate relief as the weight is lifted from my feet.

"Ev, is that you?" Cash shouts from the kitchen.

"Yeah," I yell back.

Honestly, it's strange coming home to someone waiting for me. When Landon and I were together, I was the one doing the waiting. Oddly enough, I don't mind it as much as I thought I would.

I slip off my stilettos and tuck them, along with my purse, under the bench.

Once I'm finished, I follow the delicious scent of smoky salmon, lemon, and herbs. Cash is at the counter, setting plates of food next to two glasses of water, each garnished with a lime wedge.

"Welcome home," he greets me with a grin, his hazel eyes shining enthusiastically. "I hope you're hungry."

"What's all this?" I wave at the display of food.

"Dinner. Why don't you take a seat and we'll eat, unless you'd prefer to change first?"

I shake my head. "No, let's eat now." I'm mortified when my stomach growls loud enough for him to hear.

"Sounds like you made the right choice." Cash chuckles. "Here—" He pulls out the chair on the right, motioning for me to sit down. I freeze momentarily, taken aback by his thoughtful gesture.

"Thanks," I murmur as I settle in my chair.

"I kept the menu pretty simple tonight. We've got smoked salmon, roasted vegetables, and mixed greens with a balsamic vinegar dressing," he says, pointing to each item on his plate.

"Is that all?" I tease. "This looks incredible. Far better than any takeout I would have ordered. You made all this for me?"

In the five years Landon and I were together, he never cooked for me. And I have a habit of burning anything I attempt to make, so I've grown accustomed to takeout.

"Yes, it's for you, but it's only dinner, Ev. Don't overthink it," he says, like he can read my mind.

"When you suggested I move in, I figured we'd mostly keep to ourselves. The last thing I expected was for you to be here waiting for me," I admit.

"Do you want me to leave?" he asks earnestly.

"What? No, this is your home."

"*Our* home," he reiterates. "And you can order takeout if you prefer," he taunts as he subtly slides my plate toward him with a mischievous glint in his eyes.

"Not a chance, Stafford." I intercept his attempt, firmly grabbing his hand so he's forced to release his grip, triumphantly reclaiming my plate. "I'm not passing up a home-cooked meal, even if the company is barely tolerable." I bite back a grin as I spear a piece of salmon with my fork. The moment it touches my tongue, I can't help but moan in satisfaction at the explosion of flavors. "Oh my god, this is so good," I praise before taking another big bite.

"I'm glad you like it." Cash's intense gaze doesn't leave me, and my breath hitches when he reaches over to wipe the side of my mouth with the pad of his thumb. His finger lingers over my lips, and I'm tempted to draw it into my mouth and suck on it. I imagine twirling my tongue around the tip, pretending it's something else… something bigger.

I'm in so much trouble.

My mouth turns dry at the realization I just fantasized about sucking my husband's dick. I draw back, wanting to create distance between us, and grab my glass of water, taking a big gulp.

"Sorry, you just had a little sauce on your mouth." Cash rips his gaze from mine and wipes his thumb off on his napkin.

"It's alright, I appreciate it. I had no idea you could cook," I admit, desperate to change the subject. "Remember when you tried cooking macaroni and cheese in ninth grade? Your mom made you scrape out all the burned bits from the bottom of the pan because you left it alone for too long and all the water boiled out." I smile at the memory.

"It's not like you were any better," he quips before taking a bite of his food.

"You're right. Theo has all the cooking talents. I avoid the kitchen at all costs."

My only exception is when I visit Theo at one of his restaurants. He's never turned down the chance to cook for me. He hasn't been in London as much lately, too busy with his cooking shows and other ventures I've begun to lose track of.

"Well, you're in luck because one perk of living with me is having a home-cooked meal waiting for you every night," Cash says.

"Oh, you don't have to do that. I usually stay late at the office," I warn him.

It's not by choice. My father continuously piles onto my workload, making it nearly impossible to manage it all, even with long hours. He exploits the fact that I won't say no to him, even when he's not on the same continent as me. The direct deposit that hits my account every two weeks makes it manageable, knowing that I have a reliable way to support myself and cover my mom's bills.

"That's no problem," Cash says. "Just text me when you're wrapping up work each night, and I'll have dinner ready when you get home."

I'm about to remind him that this isn't my home again, but I hold my tongue. He's doing something nice for me, so the least I can do is attempt to meet him halfway.

"Okay, I will."

"Carol prefers to leave the office by five, so I wrap up by then because she won't leave until I do. I'm usually home by five thirty."

I tense up, my fork clattering to my plate. "Who's Carol?"

"My assistant," Cash replies, upbeat. "She's great. You should stop by and have lunch with us sometime."

He has lunch with his assistant? The only other person I know who did that was Landon. I'm haunted by the memories of his assistant glaring at me from her spot outside his office as she clicked away on her keyboard. Now it makes sense why she was so bitter whenever I'd stop by to bring Landon lunch.

"And before you ask if I've done anything with Carol, the answer is no," Cash states with a softness in his eyes. "She's in her late sixties, and even if I had a thing for older women, I'm not her type. On multiple occasions, she's told me she's into ruggedly handsome lumberjacks, like the ones she reads about in her romance novels."

I laugh. That's the last thing I expected him to say.

"You might not be a lumberjack, but you have the ruggedly handsome thing going for you." The moment I realize the thought has slipped out, I glance up at Cash with a startled look, like a deer caught in headlights.

"At least half my face is," he says somberly.

That's when I realize he's sitting to my left, so I can only see the right side of his face as we eat. Something tells me that was intentional.

"Cash Stafford, have you not been paying attention? Your scar adds to your charm and makes you even more irresistible. Damn, anyone who thinks differently—they're wrong." I place my hand over his.

"Theo was right," he says, shell-shocked. "He said you liked my scar, but I didn't believe him."

"Wait. When did you talk to Theo?"

"He stormed into my office today, demanding to know why I married you. Apparently, Harrison and Dylan thought it would be funny to send him the wedding article from the *Aspen Grove Gazette*."

I gasp. "Oh my god. Did he hurt you?" I scan his body, checking for any injuries I might have missed.

That explains why Theo called me over a dozen times earlier, and when I texted to tell him I was in a meeting, he said he'd get back to me later.

"Ev, I'm fine," Cash reassures me. "My shoulder is stiff, but it's not anything a massage won't fix." He winks. "In case you're worried, I didn't tell him about the acquisition, only about our pact and getting hitched in Vegas."

"So, he thinks we're going to give this a real shot?" I motion between us.

"Yeah, for now. When you're ready, we'll tell him the truth together."

I appreciate that Cash followed the plan and didn't mention the business deal to Theo. This situation is getting messier and more complicated by the day. At this rate, I really do think we'll need a detailed spreadsheet to keep track of who we've told what.

My phone buzzes on the counter, the sound echoing throughout the mostly empty kitchen.

Theo: I'm at the airport heading to California for business. I wanted to check in before the plane takes off since we weren't able to talk earlier.

Theo: I went to Cash's office to confront him about you two getting married.

Everly: He just told me.

Theo: It sounds like I was the last person to know.

Everly: I was afraid you'd overreact, and it sounds like I was right.

Theo: My reaction was completely justified, and I'm sure Cash agrees.

Theo: Are you staying at his place?

Everly: Yes.

Theo: Fuck, I hate this. You're my sister.

Everly: And Cash is your best friend.

Theo: Exactly. He knows you're off-limits.

Everly: I'm an adult. Don't I have a say in who I marry?"

Theo: No one is good enough for you.

I take a deep breath, mentally scolding myself for sounding irritated in my last text. Theo's only looking out for me. I withheld important information from him that involves Cash and me—the two most important people in his life. And he has every right to express his frustration about it.

Everly: I love you, Theo.

Theo: I love you too, sis.

Theo: You'll always come first. No matter what. And I'm here to hide the body if things don't work out with you and Cash.

Everly: Omg, stop it. That's not funny.

Theo: It totally is.

Theo: I have to go. The plane is taking off. I'll text when I land."

Everly: Okay. Be safe.

My phone buzzes again, and I check, thinking it's Theo sending another reply, but I sigh when I see it's Landon this time.

Landon: I miss you.

Landon: I still want to take you out to dinner when I come to London.

Landon: Please talk to me, baby.

I can't resist firing off a reply.

Everly: Stop texting me. I'm busy.

Landon: I didn't tell you what day I'd be there.

Everly: I've moved on.

There, that's better. Simple yet direct—I haven't tried that approach before. Satisfied with my message, I hit send and turn my phone off.

"Is everything okay?" Cash watches me with interest.

"Yeah, it's fine," I say, avoiding eye contact.

I'm not ready to explain to my fake husband that my ex-fiancé won't stop harassing me, holding on to the false hope that we'll get back together.

Cash gives me a skeptical look but doesn't press for more information. "Save some room for dessert because we're having strawberry shortcake with fresh whipped cream."

"That's my favorite."

"I know." He grins, causing my heart to skip a beat.

God, I am way in over my head.

13

CASH

When I join the conference call, Harrison and Dylan are waiting for me.

"You're late," Harrison states with his arms folded across his chest, his white dress shirt showcasing his muscular arms. After his short stint playing professional hockey, he maintained his athletic build. He spends hours in the gym each day, meticulously sculpting his body, and follows a strict diet with the help of his private chef.

Honestly, I'm not sure how he juggles it all, especially while running a multibillion-dollar company like a well-oiled machine. I find it hard enough just managing my life and keeping the amount of stupid shit I do to a minimum.

"Sorry," I mumble.

After dinner with Everly last night, she pulled out her laptop and worked at the kitchen counter until well past midnight. When she finally came to bed—damn. It took every ounce of control not to corner her when she stepped out of the bathroom wearing another one of those sexy lace tank tops and booty shorts.

It didn't help that as soon as she drifted off, she shifted to my side of the bed and curled up next to me. She fits perfectly in my arms, and I couldn't resist holding her close.

I've never been a cuddler, not wanting to send mixed signals to the women I had sex with. Things are different with Everly. I look forward to her sleeping in my bed and waking up next to her each morning.

"Hey, little brother." Dylan greets me with a wave. "I spoke with Carol earlier, and she told me you had an unexpected visitor stop by your office yesterday." He attempts to hide his amusement but fails miserably, a grin spreading across his face.

"You're hilarious," I deadpan. "You damn well knew Theo would show up to confront me when you sent him a copy of that article."

I find their prank even less funny than I did yesterday. They better watch their backs because I'll get my payback when they least expect it.

Dylan snorts. "We figured Theo would want to congratulate you himself. For the record, it was Harrison's idea," he says, attempting to pass the blame.

"What the hell, Dylan," Harrison grumbles. "Why would you throw me under the bus like that?"

I should have guessed Harrison was the mastermind. He may be a brooding, intimidating corporate mogul, but he's surprisingly inventive with prank ideas. I usually find them highly entertaining, but not when I'm the victim.

"I didn't find it the least bit funny." I scowl. "Theo was this close to beating me to a pulp in my office." I hold my thumb and forefinger close together for emphasis. "I dodged his fist this time, but I'm a dead man walking once he finds out I didn't tell him Everly is only staying married to me because of the acquisition."

"You didn't tell him about it?" Dylan sighs, rubbing his hand across his face. "You're right. You're in deep shit when he finds out."

"Everly asked me not to," I say, recalling the urgency in her expression when we talked about it at Brew Haven.

Dylan lets out a low whistle. "She already has you wrapped around her finger, and you've been married less than a week." He gives me a smug smile as he leans back in his chair. "I'm not surprised, seeing as you've had a secret crush on her since high school."

"I have not," I lie. My ears grow warm with embarrassment, and I'm grateful my hair hides them.

"Oh really," Dylan says. "So, getting suspended for punching Jacob Barlow in the face when he dumped Everly was just for kicks?" He raises a skeptical eyebrow. "What about hanging out with her while all your friends were at prom because you didn't want her to be alone? Does that sound like something a friend would do, Harrison?"

"Personally, I wouldn't do that for just anyone," Harrison says with a smirk.

Even he's finding this amusing. I should've expected my brothers wouldn't let me off easy. Typically, I'm the one teasing them, and I'm not a fan of our roles being switched.

"That was fourteen years ago," I grumble.

"Yeah, and you're still pining for her," Dylan says.

I roll my eyes. "So what if I am?" I say coolly.

"There's nothing wrong with liking Everly. She's incredibly intelligent, funny and beautiful," Dylan says, listing off her positive attributes on his fingers.

I arch a playful brow. "Watch it," I warn.

He's teasing, but that doesn't stop the unfamiliar wave of jealousy from coursing through my veins, even though I know Dylan has found his happy ending with Marlow.

"Easy." He holds up his hands with a cheeky grin. "I was just offering her a compliment. You damn well know I only have eyes for Marlow—"

Dylan's office door swings open, and Lola rushes inside, all out of breath. She's decked out in a bright pink shirt and rainbow tutu, and her hair is styled in fishtail braids with sparkly bows tied to the ends.

"Daddy, you have to help me," she exclaims, leaping into his arms.

"Ladybug, I'm on a call with your uncles. Can it wait?" Dylan asks firmly.

"Hi, Uncle Harrison, Hi, Uncle Cash." She ignores him as she waves to the camera.

"Hey there, Ladybug. You're looking extra cute today," I say. "I love your braids."

"Thanks. Marlow did them." She affectionately runs her hands down her hair, preening for the camera.

"I figured," I smirk at Dylan, who's glaring at me.

He's never been able to master the fishtail braid, and we all like to give him a hard time about it. It's one of the many reasons Marlow is his perfect match.

"Ladybug, what can I help you with?" Dylan cuts in.

"Waffles and the puppies got into the pink finger paint again." She points to the hallway, where I can hear the dogs barking.

That's when I notice her palms are covered in bright pink paint, now smeared on the front of Dylan's shirt. I cover my mouth to stifle a laugh.

"Shit," Dylan mumbles under his breath. "Sorry, guys, I have to go." He lifts Lola, setting her on the ground, and rises from his chair. "I convinced Marlow to meet her friends for breakfast at Brew Haven, so it's just me at home with Lola and the dogs." He bends over so we can see his face on the screen.

"No problem. We'll catch up with you later," Harrison assures him.

"Thanks." Dylan drops off the conference call, leaving me to face Harrison's inscrutable expression alone.

We haven't had a one-on-one conversation since before my Vegas trip, and I'm dreading the lecture that I know is coming. I squirm in my chair, hoping he'll suggest rescheduling the meeting. After a minute goes by, I can't take it anymore.

"Can you please get on with it," I blurt.

Harrison tilts his head slightly. "Get on with what, exactly?"

"The part where you tell me how irresponsible I've been and how disappointed you are in me. Not just as my boss but also as my brother, and that if I don't get my act together, I'm fired." I sigh heavily. "You have every right to be mad at me."

Harrison has had to bail me out of several sticky situations, and if there's one thing to push him past his breaking point, it's probably my impulsive decision to get married. So I'm bracing myself for the worst.

He doesn't reply as he picks up a pen on his desk, clicking it while watching me with his icy blue gaze.

I bite my tongue, trying to be patient, but I'm practically bouncing in my chair when he finally speaks.

"I'm not mad," he states.

I give him a puzzled look. "You aren't?"

He shakes his head. "No, but I worried about you. How are you holding up?"

"I feel like I screwed all this up," I admit. "And I know that's what you've grown to expect from me." I sigh, casting my eyes down to my lap. "I'm not wired like you and Dylan. I wish I were, but I'm not."

I didn't plan on having this conversation with Harrison today, but if I'm being honest, it's long overdue.

"Why is that?" he questions.

"You command every boardroom you step into, and Dylan is a mathematical genius everyone admires. I'm the college dropout who has the position I do because I'm your brother."

Not to mention, they're both good-looking, whereas I'm flawed. The one who everyone feels bad for when they see us all together.

"You honestly believe that?" A somber expression crosses Harrison's face. "Is it frustrating when you don't log on for work on time or that you put more energy into your extracurriculars than your job? Absolutely."

I nod slowly, swallowing a lump in my throat. His brutal honesty is a hard pill to swallow, but everything he says is true.

"However, I promoted you because you have a talent for connecting with our employees, not because we're related." He taps his pen against his desk as he speaks. "You might not know this, but shortly after your accident, I overheard Mom and Dad express their concern to the doctor that you might lose your sense of humor and outgoing personality when you recovered. I didn't have the same concern."

He's right about me having never heard this before. After I woke up, I was disoriented for a while. I remember my mom crying a lot, but overall, my parents maintained a strong front.

"Why not?" I ask, my voice filled with curiosity.

"Because you're one of the strongest people I know," Harrisons replies with conviction. "The following week, you proved me right when Dad went to use the restroom in your hospital suite and discovered too late that you had covered the toilet bowl with Saran Wrap." He chuckles at the memory. "I've never seen Mom and Dad so conflicted about whether to punish you or celebrate that you were back to your old self."

When I woke up from the induced coma the doctors had put me under after my accident, I didn't feel any different. But I knew something was wrong when my parents, siblings, and friends looked at me with pity, sympathy, or a mix of both. The nerve and tissue damage was extensive, and the country's leading plastic surgeons could only do so much.

It devastated me, knowing that things would never be the same. But that didn't stop me from trying to live my life like I always had.

"Don't get me wrong. Your carefree attitude and sense of humor are refreshing," Harrison says, although I can sense a *but* coming. "But the reality is we all have to do things we don't want to do."

"When have you ever done something you didn't want to?" I scoff.

I've always envied how he makes everything look easy. He was the most popular kid in school and the star hockey player in college, and he seamlessly took over Stafford Holdings when our dad retired. He never shows weakness, and everyone takes him seriously.

"That's what you think?" He raises a brow in surprise. "Cash, I was only ten when Dad told me I would be the successor to a global empire. Long before I fully comprehended what that meant, I carried the weight of our family's legacy on my shoulders so that you, Dylan, and Presley didn't have to. I gave up my dreams so you could pursue yours."

"What dreams? I figured you wanted to be CEO." Hearing myself say it out loud sounds ridiculous, but besides hockey, Stafford Holdings is the only thing he's passionate about.

He gives a humorless laugh. "Don't get me wrong. I'm grateful for my role and wouldn't trade it for anything. But there are moments when I wish things had turned out differently," he says, his gaze distant, lost in thought.

"Why would you give up your dreams for us?"

"Because that's what big brothers do. We sacrifice our happiness for the people we love." He gives me a somber smile.

I've put Harrison on a pedestal, thinking his life was picture-perfect. Now I see how naïve I've been. He's been dealing with his own challenges, and I've been too self-absorbed to notice.

"Man, I've been a shitty brother, huh?" I mutter, running my fingers through my hair.

Harrison shakes his head. "No, you haven't. Enough about me. How are things going with Everly?" he asks, changing the subject.

"Oh, they're going great," I say sarcastically. "We just moved in together, and she's already thrown multiple pillows at my head."

Harrison smiles. "Sounds like marital bliss to me."

"I did learn that she has a weak spot for home-cooked meals," I say.

"You can't cook," Harrison states.

"Okay, fine, *home-cooked* is a stretch," I confess with a shrug. "But I plate the dishes, which is pretty impressive." My tone is teasing. "I contacted Fallon, Theo's protégé, when we returned to London. A few years ago, she ventured out on her own and now works as a private chef. She preps our dinners, and I pick them up at her pop-up shop on my way home from work."

Harrison gives me a slow clap. "I'm impressed, little brother. Have any of Theo's other students moved to New York? My chef, Steve, is retiring, and I'm looking to replace him in the fall."

"Fallon told me she's moving to New York City soon. She might be interested in the position. I'm not sure if she has a set clientele yet, but I'll ask her."

He gives me an amused shake of the head. "It sounds like this scheme of yours has an expiration date. You better brush up on your cooking skills, or you'll have some serious explaining to do when your gourmet meals start to come out of the oven as bricks of charcoal."

"The acquisition will most likely be finalized by then, won't it?" I ask wearily.

"Yeah. As long as there are no major roadblocks, it should be finalized in the next month or two."

"Right, so Everly and I won't be together anymore."

A sinking feeling settles in my stomach when I envision returning to my life from a week ago. So much has changed, and the more time I spend with Everly, the harder it'll be to say goodbye when the time comes.

"Are you still planning on getting divorced after the deal closes?" Harrison asks.

"That's what Every and I agreed on," I say, keeping my answer vague.

He furrows his brow. "Just don't make any more rash decisions, alright?"

"Yeah, okay," I say as I bring up my email on my second monitor, determined to make today productive—though I can't help but wonder, where's the fun in that?

My focus in the short term is to make Everly smile every day and keep her as happy with our arrangement as I can, given the circumstances.

She's the most important thing in my life right now, and I'll do everything I can to make her see that.

That night, I'm roused from sleep by uncontrollable need. My hard cock presses against my boxers, pulsing with desire for the woman next to me. I glance at the clock on the nightstand and groan when I see it's only 3:17 a.m.

I rarely wake up with morning wood in the middle of the night, but I'm only human. It's impossible to control my innate reaction to Everly's warm body wrapped around me like a cocoon, wearing nothing but a tank top and skimpy shorts.

The moon's silver light shines through the curtains, casting a soft glow in the darkened room. Everly is snuggled against me, her leg draped over my hip and her head resting on my bare chest. My arm circles her waist, and my hand rests on her skin where her tank top has lifted.

I use my free hand to adjust myself, careful not to disturb her.

I go still when she shifts, her thigh brushing against my dick. She mumbles incoherently, and my eyes widen when she grinds against my leg, her breasts rubbing against my bare chest as she moves against me in a steady rhythm.

My cock jerks when her moans fill the room as she rides my leg. It seems I'm not the only one who woke up sexually frustrated. I stifle a groan when Everly picks up her pace, heat from her body radiating through the fabric between us.

From this angle, I can't see her face. I assume she's too embarrassed to look at me, but she shouldn't be. I'm just as affected by her.

She digs her nails into my arm. "Cash," she moans.

"Everly?" I whisper.

I tighten my hold on her, afraid to say anything else and ruin the moment. When she clenches around my leg, I press my thigh against her core, giving her the pressure she's searching for. My hand wanders to her stomach, and as my fingers reach her lace panties, she tips her head back with a low groan, giving me an unobstructed view of her face in the dim light.

Her lips are parted, and disappointment consumes me when I see her eyes are shut.

Fuck, I think she's dreaming.

My hand lingers, tempted to give her the pleasure she's chasing in her sleep, but I force myself to pull back. My cock throbs in protest. I would like nothing more than to make Everly come, but not like this. When I bring her to ecstasy, I want her eager and begging me never to stop.

That doesn't mean I'm going to stop her from getting herself off. After all, I am her husband, and it's my job to give her what she needs.

Everly repositions herself to get extra friction. It's hot as hell watching her get herself off. She lifts her head to pepper kisses along my neck, her breath skating across my skin. It takes every ounce of restraint not to kiss her back when she squeezes my thigh with her legs.

"Oh, god," she cries as she tips over the edge. The dampness on her shorts proves her orgasm wasn't only in her dreams.

A sigh of contentment escapes her lips as she nuzzles her head in the crook of my neck. Within seconds, her breathing evens out, and she falls back into a peaceful slumber.

I'm not so lucky. My cock is still rock-hard, begging for release. I close my eyes, doing my best to ignore it. I don't want to risk waking Everly if I get up to relieve myself.

At least now I know she wants me, even if she hasn't yet come to terms with it yet. Here's to hoping her mind catches up with her subconscious soon because I'd like nothing more than to show her how much I want her.

14

EVERLY

ONE WEEK LATER

IT'S A SUNNY MORNING, THE perfect day for a jog. I'm eager for some semblance of my old routine.

I dress in a pair of black workout shorts and a hot-pink tank top and pull my hair into a high ponytail. When I step out of the bathroom, I stop in my tracks.

Cash is sitting on the edge of the bed, the brim of his ball cap covering his eyes, tying his running shoe. I'm surprised to see him since he usually goes on long runs before I wake up.

He glances up when he hears me approach and smiles. "Good morning, wifey."

"Morning," I say.

The truth is, despite my better judgment, I'm warming up to the nickname, maybe more than I should.

As promised, he's had a home-cooked meal on the table waiting for me every night when I get home from work. After dinner, I work at the kitchen island, catching up on things I couldn't finish at the office, while Cash watches a movie with headphones. I appreciate his thoughtful gesture, allowing me to work without interruption.

Since we got back to London, I've slept better than I have in years. It's purely coincidental that I'm sleeping next to Cash, or at least that's what I prefer to believe. I'm plagued with dreams of being wrapped in his arms, my thigh draped across his hips, his arms holding me tightly.

Last week, my dream turned sexual. Cash held me close as he whispered my name in my ear. With gentle hands, he stroked my body, caressing me. I arched toward him, loving the hot touch of him on my skin. I pressed kisses along his neck, desperate for him to make me come. He plunged his fingers inside my pussy, and I rode his hand as he drove me to an orgasm. It felt so real, but when I woke up, Cash's side of the bed was cold and empty.

Most mornings since, he's been gone before I'm up. This strikes me as odd, given that he seems the type who would sleep in.

"Are you going somewhere?" I ask.

"Yeah, out for a jog," Cash answers as he ties his other shoe. "Want to join me? Looks like you had the same idea?" He motions toward my workout clothes.

"Um…"

Normally, I prefer to run alone and instinctively want to decline his offer, but he must sense my hesitation.

"It's just a jog, Ev. You don't have to worry about me asking you to marry me or anything too serious," he says, flashing me a boyish grin.

Why does the reminder that we're married make butterflies take flight in my stomach? I highly doubt spending more time with him will help curb my attraction to him.

I'm not prepared when I glance over to see him standing up, giving me a full view of his bare chest—his sculpted six-pack on display.

I have to channel all my focus into appearing unaffected by his striking physique. I've gone years without having a visceral reaction to a man, and then Cash comes along and every time I see him without his shirt on, I'm like a bitch in heat.

One run together can't hurt, right?

"I'll tag along, but could you put a shirt on?" I nod toward his solid chest, feeling a flush across my cheeks.

He closes the distance between us, shamelessly devouring me with his eyes. "Suit yourself," he murmurs, his voice so soft I have to strain to catch it.

I'm disappointed when he brushes past me on his way to the closet and actually selects a shirt. He tugs it over his head as he leaves the room with a sly smirk on his face, leaving me to wonder what I've gotten myself into.

Cash's definition of a jog doesn't align with mine. He made it sound like it would be a leisurely affair—a few miles at most.

I was wrong. *Very wrong.*

Let the record show that Cash doesn't jog. He *runs.*

I consider myself in shape, doing yoga three mornings a week, and incorporating a mix of cardio and weightlifting into my routine, but Cash Stafford is on a whole other level.

We've been running for eight miles, and I'm grateful he's maintained a pace I can match.

We ran through Hyde Park, passing Serpentine Lake and catching a glimpse of the swans gracefully gliding along the water's surface. Making our way past Big Ben, we saw tourists milling around to get a glimpse of the iconic landmark.

Cash has hardly broken a sweat, but that didn't stop him from ditching his shirt twenty minutes ago, tucking it into his waistband, and leaving me to admire how his corded muscles ripple with each pump of his arms.

He looks like a model on the cover of *Sports Illustrated*, with the brim of his hat pulled low, wearing nothing but a pair of black running shorts and sneakers. The idea of climbing this man like a tree grows more enticing by the minute.

Why does my husband have to be so damn hot?

My *fake* husband, I correct myself.

Even in the early morning, the streets of London are teeming with activity, and every woman we pass can't resist gawking at him—not that he's noticed. I'm having fun giving them all dirty looks, leaving them to wonder if Cash and I are together. With my bracelet on his wrist and my ring on his finger, he belongs to me in a way he never has to anyone else, making me feel oddly territorial.

Admittedly, I can't stop ogling Cash either. I blame those rock-hard abs, tempting me to run my fingers along every ridge as I trace down toward his happy trail, slowly moving lower and lower till my fingers curl around his shaft. I haven't seen him fully naked, but judging by the bulge in his boxers that I have seen, it's safe to say the man is well-endowed.

Not that it makes a difference since I won't be having sex with him. I'm quick to check myself when my mind strays into inappropriate scenarios.

I glance over at Cash again. He's looking the other way, so I quickly swipe the sweat off my face.

Despite the mild weather, looking at me would make you think it was sweltering hot. While Cash is the epitome of sexy, I'm sweating like a pig, smelling like I didn't put on enough deodorant, and my hair is sticking to my face.

"We're almost home, wifey," he calls out.

"You mean *your* home?" I taunt him.

"Whatever you say." He glances over at me, and a grin spreads across his face, suggesting he likes what he sees.

When we're a block away from his building, he stops by a newsstand to buy two water bottles. I can't help but notice him taking a fifty-pound note from his shoe and handing it to the clerk, telling him to keep the change. He did the same for his doorman, Max, the day we got back from Aspen Grove.

His generosity only adds to his appeal. There's just something about a man who takes the time to show appreciation for those around him that makes my heart skip a beat.

"Thanks," I wheeze when he hands me the bottle. I uncap it and take a large gulp, sighing in relief as the refreshing liquid soothes my scratchy throat.

As I'm catching my breath, he moves to a nearby patch of grass. He takes his hat off and runs his finger through his sweaty tresses. I'm riveted when he pours the contents of his water bottle over his head as it trails down his chest, along his abs, and past his V-line. He shakes his head like an actor from *Baywatch* who's just stepped out of the ocean after saving someone's life.

Oh my god.

"See something you like, Ev?"

I sputter, water spraying from my mouth, my cheeks burning as I meet his hazel gaze. "No. I was just concerned about the water you just wasted." It's total bullshit, and we both know it.

"That's very considerate of you," he says with a smirk as he moves toward me. "But I think the grass was thirsty, don't you?" His eyes are fixed on me, his pupils dilating as he watches the rise and fall of my chest.

My hands tremble, and I'm not sure if it's from the long run or Cash's masculine scent permeating the air.

I step back but bump into a tree I hadn't noticed was there. Cash closes the distance so his bare chest is pressed against my breasts, causing a spike of pleasure to course through my veins and heat to rush to my core. I gasp as he trails a finger up my arm, sending goosebumps across my skin.

"I saw you checking me out while we were running. I think you like it when I'm shirtless," he says as sweat drips down his brow.

"That's your ego talking," I say, my breath coming out in ragged gasps.

"Is that so?" Cash questions with a devilish smirk.

He accepts my wordless challenge by gently cupping my chin with his hand. My breath hitches when he brings his mouth close to mine, leaving barely an inch of space between us. I can feel his hot breath against my lips like a whisper, and I can't resist grabbing hold of his waist. His skin is slippery and wet, and every cell in my body craves for him to close the remaining distance, yet my mind screams to push him away.

As if he can read my mind, he glides his hand down my neck, tangling his fingers at the base of my hairline. My physical reaction wins over as he brushes his lips against mine in teasing strokes, and a soft moan passes my lips. He's careful not to kiss me fully, only giving me a taste.

"You're right," he whispers against my mouth. "You really couldn't care less that I'm shirtless. That's a damn shame." A disappointed whimper escapes me as he drops his hand and steps back. "I better get ready for work, or I'll be late for my first meeting."

He leaves me alone on the sidewalk, my mind reeling with panic as reality sets in. The smell of his musk lingers in the air, and my bra is damp with sweat from when he pushed up against me. I feel a mix of frustration and longing, my heart racing knowing that I just let my husband kiss me… again. And it left me craving his next touch.

I'm shocked by the revelation that I want more from him… *so much more.*

After my unexpected morning run with Cash, I took a quick shower and rushed to work. The day has dragged on, and against my better judgment, I decide to take a late lunch and drop something off to Cash. He's been making me dinner every night, so I want to do something nice for him.

As I step out of the stairwell into the brightly lit reception area, I'm greeted by his assistant.

"Good afternoon, dear," Carol beams at me and pulls me into an embrace, giving me a kiss on the cheek. "Cash is going to be delighted to see you."

This is the first time we've met in person, but we spoke on the phone earlier when I asked if it would be okay to stop by. Cash gave me her number last week in case I ever needed to get ahold of her.

"I'm on my way to lunch, but he should be in his office, the last door on the left." She motions down the hall. "If you need anything, the receptionist can help you, or you can call me."

"Thank you."

She disappears into the elevator, and I move to the reception area.

I'm rummaging through my purse to find my phone when I bump into someone. I stumble backward, barely regaining my balance before I fall.

"Oh, I'm sorry—" I stop speaking when I look up to find my dad standing in front of me, his expression as cold as ice. "Dad?" His name comes out as a question. "What are you doing here?"

He wasn't due back in London until later this week, so seeing him at Stafford Holdings' London office is a complete shock. August tried calling earlier, but I was at the café ordering lunch and wasn't able to answer. He must have wanted to warn me that my dad flew into town early.

"A better question is, what are *you* doing here?" my dad snaps. "You're supposed to be working on the Camden Crest project. That's what I'm paying you for, isn't it?" His booming voice fills the reception area, causing heads to turn as people walk by.

"I'm bringing Cash lunch." I hold up the takeout bag. "Is everything okay?"

"He's got you on a short leash, huh?" He lowers his voice so only I can hear. "You're after his money, aren't you? God, you're just like your mother. Be careful, *little* girl. Don't forget who you work for."

My eyes widen as he gets in my face. I can't understand why he's so angry when he's the one who insisted I go through with this charade. Now he's outraged to find Cash and I are getting along? There must have been a setback or complication with the acquisition. It's the only explanation for why he's acting this way.

"Ev, there you are." Cash's voice startles me, and I glance over to where he's standing near the reception desk, his gaze narrowing in on my dad. "Richard, do you need a map to find your own personal space?"

If we weren't in an office with people milling around, I doubt he would be so calm.

"I was reminding Everly of her place," my dad sneers.

"And I'm reminding you of yours," Cash growls, striding toward us with purpose.

When he gets close, my dad shrinks back. Cash locks eyes with me, silently confirming that I'm okay before stepping between me and my dad.

"What the hell are you doing here, Richard?" Cash glares at him.

Dad adjusts his tie and clears his throat. "I had a last-minute change in my schedule, so I came to London early. I stopped by the Townstead offices first, and the receptionist told me Everly took a late lunch to come here."

"And what was so important that you couldn't wait until she was back at her office?" Cash asks.

"I got a concerning call from one of my lawyers when I landed. The Stafford legal team wants to do a deep dive into Townstead's financials, but my team already provided the standard information required."

Cash raises a brow. "That doesn't explain why you're here. You damn well know all communications regarding the acquisition should go through our lawyers."

"This is an extenuating circumstance, and I knew you would be able to get me in touch with your brothers. Considering we're family now, it's the least you can do."

Translation: He figured he could use me to get to Cash and his brothers—unbelievable.

Cash snickers. "What do you think my brothers are going to do about it? They're investing millions into this deal. As far as they're concerned, *all* your financial records are fair game. It's called enhanced due diligence, in case you haven't heard of it."

I put my hand over my mouth, stifling the surprising urge to laugh from watching Cash put my dad in his place.

"I don't give a shit what you think. Get your brothers on a call right this instant so I can talk to them," my dad demands, the vein in his forehead bulging. "It's urgent."

Cash folds his arms across his chest, his gaze cold. "Did you make an appointment with my assistant?"

My dad rears his head back. "Why the hell would I need an appointment?" He scoffs.

"Because I have a busy schedule, and my afternoon is booked solid." Cash shrugs.

"What are you playing at, *boy*," my dad spits out.

"I don't have time for bullies who threaten their own daughter," Cash hisses in a hushed tone. "Everly and I stayed married like you wanted, so what the hell do you have to complain about? You work her to the bone, and I refuse to let you ruin what little time I have with my wife."

My gaze darts between them. Cash's fists are clenched at his sides, his posture rigid, and the vein in his neck pulses. My dad tries to maintain an indifferent front, but the sweat on his brow is a clear giveaway that he's scared shitless.

Cash can be intimidating when he wants to be, and it's such a turn-on that he's willing to stand up for me.

"I'll make sure Harrison hears about your blatant show of disrespect," my dad seethes.

"Something tells me he'll take my side when he finds out you raised your voice at his sister-in-law." Cash turns to me and places his large hand on my lower back. "Come on, Ev, let's go."

With no argument from me, he leads me past the reception desk and through a pair of glass doors, leaving my dad behind with his mouth hanging open in disbelief. He guides me to his office, shutting the door once we're inside.

Like his home, the room is sparsely furnished with only a desk, a leather office chair, and a budget rolling chair in the corner.

I glance up at him. "Did you move to a new office recently?"

He shakes his head. "No, why?"

"Because there's nothing here," I say, stating the obvious. "My workspace has a cozy couch, a couple of plants, and some knickknacks to make it feel more like home since I spend so much time there."

Cash perches on the edge of his desk and pats the wood for me to join him.

"Having me work in the London office was meant to be temporary," he explains. "Harrison hasn't given a specific timeline, but I didn't think it was worth settling in fully."

I take a seat next to him, not bothering to move away when he scoots closer so our legs are touching. "Is your office and apartment in Maine furnished?" I ask, curious about his life in the States. I imagine he'd have a nice setup based on the penthouse he owns here.

He glances over at me. "No. I'm traveling more than I'm in Maine, and when I am in town, I spend my time with my family."

My heart aches for him. Now I see the reality behind his carefree attitude and unbothered demeanor. The easy smiles, flirtatious gestures, and playful antics serve as distractions, concealing the scars of his past—both seen and unseen.

His insecurities related to his physical appearance and how others see him have clouded his perception of reality. He avoids attachment, whether with people or places, the ever-present fear of rejection haunting his subconscious.

It hurts me to think he believes he can't find happiness because of his flaws. What he doesn't realize is that we all have imperfections. Some are visible, while others linger in the shadows of our minds.

In some ways, we're so much alike, both afraid of trusting someone with our fragile hearts and unable to see past our own misgivings. Maybe that's why I'm drawn to him. He makes me feel safe and secure, and everything he's done since our night in Vegas has been to make my life easier.

Whenever I complain or grumble about our situation, he counters with a compliment or words of encouragement. His positive outlook is gradually breaking down the barriers I've built to protect myself, and I don't know how to stop it—or if I even want to anymore.

A lump forms in my throat when I catch Cash watching me intently.

"My dad is going to lose his shit after the stunt you pulled out there," I say, nodding toward the lobby. "He's used to having the upper hand in any situation."

It's frustrating that I haven't found the courage to stand up to him, but after his erratic behavior this afternoon, I don't think I have a choice anymore.

"I don't give a damn," Cash declares boldly. "Once he sells his company, he'll have no control left, so he better get used to it."

It makes me think there's more at stake than my father is letting on. He'd never relinquish control unless he was out of options.

"I'm done standing by while your piece-of-shit father treats you like garbage. You deserve better." Cash's eyes convey unwavering conviction as he gives my hand a gentle squeeze.

My chest tightens. His steadfast support means more than he'll ever know, and he's quickly becoming my constant.

A twist of guilt winds through me as I remember all the assumptions I've made about Cash since I saw him in that hotel bar in Vegas. My prejudices blinded me, and I didn't hesitate to label him as a playboy with no regard for women.

I couldn't have been more wrong, and the idea of walking away after this is all over makes me physically sick. Needing a distraction from my conflicting emotions, I open the bag of food I brought for lunch.

"I appreciate you standing up for me." I give Cash a feeble smile as I hand him a turkey and Swiss cheese sandwich.

"That's what husbands are for," he teases as he takes a large bite of his sandwich. "Oh my god, this is great. Thanks for bringing lunch. Any chance I can convince you to stop by every day?"

"I wouldn't count on it." I playfully slug his shoulder. "It's been so nice of you to make dinner every night, and I wanted to show my appreciation."

"You should never feel pressured into doing anything you don't want to, but I admit, I look forward to spending time with you, and I'll take it any way I can."

"I enjoy spending time with you, too," I murmur as I unwrap my sandwich.

My resolve is crumbling fast, and I'm afraid there may not be a chance to reinforce it before Cash Stafford has stolen my heart completely.

15

CASH

I LOOK OVER AT EVERLY, who's been typing furiously at my desk for two hours straight.

Carol gave me a heads-up that she was coming after I asked her to pick up lunch, but she asked me not to tell Everly that I knew. Regardless, I'm glad Everly came.

After we ate, she checked her email on her laptop, and I suggested she finish her workday here with me. The security guard stationed in the building's lobby confirmed Richard had left the building shortly after our confrontation. Still, I didn't want to risk Everly going back to the Townstead offices if he was there waiting for her.

Seeing him stand so close to her while he reprimanded her filled me with rage. It brought back memories of the awful things he said to her over the phone when we were in Aspen Grove.

I instructed security to prevent him from entering the building in the future. Then I emailed Harrison to loop him in on what happened. I told him to keep Richard away unless he wants me facing legal action for battery and assault.

Regardless of what happens with Everly and me after we settle this business arrangement, I'll make sure she never has to work for her dad again. Hell, I'll do everything in my power to ensure she never has to see him again if she doesn't want to.

"Is everything okay?" Everly asks when she catches me watching her.

"Yeah, but it's getting late." I gesture to the darkening sky outside the window. "We should head out soon."

"Oh, okay." She frowns. "But I still have a lot of work to finish."

"Why don't we grab a bite to eat, and you can finish once we get back to the apartment?"

I text Fallon to say I won't pick up our usual meal tonight. If the circumstances were different, I would be more remorseful for giving Everly the impression that I cook for her, but it's been a way to get her to lower her defenses and spend time with me.

My phone vibrates in my pocket, and I take it out to see that I have an unread text.

Mom's Favorites Group Chat

Mom: I haven't heard from either of you for days. Are you alright?

Cash: I'm in my honeymoon phase. What's your excuse, Presley?

Cash: Unless you have some news to share?

Mom: Presley?!?!

Presley: Very funny Cash.

Cash: I thought so.

Mom: So you and Jack still aren't engaged?

Presley: Sorry to disappoint you mom.

Mom: As long as you're happy, I'm happy too.

Cash: She wouldn't say that if you and Jack broke up.

Mom: Cash, don't joke about that.

Cash: You're right. Then you'd have to work overtime to find Presley another man.

Mom: I have no idea what you're talking about.

Presley: Don't worry Mom, Jack and I aren't breaking up.

Mom: Thank God.

Mom: Cash, how is Everly?

Cash: Good. She stopped by my office this afternoon so I'm taking her out to dinner.

Mom: I'm happy to hear that. She deserves to be spoiled.

Presley: Mom's right. The best way to a woman's heart is with food and with her favorite things.

Cash: Thanks for the advice.

Presley: That's why I'm your favorite.

Mom: We don't have favorites in this family.

Cash: Is now a good time to remind you to check the name of the chat?

Mom: Presley, you promised you'd change it.

Presley: I have to go. Jack just walked into my office.

Cash: Talk to you both later.

I put my phone away before my mom asks me to change the chat name That's between her and Presley, and I know better than to intervene.

I let out a low groan when I stand up. My back is stiff from sitting on the uncomfortable rolling chair for hours. I had Everly use my desk while I used the one I found in the janitor's closet during my first week here. Carol told me I should get an extra chair in my office for visitors, even offered to order me one but I refused.

I make a mental note to contact Marcus, to decorate my office with more comfortable chairs, a bookshelf, and a few plants. When Everly visits my office, I want her to feel at home.

That means I should also have Marcus decorate my place too.

Everly's asked about it in passing, but I've deflected by telling her Marcus has been busy with another project, which is somewhat true. He's currently decorating some pop star's

London apartment, but he would make time for another project if I asked.

I'm not ready for Everly to have her own room. We've only lived together for a short time, but now my entire world revolves around her. Every morning, I wake up with her snuggled beside me, then spend the day counting the hours until I can see her again.

We've fallen into a comfortable routine, and I'm getting attached. I might be playing with fire, but being near Everly makes me want more time with her.

"Have a wonderful night," Carol says, waving from her desk as we leave my office.

Everly waves back with a grin. "Thanks, you too."

I can't shake the pang of jealousy I feel at how freely she shows fondness for Carol, even though they just met in person today. Meanwhile, I have to work around the clock to earn every smile, laugh, or hint of amusement. I'm addicted to the sound of Everly's melodic laugh and the way her face lights up when she smiles. Her happiness makes all the effort worthwhile, though, and I'll keep at it for as long as she lets me.

"Oh, Cash, hold on a sec," Carol says, motioning me over to her desk. "Before you leave, I think there's something wrong with your calendar."

"What is it?" I ask, leaning in to look at her computer screen.

"You have an interview scheduled tomorrow for 8:00 a.m." She points to the early morning meeting. "Should I call the candidate and reschedule?"

"No, eight works for me," I assure her. "But thanks for confirming."

My chat with Harrison last week prompted me to reflect on my current role at Stafford Holdings. I genuinely enjoy the work I do as COO, but my bad work habits aren't doing anyone any favors, including myself. I'm tired of being perceived as the guy who coasts on his brothers' achievements.

More importantly, I want Harrison to be proud of me and to prove my worth, which starts with arriving at the office on time and putting in a full day's work. As a first step, I updated my availability for interviews I have scheduled in the upcoming weeks.

"Yeah, no problem," Carol says, jotting on a sticky note. "I'll see you bright and early then." She appears uncertain about how to interpret my newfound commitment.

"Sure thing." I nod. "Ready to go?" I ask Everly.

"Yup, lead the way."

As we walk past the reception area toward the bank of elevators, the only sound is the click of Everly's red stilettos against the marble floor. I can't resist stealing a glance downward, admiring the sight of her smooth, toned legs.

The other night, I caught a glimpse of red-laced panties in her laundry basket, and I immediately picture that she has them on now under her black pleated skirt. God, what I wouldn't give to trace my hand up her thigh, lifting her skirt to get a peek.

The ding of the elevator grabs my attention, breaking me out of my fantasy.

When the elevator doors open, I motion for Everly to enter first and follow after her. We're the only two in the confined space, so I press the button for the lobby.

Everly lets out a loud inhale as we begin our descent.

"Are you ok—"

The flickering of lights cuts my question short, and the elevator comes to a grinding halt halfway to the lobby.

I glance over to see Everly move to the back of the elevator, staring wide-eyed at the doors. Despite my repeated attempts, they remain shut when I press the lobby button. A growing sense of unease washes over me when I pick up the emergency phone and no one answers.

My worry eases slightly when I check my phone to see that I have service. I try calling Carol, but she doesn't pick up. I send texts to both her and the building maintenance supervisor, informing them that Everly and I are trapped and require immediate help.

The lights flicker again before going out completely.

Fuck, that can't be good.

This is a recipe for disaster. We're confined in a small, dark box—a scenario straight out of Everly's nightmares—and there's nothing I can do except wait for someone to rescue us.

"Oh my god," she cries, her breathing growing panicked. "We're literally hovering in midair without power. We're definitely going to die."

I'm quick to turn on the flashlight on my phone and set it on the ground to illuminate the space. When I turn around, Everly is now cowering in the corner, clinging to the railing.

"Ev, I'm right here. Everything will be okay," I reassure her as I rush to her side.

I encircle her with my arms, guiding her to the nearest wall and coaxing her to the ground. Once we're both settled, I bring her onto my lap, her lack of protest indicating shock.

I stretch out my legs, figuring I might as well get comfortable since there's no telling how long we'll be here. Everly tightens her grip at the nape of my neck, resting her head against my chest, gasping for air.

"Shh, I've got you. You're safe with me," I whisper against her ear. "Take a deep breath for me, okay? Inhale deeply for five counts, then exhale slowly for another five." She mimics the exercise, her lip quivering as she does. "You're doing well. Let's do it again," I praise, encouraging her to continue.

She nods as she takes another deep breath, this time counting out loud with me. "One, two, three, four, five…"

We repeat the routine several times, and her breathing evens out. I'm surprised when she cuddles into my chest, nuzzling her nose into my neck.

"This is why I prefer taking the stairs," Everly rasps, her voice trembling. "What are the odds we'd get stuck in this death trap?"

I suppress a laugh, not wanting her to think I'm not taking her concerns seriously. I have the most beautiful woman in my arms, so it wouldn't be the worst way to go.

"We could set up caution tape in front of the elevator, like they do on *The Big Bang Theory*," I suggest. "Then we'll never have to worry about anyone getting stuck again."

Everly chuckles at my suggestion. "I'm glad you're here," she murmurs, gazing up at me with those big brown eyes.

"There is nowhere else I'd rather be," I assure her as I tug her closer, kissing her on the forehead.

"I have a phobia of being trapped inside small spaces, particularly when they can move." She plays with the top button of my shirt while she explains. "When I was eleven, my mom and I got stuck in an elevator at my dad's office. The lights went out and she didn't have her phone, so we sat in the dark for an hour before we were rescued. Since then, I've avoided elevators when I can."

"I'm afraid of clowns," I blurt, wanting to make her feel better about her fear. "When I turned five, my mom hired a clown for my birthday party. An hour before the party started, I fell asleep on the couch in the living room. When I woke up with a clown hovering over my bed, it scared the living shit out of me." I shudder at the memory.

"Clowns?" Everly chuckles. "The great Cash Stafford is afraid of clowns? Oh, this is too good."

"I swear to god, Ev, if you tell my brothers, I'll never forgive you," I warn.

I'm only half joking. I've gone to great lengths to keep my fear under wraps because Dylan and Harrison would tease me mercilessly if they ever found out. The idea of enduring years of clown-related pranks sends a chill down my spine.

Everly brushes her thumb against my scar, her brow deepening. "Thanks for trusting me enough to share. Your secret is safe with me," she vows.

I rest my hand against hers, holding it in place. Who knows when I'll get another chance to hold her this close again (when she's awake), so I'm savoring her touch while I can.

"What are you thinking?" I ask.

"Would you do anything different the night of your accident if you could go back?" she whispers as she runs her finger along my scar.

That night, I'd been on my way to Theo and Everly's house during a bad snowstorm. I stopped to help Ruth, an elderly woman who lived in Aspen Grove. Her car had broken down and I offered her a ride into town. After I helped her into my car, she remembered she'd left her purse in the passenger seat of her vehicle.

I had just stepped out of my car when an SUV came barreling around the bend and hit a patch of ice. The last thing I saw were two headlights coming straight toward me, and then everything went black. The police report said I was thrown into the vehicle's windshield.

I woke up in the hospital a week later with bandages covering half my face and had to undergo multiple reconstructive surgeries. Even with all that work, the left side of my face was still a mangled mess.

"There's nothing I would change," I state. "I might have a fucked-up face, but there's no telling what would have happened if Ruth had been standing in the road instead of me."

The doctors said it was a miracle that I didn't suffer more severe injuries and credited it to my youth and resilience. It also helped that my parents flew in the best surgeons to help with my recovery.

"Oh, Cash," Everly sighs. "I wish you could see yourself the way I see you. When I said your scar was sexy, I meant it." She shakes her head, dismissing my attempt to argue. "It's a testament to the sacrifice you made to help someone in need. Sure, you're undeniably attractive, but it's your compassion, charisma, and personality that make you irresistible. You're a genuinely good person, and that can't be replicated."

God, how does she do that? With a few simple words, she makes me feel like I truly matter. Everly sees the best in me, even when I can't, and is helping to shift my perspective.

She adjusts in my lap, pausing when her ass brushes against my cock. Her eyes widen as she sits up, glancing down to see how much she affects me.

Unable to resist, I move my hand to the small of her back, trailing my fingers along the fabric of her shirt in a hypnotic fashion. She doesn't move as I lean in to tuck her hair behind her ear, pressing a chaste kiss to her temple. I exhale slowly, the air brushing against the side of her face, and a soft moan escapes her lips. She moves her hand between us to rest against my slacks. At first, I think it's an accident until she grazes the outline of where my cock is pressing against the fabric.

Her action leaves me stunned, caught up in a lust-induced haze. I don't dare break the silence, unwilling to shatter the spell of the moment.

I groan when she moves her fingers in a circular motion, teasing me. Even with material between me and her hand, it feels like fucking nirvana.

God, this woman is trying to kill me.

Everly gazes up at me with a mischievous glint in her eye. "This doesn't mean I'm going to sleep with you, Stafford," she whispers, moving forward to nip at my bottom lip while her hand is still on my crotch.

"Are you trying to convince me or yourself, Ev?" She moans when I run my tongue across the seam of her lips. I grab her hand and push our joined fingers firmly against my hard-on. "After this, you'll be consumed with thoughts of my cock deep inside you, claiming you as my wife, inch by inch."

Just as her mouth parts, welcoming me in for a taste, the lights come back on. I blink rapidly as I adjust to the brightness. As the doors squeak open, Carol and the maintenance supervisor poke their heads inside.

"Are you alright?" she asks us with a knowing smile.

"We're fine," Everly squeaks as she scrambles from my lap.

She acts like we're high school kids getting caught behind the bleachers. As far as Carol knows, I was getting frisky with my wife, making the most of the honeymoon stage, and she doesn't seem fazed one bit.

Everly straightens her skirt and retrieves her purse from the ground.

"Thanks for saving us," she says to the maintenance man before darting past him and disappearing down the hall.

"Great timing," I mumble.

"You're not the first man who wasn't happy to be rescued," he says with a chuckle.

"How many times has this elevator broken down?" I ask, alarmed.

He shrugs. "A few."

Everly's preference for the stairs might be a smart move, but if another elevator mishap means we can continue where we left off, I'm game for it any day.

16

EVERLY

I HALF EXPECTED TO FIND my dad in my office this morning, but I was relieved when I got to the office and August told me my dad flew back to New York last night. After his impromptu visit to the Stafford Holdings office yesterday, he came back to Townstead International to meet with August and Liam.

That hasn't stopped him from tormenting me with a barrage of emails. There was no mention of the incident at Cash's office, just a mountain of work he insisted was urgent. He's a master at psychological warfare.

His version of love has always come with conditions. He's incapable of feeling genuine love for anyone, not even me or Theo. It's a sobering reality that I've struggled to grapple with since I was a kid. He had me convinced that it was my fault whenever he got angry at me for not doing things his way, and believed that if I could meet his expectations, he'd finally give me the affection I craved.

I was wrong.

I'm drawn out of my thoughts when August strolls into my office without knocking. "Good morning," he chirps. "Figured you could use this." He sets a cup of coffee on my desk before taking a seat on the couch in the corner. "Dark roast with two pumps of creamer just the way you like it."

"God bless you," I smile. "It's been a hectic morning and I haven't had my caffeine fix yet." I take a long sip, exhaling in satisfaction.

He leans back, crossing his legs like he plans to stay a while. "Glad I could be of service," he grins.

Today he's wearing a light gray suit with cropped pants, paired with a black shirt underneath, and stylish black loafers. He refuses to adhere to a typical business dress code, opting to showcase his individual style. My dad gives August hell for it whenever he's in town.

"What I would give to have been a fly on the wall during Cash's interaction with Dick yesterday."

I looped August in on the details of my dad's unwanted visit to Cash's office earlier.

I roll my eyes. "You're just jealous Cash got to stand up to him, while you have to stay silent."

He tips his head, giving me a hard look. "I'm not the only one."

"Touché," I say, taking another drink of my coffee, savoring its rich flavor.

We've both been guilty of letting my dad treat us with disrespect over the years.

"So, how's that sexy man of yours anyway?" August asks. "Have you fucked him yet, or are you still trying to convince yourself that you're not going to sleep with him?"

Coffee sprays from my mouth, and I'm quick to wipe my mouth on the back of my hand. When I look down, I spot a coffee stain on my sleeve.

"Damnit," I mumble. "Give me a warning the next time you switch topics to my sex life," I deadpan.

I grab a single-use stain remover packet from my drawer, tear it open, and dab the spot on my blouse until it's hardly noticeable. Thank god I'm always prepared.

"You know I don't have a filter," August shrugs. "Hell, if I were in your shoes, I'd be fucking that man six ways to Sunday."

"You do know you're talking about *my* husband, right?" I try to sound nonchalant, but a flicker of possessiveness sparks inside me.

"So, you have fucked him?" August smirks.

I nibble on my lip as a blush rises up my neck. It feels hot in here, like the temperature has spiked. "It's none of your business," I say, trying to brush him off.

Cash and I might not have had sex on the elevator, but I recall the way his strong arms felt wrapped around me as he held me close. As though I were the center of his universe, and he would do anything to protect me. There was no judgment or criticism, only tender caresses and soft-spoken words. My mind drifts to his cock pressed against his pants, the swollen tip jerking as I traced the outline with my finger.

August leans forward in his seat. "Come on, Everly," he says, pointing at me. "It's obvious by the flush in your cheeks you and Cash have hooked up, or at least you want to."

"We haven't slept together," I say, hoping he'll drop the subject.

That doesn't mean I don't want to.

It's a good thing August can't read my mind or I'd never hear the end of it.

"Mark my words, Ev. It's only a matter of time before you two are fucking like rabbits."

His conclusion catches me off guard. Thankfully, my coffee is safe on my desk this time, or I would have spilled it on my lap and needed a whole box of stain-remove wipes.

I'm just about to deny his assumption when we're interrupted.

"Everly, have you seen—" Liam stops short in my doorway when he spots August lounging on my couch. "There you are," he sighs.

"Here I am," August quips. "Do you need something, or are you just keeping tabs on me, brother?"

Liam pushes his thick-rimmed glasses up his nose. His wardrobe is strictly professional, in contrast to August's relaxed business style. He's the epitome of a well-dressed businessman in his charcoal-gray suit, cobalt tie, and leather dress shoes. His hair is styled in a crew cut, a striking contrast to his midnight blue eyes.

"Richard wants the proposal for the Thames Park Towers project sent to him by the end of the day," Liam says.

August narrows his eyes. "You're joking. The bastard told us about the project yesterday. How the hell does he expect us to prepare an entire proposal in one day?"

"This is all my fault," I interject.

August arches an eyebrow. "How do you figure?"

"If Cash and I hadn't provoked my dad yesterday, he wouldn't be piling all this extra work on us."

"Yeah, right," August scoffs. "The prick is always looking for an excuse to make our lives more miserable. Even if he hadn't turned up in London yesterday, he'd still want this proposal finished today."

"He's right. This has nothing to do with you," Liam states. He leans against the doorway with his arms folded across his chest. "I've been meaning to ask. How are you holding up? The news about Stafford Holdings buying out Townstead International was shocking, and I can only imagine how difficult it must be for you. Richard should never have asked you to stay married to Cash to keep the deal from falling apart, and I told him so yesterday."

In some ways Liam reminds me of Harrison. He's a fierce protector and takes his big brother role seriously. The difference is that he's the reserved genius type who prefers to keep to himself. When he does speak, his calm and measured tone gives weight to his words.

"I appreciate you standing up for me," I say. "We've put our blood, sweat and tears into this company, and I'll be damned if it's jeopardized. Whatever my dad is up to, we'll be better off with the Staffords owning the company." Liam gives me a wary gaze. He doesn't know their family like I do, but he'll see the truth in time. "And don't worry about me. Cash and I are getting along well and spending time reconnecting with each other."

I'm happier than I've been in a while. My pulse quickens whenever I see Cash, and I find myself looking forward to our evenings together. He's kept his promise to make me smile every day, and I think it's fair to say I'm rather fond of my husband—more than I like to admit.

"Cash doesn't know you as well as he wants to," August says with a sly grin.

"Shouldn't you be getting back to work? That proposal isn't going to finish itself," I quip.

"Yeah, I'll go, but I'm reserving the right to tell you I told you so when you're head over heels for Cash."

I think I'm already halfway there.

"Leave her be," Liam chimes in. "Oh, I almost forgot. Everly. There's a giant bouquet of flowers at the reception desk for you," he says.

I have a sneaking suspicion I know who they're from, and it's not Cash.

As I climb the last flight of stairs to the penthouse, I'm exhausted. The rest of my day at the office went by in a blur, helping Liam and August prepare the Thames Park Towers proposal.

When I enter the kitchen, I see Cash placing a perfectly assembled margarita pizza into the oven. My mouth waters. He spoils me with his home-cooked meals, and there's a good chance I'll starve when it's time for me to leave.

A pang of sadness passes through me when I consider the prospect of moving out of the High Rise and no longer sharing my evenings with Cash.

"Woah, those are nice flowers." He gives a low whistle, nodding to the giant bouquet in my hands. "Who are they from?" His tone carries a hint of jealousy.

I place the vase on the counter, stretching my arms out after carrying them all the way home and up several flights of stairs.

"Can you take these to your office tomorrow? I want Carol to have them," I say, sidestepping his question.

"I'm sure she'd appreciate the gesture, but wouldn't you rather keep them?" He gives the gaudy arrangement another critical once-over.

"No. I hate roses," I mutter glaring at the offending arrangement.

I was furious when the local flower shop dropped them off with a message from Landon that said *Miss you*. It was oddly satisfying to tear the note to shreds.

The bouquet seemed to mock me throughout the afternoon, but I resisted the urge to toss it out. I knew Carol would be delighted to keep the flowers at her desk for some added cheer, given that Cash's office is so drab.

"Sounds like whoever gave you those doesn't know you very well." Cash's gaze bores into mine. "Do you want to talk about it?"

I wring my hands together as I look at the ground. "I'm not sure," I answer honestly.

I've avoided the subject of Landon until now, unsure how Cash would react. Given his reaction to my dad's unannounced visit and how he cornered me, I doubt he'll take it well.

He checks his watch. "We have sixteen minutes until the pizza is done. Why don't you sit down and you can *not* tell me about it?"

"I won't say no to sitting down. My feet have been aching all day."

He leads me to the loveseat in the living room, and I sink down into it, leaning against the armrest. I'm perplexed when Cash slides to the other side and lifts one of my nylon-clad feet into his lap.

"What are you doing?" I squeal, attempting to pull away. "My feet are sweaty and gross."

"Ev, please relax," he says, not loosening his grip. "Let me take care of you." He pauses, waiting for my permission.

"Okay," I murmur. "But just for a few minutes."

"Whatever you say, pretty girl." He smiles.

A blush creeps up my cheeks at his compliment. His smile is dangerously captivating, the perfect blend of charm and mischief, making my heart race. And I wish he would stop looking at me as if he plans to keep me forever when this arrangement is only temporary.

I'm sidetracked when he presses his thumbs into the sole of my foot.

"Oh my god," I breathe out, my eyes falling shut.

"That good, huh?" His voice is raspy.

"So good." I groan in relief.

His gentle touch works wonders, melting away the tension. The rhythmic motion lulls me into a tranquil state.

"You might want to ask your questions while I'm under the influence of your magic touch," I warn him.

Given my current state of calm, I'll likely answer almost anything he asks.

"I'm going to take a wild guess that whoever sent you those roses is the same person who sent you those late-night texts." Cash sets my foot back on his lap and gives the other one the same treatment.

"That wasn't a question," I retort.

"No, it's a statement. Most guys who do something wrong start with a text or call. If that doesn't work, they resort to sending flowers. The bigger the screwup, the bigger the bouquet."

"Are you saying you'd do something different?" I peek my eyes open, wanting to see his response.

"When I do something stupid, which will happen on occasion, I'll apologize in person and make it up to you with toe-curling sex." I gasp as he pushes on a pressure point at that exact moment. "When I bring you home flowers, it'll be to brighten your day, not because I need your forgiveness. And it won't be one bouquet—it'll be an entire roomful to show how much I care."

I try to calm my racing pulse as I process my fake husband telling me he's going to fuck me and dote on me endlessly. His eyes are blazing with lust, and I have to redirect this conversation before we end up naked on this couch.

No matter how enticing that sounds.

"My ex-fiancé, Landon, sent the flowers." I take a piece of lint from the couch as a distraction while speaking. "I called off our engagement two years ago when I caught him cheating, but that hasn't stopped him from sending texts and calls whenever he gets it into his head that there's a chance we could get back together."

"Have you told him you're married?" Cash frowns.

"I texted him a few days ago and told him I've moved on," I say defensively.

"Well, clearly, that didn't work." He gestures to the bouquet in the kitchen. "Why don't you like roses?"

When he's finished my massage, I sit upright and curl my feet underneath my legs. I've kept the memories locked away, avoiding the pain of old wounds. But with Cash by my side, I find the courage to share it.

"My dad used to bring my mom jewelry and a bouquet of two dozen red roses after every business trip. The year before their divorce, the jewelry he brought home was more expensive, and the flower arrangements larger." I take a deep breath as I collect my thoughts. "My mom became suspicious and hired a private investigator to follow my dad, and that's when she found he was cheating. When he came back from his next trip, she hurled the vase of roses he brought with him across the room. It shattered on impact." I shudder at the memory. "My dad left a week later."

The combination of my mom's unpredictable behavior and my dad's selfish tendencies was a recipe for failure. My parents never physically caused each other harm, but it was painful to watch the love they once shared shrivel away until there was nothing left but decay.

"What kind of flowers do you like?" Cash asks in a husky tone, pulling me away from the somber memories.

I offer him a soft smile, grateful that he doesn't press me for more details. "Daffodils. They're my favorite." They're vibrant and cheerful and symbolize the fresh start I desperately crave.

"Daffodils," he repeats. "Noted," he adds with a mischievous grin.

I'm not sure whether to be excited or concerned about what he's plotting.

17

EVERLY

IT'S BEEN ANOTHER LONG DAY at the office after a brief reprieve last night, complete with a foot massage, gourmet pizza, and a pleasant conversation with Cash. It's past lunchtime, and my stomach is growling in protest.

After a meeting with a client in the conference room, I step into my office and freeze when I find Landon sitting at my desk. His hair is disheveled, his eyes bloodshot like he's been sleep-deprived for days, and his white button-up shirt is wrinkled.

He's a far cry from the sharply dressed, accomplished lawyer I fell for. Now, my feelings have turned to pity and frustration at his insistence on trying to hold me back from moving on.

"What are you doing here?" I sigh, hanging my purse on the coat rack in the corner.

He gives me a weary smile as he jumps out of the chair to approach me. "You're back."

"How did you get in?"

"I walked in." He shrugs.

He must have slipped past the front desk while the receptionist was on her lunch break. She wouldn't have allowed him in my office without checking with me first.

"You need to leave," I state firmly, pointing to the door.

I'm sick and tired of the unwelcome men in my life dropping by whenever they please. It's clear that I've allowed things with Landon to drag on for far too long, and it's time to put an end to it once and for all. Cash is right; I have to be more direct.

"Come on, don't be like that, baby," Landon pleads, moving closer. "You haven't responded to most of my texts or calls lately, so I had to visit you in person while I'm in town. Did you like the flowers I sent yesterday?" He glances around, frowning when he doesn't see them.

One silver lining after our breakup was that his law firm relocated him to their New York office, making it much easier to have the space to grieve the loss of our relationship, and his unwelcome advances.

"If I wanted to see you, I would have reached out," I point out. "Can't you see that this is over? Our relationship ended two years ago, and you need to accept that we're never getting back together."

A sense of relief washes over me at finally being able to say those words to his face.

"You don't mean it," he bristles, becoming more agitated. "I made a mistake, baby, but we can move past it. We belong together. Can't you see that?"

He closes the distance between us and I recoil when his hand grazes my arm, not out of fear, but because I find the cold and clammy sensation unpleasant. It's different from Cash's touch, which is warm and inviting.

"Landon, this has got to stop. We're never—"

"What. Is. That?" he interrupts, eying my ring with disdain.

"My wedding ring," I state with a genuine smile. "I told you when I texted you the last time that I had moved on."

"I figured that was your way of playing hard to get. How could you do this to us?" Landon cries as he pulls at his hair in agitation.

I let out a humorless laugh. "Do this to us? There is no *us*. There hasn't been since the day I found you fucking your assistant in the same bed you and I had slept in together the night before."

"Everly, if you let me walk out of here, you'll regret it," he says with a vacant tone.

His empty threat sounds like something my dad would say. How did I not see it before? They have so much in common— always needing to have the final word, wanting things done their way, and unwilling to accept when an outcome isn't in their favor. If Landon and I had stayed together, I would have been subjected to a lifetime of emotional tirades and criticism.

Cash would never treat me like this.

He's the opposite of Landon in every way—loyal, protective, and attentive.

"If you don't walk out of here, *you'll* be sorry." As if I conjured him from thin air, I'm relieved when I hear Cash's voice. I look over to find him standing in the doorway, holding a bag of takeout.

He strides toward me, wrapping his arm around my waist, pulling me behind him in a protective gesture.

The strong-willed part of me can't help being offended, but the hopeless romantic in me swoons at his instinct to shield me from harm.

"You have no right to talk to me that way. I'm Everly's fiancé," Landon declares, feigning confidence.

"You mean ex-fiancé," Cash corrects him. "It's been over two years since you broke up, so why are you still harassing my wife?"

Landon looks like a mouse cornered by a cat, his gaze darting to Cash's scar as he tries to gauge if he's in danger.

"Everly, come on babe, please tell me this is a joke," Landon whines, cautiously glancing over Cash's shoulder to get a look at me.

"We're done," I reiterate. "Now, leave."

"Baby, pl—"

"You work at Thompson & Tate, right?" Cash interrupts him with a menacing tone.

Landon's eyes grow wide, like a deer caught in headlights. "Uh, yeah."

"Dawson Tate and I go way back. In fact, we met up for drinks on the Upper East Side two months when I was in New York. If I called him right now, I bet he'd answer," Cash says, pulling his phone from his pocket. "He'd be very interested to learn that one of his employees is harassing my wife."

"Woah, hold on a minute," Landon rushes out. "Let's not do anything rash."

Cash grins like he has the upper hand. "This is how it's going to go. Get the hell out of Everly's office and stop contacting her. If you try reaching out, I'll know. You had your chance with her and wasted it. That's not my problem. She's mine now." I fight the smile lifting my lips when he draws me into his side.

"Okay, fine. Geez, call off your guard dog, Everly," Landon says to me, holding out his hands in defense. "I'll go, just don't let him call Dawson."

"Goodbye, Landon." My voice is devoid of emotion.

I ignore his request, liking the idea of him being on edge.

He doesn't bother with a response as he leaves my office like a bat out of hell. The second he's gone, it's like a weight has lifted off my shoulders. Something tells me today was the last time I'll hear from him. Cash can be very convincing when he wants to be.

"How do you know Dawson Tate?"

He's one of the most ruthless lawyers in New York City and the last person I imagined would be in Cash's inner circle.

"I've never met the guy," Cash says.

My eyes widen. "But you just said you had drinks with him two months ago."

"That was Harrison. It wouldn't sounded as intimidating if I had said my brother knew him now, would it?" He smirks.

I raise a brow. "And what would you have done if Landon had called your bluff?"

"Easy. Called Harrison, pretending I was talking to Dawson. He would have gone along with it."

"Thanks for getting rid of Landon. It's not your problem to deal with but I appreciate your help, regardless."

"You're my wife. Your problems *are* my problems. What do I have to do to make you see that?"

He lifts my jaw so I'm met with his soft gaze.

"I think you need to remind me again, just to drive your point home," I mock him playfully.

"I mean it, Ev." He swipes his thumb along my cheek. "You belong to me, and I protect what's mine." I swear he lets out a low growl, but I can't be sure.

"I'm really glad you showed up," I say, leaning into his touch.

"It was my turn to bring you lunch." He smiles, holding up a takeout bag from my favorite bistro down the street.

I've come to discover that Cash is unlike any of the men I've been with in the past. Everything he's done since the night at the bar has been to make my life better and show me how much he cares. Instead of being on guard, ready to push him away, maybe it's time to give him a real chance.

18

CASH

"YOU'RE LATE." HARRISON FROWNS AS he taps his watch.

"I'm sorry," I say, settling into my office chair and looking into my laptop's camera. "I ran all the way back, but I took Everly lunch, and I didn't want to rush—" I stop when I see Harrison and Dylan giving each other looks at the conference table in our Maine office.

Nowadays, it's rare for them to be in the same room during our meetings since Dylan works from home most days, and Harrison spends a lot of time at our New York office. While it's only an hour's plane ride into the city, going to the headquarters in Maine has become an inconvenient detour for them both.

"You had lunch with Everly?" Dylan asks as he adjusts his glasses.

"Yeah, of course I did. She's my wife." I'll never tire of calling her that. "You and Marlow go out during the day all the time, and you're not even married yet," I taunt him.

He gives me a sideways glance in response. If it were his call, they'd get married today, but she wants to wait until she's officially adopted Lola before they exchange their wedding vows.

"At least Marlow wants to be my wife," he says with a smirk.

I shoot him an annoyed glare. "Everly has bigger issues to deal with, like her ex-fiancé showing up at her office, begging her to take him back."

When I went to take her lunch this afternoon, her office door was open. Curiosity got the best of me when I saw her talking to another man, and rage surged through me when I realized it was Landon. The cheating bastard had the nerve to beg Everly to take him back, then lashed out when she stood her ground. He betrayed Everly's trust, and I was more than happy to help put him in his place.

"Wait, are you serious?" Dylan asks. "That happened today?"

"Yeah. I walked in just as she was telling him she got married. I told him to get out of her office, among other things." I shrug a shoulder.

"What did you do, Cash?" Harrison looks alarmed. "Please tell me you're not going to be slapped with assault charges."

"No, it's not as bad as it sounds," I assure him. "He works for Thompson & Tate, and I may have hinted at being friends with Dawson. So, could you make a call and have Landon fired?" I ask like it's the simplest favor in the world.

Harrison rubs his temples, letting out an exasperated sigh. "Let me get this straight. You want me to call up Dawson Tate, the guy who has a reputation for making grown men cry on the stand, and ask him for a favor? He doesn't do things for free."

"Do it for Everly," I encourage him. "Her douchebag ex cheated on her and deserves what's coming to him. I'm sure Dawson would gladly channel his pent-up frustration into seeking revenge for a cheater and a liar."

"Fine," Harrison concedes with a resigned sigh. "But when Dawson calls to cash in his favor, it's on you to handle it."

"Sure, no problem." I wave him off.

I would do anything for Everly, even make a deal with a devil who wears custom-made suits and thrives on ruining his enemies without mercy.

Settling back in my chair, a satisfied grin curves my lips as I picture Landon's reaction to losing his job. With any luck, Dawson will bring him to tears while breaking the news. It's the small victories that bring me joy.

"You owe me a hundred bucks." Dylan nudges Harrison. "Bringing lunch to Everly and seeking vengeance on her ex totally counts."

"No, it doesn't. He hasn't said the L word yet," Harrison counters, swatting Dylan's hand away.

My eyes ping between them. "What the hell are you talking about?"

Now I understand how Everly felt when my brothers and I discussed the acquisition at my parents' house, and she didn't know what was happening.

"Oh, nothing much. We were wagering on how long it would take you to stake your claim on Everly. I bet less than three weeks; Harrison said a month."

"She's my wife, why wouldn't I?"

"Oh, for crying out loud," Dylan complains to Harrison. "That's as close to a declaration of love we're going to get."

"Fine," Harrison grumbles as he retrieves his wallet and pulls out a hundred-dollar bill. He places it in Dylan's outstretched hand.

"I think this is the first time I've ever won a bet with you. I'm totally framing this." Dylan holds the bill up with a triumphant grin.

"Don't get used to it," Harrison taunts.

Could I love Everly? I've never felt this way about anyone else. I miss her when we're not together, and she's constantly on my mind. My heart races when she walks into the room, and there's nothing I wouldn't do for her. And the very idea of this thing between us ending makes me physically ill. But is that what love feels like?

"Why don't we talk about work since this *is* a work meeting," I interject.

I'd rather discuss anything other than the complex emotions I have for my wife.

Harrison and Dylan look at me as if I'm speaking gibberish.

"Who are you, and what have you done with Cash Stafford?" Dylan mocks playfully.

"He has been working longer hours and logging in earlier than normal," Harrison adds.

"Isn't that what you wanted?" I deadpan.

"I appreciate you stepping up. It seems like Everly has been a good influence on you." He clears his throat. "You're right. We should get down to business since I have a virtual meeting with the board in twenty minutes," he says, checking his watch. "They want an update on the acquisition and are eager to know how the newlyweds are doing."

My eyebrows shoot up. "What did you tell them?"

"That you're enjoying every moment of newlywed bliss and are staying out of the majority of the acquisition discussions."

The week Everly and I got back to London, Harrison broke the news of our marriage to the board. As anticipated, there were concerns about our wedding taking place before the business deal was finalized, but Harrison eased their concerns by convincing them that we'd fallen in love after reuniting and couldn't wait to get married.

"How is the deep dive analysis on Townstead International going, Dylan?" Harrison asks.

I lean forward in my seat, my interest piqued. Since I've had to stay out of the day-to-day discussions of the deal, I'm eager for the sporadic updates that I get on our calls.

"We've run into some anomalies in the finances that warrant further investigation," Dylan explains as he pushes his glasses up on his nose. "The financial records for Europe are in perfect order; the issue appears to be with their North America division. It took us a while to get the additional records, but we have them now, and my team and I will have a full report over to you by the beginning of next week."

I'm not surprised that there's something questionable going on with the part of the business Richard manages. From what I've observed, Everly and her step-siblings run their London office like a tight ship. If you ask me, they should run the entire company.

"Has Richard tried coming by your office again?" Harrison asks me.

"No, he hasn't been back to London, that I know of."

He hasn't directly contacted Everly since the incident at my office, but that hasn't stopped him from emailing her assignments that have her working well into the night once I go to bed.

"Good. His lawyer instructed him to steer clear of all Stafford Holdings offices and informed him that anything related to the acquisition has to go through our legal teams."

"Please keep me in the loop. I don't want to keep anything from Everly, especially when it concerns her."

If her dad is involved in any questionable activities, I want to make sure it doesn't negatively affect her. And she deserves to know the truth if he is involved in something he shouldn't be.

I wake up as the first rays of sunlight stream through the window.

The clock on my nightstand reads 6:13 a.m. I groan, frustrated by being wide awake with no hope of falling back asleep. Like every morning, Everly is sprawled across my chest, with her arm draped over my stomach. Her pouty lips are slightly parted as she sleeps soundly. My rigid cock presses against her thigh, straining against my boxers.

I slip out of bed, careful not to wake her, and head straight for the bathroom, shutting the door behind me. If I had any self-control, I'd take a cold shower like I've been doing most mornings lately, but I'm desperate to relieve my aching cock.

After turning on the faucet, I strip out of my underwear and step under the stream of hot water.

My eyes fall shut as I imagine Everly is here with me.

In my mind's eye, I kneel in front of her and spread her legs open, peppering kisses along her skin. My hands grip her quivering thighs as I lick her pussy in long, steady strokes. I gaze up to find a wanton expression on her face as I plunge two fingers inside her tight cunt. Her fingers tangle in my hair as I work her clit hard, telling her to be a good wife and come for me. She arches her back as she comes, shouting my name.

A low groan escapes my mouth as the vivid scene plays in my mind. I put my hand against the wall for support, stroking my rock-hard cock with the other, desperate for relief. My breath comes out in pants, and I squeeze harder as another fantasy enters my thoughts, clear as day.

I've got one hand gripping Everly's hip and the other on her breast as I drive into her from behind. I tilt her head back so I can see her unbridled expression as she takes my cock inside her slick pussy.

"Holy shit, Ev, that feels so good," I moan, pumping my dick.

There's a subtle chill in the air, and I look over to find Everly standing in the doorway. She's real. Her mouth hangs open as she stares at me through the glass, her gaze zoned in on my dick.

Despite the steam and my lust-filled haze, I can't help but notice that she's braless, her pebbled nipples poking through her white tank. I lick my lips, thinking about wrapping my mouth around one of them. If I were a better man, I'd stop immediately, but I'm a selfish bastard who can't resist the urge to watch her unfiltered reaction as I come to visions of worshiping her only the way I could.

I continue stroking my shaft, my eyes locked on Everly. Her grip tightens on the door handle, her cheeks flushed. I pick up my pace as I watch the rapid rise and fall of her chest and the way her lips part when I squeeze my cock tighter.

"Fuck, Ev," I say her name like a prayer as my orgasm hits me like a freight train.

Her hand drifts to her mouth, her fingers brushing against her lips as she takes in the scene before her. She stares at me, eyes wide as saucers as ropes of cum spurt onto the shower floor. It ends all too soon when I briefly glance down, and when I look back up, she's bolted from the room.

Damn, that was hot as fuck.

19

EVERLY

I'M FLUSTERED AS I FLEE from the bathroom, heading straight to the walk-in closet. I grip hold of the doorframe, breathing heavily as visions of Cash standing under the water with his hand wrapped around his cock flash through my mind.

When I woke up and he wasn't in bed, I assumed he went for a run—until I heard the shower running. Curiosity got the better of me when I saw the door was ajar. I expected to find him naked, not jerking off as he called out my name.

Feeling flushed, I strip out of my tank top, shorts, and underwear and grab my white robe from its hanger, tying it around my waist.

I freeze when I hear the shower turn off. Coming into the closet was a bad idea. Cash is going to have to get dressed, and I'll be forced to confront him. If I go now, I should have enough time to leave the room before he's finished drying off. I wonder if he'll come in wrapped in a towel or stark naked.

God, what is wrong with me?

I rub my hand across my face. Cash is my fake husband, not a piece of meat. And yet I'm lusting after him like he's forbidden fruit that I'm desperate to sink my teeth into.

I've just made up my mind to make a break for it when I hear him enter the closet.

"Do you need something, Stafford?" I ask, pretending to look through my skirts. We both know it's an excuse to avoid looking at him.

"Did you like what you saw in there?" he asks point blank as he approaches me.

Yes, it was the most erotic moment I've ever witnessed.

"I don't know what you're talking about," I reply, feigning indifference.

"Oh, really?" Cash's tone is skeptical. "Because from where I was standing, you couldn't pull your eyes away as you watched me jerk off. Curious as to what I was thinking about?" He pauses briefly. "I'll tell you." He leans in, his breath warm against my neck. "I was thinking about what you might taste like with my face buried inside your pussy."

My legs instinctively clamp together as the image flashes in my mind.

I glance over my shoulder at him. "And suppose I did like what I saw. What would you do about it?"

I lose my train of thought as he winds his arm around my waist, my back pressed to his front.

"Do you have any idea how much power you have over me, Ev?" he murmurs in my ear. "All I can think about is our moment in the elevator, with your hand pressed against my cock, the impulse to kiss those perfect lips consuming me."

"This isn't real." My breathing quickens as I track his every move. "Our marriage is fake, remember," I whisper, a last-ditch effort to convince myself.

Cash shakes his head in mock disappointment. "That's a damn shame."

He brushes my hair over my shoulder, holding me captive with his touch. I'm rooted in place, my skin tingling with heat as his soft lips brush against the shell of my ear, leaving me gasping for air.

"Why do you say that?" My question comes out breathless.

He spins me around to face him, his intense hazel gaze holding me captive. My eyes trace the jagged scar spanning from his ear to his mouth. Despite the imperfection, he's every bit an Adonis, a living work of art whose flaws make him even more appealing.

"Rumor has it that newlyweds have some of the best sex of their lives." His eyes dip to where my robe opens, and my nipples ache under the intensity of his gaze. "Aren't you even a little curious about how my fantasy could play out in real life?"

Oh god, yes.

I bite back a groan, finding it more difficult by the minute to tamp down my instinctive response to him.

"Why don't you show me." The words escape my mouth before I can stop them.

I'm stunned speechless when he scoops me into his arms and carries me over to the large upholstered bench in the corner. It's identical to the one in the entryway. Now that I think about it, both showed up the day after we returned from

Aspen Grove. One of Cash's sweet gestures, giving me a place to sit when I take my shoes on and off.

Why does he have to be so damn thoughtful? It makes it so much harder to resist him.

Once he's eased me down onto the bench, he kneels before me. He's wearing only a pair of black boxers, his bare chest glistening with water droplets. He must have rushed to dry off before coming to find me.

"What are you doing?" I squeak.

"Showing you what it feels like to have a man worship at your feet."

I can feel a blush spread across my cheeks as he brushes his hands along my legs, leaving a trail of goosebumps in their wake. When he pushes the silky material of my robe to the side, the belt comes undone, and Cash lets out a guttural groan when he glimpses what's underneath—nothing.

I wait with bated breath as he leans into the apex of my thighs, nipping at my sensitive skin. When I try to shift in my seat, he holds my legs apart, pressing his nose against my core, inhaling my scent.

God, why is that so hot?

He coaxes me to lie back on the bench, lifting my legs over his shoulder. I should be mortified that I'm laid out bare for him, but a rush of heat courses through me, and my thoughts are consumed with what he might do next.

I weave my fingers into his hair, wrestling with the desire to draw him closer and the impulse to push him away. The former wins when he licks along the seam of my pussy in teasing strokes, and I instinctively push his head into my thighs.

I moan. "Fuck, Stafford. Your mouth feels so good."

"I'm just getting started." He says it like a promise. As if this is a small taste of all the wicked things he could do to me if only I'd let him.

I'm dripping with arousal as he alternates between licking and sucking. I moan louder as he grazes my clit, focusing his attention on the sensitive bud.

"Oh my god," I gasp out as I dig my nails deeper into his scalp.

"Fuck, Ev, you're so damn sweet," he murmurs before burying his face back between my legs.

I pant heavily as my climax draws near, and Cash locks his mouth around my clit. As I cry out begging for more, he bites down firmly, and the room fills with my screams as I erupt, tumbling into orgasmic bliss.

When I finally come down from my high, Cash helps me sit up, the evidence of my pleasure on his lips.

When his gaze meets mine, I reach out to touch his cheek, softly running my thumb over the raised skin of his scar. He briefly closes his eyes as if savoring my touch.

"Are you okay?" he asks, holding my hand against his cheek.

Being with Cash feels like finding refuge from a storm. More than anything, I want to tell him that he has a wicked mouth and there's nothing I'd like more than to spend the day locked away with him. But I hold back, my doubts outweighing the longing to surrender to my feelings.

For so long I'd been convinced that men were all untrustworthy and after Landon, I avoided them at all costs. Now that I've met someone who wants to cherish me and shower me with affection, I'm unsure how to reconcile my newfound hope with my lingering fears.

I nod. "It's getting late. I should get ready for work," I say, flinching when the words come out of my mouth.

"Yeah, okay," Cash reluctantly agrees. I don't miss the hurt in his voice as he stands, extending his hand to help me up. He gives my fingers one last squeeze before he steps away.

He's halfway across the room when I stop him.

"Cash?" I whisper.

He turns around to face me. "Yeah?"

"You should know, that was the best orgasm I've ever had."

He gives me a sly smile. "Don't worry, it won't be your last. Mark my words, Ev. When you're ready to accept what's happening between us, I'll make sure you're screaming my name while I'm deep inside you," he promises, his eyes ablaze with determination.

The mental picture of him hovering above me on our bed, fucking me without restraint, enters my mind. My mouth falls open when he leaves me alone with my runaway thoughts, wishing I had the courage to ask him to stay.

Squinting down at the screen, I struggle to make sense of the email I'm reading. I should have left an hour ago, but after my encounter with Cash this morning, I'm stalling.

My face turns bright red just thinking about his head pressed between my quivering thighs, with my fingers tangled in his hair as I screamed out in ecstasy.

I'm not ashamed of what we did—in fact, I want to do it again—but that means our relationship would become even more complex, if that's even possible at this point.

I'm startled when my phone rings on my desk, but I smile when I see who it is.

"Hey, Theo," I answer cheerfully.

"Hey, little sis," he teases.

"Are you forgetting we're the same age?"

"I'm two minutes older," he retorts smugly, a detail he never fails to remind me of.

I hear someone shout "Order up," in the background, followed by another voice yelling "Cut." A chorus of arguing voices follows.

"Where are you?"

"At the studio in LA. Hold on just a second." The voices fade and a door slams shut. "Are you still there, sis?"

"Yeah, I'm here." I wedge my phone between my shoulder and ear as I finish typing an email.

"Sorry about the noise. We're filming a pilot for *The Great Cook-Off Challenge*, and not all the cast members are on the same page with the show's direction."

"It's no problem," I assure him. "I miss you. When are you coming back to London?"

"Within a few weeks," he answers. "After we're done filming here, I'm flying to Paris to visit La Maison de la Lune before its grand opening. I'm collaborating with another chef in Barcelona after that."

Theo has been a culinary genius since he was a kid. He had a gift for turning a simple box of macaroni and cheese into a

ANN EINERSON

decadent dish with household staples like bacon, parmesan cheese, and breadcrumbs.

He was always bound for greatness. After he graduated culinary school, a celebrity chef dropped by the restaurant he worked at and was so impressed she requested to meet the chef. They had a long conversation, and she gave Theo her card before she left. Within two years, he'd opened his first restaurant.

"Okay, hotshot," I say. "Well, I miss you." The main reason I asked my dad to work in the London office was to be close to Theo, but lately, he's been traveling more than he's home.

"I miss you too," he says with a hint of sadness. "We have a lot to talk about when I get back to London, don't we?"

I sigh. "Yeah, we do." I send off the email I was working on, and lean back in my office chair.

"Like the fact that you married my best friend because of a silly high school marriage pact," Theo mutters, his dissatisfaction evident.

Since his confrontation with Cash, we've had several brief phone calls and text each other daily, but we haven't had a chance to properly discuss things because he flew to the States that night. Honestly, it might be for the best because I'm not sure how long I could withhold the truth about the acquisition if he were here in person.

"Is this a conversation you really want to have over the phone?" I ask him.

Theo falls silent for a minute. "No, but I don't like that you two are playing house when I still don't have all the details." I

236

hear someone calling Theo's name in the background, followed by him cursing under his breath.

"Listen, I know you have to go, but I don't want you to worry about me."

He scoffs. "You're my sister—I'll always worry about you."

His simple declaration is like a warm blanket of assurance that, no matter what, I will always have his unwavering love and protection. It's difficult being so far away from him. We were inseparable as kids, and the distance between us never gets easier.

"Theo, I appreciate it, but I promise I'm okay... more than okay."

"Is Cash treating you well?" he asks, the discomfort in his voice obvious.

"Yes, I couldn't have asked for anyone better," I state with conviction.

"I guess I'll have to live with that answer for the time being." There's more commotion in the background. "I wish we could talk longer, but I have to get back to filming. I love you, sis. I'll talk to you soon."

"Love you too, Theo."

As I glance around my office, I realize how absurd it is that I'm hiding out. I'm lucky enough to have someone waiting at home for me, and I shouldn't take that for granted. I pack up my bag, curious how things will play out when I get back to the apartment. A part of me is hoping that Cash meant it when he said what happened between us was just the beginning.

The apartment is quiet when I step inside. When I texted Cash to tell him I was on my way home, he said he was working out in the gym on the floor below and would be back in a couple of hours. Which surprised me, considering he's always here when I get home from work.

What if my cutting things short this morning pushed him over the edge. He could have decided I'm more trouble than I'm worth.

The thought enters my mind like a whisper of smoke, clouding my judgment, but I'm quick to push it to the side. I consider going down to the gym to see him, but I decide against it, not wanting him to think I miss him… even though I do.

After confirming he isn't in the apartment, I go to our bedroom, heading straight for the closet. I strip out of my blouse and skirt, tossing them into the laundry basket in the corner. I leave on my matching set of black lace lingerie and retrieve the floral shoebox stashed on the bottom shelf of the far wall of built-in shelves.

Whoever boxed up my belongings in my apartment packed my sex toys for me. I was mortified when I found them in Cash's room while organizing my things. At least the movers had the good sense to keep my collection together.

I open the lid and dig through the vibrators and dildos until I find my favorite blue rabbit vibrator. It's been ages since I've used it. Aside from the mornings when he goes for a run or works out in the gym, Cash is always home, and I haven't wanted to chance him walking in on me pleasuring myself.

Tonight is the exception. I've been wound up like a spring all day and can't wait any longer for my next release.

When I go back to the bedroom, my gaze drifts to the bathroom, thinking of Cash stroking his thick cock, precum leaking from the tip. My breathing picks up as I recall when he came, ropes of cum spurting to the shower floor.

My gaze shifts to the door, deciding to keep it open so I can hear if Cash comes home. I already know this is going to be quick.

Vibrator in hand, I crawl to the middle of the bed and lie on my back. I shimmy out of my underwear, tossing them to the floor.

Anticipation crackles in the air as I push the vibrator inside myself, groaning at the welcome intrusion. There's no need for lubricant since I'm already wet from fantasizing about Cash's thick cock. The sensation feels incredible, given my heightened state, and a jolt of pleasure shoots through my core when I turn the device on.

A soft hum buzzes through the air, and my hands tremble as I ease the vibrator in and out in uneven strokes. I think of the mind-blowing orgasm Cash gave me with his skilled mouth. The way his tongue licked and sucked, coaxing pleasure from my body as his fingers pressed into the supple flesh of my thighs.

"Oh, Cash," I moan, remembering how he latched onto my clit as I tumbled into a blissful orgasm.

I push the device deeper, frantically searching for a similar result. The added pressure has me groaning, my muscles taut with the prospect of a climax. I'm startled from my elevated state when I hear movement.

My pulse quickens as I raise my head, my gaze darting to the open doorway where Cash is standing with his hands at his side. His eyes are blazing with lust as he shamelessly peruses my nearly naked body.

How did I not hear him come home?

Despite being comfortable in my own skin, it's difficult not to feel self-conscious when I'm lying spread eagle on the bed with a vibrator shoved in my pussy while my husband stands a few feet away, looking at me like he's starving.

I ease the vibrator out of me, pausing when Cash speaks.

"Don't stop on my account," he says in a husky voice.

The idea of him watching me climax sends another ripple of ecstasy through my body as the tip of the vibrator continues to pulsate at my entrance.

I surprise even myself when I say, "You can watch from there."

"Whatever you want, wifey," Cash says.

God, why do I like that nickname so much.

With one shoulder against the doorway, he folds his arms as though preparing to watch a performance.

I prop myself up on my elbow so I have a better view of him. He's shirtless and wearing sweats that hang low on his hips. His well-defined muscles and confident stance make him positively mouthwatering.

Before I can overthink my invitation, I take in a deep breath, pushing the humming vibrator back inside my pussy.

Cash doesn't move as he watches me plunge the device in and out. The bulge in his sweats grows larger when I let out a guttural moan.

"Fuck," he mutters under his breath as he palms his shaft through his sweats.

My eyes flutter closed as the pleasure intensifies.

"Keep those beautiful eyes open, Ev," he instructs.

I obey, snapping them open. Part of me longs for him to share this moment with me, and I don't want to miss a single second of it.

"God, it feels so good," I murmur.

"It's nothing compared to what it would feel if it were my cock instead. I'd grip your thighs, my fingers making imprints on your skin." My breath hitches when I turn up the speed of the vibrator. "I'd thrust inside your tight pussy while playing with those delicious nipples."

I pump the vibrator faster in frantic strokes.

"Fuck, Cash, what are you doing to me?"

"I could ask you the same thing." He groans. "Put more pressure on your clit, Ev. Get yourself there."

He doesn't have to tell me twice. My eyes remain locked on him as I push the fluttering ears of the device onto my clit like he ordered, crying out as I fall off the edge.

As I come down from my release, I'm disappointed to find that it left me unsatisfied and longing for more. One glance at Cash's abs, glistening with sweat, and the pressure inside builds again.

"Want to test a theory with me?" he asks, remaining rooted to his spot by the doorway.

"Which is?" I whisper.

"That the real deal is much better than those toys of yours."

It's like he read my mind.

"Yes, let's test your theory," I say, frowning when he doesn't come closer. "Stafford, I want you."

"Fuck, Ev." He stalks into the room, his eyes never leaving mine. He's still palming his cock through his sweats, and his hair has fallen over his scar, making him look deliciously irresistible. "If I get on that bed, there's no going back. You'd be my wife in both word *and* deed, and that's not something I take lightly. Do you understand?"

I pause for a moment. He's not asking me to be his forever… just his *right* now. We've already crossed so many other boundaries. What's one more? Especially when it means mind-blowing sex from a man who I can't stop obsessing about.

Determined to make the most of the situation, I toss the vibrator on the nightstand and crook my finger in Cash's direction, inviting him to join me on the bed.

"Let me hear you say the words, wifey," he murmurs, his eyes burning with longing.

"I understand… hubby."

Tonight holds the promise of being unforgettable, and I'm eagerly anticipating what's to come.

20

CASH

AFTER EVERLY RUSHED OUT OF the closet this morning, I was concerned I had scared her off for good. My fears amplified when she didn't come home at her usual time tonight. To calm my nerves, I spent hours at the gym burning off my pent-up energy.

What I didn't expect to hear when I stepped into the apartment were moans coming from down the hall. I froze in place when I found Everly in our bedroom, lying on the bed, wearing nothing but a black lace bra. My name passing her lips while one hand gripped the sheets and the other pushed a vibrator into her pussy.

Everly sits up in the bed. My cock twitches in my pants as she slowly unfastens her bra, enticing me to draw closer. I'm riveted as her supple breasts spill out, begging to be touched. She pushes her hair behind her shoulder, giving me an unfiltered view of her naked body.

"Fuck, you're a goddamn vision," I murmur.

I'm captivated by her hourglass figure and sinful curves. Her body is a work of art, and I have the privilege to experience it firsthand. I'm damned lucky she's all mine.

For now.

Our future may be uncertain, but I plan to savor every precious moment I have with Everly... my Everly.

Her eyes track my every move as I stride toward the bed, pausing to tug off my sweats and boxers.

She's still as I crawl onto the bed beside her.

"This is your last warning. Are you absolutely sure you want this?" I ask, grazing my knuckles against her cheek.

I would be disappointed if she backed out now, but I will never push her into doing something she's not ready for.

"Yes, now please stop talking and put your mouth on me," she demands.

"With pleasure."

I bend and kiss the valley between her breasts, and she draws in a sharp breath when I flick one of her nipples with my tongue. The small bud hardens at my touch, and I greedily wrap my mouth around it, biting down on the soft flesh.

"Oh, god," she cries out.

Everly puts her hands on my shoulders, her nails sinking into my bare flesh, and I welcome the pain. Her moans grow louder as I alternate between licking, biting, and sucking her sensitive breasts. She clings to me, and I fucking love it.

A pleading whine escapes her lips when I pull away.

"Don't worry, I'm just getting started," I promise.

I glance down to see her pussy is already wet for me, and I shoot her a wicked smile as I sink two fingers inside her tight heat. Her gasp fills the room.

"Damn, you're soaked, Ev. Is this all for me?"

"Yes. For you," she pants.

I drag my tongue along the column of her neck and pepper kisses across her collarbone. When I add a third finger, she lets out a strangled sound of arousal, and my cock aches with need. It's the most sensual sound I've ever heard, making me want her—want *this*—even more, if that's possible. All the waiting and the anticipation leading up to this moment makes it even sweeter.

"Are you going to come on my hand?" I whisper.

She nods as she clenches tighter around me. "You better not stop, Stafford," she breathes out.

"Not until you come for me."

I can sense that she's close to the edge, her body coiling tighter with each plunge of my fingers. I thrum her clit with my thumb, and within seconds she shatters around my hand.

Her head falls back on the pillow as she lets out a strangled cry of pleasure, plummeting off the precipice. She doesn't stop riding my hand until I've wrung every drop of desire from her core.

Everly is utterly captivating when she's on the verge of release, but watching her lose control as she comes is something else entirely.

"Taste how delicious you are." I lift my fingers to her lips, my gaze glued to her mouth as she sucks them clean. "Your next orgasm is going to be around my cock," I murmur.

"There's no way I can have another orgasm tonight." She drops her head back against the pillow.

"Is that a challenge?" I ask as I rock into her, my cock pressing against her thigh. "You're coming at least three more times tonight."

"I'll believe it when I see it," she taunts.

"Challenge accepted."

I reach over to the nightstand to grab a condom, ripping the package open with my teeth. Once it's on, I grab hold of my shaft and line myself up with Everly's entrance. I run the tip of my dick along her seam in teasing strokes. Fuck, I'm not even inside her yet and I'm already finding it hard to control myself.

"You sure you want my cock?"

"Oh god, yes," she says.

I push inside slowly, and her cunt clenches around me at the intrusion. She threads her fingers through my hair, tugging me closer as our intermingled groans fill the room.

Once I'm fully seated, I pause to give her a moment to adjust. "Holy shit. You're so goddamn tight," I grit out, my voice strained.

"You were right. My toys are nothing compared to your big cock," she gasps.

I chuckle. "As long as you're mine, you won't need them." My muscles quiver from the strain of holding back while she acclimates to my size. "Unless we play together."

"I like the sound of that," she murmurs.

I intertwine our fingers, guiding her arms above her head, and begin moving in a steady rhythm. Everly meets me thrust for thrust, and I embrace the warmth as she welcomes me into her pussy. She has me under her spell, and I'm relishing the feeling of being owned by this woman. I'd willingly bind myself to her for all of eternity if I could. Marrying her was hands down the best decision I've ever made.

I brush my tongue against her lips before slipping it inside her mouth. She moans loudly as I pick up my pace and shift the angle of my cock to press against her G-spot.

"I'm so close, Cash," she pants out.

"How badly do you want to come for your husband?"

When she doesn't respond fast enough, I slow my pace, pushing into her with short, shallow strokes. She writhes beneath me, desperate for release. Little does she know that teasing her is torturing me just as much, if not more.

"Tell me, Ev."

She wraps her legs around my waist, digging her heels into my back. Her blazing gaze locked on me. "Stafford, if you make me wait another minute, I will get one of my toys and do it myself." She pants in frustration.

I press my lips together, stifling a laugh at her impatience. God, her fiery spirit is irresistible, notably when she's on the cusp of an electrifying orgasm.

"Don't worry, Ev, we're going to come together soon," I say, kissing her forehead. "This pussy belongs to me, doesn't it?"

She nods. "Only yours."

Her confession leaves me undone as I pound into her without restraint. All rational thought is gone as the primal sound of flesh slapping against flesh resonates in the air. Everly flies higher into a state of euphoria, digging her fingernails into my palms. She looks up at me with her captivating brown eyes, filled with lust, silently begging for more.

"Come for me, beautiful," I command, changing my angle to hit her most sensitive spot. When she shatters, I'm right behind her, letting out a guttural groan as we tumble into a state of oblivion together.

"You're fucking perfect, and you're mine," I murmur as I collapse on top of her, resting my head against her chest as we both catch our breath. "Are you okay, Ev?"

She runs her fingers through my hair. "Yes, but we have a problem," she tells me, her eyes shimmering with amusement.

"And what is that?"

"You promised me at least two more orgasms tonight."

I chuckle, lifting my head to press a kiss to her nose. "Don't worry. Now that I've had you once, I'm never stopping.

21

EVERLY

I STARE AT MY WEDDING ring sparkling in the light. Even though it's early, I'm curled up on the couch with a cup of coffee and my laptop. I haven't made an effort to start working yet, though. My thoughts are too chaotic to focus.

Last night, I couldn't resist the magnetic draw to Cash any longer, and after our mind-blowing sex in the bedroom, we had sex in the shower and again on the bathroom counter. He treated me like a queen, showering me with words of affection and praise.

Something has changed between us, our connection going beyond physical attraction. It's an emotional bond, a tether holding us together, pulling me back to memories with the boy I grew up with—cruising around Aspen Grove listening to Linkin Park, catching Saturday morning matinees, and him showing up with a cheeseburger and milkshake when I needed a pick-me-up after my heart was broken.

When I woke up wrapped around Cash like a koala bear, his arms securely banded around my waist, reality set in. This arrangement was never supposed to be more than a marriage on paper, but despite my attempts to remain detached, my husband is finding his way into my heart. What scares me the most is how vulnerable that makes me feel.

I close my eyes, and think back to our wedding night.

We exit the chapel hand in hand, and I can't hide the grin on my face. He shamelessly looks me up and down, letting out a low whistle. "You're so goddamn beautiful."

"I don't think you've complimented me nearly enough tonight," I tease, batting my eyelashes.

He hasn't taken his eyes off me since I stepped out of the dressing room at the boutique in The Shoppes at Premiere. In the span of an hour, he's called me some variation of stunning, beautiful, and gorgeous countless times. It's clear he knows how to make a woman feel good about herself.

He gently tugs my hand, drawing me against his chest. "In that case, I'll have to remind you every five minutes that you're fucking sexy in that dress."

The white satin contours to my curves, with a classic A-line silhouette and an off-the-shoulder neckline.

I wanted to wear a white dress for the ceremony but was worried when we got to the boutique only ten minutes before closing. When the sales associate found out Cash's family owns the hotel, she was more than happy to accommodate us. After browsing the store, I finally found my dress at the back of a rack of sample wedding dresses that just so happened to be in my size.

A shiver runs down my spine as Cash brushes a strand of hair from my face. His gaze lingers on my mouth, and I think of the kiss we just shared at the altar. The way he took charge, flicking his tongue along the

seam of my lips, coaxing me to let him in, and the warmth of his mouth…
It was incredible.

"You're perfect, Ev," he whispers. "And you're mine."

His declaration sends a flurry of butterflies through my stomach, making me wish he'd kiss me again.

"Ready for your close-up, lovebirds?" We both lift our heads to find a photographer observing us with an amused expression. He taps his foot impatiently, waiting for us to get a move on.

"Yeah, we're coming," Cash says.

He was adamant about getting the complete wedding package, including having photos taken during the ceremony and outside afterward.

Cash leads me to the pink Cadillac parked in front of the chapel. The top is down, making for the perfect photo opp. He opens the door to the back seat, extending his hand to help me inside before circling around and hopping in next to me.

He slings his arm across the back seat, placing his other hand possessively on my hip. I lean against his chest, propping my feet up on the window ledge. My body naturally eases into him as I place the bouquet of daffodils we purchased at the chapel in my lap.

"Look at me and smile," the photographer says.

He remains stoic as he snaps several photos, undoubtedly used to the light-night stream of tipsy couples tying the knot.

When he pauses to look down at his camera, I tilt my head back to glance at Cash. He's dressed in a black suit he packed for his work trip. The sleeves are rolled up to his elbows, drawing attention to the bracelet on his wrist. My chest tightens knowing he kept it all these years because it meant something to him, implying that I matter to him too.

Warning bells sound in my head, reminding me why getting married was a bad idea. We hadn't seen each other in fourteen years, and I swore off serious relationships after breaking up with Landon. Yet, none of that matters as the alcohol's effects still linger, keeping me on cloud nine.

When Cash catches me admiring him, he offers me a warm smile.

"I can't believe we really got married." I giggle.

"I can't believe you're my wife," he murmurs, nuzzling his nose against my neck.

Being this close to Cash gives me a sense of peace and comfort I haven't felt in a long while, and for the moment, all my worries disappear, content in the warmth of his embrace.

I'm pulled from the memory when I hear movement down the hall.

"Everly, where are you?" Cash calls out, bursting into the living room seconds later. He's shirtless, with his hair disheveled and his black joggers hanging low on his hips.

I raise a brow at his ruffled state. "Everything alright?"

"You weren't in bed when I woke up; I wanted to make sure you were okay."

My chest tightens with affection. "I couldn't sleep," I admit, setting my cup of coffee on the barstool that I brought over from the kitchen.

"I must not have given you enough orgasms," he teases.

I give him a crooked smile, unable to resist goading him. "You'll definitely have to up your game next time."

"You're right. I look forward to making up for my less-than-stellar performance last night." He gives me a cheeky grin.

We both know his performance last night was exceptional. There's no denying I want there to be a next time, but that doesn't mean I'm not conflicted.

The tequila shots played a part in my impulsive decision to marry Cash, overriding my usual judgment. When I found out about Stafford Holdings buying Townstead International, I thought I could compartmentalize my emotions. Yet, the more time I spend with Cash, the more he brings me the same peace and comfort he did in Vegas.

He strides across the room and crouches in front of me, using a finger to lift my chin so our eyes meet. "You seem lost in thought. Do you want to talk about what's bothering you?"

"What makes you think something is wrong?"

He kisses my forehead. "Because I can see it in your expression."

I take a deep breath, considering how to express what's on my mind. "Our marriage was meant to be temporary." I motion between us. "And now that the lines have been blurred, things feel much more confusing."

"I like blurring the lines with you," he murmurs.

When Cash caresses my cheek, I close my eyes and lean into his touch. He has a way of making me feel safe and secure when my thoughts are chaotic.

He has become my anchor, steadying me through turbulent waters—my shelter from the storm. Since the moment we agreed to stay married to keep the acquisition from falling apart, every decision he's made has been with my best interest in mind.

I never witnessed this kind of adoration between my parents. Their relationship was centered around maintaining their social status rather than genuine affection, so it was no surprise when it fell apart. That doesn't mean it hurt any less to watch, but my distorted view of romantic relationships has clouded my judgment, making me believe that what Landon and I had was genuine, when it was superficial at best. He never looked at me the way Cash does—like I'm the center of his universe.

"Last night was incredible," Cash says. "As far as I'm concerned there is no timeline or expiration date. There's only you and me, and I'd like to enjoy every moment we have together, however long it may be."

I smile. "I want that too."

More than anything.

"I have something that I think will lift your mood," he says.

Before I can ask what it is, my phone pings. I look down to find a text from August.

August: Have fun playing hooky today.

Everly: ???

August: Ask your husband.

When I glance up at Cash, he's watching me as he taps his fingers against his leg.

"Do you know anything about this?" I ask, holding my phone out for him to see.

"Yeah," he confirms once he's finished reading the message. "I told August you were taking the day off."

When we got back to London, I gave August's number to Cash in case of an emergency but failed to specify that plotting ways to convince me to skip work doesn't qualify as an emergency. It's not surprising since they are similar in their need for adventure and taking risks.

"Cash, it's Tuesday. I can't just skip out on work without giving notice."

"Today is special." His face lights up like a kid on Christmas morning.

"How so?"

"I have a surprise for you."

A surprise?

He's piqued my curiosity, but I haven't taken a day off work in years. I'm sure my dad will have something to say if I don't go into the office today, but then again, why should I care?

My phone pings again.

August: Don't overthink it. You deserve a break. Liam & I will hold down the fort until tomorrow.

Everly: Traitor.

August: Have fun!

There's my answer.

I set my laptop and phone on the couch.

"Alright, you have my attention," I tell Cash, folding my arms across my chest. "What's the surprise?"

"It wouldn't be a surprise if I told you, now would it?" he says with a twinkle in his eye. "Go get ready. We leave in an hour." He walks out of the room, pausing halfway then turning around to add, "Oh, and you should wear a sundress." He winks, leaving me sitting alone, puzzled by his cryptic request.

Regardless, a warmth spreads through my chest. He's planned something special for me; the least I can do is push aside my inner turmoil for one day.

When we pull up outside a nondescript shop, Cash helps me out of the vehicle. There's no name on the door, the lights are dimmed, and there's a Closed sign in the window. Despite its inconspicuous appearance, I recognize it. We're at Belgravia, a luxury shoe boutique that exclusively operates by appointment only.

Cash strolls inside like he owns the place, and I follow, curious as to what he has up his sleeve.

We enter a room with plain white walls, a reception desk, and a pair of upholstered pastel blue chairs in the corner.

A woman with chestnut-colored hair, dressed in a tailored black suit, emerges from behind the reception desk to welcome us. She strides over, her designer heels with distinctive red soles clicking against the floor.

"Mr. Stafford, I presume?" She reaches out to shake Cash's hand.

"Please call me Cash, and this is my wife, Everly." He gestures toward me.

"It's a pleasure, my dear. My name is April," she says with a warm smile, then turns back to Cash. "I've arranged everything to your specifications."

She leads us through a door into a luxurious showroom with cream-colored walls and gold crown molding. In the far corner, there's an ornate full-length mirror positioned next to a dressing platform, which is ironic considering there are no clothes here. Instead, three walls are lined with shelving and track lighting to showcase an extensive collection of shoes.

There's a cream wingback sofa in the middle of the space, surrounded by several stacks of shoe boxes.

"Everything looks good, thank you," Cash says, nodding in approval. "We'll let you know if we need anything."

"Yes, of course. I'll be out front if you do," April says. With that, she turns and leaves, closing the door behind her.

"What are we doing here?" I ask, moving closer to one of the shoe-filled walls.

As I assess the extensive selection, it becomes clear that there's not a single pair of shoes in this room that doesn't retail for at least £2,000.

"I know how much you love high heels, and I wanted you to have your pick of the most sought-after shoes in the world. I've been told that many of these styles haven't been released to the public yet."

My eyes widen in shock. "You did this for me?"

This is beyond my wildest dreams. Although I have a fondness for luxury shoes, most of my collection are budget brands. Occasionally, I'll splurge if I find a pair that I can't live without, but never shoes on this grand of a scale.

I can't believe Cash arranged a private appointment at the city's most elite shoe boutique, all because of my fondness for high heels.

I swear I hear him say, "I would do anything for you," but he speaks so quietly that I can't be sure. "We have the place to ourselves for the rest of the morning, so why not indulge me and try on some of these beautiful shoes?" He motions around us.

"What are all these boxes?" I gesture toward the stacks next to the couch, estimating at least fifty pairs.

"I called ahead and had April pull every high heel they had in your size," he says.

"Cash you didn't have to—"

"I wanted to," he interrupts me, placing his hand over mine. "Now, why don't you take a seat so we can get started?" He guides me to the sofa.

I do as he asks, noting that the couch is surprisingly comfortable.

Cash picks up the nearest box and opens it to reveal a pair of gorgeous black open-toed high heels with a diamond-encrusted ankle band. They're part of an upcoming collection for a high-end designer known for red soles, set to be released next month.

I trace my finger over the material of one shoe like it's a priceless artifact.

"I take it you like these?" Cash asks with an amused smile.

"They're stunning."

"You should try them on." He kneels in front of me, placing the box on the ground.

"I can put them on myself."

"You could, but it'll be more fun if I help, don't you think?"

"I do like you on your knees," I say with a smirk playing on my lips.

He removes the red pumps that I'm wearing and lifts my foot in his hand, slowly brushing his hand down my leg, causing a shiver to snake down my spine. My breath hitches when he places a tender kiss on my calf. His heated gaze never leaves mine as he slides the black heel onto my foot and fastens the buckle in place. His hand lingers as he traces the band around my ankle.

He repeats the process for my other foot with equal precision, and I bite down on my lip as he teases me with his touches.

"You're the most beautiful woman I've ever met," he rasps as he looks up at me. "And you're my wife."

"Yes, I am," I say, flashing my ring. "And you're my husband."

I finally understand why he loves calling me *wifey* so much. There's a heady thrill in claiming someone out loud, knowing they belong to you, for better or worse, even if it's only temporary.

"You're right, and as your husband, my most important duty is to bring you unmatched pleasure."

"Is that so?" My pulse races. "In that case, I'd like a demonstration, please."

"Who am I to tell my wife no?"

He presses his lips to my calf, slowly trailing upward as he peppers kisses along my leg. When he gets to my knee, he pushes my dress aside, moving up my thigh inch by agonizing inch. My breath hitches when he leans forward to press his nose against my panties, inhaling deeply.

My cheeks flush when he tugs down the waistband of my underwear. I lift my hips so he can slide them off and watch as he tucks them into his pant pocket for safekeeping. I can't believe I just let him take my underwear off in the middle of a store, but I can't seem to bring myself to stop him.

"God, you're perfect, Ev," he groans.

My mouth falls open as he traces my seam in gentle strokes. He lifts my leg over his shoulder, the move giving him an unobstructed view of my pussy.

I gasp when he plunges two fingers inside me, pushing them in and out at a steady pace. His eyes remain fixed on mine as he watches my reaction to his touch. I tighten my grip, digging my nails into the fabric of the couch as he massages my clit with his thumb in languid circles, my body coiling tighter with each thrust of his fingers inside me.

"Does it turn you on knowing that someone could walk through that door at any moment?" he whispers.

I nod as the sound of my arousal fills the room.

He asked for us not to be disturbed, but it doesn't stop me from liking the idea of someone overhearing us like this. My husband kneeling before me, his hand under my dress as he fucks me with his hand.

My head lolls back against the sofa when he adds a third finger. He keeps teasing me, pulling out whenever I'm close to climaxing. I'm teetering on the edge, desperate to lose all control, as he draws out my impending orgasm, toying with my mind.

"Cash, I need to come," I moan. My body is strung tight with tension.

"Who do you belong to?"

"You," I murmur.

"I couldn't hear you, Ev. Who do you belong to?" he groans as he pushes his fingers back into me.

"You," I cry out, not giving a damn who hears my declaration.

"That's right. You're all mine," he rasps before he flicks my clit repeatedly, giving me the added friction I've been begging for.

I detonate like a bomb, my body shuddering from the intensity of my release.

Once my orgasm subsides, Cash brings his fingers to his mouth, sucking them clean, one by one. I watch with rapt attention as he tastes my essence on his tongue.

"Delicious," he says, flashing me a wicked grin.

When he's finished, he leans forward so our mouths are only inches apart. He closes the distance, nipping at my lips before plunging his tongue into my mouth. Our moans fill the air as he explores my mouth with fervor.

When he pulls back, I'm left dizzy. He straightens to his full height and holds out his hand for me, smoothing out my dress and hair when I get up.

"I think you have a possessive streak," I say playfully.

"Only with you," he replies before he gives me another kiss that steals my breath.

After he releases me, he heads over to the closest wall and pushes a silver button in the corner.

Seconds later, April opens the door. "Is everything alright?" she asks, glancing around the room. If she overheard anything that just happened, she keeps it to herself.

"Yes, great." Cash flashes me a mischievous smile. "We'll take everything you pulled. I'd like it all delivered to my apartment."

My mouth gapes open, and when I look over, April blinks in disbelief, as if doubting she heard him right, until Cash hands her his black card.

"Yes, of course," she exclaims, accepting the card. "I'll start ringing these up right away." She rushes out, leaving the door open behind her.

"Cash, what are you doing?" I whisper. "The heels I have on are more than enough. There's no way you're buying me all these shoes. It'll cost a fortune."

"Clearly you don't know how to be spoiled. Don't worry, I'll show you how it's done, wifey." He winks.

His statement causes a frenzy of butterflies to swarm in my stomach as another one of my defenses crumbles.

22

CASH

THE PAST TWO WEEKS HAVE flown by. Everly and I have spent most of our free time together, and I wouldn't trade it for anything.

She asked to join me in the gym today, and now I'm regretting saying yes because I'm having a hell of a time concentrating.

I use every ounce of willpower to stay focused while running on the treadmill. Unfortunately, it's impossible when she decides that the section on the mat a few feet in front of me is the perfect spot for yoga.

Everly's dressed in tight black yoga pants that showcase her perfect ass and toned legs. Her neon green sports bra does nothing to hide her pebbled nipples, and she's barefoot, her red-painted toes matching her fingernails.

I push a loose strand of hair back under my hat as I watch Everly bend forward into a downward dog pose. She has her backside turned toward me, giving me the perfect view of her ass. My cock strains against my shorts, eager to play.

It's a damn good thing I have a private gym because there's no chance in hell I would allow another man to see her like this. She's mine.

In the past two weeks, she's been insatiable. We've fucked on every surface of the apartment and once in the stairwell when we couldn't wait to get up the last flight of stairs.

Sex used to be a fleeting thing—a single night of untold pleasure. Anyone I took to bed knew my terms—no strings attached and no misconceptions of a commitment. Not because I didn't care for the women I've been with but because I refused to give anyone the chance to break my heart.

With Everly things are different, and not just because we're married. She's given me a renewed sense of purpose, something that has long been absent in my life.

She peers at me through the gap between her legs, a smile on her lips.

Fuck, I love that smile.

"Enjoying the view?" she calls out in a sultry tone.

"What do you think?"

She releases from her position, lowering herself to the ground. I'm riveted as she lies on her back with her knees bent and her hips and breasts lifted toward the ceiling in a bridge pose.

I slam the stop button on the treadmill and snatch the towel draped over the handrail, unwilling to watch from a distance for another second.

She raises a brow. "Yes?"

"I think you need some help with your posture." My voice comes out husky as I dab away the sweat dripping down my forehead and toss the towel into the nearby bin.

Everly gazes up at me with an impish smile as I cross to her. "And you think you can help me fix it, Stafford?" She keeps her hands at her sides.

When I get to her, I kneel down and slide my hand under her lower back, encouraging her to lift her hips upward, and put my other hand on her stomach to keep her steady. Her posture was already perfect, but I couldn't resist the urge to touch her.

She watches me closely as I lean down to kiss her exposed belly. I trace my tongue across her navel, drawing out a soft moan which goes straight to my dick.

She lowers her back slightly, and I apply pressure to keep her in place.

"Maybe working out together wasn't such a good idea," Everly whispers as I press a kiss to her hip.

"It's the best idea," I say. "But I should let you finish because you're mine for the rest of the day."

"I'll have to check my schedule," she says, taunting me.

"In the meantime, be a good wife and finish your yoga flow," I order playfully, planting a kiss on her other hip.

She gives me a pout when I move my hands away, forcing her to hold her bridge pose on her own. After grabbing a water bottle from the nearby mini fridge, I sit against the closest wall.

Everly tilts her chin up to look at me. "Are you going to watch me the whole time?"

"Absolutely." I grin as I take a swig of water.

Once Everly is finished with her yoga sequence, she comes to sit next to me against the wall.

I take my hat off and sweep my hair away from my face.

Everly nibbles on her lower lip before she says, "Can I ask you something?"

"Anything," I answer, taking her hand in mine and giving it a reassuring squeeze.

"Is there a reason you keep your hair longer?" She tenderly cups my cheek, caressing my scar with her fingertips. "I like it, but I remember you wore it short in high school, and I was just curious."

I nod slowly, considering my response. "Growing my hair out didn't start on purpose. I didn't get it cut for a while and discovered it drew attention away from my scar. It became a protective shield against unwanted stares and questions from people who were quick to judge me based on my appearance."

Similar to Everly, I've masked my true identity, afraid of getting hurt and not wanting to burden anyone with my insecurities.

A part of me believed being different was a negative, that I was flawed, and I constantly compared myself to those around me. I overlooked the reality that everyone faces internal conflicts, each trying to overcome their own challenges. I'm starting to realize that standing out because of my differences isn't a bad thing.

"Oh, Cash," Everly utters, leaning her forehead against mine. "I'm sorry you felt like you had to hide who you are. Your scar is an important part of your story."

"Thank you," I murmur. "From day one, you treated me like I was still *Stafford*, the captain of the lacrosse team and the guy who could make you laugh." I tip her chin up so I'm met with her warm brown gaze. "Since our paths crossed in that bar in Vegas, you've continued to remind me that it doesn't have to define who I am." Everly rests her head against my shoulder.

Even around my family, I've sometimes hidden my insecurities or true feelings about my scar. Everly is the only one I feel like I can truly be myself around. Like I've become her confidant, she's becoming my safe haven. She once asked me if I believed in soulmates, and I said I wasn't sure. Now, I'm beginning to think they might exist after all.

"Cash Stafford, you are sexy as hell. Scar and all," she murmurs as she straddles my hips. "And I'll say it as often as I have to until you believe it."

"In that case, I'll never believe, so you'll have to stay here forever."

Everly leans in to kiss the puckered skin of my scar, her lips tracing the uneven ridges and the distorted edge of my mouth. My pulse races as she grinds against me, and I capture her mouth in mine, grinning when she moans. All these endorphins have me in a cloud of euphoria, and the smoldering desire I've tamped down bursts to life, igniting like a fuse.

She tangles her fingers in my hair, holding on tight to keep me close. In response, I grip her hips in a firm hold, pressing my thumbs into the supple flesh of her thighs, secretly hoping there are faint bruises tomorrow as reminders that this is real… that she's real.

Everly slips her skilled tongue inside my mouth, leaving me breathless. Our electric chemistry is all-consuming and I'm prepared to rip her clothes off when she tugs on my hair, triggering a thought to cross my mind that I can't ignore.

"Hey, Ev?" I say it like a question as I pull away from her pouty lips.

"Yeah?" She blinks up at me.

"I want you to cut my hair."

She gives me a puzzled look. "Cash, I didn't ask about it because I thought you should cut it. I'm sorry I gave you that impression."

"You didn't," I assure her. "It's time for a change."

"I've never cut hair before. Let me call August and see who he recommends in the city."

I shake my head. "No." I tug her closer, my hands securely wrapped around her back. "I want you to do it… please," I add when I sense she might say no.

She gives me a soft smile like she knows how important this is to me. "Okay, I'll do it, but don't come complaining to me when you end up with a botched haircut."

"I'll show it off with pride because you'll have been the one who cut it," I say with a playful smirk.

An hour later, I'm patiently waiting on a bar stool in the kitchen. Several towels are spread out on the ground beneath me, and I'm wearing the barber cape that came with the hair-cutting kit my mom gifted me this past Christmas—a not-so-subtle hint if there ever was one. I've used the scissors to trim my ends, but for the most part, it's remained stashed away in a cupboard.

Everly leans against the counter, her lip caught between her teeth in deep concentration. She's watching yet another tutorial on her phone, determined to do her research before she starts.

After several more minutes, she puts her phone away and looks over at me. "Okay, I'm ready. Last chance to back out, Stafford." There's a hint of hesitancy in her tone.

"Let's do this," I say, glancing over to give her a reassuring smile.

Everly carefully examines the contents of the kit I laid out on the counter.

She picks up the spray bottle and comes to stand in front of me, moving her hand to shield my face. "Close your eyes," she cautions.

I follow her instructions, and once my entire head is damp, she runs her hands over my hair, smoothing out the strands. When she kneads my scalp in a small, circular motion, a sigh passes my lips. I'm lost in the feel of her touch, the tension melting away like ice under her warm fingertips.

"Okay, you can open your eyes now," she says, making me wish the moment could have lasted longer. I wouldn't mind if she spent the whole day exploring me with her hands.

My gaze briefly meets hers before she turns her attention back to the counter. Her hands tremble as she picks up a pair of scissors and an alligator clip.

I reach out my hand, giving her wrist a reassuring squeeze. "Thanks for doing this."

"Wait to thank me until I'm finished," she teases.

"I'm going to like it no matter what," I promise.

She steps behind me, and then uses the clips to section off my hair. Tentatively, she picks up a strand, taking a deep breath before making the first snip. Her initial hesitation is palpable, but with each cut, her movements grow more fluid, reflecting her growing confidence.

My eyes drift to the growing pile of hair on the ground—a tangible symbol of the cathartic release I've put off until now. Each strand that falls makes me feel lighter and freer than I have since before my accident.

I stiffen in my chair when Everly softly blows hair off the nape of my neck, her breath grazing my skin, sending a tingle up my spine. It requires all of my self-control to stop from turning around and fucking her like I've wanted to do all morning.

After finishing the back, she steps around to face me, tilting my chin and directing my gaze ahead before starting on the front.

I place my hands on her hips, needing to touch her, but she gives me a warning look before going back to the task at hand.

My eyes drift to her tits. In this position, they're just inches from my face, and her rosebud nipples are visible through her sports bra. I hold back a groan when she moves closer, fighting the urge to yank her bra down and put one of her nipples in my mouth.

I allow my hands to wander, sliding down her back toward her ass.

"Stafford," Everly warns with a gasp. "Do you want me to mess up?"

"You won't."

"You should keep your hands to yourself just to be sure."

"I can't," I admit, giving her ass a squeeze to prove my point.

Her breath hitches, but she keeps her eyes on my hair as she cuts. I occupy myself by tormenting her as I run a hand along the outside of her legs, following the curve of her hip. Goosebumps spread across her skin. I occasionally lean forward to kiss the swells of her breasts peeking out from her bra. When it comes to Everly, I have no control.

Just as I begin to inch my hand up her thigh, she steps back.

"Okay, I'm finished." Her voice is breathless. "Why don't you take a look." She moves behind me to remove the cape, then offers me a handheld mirror from the counter.

I tap my foot against the stool, anxiety coursing through me as I stare at her outstretched hand. Our eyes lock as I summon my courage and steal a glance in the mirror.

My hair falls below my ears, still long enough to run my hand through it. The only difference now is my scar is fully visible with no way to hide it.

I remain motionless as I study my reflection. My hand trails along the jagged scar, starting at my left eyebrow, moving over the rough ridges along my cheek, and down to the corner of my mouth. After fifteen years, the once angry red has faded to pink, but it doesn't make it any less a part of my identity.

For the first time in my adult life, the sight of it doesn't evoke a sense of dread.

Somehow, it's been transformed from something I once found repulsive into a hopeful reminder that healing can take many forms and that it's never too late for a new beginning.

And I want Everly to be a part of mine.

"Are you okay?" She asks, tightening her grip on the mirror. "If you don't like it, we can find a barber to fix it."

I shake my head, pulling the mirror from her hand and setting it on the counter.

"I love it, Ev." I draw her close, giving her a kiss.

I think I'm falling in love with you.

"I'm glad." She smiles as she traces my scar with her finger. "You're incredibly handsome."

"I need you right now," I say, my voice hoarse.

"You had your chance to tease me. Now it's my turn."

Everly's gaze is unwavering as she steps away from me to take off her yoga pants. She shimmies them down her legs, kicking them off to the side. Next is her panties. She slides them past her hips, toying with me as she slowly lowers them down far enough for me to see her pussy. Once she pulls them off, she holds them out toward me.

My patience has reached its limit, and I get up to close the distance between us. I grip Everly's hand in mine, pushing her panties to my nose, drawing in a deep breath. She drops them to the floor, her brown eyes filled with lust.

I tug the bottom of her sports bra, lifting it over her head to expose her full breasts.

"Damn, these tits are perfect, Ev. I'll never get enough."

I lift her onto the island counter and eagerly suck a nipple into my mouth, biting down on the soft flesh just the way I know she likes.

"Oh, god," Everly cries out as I lavish her breasts with attention. "Fuck me, Cash. Don't you dare hold back."

"I don't have a condom."

"It's okay, I have an IUD."

I furrow my brow. "Are you sure?" We've been using condoms religiously up until now. "I'm clean, and I've never gone without a condom before. But if you're not ready…" I trail off, my hand twitching slightly.

"I'm positive. I want to feel you without any barriers," she says, giving me a soft smile. "I trust you, Stafford."

A warmth spreads through me when those words pass her lips. Until now, she's been battling her conflicting feelings toward me, and I'm aware of the magnitude of her putting her full trust in me like this.

Within seconds I have my shorts and boxers shoved down, my rigid cock springing free. I drag Everly closer to the edge and push myself to the hilt in a single thrust. She throws her head back, crying out as she clenches around me. Fuck, she feels so good without any barriers.

Something spurs me on as if we're in a race against the clock as I fuck her hard, letting go of my last ounce of self-control. With every thrust, I revel in the feeling of my dick shoved deep inside her.

My senses become heightened, and I'm acutely aware of her sweet groans as she flies higher into oblivion, her arms wrapped around my neck, her fingernails sinking into my skin, holding on to me for dear life.

Everly has breathed new life into me; reawakening my heart, mind, and soul, and I don't know how I'm ever going to let her go.

"Damn, you were made to take my cock." I slant my mouth across hers, kissing her fervently as I buck my hips, picking up my pace. We kiss roughly and I'm aware of the faint, metallic taste of blood when she bites down hard on my lip.

The tinge of pain causes my release to barrel forward like a freight train, and I reach between us, moving my thumb in circles against Everly's clit until she's writhing beneath me, begging for her release.

"That's it, beautiful, come for me," I say.

She calls out my name as she chases euphoria, and I roar as unfiltered pleasure surges through me at the intoxicating sight of her unraveling beneath me. As we come crashing down together, she cries out.

"You're a fucking vision, coming all over my dick, Ev." I rest my head against her shoulder and carefully pull out of her, not wanting to cause her pain. I stifle another groan as I watch our mixed cum drip down her thigh.

"You're only going to fuck me once?" she pouts, teasing me with a glint in her eye.

It's adorable that she thinks I'm done with her. We won't be stopping until we're both boneless and sated.

"I'll never be done with you, Ev," I vow.

She is my wife in every sense of the word. There's no chance I can let her go when the acquisition is finalized. I'll have to do everything I can to show her this is real and that we belong together.

23

EVERLY

EVERY TIME I SEE CASH'S short hair, it almost brings me to tears. Not because I don't like it—he's sexy no matter the length of his hair—but because of what it represents.

He's used it as a shield for all these years, and I'm honored that he would ask me to be part of his healing process. It serves as a reminder of his willingness and courage to step outside of his comfort zone.

His example has made me consider my situation with my dad. I've avoided a confrontation with him out of fear that I'll lose my job, financial security, and any chance of having a working relationship. However, I'm learning that my happiness should come first, above all else. When the next opportunity presents itself, I won't pass up the chance to stand my ground.

I'm yanked from my thoughts by the sound of the fire alarm.

"Oh no," I shout, leaping from my chair. I rush to the oven and yank out the burned casserole, dropping it into the sink—dish and all. Plumes of smoke surround me as the alarm continues to blare.

Cash chooses this exact moment to come home, rushing into the kitchen with a startled look on his face. His eyes dart to me before jumping onto the kitchen island and turning off the smoke detector.

I sigh in relief when the apartment finally falls into silence. It's a good thing his gym is on the floor below, or we'd have angry neighbors demanding to know what all the commotion was about.

"Ev, are you okay?" He climbs down and stalks toward me, gently cradling my face with his hands.

"Yeah, I'm so sorry," I mutter, my face flushed with embarrassment. "I was baking a shepherd's pie for dinner but burned it."

He's been so incredibly thoughtful since I moved in, and I wanted to do something special for him in return. I left work early to pick up a bake-at-home pie from a nearby restaurant, figuring it would be easy to prepare. The only problem is that I forgot to set a timer when I put it in the oven and got distracted.

"At least now we know the smoke detector works." Cash offers me a reassuring smile. "I'm just glad you're okay." I melt into his touch, inhaling the comforting scent of citrus, musk, and sandalwood.

Our domesticated marital bliss feels more real by the day, especially now that we're having sex every chance we get.

Something about our new intimacy has brought us closer despite the lingering doubts in the back of my mind.

I meant it when I told him that I trust him, but I can't help waiting for the other shoe to drop. In the past, whenever things started to look up, that's when they fell apart.

I narrow my eyes at Cash when he laughs. "What's so funny?" I frown.

"I'm not laughing at you, Ev. It's just amusing how neither of us can cook worth shit."

I tilt my head, my brows furrowing in confusion. "What do you mean? You've made dinner almost every night, and every dish tastes like it came out of Theo's kitchen."

He bites his lip, stifling another burst of laughter.

"Cash—"

He holds his finger out to stop me. "Hold that thought. I have something to show you."

He leaves me in the kitchen, returning a few moments later with a canvas tote bag. From it, he takes out a tray of grilled lemon herb chicken, a container of roasted vegetables, a garden salad with a separate container of vinaigrette dressing, and two fruit tarts.

"What's all this?" I ask.

"Our dinner," he admits, shifting from foot to foot. "Do you know Fallon? Theo mentored her, and she worked for him for years."

I nod. "Yeah, I used to see her all the time when I'd visit Theo's restaurant in the West End. She left last year to launch her private chef service…" My voice falters as the pieces fall into place. "You hired her to prepare our dinners, didn't you?"

"Guilty," he says with a sly grin.

I frown. "Why would you do that?"

It doesn't matter to me if Cash can cook. I survived on fish and chips, Thai food, and sandwiches from the pub down the street from my office for years, and I would be fine doing that again. Or if he had told me upfront that he wanted a private chef to cook our meals, I would have been okay with that. I'm struggling with the fact that he wasn't honest from the start.

His confession stirs memories of Landon lying about his whereabouts and who he spent time with when we were dating. When the truth came out, my pride was bruised, and I felt foolish for missing the warning signs.

Cash fidgets with his bracelet as he looks at me apologetically. "I figured you'd appreciate it more if you believed I was cooking dinner rather than someone else doing it." He's not wrong. It's one of the primary reasons I began feeling at ease with him. "I saw how hard you work and wanted to make the transition easier for you, especially since moving in with me wasn't your first choice. You deserve to live somewhere that feels like home, and I thought coming back to the apartment to a home-cooked meal every night would help." He stops in front of me, and I'm met with his earnest gaze.

His admission tugs at my heartstrings. It would have been better if he'd told me upfront, but I can understand why he didn't. He may be too laid-back at times, but he's also kind-hearted and patient.

I have to remind myself that Cash is nothing like Landon and would never deliberately cause me harm. He goes to great lengths for the people he cares about, and I'm fortunate to be counted among them.

"I appreciate the gesture, but it hurts that you kept this from me. It's important that we don't keep secrets—big or small." I place my hand in his. "Can we agree on being open with each other moving forward? It's a hard limit for me."

Cash squeezes my hand as he looks into my eyes. "There's one more thing I have to tell you," he confesses.

"Which is?"

"Marcus didn't put off decorating the apartment. I waited to call him until yesterday." He holds his hand out to stop me when I go to speak. "I wasn't ready to have you sleep in a separate room. What if you got scared of the dark or needed me to kill a spider?"

"You can tell the truth and admit that you like having me in your bed." I rise on my toes to press a kiss to his lips. "Don't worry, Cash, I like being there too."

"No more secrets," he promises.

"You said you called Marcus yesterday. When is he stopping by?"

"Later tonight, actually," Cash tells me. "It's about time we made this place a real home."

My heart races every time he calls it *our* home. This arrangement was supposed to be temporary, but right now, it feels like anything but.

When the elevator doors open, a man enters the penthouse's entryway. He's clad in designer jeans, a blazer layered over a graphic tee, and a stylish blue scarf. He strides in with a leather portfolio tucked under one arm, scanning the space with a discerning eye.

"Marcus, it's great to see you. Thanks for coming," Cash says, giving him a pat on the back.

"Sure thing. I've been itching to decorate this space since you bought it." Marcus looks around. "I'll admit, I didn't think you'd ever take me up on my offer, given how set you were on keeping it looking like a permanent bachelor pad."

"He had no choice," I interject, coming to stand next to Cash. "This apartment is too stunning to stay empty."

"And who might this lovely creature be?" Marcus asks, his face lighting up as he glances between Cash and me.

"This is Everly, my wife," Cash states, beaming with pride.

"It's a pleasure to meet you," Marcus says, offering me his hand. I mirror his gesture and he presses a chaste kiss to my hand. "It's about time you finally settled down," he tells Cash.

"I got really lucky." Cash puts his arm around my shoulders, silently staking his claim.

"How do you two know each other?" I ask.

"We worked in the mailroom of the Stafford Holdings New York office. I was saving up to move to London, unaware that I was working with the future Chief Operations Officer of the billion-dollar conglomerate," Marcus says.

With a sheepish look, Cash lifts his arm from my shoulders and rubs the back of his neck. "I didn't want people to know who my family was."

"This guy was everyone's favorite co-worker." Marcus points to Cash. "He brought lunch for our department every Friday and gave everyone gift cards to their favorite restaurant for their birthday and Christmas."

I'm not surprised. Cash is the most compassionate and generous person I know. Even if he didn't have a dollar to his name, he would give the shirt off his back to help someone. It's one of the reasons I'm drawn to him.

"Now, where should we start with this blank canvas?" Marcus waves around the apartment.

"Everly, what do you think?" Cash nudges me for my opinion.

Admittedly, I've been fantasizing about how I'd decorate the place since the first time I stepped inside, and I appreciate him giving me a say.

"Why don't we start by giving the primary bedroom a refresh," I suggest to Marcus. "A cozy loveseat and paintings will brighten up the room. Plus, with my growing shoe collection, I could use your expertise on how to optimize the space we have." I glance over to give Cash a knowing smile.

The shopping trip to the boutique last week was incredible, and I couldn't believe it when all the shoes he bought me showed up at the apartment. It's surreal having a sexy billionaire insistent on buying me a store full of heels simply because they're my favorite. Now it's just a matter of finding a place to store them all.

Marcus nods as he jots down notes in his binder. "What else?"

"For the living room, I would like to incorporate a few high-quality pieces, a painting or two, and some plants—keeping it elegant yet understated." I've grown to appreciate the apartment's simplicity and want to keep the minimalist style, but want to add a few elements to make it more inviting.

"As for the kitchen and dining area, I'd like to include a dining room table for when we have guests over."

"Anything else?" Marcus asks as he glances up from his binder.

"What about the guest bedroom?" Cash chimes in, his expression wary.

"Oh, yeah, that's right." I hold my finger in the air. "I'd like the guest room closest to the kitchen to be furnished and decorated for when we have family or friends come to stay. What do you think about including some nods to London?"

"That's a great idea," Marcus agrees. "I'm going to look at the bedrooms to get some measurements. Is that okay?" he asks, taking a small measuring tape from his binder.

"Yeah, be our guest." I wave down the hall.

"Perfect, I'll start with the primary," he calls out as he walks away.

Once he's out of view, I turn to see Cash staring at me with an unreadable expression, which isn't like him. Normally, he's an open book.

I furrow my brow. "What's wrong? Did you not like one of my suggestions?"

He shakes his head. "You didn't ask Marcus to furnish a separate room for you. Unless you plan to stay in the London-inspired room when we don't have guests."

"I don't."

I tuck a piece of hair behind my ear as I wait for him to respond, fully aware of the weight those two simple words carry. Telling him I like sleeping in his bed is one thing, but admitting I want to keep sharing a room is another.

Cash's gaze turns heated as he tugs me closer to his chest. "You mean it, Ev?"

I nod. "As long as I'm here, I'm staying in our bedroom."

"Say it again," he demands.

"I'm staying in *our* bedroom," I repeat.

He tips my head back, kissing me like he's been starved for my admission, making me want to give him everything he asks for and so much more.

My moan reverberates through our kiss as his tongue dances with mine, leaving me breathless. Our intoxicating chemistry is dizzying, and while my focus is on his hand sliding down my thigh, I have enough sense to remember that we're not alone in the house.

"We have a guest," I murmur against his lips with a smile.

"That's alright, I can wait until later tonight to fuck you." He flashes me a sexy grin. "After all, we do share the same bed."

24

CASH

I WAKE UP AND AM GREETED by the faint scent of jasmine, lavender, and vanilla.

Everly and I are entangled in a mess of limbs—she's draped across my chest, her legs intertwined with mine, her head nestled in the crook of my neck.

God, I'll never tire of waking up like this.

I can't help drifting back to the night it all began.

Everly squeals as I lift her into my arms and carry her down the hall. "Cash, what are you doing?"

"Haven't you heard? It's tradition to carry the bride over the threshold."

My pulse races when she winds her arms around my neck, resting her head against my shoulder. I've waited so long to have her in my arms, and it's hard to believe this is real.

Once we're inside my hotel room, I shut the door behind us and bypass the living room, taking her straight to the bedroom.

When I set Everly on the ground, she looks up at me with wide eyes. Her pouty lips part slightly, begging to be kissed. I trace her jawline with my thumb, like I did at the chapel, savoring the feel of her surrendering to my touch.

Everly is my wife.

It's our wedding night.

The desire to claim her pulses through my veins as she licks her lips and watches me with her chocolate-brown eyes. It's on the tip of my tongue to promise her a night full of bliss, where we'll fuck until morning, but my conscience holds me back.

Everly isn't a one-night-stand conquest. She's the one I've wanted since high school. Now that she's mine, I can't risk losing her. No matter how much I want to spend the night memorizing her body like it's a timeless work of art.

I can't believe she's really my wife.

Everly chews on her lower lip. "Cash?"

"What is it?"

"I'm hungry," she says, giving me a sheepish grin when her stomach growls loudly in agreement.

We've been married for less than an hour and I'm already failing as her husband. We haven't eaten since I found her at the bar. She must be starving.

I pull her in for a hug, pressing a chaste kiss to her forehead. "I'll order room service."

"Thank you," she says.

By the time our food arrives, Everly has discarded her wedding dress on the floor, and made herself comfortable on the king-sized bed, watching a The Big Bang Theory rerun.

She's wearing nothing but her bra and panties. The swells of her breasts peek out of her white lace bra, tempting me. It takes every ounce of restraint not to draw her into my arms. Luckily, I'm quickly distracted by her face lighting up when I push the room service cart through the door.

"It smells so good," Everly says.

"Wait until you taste it."

The Premiere hotel has world-class chefs in the kitchen, and the food is amazing.

Everly rubs her hands together with anticipation when I set a tray on the bed that includes two cheeseburgers, a mountain of fries, and a bottle of champagne the staff sent up to celebrate our nuptials.

I settle in next to Everly, and we both dig in while watching another episode. Once we've polished off our meal and the bottle of champagne, she falls asleep cradled in my arms.

As I absentmindedly play with her hair, I lean in and whisper in her ear, "I'm never letting you go, Everly Stafford."

We've come a long way since that night, and I shudder at the thought that not being transparent with her about Fallon preparing our meals and not contacting Marcus sooner could have jeopardized our future together, no matter how insignificant it might seem in the grand scheme of things.

I half expected Everly to storm out yesterday after she learned the truth. The reasons for keeping those things from her felt harmless, but in hindsight, I can see how challenging it must have been for her, given her past with her dad and Landon.

I'm beyond grateful she was willing to listen to my reasoning. She made it clear that she would not tolerate any more secrets between us, which I agreed with. *Although, she said nothing about surprises.*

She deserves the world, and I want to be the one to help make all her dreams come true.

We've danced around the topic of our future post-acquisition, but with every day that passes, I'm more determined to prove to her that we can build a future together. A real marriage. I never thought settling down was in the cards for me, but Everly has changed everything.

She stirs beside me, and when her eyes flutter open, I'm met with her sleepy brown gaze.

"Good morning, Ev," I say, showering her shoulder with kisses.

"Good morning, Stafford," she murmurs, her voice husky from sleep.

"Do you have any meetings this morning?"

"Yeah, I have one with August and Liam at nine o'clock. Thank god it only takes fifteen minutes to get to the office, so I don't have to leave so early."

"And to think you wanted us to live at your place," I say, drawing her in closer.

"At least my apartment is fully furnished," she quips.

"Not for long. Marcus will have this place furnished and decorated in no time."

Our meeting with him went well last night. Everly's face lit up as she shared her decorating ideas, and it made me happy to see how excited she was to transform this place into a real home. I admit I wasn't expecting her to say she wanted to stay in our bedroom with me.

It would have been hard to accept her sleeping in another room, but I would have respected her decision.

I'm so glad she didn't.

Everly beams. "I can't wait to see what he comes up with."

"Do you enjoy living in London?"

"Oh, absolutely. I love the culture, the food, and the stunning architecture. It's a welcome change from living in California when I was in college."

"Would you ever consider moving back to Aspen Grove?"

She shrugs. "I'm not sure if I'd ever live there full time, but going back with you made me realize how much I miss it. I wish we could have driven by the old Miller place when we were in town."

"How come?"

"When I was younger, I dreamed of buying it," she reminisces. "I pictured it with a manicured lawn, a white-picket fence, a porch swing facing the side of the house, black shutters... The inside would have a rustic feel with exposed beams, a sliding barn door leading to the pantry, and a farmhouse table. And the loft would be transformed into a cozy reading space." She lets out a wistful sigh as she gazes off into the distance. "Honestly, I can't even remember the last time I read an entire book from start to finish."

The abandoned Miller house sat untouched for years, sitting on the outskirts of town, its existence ignored by most. But not by Ev. She finds beauty in imperfect things, giving them new life—like she's done with me.

Since our visit to Aspen Grove, the day after our impromptu wedding, I've been working on a surprise for her— something that holds meaning for us both. It was a spur of the moment decision, but now I'm more eager than ever to reveal the final result to her now that I'm certain it will hold special significance for her.

"Sounds like a scene straight from *The Notebook*," I playfully remark.

She whips her head to look at me, eyes wide. "You've watched it?"

"Yeah. When Presley moved to New York, she was lonely, so we'd hop on a video chat every Friday night and watch the same movie together. We switched between chick flicks and action movies, but let's be honest, she usually had the final say."

Everly grins. "She's lucky to have you as her older brother."

Presley and I have always shared a close bond. Despite our seven-year age gap, our connection is special. Growing up, she was like my shadow, and I felt a sense of duty to protect her at all costs.

I was skeptical when she started dating Jack, but my reservations disappeared after seeing firsthand how happy he makes her. The one drawback to her having a boyfriend and me living on another continent is that we don't get to talk on the phone as often as we used to. As much as I complain about the group chat with her and my mom, it gives us a way to stay in touch when life gets busy.

"Do you have time for a quick run on the treadmill?" I ask.

"I'd rather stay in bed a little while longer. I'm extremely comfortable right now." Everly sighs with contentment. "Aren't you?"

"Staying cuddled in bed with a beautiful woman? Sounds like a hardship."

"If you need convincing, I had something more than just cuddling in mind," she murmurs, leaning in to kiss me.

She trails her hand down my stomach, and my cock springs to attention as her fingers glide over my skin, sparking an electric heat to course through me. Thank god, we slept naked last night.

"Were the six orgasms I gave you last night not enough?"

Everly bats her eyelashes, feigning innocence. "Last night? What happened last night? I think I need a refresher." She grips my hard-on, and I groan at being held by her.

This woman is insatiable. I fucking love it.

Without warning, I move her onto her back, settling above her with my legs on either side of her hips, locking her arms in place above her head. "God, you're going to be my undoing, Everly Stafford."

Her eyes widen at hearing me use her married name, and a ghost of a smile tugs at her lips. "Are you going to keep staring, or are you going to fuck me?" she goads.

"Be careful what you wish for. You're going to be deliciously sore by the time we're done," I whisper as I drive into her with abandon.

Everly and I are cuddled on the couch, watching a movie, as I absentmindedly stroke her hair, savoring the domestic bliss of spending the night with my wife.

It took some effort to convince her to break away from her work, but after I compromised with the promise of multiple orgasms later, she was all in.

She tilts her head to look up at me when the elevator dings. There's only one other person who has access to my apartment, and we thought he was still out of town.

"Everyone decent?" Theo's voice echoes through the entryway.

Everly scrambles from the couch and runs to meet him. I pause the movie and get up to follow her. When I round the corner, she's throwing her arms around Theo's neck.

"You're here," she exclaims. "I missed you so much."

"I missed you too, sis." Theo holds her close, pressing a kiss to her hair.

Their twin bond was evident growing up, and I can only imagine how difficult it is for them to spend long periods of time apart now that they're adults.

Everly pulls back to get a better look at Theo. "How are you here?"

"I finished in Barcelona early and came straight to see you. My driver was halfway to your apartment before I remembered you were staying here." He side-eyes me.

"Why don't we all go into the kitchen, and I can make us ice cream sundaes?" Everly suggests, doing her best to defuse the situation before it escalates.

Theo gives me a curt nod as he passes.

Him visiting us is a good start, but it's obvious he's still not thrilled that I married Everly. Normally, we keep in touch when he's away on business, but this time, he's been quiet, offering only a brief response when I've reached out. I get why he's upset, but I'm confident he'll eventually come around.

At least, I hope so.

He's the most important person in Everly's life, and I'll do whatever it takes to make sure she's able to maintain a healthy relationship with us both.

We follow her into the kitchen, watching as she removes a tub of vanilla ice cream from the freezer and grabs bowls from the cupboard.

"Why am I not surprised you bought the cheap ice cream?" Theo teases her as he sits on a barstool and leans his arms on the countertop.

"My unrefined palate thinks it tastes just as good as the artisan ice cream you prefer that costs double the price." She gives him a coy grin. "Besides, you won't notice the difference once it's slathered in chocolate syrup and whipped cream."

Theo shakes his head and turns to me. "She'll never learn, will she?"

"Ev's got a point," I say. "She made chocolate fudge sundaes the other day, and you can't tell the difference."

I grab the basket of toppings Everly brought home from the store last week when she was craving something sweet.

Theo rolls his eyes. "Oh, this is just great. You've only been married for a hot minute and are already ganging up on me?"

"Consider it payback for all the times you and Cash made me sit in the back seat in high school," Everly sasses.

She scoops ice cream into three bowls, and I assist by adding the toppings—chocolate syrup, peanuts, caramel sauce, whipped cream, and a cherry. After finishing, I take my bowl and sit next to Theo, who's reading something on his phone. Everly joins us, handing Theo his dessert with a warm smile. She hops up on the counter between us, her legs dangling off the edge.

"Thanks, sis," Theo says, tucking his phone in his pocket before digging into his ice cream.

"Yeah, thanks, Ev. This looks delicious," I say as I take a big bite.

"You did most of the work." Her gaze locks with mine as she twirls her tongue around her spoon, licking the ice cream off.

I'm fucking jealous of a spoon.

"I'm shocked you're eating this," Theo says to me.

I snap my head to look at him. "I still eat healthy," I retort. "For the most part."

"Yeah, and he gets plenty of exercise," Everly chimes in with a sly smirk.

I shoot her a warning glance, but Theo doesn't seem to catch on to her double meaning.

My mind goes blank when she picks up her cherry with her fingers and wraps her lips around it as she slowly sucks it into her mouth.

Ice cream sundaes are officially my new favorite dessert.

"Cash, are you listening?" Theo's voice snaps me out of my daydream.

"Huh?" I look over to find him frowning at me.

"Jesus Christ. Everly has you wrapped around her finger, doesn't she?" His gaze pings between us, noting how I can't seem to stop staring at her.

"I do not," Everly says defiantly.

"Oh, really? Then why hasn't Cash taken his eyes off you since we sat down?" He raises an eyebrow.

Busted.

"Because we're newlyweds." she sasses back.

Theo pushes his bowl to the side. "Don't remind me," he grumbles.

"Is there something you want to say?" I ask.

His true feelings about me and Everly being together were bound to come out tonight, and it's only fair to let him express those.

"Honestly, I figured one of you would come to your senses and realize how absurd this is. I mean, a Vegas wedding? You can't get more cliché than that." He sighs. "I just don't want to see either of you get hurt when this doesn't work out."

I turn to face him. "Everly is my wife, and unless she tells me she wants to end this, I'm all in." I direct my words to him, but my gaze stays fixed on his sister. "There's nothing I wouldn't do for her."

Everly's mouth falls open at my confession, but she composes herself, schooling her expression.

Theo lets out a low whistle. "Damn, sis, you've achieved the unthinkable."

"What's that?" Everly asks with a raised brow.

"I never thought I'd see the day when Cash Stafford is head over heels for a woman. Although I would have preferred it to be someone other than you," he complains.

"Too bad we don't always get what we want, huh?" Everly smirks, giving him a playful slug on the shoulder. "Why don't you stay and watch a movie? We just started *What Happens in Vegas.*"

"How fitting," Theo snickers. "I'll stay, but I'm sitting in the middle."

I give him an amused scowl as he heads into the living room.

At least he's warming up to the idea of us being together. Now, we just have to find the right way to break the news about the acquisition to him. Even though it was the reason for Everly and me staying married, it's no longer relevant… at least not to me.

25

CASH

EVERLY HAS BEEN IN HIGH spirits since Theo stopped by our apartment last week. It's been fourteen years since the three of us have hung out together, and it felt like old times. Since then Theo has texted me a few times, and even suggested we all go out for drinks once he gets back from his current business trip.

It's Sunday morning, so I surprised Everly with a full-body massage at the spa on the second floor of the High Rise. It's one of the many perks of living in one of London's most coveted complexes. However, the penthouse apartment is the only one with a private gym, which is why I couldn't resist buying it when it became available last year.

I'm finishing up a weightlifting session before meeting Everly downstairs when my phone pings. I set the barbell to the ground and retrieve my phone from a nearby bench to find that I have a text.

Presley: Are you awake?

Cash: No, I'm texting in my sleep.

Within seconds, my phone rings with an incoming video chat, Presley's name popping up on the screen.

"Hey, Pres," I answer, taking a seat on the bench.

She appears on the screen, lounging in bed, her hair tied in a messy bun. She's wearing an oversized button-up shirt, which I assume belongs to Jack.

"It's early in London. I'm shocked you're awake," she says.

"It's the middle of the night in New York. What are *you* doing awake?" I counter.

"You're such a smartass," she remarks in a snarky tone. "One of Jack's clients in Chicago has a critical issue with a multimillion-dollar project launching on Tuesday, so he had to spend his weekend helping them in person. I have an important presentation tomorrow afternoon, so I couldn't go with him." She pouts as she leans back against the headboard.

I chuckle. "That doesn't answer my question."

"We've only spent the night apart from each other a handful of times, and I can't sleep without him here," she admits.

I can relate. I've grown so used to sleeping next to Everly, and I don't like thinking what it would be like if she wasn't there anymore.

"I'm touched you'd call your big brother to keep you company," I say, grabbing the towel next to me to wipe my brow.

"I would have called Dylan, but I'm sure he's asleep, and Harrison's likely up working late or on a call with a client overseas, even on the weekend."

"Glad to know I'm your last resort," I say wryly.

We both know I'm the one she reaches out to first when she needs to talk to someone.

"Honestly? I miss our daily phone calls." She sighs. "Getting married doesn't give you the right to disappear on me."

"Oh, you mean like you did when you and Jack first got together?" I ask with a raised brow.

"What are you talking about?"

"Pres, when you two started dating, we didn't talk on the phone for an entire month after you went back to New York." I grab my sports drink from the ground and take a big gulp.

There's silence on her end as she looks at me with a perplexed expression. "Okay, fine. I guess you're right."

"I'm sorry. What was that?" I cup my ear.

Presley shakes her head. "You're so annoying," she huffs.

"No, that's your job, little sis."

"It's a good thing I take my job seriously then," she quips. "Are you and Everly planning to visit Aspen Grove soon? Every time I talk to Mom, she asks if you've mentioned anything to me." Presley goes out of view briefly when she leans over to grab a Chapstick from her nightstand. "She still seems upset that you didn't invite us to the wedding. Honestly, I don't blame her. We're your family and should have been there. I wanted to see my favorite brother get married."

I grin. "I'm totally telling Harrison and Dylan that you called me your favorite."

"Go right ahead. I tell them they're my favorite, too."

I understand why Presley and my mom are unhappy about the wedding. They assume we eloped and chose not to invite our families. The truth is far less glamorous.

A sign of resignation escapes me. "Presley, I have something to tell you." I take my baseball cap off and run my fingers through my hair.

"Oh my god." Her eyes widen as she holds the phone closer to her face. "You cut your hair."

I fidget with my bracelet. "Yeah, I did."

"It looks so good," she says.

"What? No jokes?"

She shakes her head. "Not about this. You seem more content, happier even. Like a weight has been lifted off your shoulders."

It's like she can read my mind.

My scar is permanent, and I know some days I'll still struggle with that reality. The difference now is that I'm learning to turn the pain into resilience and accepting myself for who I am.

"I do feel lighter," I tell Presley with a chuckle.

"What does Everly think about your haircut?"

"She's what I wanted to talk to you about. Well, sort of."

Presley's smile drops. "Please tell me it's not bad news," she begs, sitting up straight in bed.

"Depends on how you look at it. Everly and I got married on accident," I admit, glancing down at the ground.

"What do you mean?"

"We hadn't seen each other since high school until the weekend in Vegas. I saw her at the hotel bar and I invited her to hang out. After a few too many drinks, we spontaneously got married because of a marriage pact we made in high school."

"Shut the front door." Presley slaps her hand over her mouth.

"I was supposed to tell the family when we got to Aspen Grove, but I couldn't when I saw how excited you and Mom were."

Presley holds up her hand. "Wait, why didn't you get it annulled if that's the case?" Her eyes widen as realization strikes. "Does this have something to do with the Townstead acquisition?"

She might not work for Stafford Holdings, but she owns stock in the company, and Harrison keeps her in the loop on what's coming down the pipeline.

"Harrison and Dylan confronted Everly and me before family pictures, and they advised us against ending things before the deal was finalized to avoid bad optics." I wince at the admission.

"How could I miss all of that?" She shakes her head. "That's what I get for making out with Jack in the bathroom instead of being nosy like Harrison and Dylan. But you should have told me later," she scolds.

"Oh, come on, Pres. There's no way you could have kept that from Mom. You might be good at keeping your own secrets, but you're terrible at keeping other people's."

"If that's the case, what makes you think I won't call Mom right after this and spill the beans?"

"Besides it being the middle of the night? I'm giving you the benefit of the doubt. And if you do tell, I know never to trust you with another secret."

"Cash, that's not fair." She flops down on her bed, her head landing on the pillow. "You shouldn't have told me."

I arch a brow. "Weren't you just scolding me for not telling you sooner?"

"Ugh." She sighs. "Fine, I'll keep my mouth shut. So how does this work? Are you and Everly supposed to get divorced after the deal is done? I know you better than anyone, and it's clear that you care about her." Her tone changes to one of concern. "I might have been a kid at the time, but I could see how much you liked her in high school. Plus, you've worn the bracelet she made you for the better part of fourteen years. If that's not a foundation for true love, then I don't know what is."

"It's complicated, Pres." I rake my fingers through my hair. "I want to be with Everly, but—"

"Uncomplicate it," she states, cutting me off. "You can't let the chance of being with the one person you've always wanted fall through your fingertips."

I raise my brow. "Since when did you become the relationship expert?"

"Since I was the first sibling to be in a serious relationship."

"Yes, you're so much wiser than the rest of us," I mutter sarcastically.

"Naturally," she chirps. "Now if only you'd take my advice and tell Everly how you feel."

"Okay, I think it's time for you to go to bed now."

She sticks her tongue out at me. "You're no fun."

"I'm still your favorite brother."

"Only if you and Everly stay together." She smirks. "I mean it when I say you two could be happy together. Fake marriage or not. I mean, Jack and I started out fake dating, and look how that turned out." She gestures around their bedroom.

"Yes, shacking up in a penthouse in New York. Mom and Dad are so proud." I wink.

My mom is thrilled that Jack and Presley are living together. She only wishes they'd get married and give her grandbabies. But for now, she'll have to settle for them being madly in love.

"At least we came clean about our relationship early on. Imagine how she'll react when you finally tell her."

If I can convince Everly to give me a real chance and agree to stay with me long-term, something tells me my mom will be okay with it.

"We'll have to wait and see. Listen, I have to go, but I'm glad you called," I say.

"Yeah, me too. Don't be a stranger."

"I won't. Good night, Pres."

"Good morning, Cash." She grins before ending the call.

I tuck my phone in my pocket and head down to the spa to meet Everly.

She's the person I want to grow old with, to create a lifetime of memories with. As far as I'm concerned, this thing between us should be permanent, but she has the final say. All I can do now is show her how much she means to me and that my future belongs to her.

The first step is figuring out how to tell my wife I don't want a fake marriage anymore.

"Tell me again why we haven't come here yet?" Everly says over her shoulder as I follow her down the hall toward the sauna. When we get to the entrance, we take off our robes and hang them on the designated hooks. She keeps the towel she took from the front desk tucked under her arm, and I open the door for her, motioning for her to go in first.

"Thank you," she says.

As soon as we step into the sauna, I'm hit with a wave of intense, dry heat.

We're the only ones here, and I follow Everly to the bench in the far corner. She's wearing a bold red bikini that makes my mouth water. Her breasts spill out over the strapless top, and her high-cut bottoms hug her hips. I can't take my eyes off her—she's a total knockout.

And she belongs to me.

Everly settles into her seat and sets the towel down on the bench next to her. She leans back against the wall, her arms resting at her sides as her entire body visibly relaxes.

I sit next to her, scooting closer until our legs touch. Her skin glistens with oil from her massage, enhancing its natural glow, and the subtle scent of lavender and eucalyptus wafts through the air. The sound of her steady breathing fills the room. I'm spellbound by her alluring beauty as I study her heart-shaped face, pert nose, and pouty lips.

My hand moves to her leg, and her eyes fly open, accompanied by a soft gasp. I slowly trace my hand up her thigh in teasing strokes before slipping my hand inside her bikini bottoms, welcomed by her warmth.

"Someone could walk in here at any moment," Everly warns, glancing toward the door.

She nibbles on her lip as I trail my finger along her seam.

"The idea didn't seem to bother you when we were in the shoe store," I remark, leaning across her to grab the towel she brought and drape it across our laps. "There. Now if anyone comes by, all they'll see is a couple sitting side by side with a towel over their laps. It's completely innocent."

"That's not—"

Everly abruptly stops speaking when I plunge a finger inside her. She clutches the edge of the towel, digging her fingers into the fabric.

"Fuck, you're soaked, Ev." I lower my mouth to her ear. "Does the idea that someone could walk in and catch us at any moment make you wet?"

She looks up at me, nodding as she swallows hard.

Her legs fall open for me, making it easier for me to pump my finger in and out in a steady rhythm while massaging her clit in languid circles. When I add two more thick fingers, her head lolls back against the wall, and her eyes flutter shut.

My movements slow subtly until my hand goes completely still.

Everly's eyes snap open as she gives me a discontented pout. "Why did you stop?"

"Because you're so damn beautiful, and I want to watch your reaction when you finally come undone for me," I say, her entranced gaze locked on mine.

I move my fingers again, teasing in quick strokes, never going more than knuckle-deep. Everly puts her hand under the towel and grabs my wrist, urging me to give her the gratification she's searching for. She squirms against me, and despite knowing full well her body is begging for release, I continue to draw out her approaching orgasm.

My breath quickens as I toy with her. The scent of her arousal mixes with the smell of the oil, and I welcome the taste of her as she brushes her tongue against mine.

We both freeze when we hear voices outside the sauna. My hand remains buried inside Everly's pussy as we wait with bated breath. When the voices grow fainter, sounding more distant, I thrust my fingers deep inside her, angling toward her G-spot.

"Oh, god." She breathes.

"It's intoxicating watching you unravel, knowing there could be people within hearing distance." She moans as I pump my fingers in and out. "Are you going to be a good wife and come on my hand?

"Fuck, yes," she cries.

After a few firm strokes of her clit with my thumb, she detonates like a bomb. My cock becomes harder than steel as her orgasm rips through her, and tremors course through her body.

"I'll never get tired of watching you come for me."

Just like I did at the shoe store, I bring my fingers to my mouth, groaning as I suck them clean. Everly's eyes widen as she watches me savor her essence.

"Delicious." I flash her a wicked grin of satisfaction.

"Let's go back to the apartment," she says with a heated gaze. "What I want to do with you next can't be hidden under a towel." Her eyes sparkle with mischief.

"By all means, lead the way."

I'd follow her to the ends of the earth and back again.

26

EVERLY

AUGUST GIVES A LOW WHISTLE when I walk into the break room and points to my four-inch suede red heels. The rest of the office is at lunch so we have the place to ourselves.

"Damn, Cash wasn't messing around when he took you on a shopping spree. You've worn a different pair of heels every day since he took you to Belgravia," he remarks.

I take my lunch and a bottle of water from the fridge, twisting off the cap to take a sip.

"You deserve some credit for convincing me to ditch work," I tease.

August laughs. "Rebellion looks good on you. It's about damn time one of us found a way to stick it to Dick. He's been even more difficult to deal with lately if that's possible."

I sit down at a table and unwrap the chicken sandwich that arrived an hour ago. When Cash and I can't have lunch together, he arranges to have something delivered to me.

"Thank god, he lives on a different continent," I say.

Since my dad showed up in London unannounced, he's limited his communications with me to emails and messages. However, he has continued his onslaught of short turnaround times for projects—not just for me but the whole London team. He's clearly on edge, and the longer the due diligence phase of the acquisition plays out, the more irritable his commutations become.

Cash and I have avoided discussing the deal whenever possible. I prefer to keep it separate from our personal lives, avoiding the constant reminder that this arrangement could still have an expiration date.

August grabs a granola bar from the snack basket on the counter and takes a seat next to me. "How are you holding up?" he asks. "Don't think I haven't noticed that you've been smiling more lately and leaving at a reasonable time most nights. Can I assume it has something to do with Cash?"

I shift in my seat, looking down at my sandwich. "Maybe."

It has everything to do with him.

My cheeks flush just thinking about our visit to the spa yesterday. All rational thought went out the window the second he slipped his hand inside my bikini bottoms. Occasionally, Cash's blasé attitude rubs off on me, making me feel more carefree and adventurous than I've ever thought possible.

August studies my face.

"You're totally sleeping with him now, aren't you?" he asks bluntly.

"Yes, I am," I say confidently.

There's no point in denying it.

He grins from ear to ear. "Is now a bad time to say I told you so?"

I roll my eyes. "You're unbelievable."

"Is it serious?"

"More serious than a marriage?" I deadpan.

August bursts into laughter. "Well, when you put it that way…"

Cash and I haven't defined whatever this thing is between us aside from agreeing that we're not putting an expiration date on it. But there is no question we're both enjoying our time together.

"We're still deciding where we go from here," I answer honestly. "When we agreed to this arrangement, we knew the score—once the acquisition is finalized, our marriage would end. Now, I'm not sure what's going to happen. We've sure made a mess of things," I say before taking a bite of my sandwich.

August shakes his head. "Nope. I won't stand by and let you second guess yourself. After you broke things off with Landon, you avoided men like the plague and spent two years going through the motions. With Cash you're more at ease. If things don't work out between the two of you, I have no doubt you'll come out of it stronger."

"I sense a 'but' coming," I say.

"*But*, in my opinion, Cash is a keeper," August says. "It's clear that he wants the best for you and is committed to making you happy."

"You're absolutely right." I pause to take a long drink of water. "I just don't want to get hurt again," I admit.

Cash has the power to cause me more pain than Landon ever could. Not because I'm worried he'll betray me, but that he'll decide he doesn't want to stay married when the acquisition is finalized. My feelings for him run deeper than anyone before, and it frightens me to think I might get left behind in the end.

"I know it's hard to move on after a heartbreak, but you deserve happiness. If Cash makes you happy, you should go for it.," he says, leaning over to give my hand a squeeze. "Just know that whatever happens, I'm in your corner."

"Thanks, August," I smile. "I'm lucky to have you."

"Hell yeah, you are," he says playfully. "And I'm grateful for you, too."

I've just stepped in the door from work when my phone rings. I let out a sigh when I see that it's my mother... again. She's called nonstop for the past couple of days, but I haven't had the patience to deal with her. It's only Monday, and work has already been unbelievably chaotic. August's presence makes things bearable at the office, and coming home to Cash is my saving grace.

I draw in a deep breath and prepare myself for our call. I care about my mom and want to be there for her, but our conversations often leave me feeling emotionally drained.

"Hello, Everly."

"Hey, Mom."

I tuck my shoes and purse under the bench in the entryway and head into the kitchen. Cash is nowhere to be found, but I can smell something baking in the oven.

We agreed to have Fallon continue preparing our meals for now. She'll be moving to New York soon, so we're making the most of her exceptional cooking skills while she's still in London.

"What's going on?" Mom says, sounding annoyed. "You haven't returned any of my calls."

"I'm sorry. I've been busy." I grab a bottle of water from the fridge and take a seat at the counter. "How are you?"

"Wonderful. You won't believe where I am," she chirps with excitement.

"Where?" I place my phone on speaker and set it on the counter next to me.

"Miami," she exclaims. "Oh, Everly, things are finally turning around. I met a handsome surgeon online, and he invited me to stay with him for a month at his vacation house. It has a home theater and a pool with a waterfall. It's incredible."

"What's his name?" I sigh.

"Mark."

"What's his last name? Does he live in Miami?"

"I'm not sure what his last name is—that's unimportant," she says, brushing off my question. "He's from Colorado and comes here when he needs a break from work. He's such a gentleman and is a dynamo in the sack." I cringe, rubbing my temples as she giggles like a schoolgirl. Clearly, my mom doesn't understand the concept of TMI. "Honey, I think he's the one."

I rub my forehead, trying to ward off an impending headache. This is so typical of her—going away with a man she barely knows. He could be married with kids and using his vacation house to keep his affairs hidden from his family, or a scam artist who thinks my mom has money of her own. It wouldn't be the first time she's gotten involved with someone like that.

"What happened to the guy you met in Bali?" I ask, taking a sip of water.

"You mean Jonathan?" She scoffs. "He was just a fling."

That's funny, considering she called him her soulmate the day she was packing for her trip to meet him.

"What happened?"

"The spiritual retreat he took me on was fabulous, but afterward, we stayed in a resort for a few days." I hear the abrupt slam of a door in the background and the sound of shoes slapping against concrete. "The room had a terrible view, and he opted for the cheapest meal plan, then he had the nerve to get upset over my spa bill. I can't be with someone unwilling to support the lifestyle I deserve." She lets out an exasperated sigh.

"Mark treats me like royalty. I'm lounging out by the pool right now while his personal chef prepares dinner. Did I mention he's filthy rich?" She laughs with glee. "Oh, that reminds me—I was in Aspen Grove last week and stopped by Main Street Market for some wine. Imagine my surprise when Willis, the owner, offered his congratulations on your marriage to Cash Stafford. Is there a particular reason you didn't tell your mother you got married, and to a billionaire, no less?"

There are plenty of reasons, but none of which I want to share with her.

"We eloped in Vegas, just the two of us." I keep my answer brief.

"Darling, this is amazing news," she squeals. "I always knew Theo's connection to the Staffords would pay off eventually. Please tell me you didn't sign a prenup. You need to get every penny you can before Cash leaves you."

I close my eyes, praying for patience. "Mom, I didn't marry Cash for his money."

He's never brought it up, but I assume when this marriage ends, we'll each leave with what we came in with. I would never exploit him like my mom has so many of the men she's dated.

My stomach turns at the word *when*. There's a voice in the back of my mind urging me to consider the possibility that this could be more than an accidental wedding turned marriage of convenience.

"Well, it doesn't hurt to have unlimited access to it," Mom says. "I'm sure he wouldn't mind if you sent me five grand. I found the most beautiful, limited-edition designer bag I can't live without. It's the least you could do for not inviting me to your wedding."

It's ironic how Johanna wanted pictures of Cash and me as a couple because she wasn't at the wedding, while my mom wants a designer bag she'll use once before she finds another she can't live without.

I sigh. "Mom, I'm not sending you money for a bag."

We've had this discussion hundreds of times. I never send her money outright and refuse to pay for anything that isn't a necessity.

313

I cover her mortgage and utilities and have food delivered when she's home in Aspen Grove. It's important that she has a safe place to return to whenever her latest conquest doesn't work out. She's never worked a day in her life, and I'm not naive enough to think that'll ever change, even if I cut her off. She'll keep seeking new men to exploit as long as she can.

"How about for Christmas? Maybe by then, Mark and I will be married too, and he'll buy it for me," she exclaims.

"Yeah, maybe," I say, sounding skeptical.

Despite her shortcomings, she's still my mom. I respect Theo's decision not to have contact with her, but I can't do it. Unlike my father, she's never belittled me or made me feel less than the gum on her shoe. Yes, she's immature, materialistic, and self-centered, but that doesn't mean she doesn't care about me in her own way.

Our contact will remain limited, with infrequent phone calls, but I'll make sure that when she has her next messy breakup, her house will be waiting for her.

When I look up, Cash is walking into the kitchen and heading to remove a casserole from the oven.

"Mom, I have to go," I tell her. "I'm glad you're happy."

"Oh, okay, darling. I'll call you soon. Bye."

"Bye," I say, hanging up the phone.

Cash leaves the dish on the stovetop to cool and comes to take a seat next to me.

"How much of that conversation did you hear?"

He takes my hand. "Enough to better understand why you no longer believe in soulmates and steered clear of relationships after what happened with Landon."

314

"You have a bad habit of eavesdropping on people's conversations, don't you?" I needle him.

"Maybe I wouldn't be tempted if you didn't use speakerphone," he quips.

"Did you catch the part where my mom implied I should rob you blind before you decide to leave me?"

"I'm not leaving you, Ev. Besides, you don't have to steal anything—it belongs to you."

I scrunch up my nose in confusion. "What do you mean?"

"What's mine is yours," he states.

I gape at him in disbelief when he takes out his wallet and places a black card—with my name etched on the bottom—in front of me.

"When did you have this made?" I ask, tracing the golden lettering with my finger.

"The day we got back to London. I held on to it until I thought you might accept it."

"I don't need your money." I slide the card back to him.

"Maybe not, but it would mean a lot if you kept it, just in case." He pushes it back. "There's something I have to say to you. I don't know how you'll take it, but it's important that I get it off my chest."

"I'm listening," I encourage him.

"When all is said and done, and the acquisition has been finalized, I don't want this to end in divorce," he states firmly. "What we share is real… at least it is to me." He reaches over to caress my cheek. "Whether that means we legally end our marriage and explore dating each other until you're ready for more, or we renew our vows surrounded by our loved ones, it doesn't matter. In the end, I want you as my wife forever."

My head spins at his declaration. I'm still reeling from the conversation with my mom, and adding Cash's declaration to the mix... It's a lot to process. I never expected those words to come out of his mouth. Before me, he had never committed past a one-night stand. Now, he wants to spend his life with me? My breaths come out short and ragged, my chest tightening with each inhale.

"Cash, this isn't... I'm not sure..." I trail off, struggling to find the right thing to say.

Aside from Theo, he's become the most important person in my life. Our bond grows stronger with each passing day, and when we're not together, his absence leaves a void only he can fill.

It's clear that I'm falling head over heels for Cash Stafford, but my lingering reservations hold me back from diving headfirst into long-term commitment, even though the hopeless romantic in me is screaming at me to let go of my fears and follow my heart.

Cash takes my hand in his. "You don't have to give me an answer now. This was supposed to be a marriage of convenience, plain and simple. All I'm asking is for you to think about what I said and decide if you can envision a life without me. If the answer is yes, I'll let you go when the time comes. It will break me, but I'll do if it makes you happy." He brings my hand to his lips, pressing a kiss on the back before getting up to go over to the stove. "We better eat before it gets cold," he says, dishing up casserole for both of us.

"Thank you," I say when he sets my plate in front of me.

For everything.

"You're welcome." He smiles.

I take a bite of casserole, my mind racing, knowing this will be one of the most important decisions I've ever made. While I don't have an answer for Cash right now, one thing is certain—life without him seems unimaginable.

27

CASH

As I ANXIOUSLY WAIT FOR Everly to get home, I pace the length of the foyer, stopping at one end before turning around and striding to the other.

I tasked August with letting me know when she left the office, and he texted me fifteen minutes ago, so she should be here any minute.

Something has changed since her conversation with her mom at the beginning of the week. She's been more withdrawn, keeping her thoughts to herself.

Her parents are toxic, and if it were up to me, I'd cut them both out of her life completely. While I think she'll appreciate my efforts to remove Richard from the equation, she'll never stop taking care of her mom. Everly views her mom like she would a child who makes irresponsible decisions and needs supervision. Regardless, I'll stand by her side and support her, no matter what she decides.

A persistent thought nags me, wondering if my statement about not wanting this marriage to end is part of what has led her to withdraw. I don't regret what I said. The acquisition will be completed soon, and I had to let her know my intentions—for better or worse.

For now, all I can do is give her time to consider what she wants and demonstrate her importance in my life.

As soon as the door to the stairwell opens and Everly steps out, I stride over and pull her into a hug.

"Is everything okay?" she asks, her gaze darting to the two suitcases resting against the wall.

"I have another surprise for you," I tell her as I hold her close. "August told me you have Monday off, so I planned a last-minute trip for us over the long weekend."

"Oh." She glances between me and the stairs like she's unsure what to do. "I figured I would work from home and catch up on a few projects."

"You can work on the plane. Besides, Marcus texted me earlier today to say all the furniture he ordered has arrived at his warehouse. He and his team can get everything set up while we're out of town. It'll be much easier if we're not at the house."

Everly steps closer, tugging my collar, and leans in for a kiss. "Does this surprise come with another closet full of shoes?" she murmurs against my mouth.

I wind my hand around her waist, nipping at her lips. "I'm afraid not, but it does come with a gift at the end," I say, hoping a little bribery will entice her to agree.

She taps her finger on her chin. "What is it?"

"You'll have to come with me to find out," I say with a sly smirk.

She frowns when I take a step back and pick up our suitcases. "You want to leave now?"

"Yeah, I've already packed for us, and the plane is waiting."

She raises a brow. "How do I know my suitcase isn't packed full of lingerie?"

"It would be fitting if I were planning to lock you inside a hotel room and have my way with you all weekend. Unfortunately, that's not the kind of trip we're taking this time."

I recruited my mom and Presley to help me pack her suitcase. They walked me through what to bring in our group chat. Living with Everly has given me a good idea of her skincare and makeup routine, as well as her style preferences, but I didn't want to chance forgetting anything.

I call the elevator and put the two suitcases inside once the doors slide open, sending them down before heading toward the stairs.

"You coming, Ev?"

"I can't let your planning go to waste, now can I?" she teases, following me into the stairwell.

Here's to hoping this trip goes off without a hitch and that when we get back, Everly will be irrevocably and unequivocally mine.

ANN EINERSON

"You're really not going to tell me where we're going?" Everly asks, turning her head in my direction when we pull up to the tarmac.

I give her a cheeky grin. "It's a surprise, remember?"

"Is it somewhere tropical? Are we leaving Europe? Is there a beach?" She ticks each destination option with her fingers.

My face falls as I rub the back of my neck. "Maybe I set your expectations too high."

"I'm just wondering if I'll have access to the internet in case I'm not able to get all my work done on the plane."

"Yes, you will."

She studies me closely as if trying to read my mind. "Are we going to Aspen Grove?"

I lower my gaze. "Yeah," I admit. "We were only there for a day last time, and you said you missed it. I figured it would be a nice change of pace for a few days. Plus, your mom won't be in town, so I didn't think—" I lose my train of thought when Everly places her hand on my cheek.

"Cash, I'm glad we're going there." She offers me a reassuring smile.

"You are?"

She nods. "Yes, and I'm looking forward to spending time with your family."

"How do you know we're going to see them?"

Everly cocks an eyebrow. "There's no chance your mom would let us visit Aspen Grove and stay somewhere else."

She's right. When I told my mom this morning about our impending visit, she was overjoyed, insisting that we stay with her and dad. If everything goes according to my plan, this will be our last opportunity to do so, and my mom knows it.

322

"Are you sure? That means we'll be sharing a bed, wifey," I taunt her.

"I'm looking forward to it, hubby." She leans in to give me a kiss on the lips. "Does Harrison care that you're using the Stafford Holdings jet for personal use? Last time, you were technically on business, aside from the detour in Aspen Grove."

I scrunch my nose in confusion. "It's not the company jet. It's ours."

"How did I not know you owned an entire plane?" She laughs.

"We own a plane," I state.

"I'm sorry?"

"We're married, so it's our plane, and you're welcome to use it anytime you want."

I meant what I said. What's mine is hers. There's nothing more important to me than Everly, and no matter what she decides, that will remain true.

Her mouth hangs open in disbelief as I open the car door to help her out and tip the driver. I hold her hand as we climb the stairs to the plane. The last time we flew together, she refused my help, and claiming her as mine, beyond a legally binding document, was a pipe dream.

The flight attendant stands inside the plane's entrance, ready to greet us. This time she doesn't offer us champagne. Everly and I have both avoided alcohol since our night in Vegas.

"Welcome back." She smiles at Everly. "It's good to see you, Cash." She gives a nod.

"Thank you," Everly says as she passes her, walking into the cabin.

She moves to the farthest row from the aircraft door, checking over her shoulder to make sure I'm following. I stop short, taking the seat in front of her, noticing her frown with disappointment.

She leans over my seat. "Why are you sitting up there?"

I tilt my head back to look at her. "Last time, you wanted me to sit somewhere else, so I figured I'd spare you the trouble." I bite my cheek to keep from grinning when she sighs and comes around to sit next to me.

"Well, this time, I want to sit next to my husband, if you don't mind."

"Not at all." I lean in close so only she can hear. "Want to see the bedroom once we're in the air?"

"There's a bedroom?" she asks with a raised brow, turning to look behind us. "I can't believe I didn't notice when we were here before."

"Maybe if you hadn't been so busy working, you would have." I wink.

Just then, the flight attendant stops by to hand us bottles of sparkling water.

"Thanks," I say. "Once the plane takes off, we'd like complete privacy. I'll let you know if we need anything later on."

"Yes, of course." She hurries to the front of the plane.

I take a casual sip while pulling a random book from my bag. Everly said she doesn't get to read much, so I packed several romance books for her that Carol let me borrow.

They're all small-town romances with rugged lumberjacks, apparently.

I fully support Everly reading them as long as she doesn't decide she needs a small-town lumberjack in her life. Considering we live in the heart of London, I think we're safe from that scenario. Then again, I wonder if I have any flannel shirts at the back of my closet. I wouldn't mind doing a little role-play if that's something she's into.

Everly glances at the book in my hands. "What's that?"

"I brought along some novels I thought you might like."

She narrows her eyes at me skeptically. "Lumberjack romances?"

"I have it on good authority they're the best kind. If Carol likes them, they must be harmless."

Everly laughs. "You might want to read one first before assuming anything."

Now I'm curious as to what could possibly be in this book that has her so amused.

I open up to a random page and begin reading out loud.

"*When I've caught my breath, I flip Cassie back to her hands and knees, taking hold of my shaft, and guiding it back inside her slick cunt. She tilts her head back to look at me, a low moan passing her lips at the first hard thrust.*"

A quick glance at Everly, out of the corner of my eye, shows me she's gripping the armrest, her mouth slightly parted and her attention unwavering. So, I keep going.

"*My grip tightens on Cassie's hips, and I pound into her mercilessly. The sound of flesh slapping against flesh fills the air. She clenches tightly around me, crying out when I reach my hand around her front to pinch her clit, sending her careening off the edge of sanity. A guttural groan passes my lips as I come alongside her."*

Everly's eyes fall shut, and her hold on the armrest is so tight her knuckles have turned white. She nibbles her bottom lip like she's trying to suppress a moan.

"I ease Cassie down until she's lying flat on her belly, and I lie on top of her with my softening cock still inside her. This is the third night in a row we've gone bareback, and the idea of her belly swollen with my kid has my dick growing firm again. 'You're such a good girl, Cass. My good girl,' I praise, stroking her hair as I gear up for round three."

By the time I've read seven straight chapters of smut, my cock is hard, straining against my pants. Everly's eyes are now wide open, her gaze locked on me. Her legs are squeezed together, and she's practically vibrating in her seat.

We're going to have to read lumberjack erotica more often if it gets my wife this hot and bothered.

As soon as the pilot announces that it's safe to move around the cabin after reaching cruising altitude, I throw down the book, unbuckle Everly's seat belt, and usher her to the bedroom.

I gesture for her to step inside. "Ladies first."

She blushes. "Thank you."

Despite my past reputation, I've never brought another woman here. Joining the mile-high club never appealed to me, until now.

The room is a smaller version of a swanky hotel room decorated in shades of gray and white. The bed is positioned against the wall, concealing a bathroom on the other side. Everly spins around in a slow circle, taking it all in.

She saunters over to the bed, perching on the edge, and crooks a finger in my direction.

"Aren't you going to join me?" she asks.

"I'm rather enjoying the view from here," I say, leaning against the door with my arms folded across my chest.

"Suit yourself."

My mouth goes dry when she reaches up with steady hands to unbutton her blouse. The suspense is unbearable as I track her delicate fingers unfastening each button with precision. A grunt of approval passes my lips when she tosses her shirt to the ground, revealing a lacy red bra.

She unclasps it, and her ample breasts spill out. I clench my fists, forcing myself to remain in place. Everly gives me a sultry smile as she tugs off her skirt and underwear, throwing them to the floor in a haphazard pile.

My gaze is glued to her as she approaches me, her hips swaying with each step. My throat tightens as she drops to her knees in front of me.

"Ev, what are you doing?" My voice is strained.

"Something I don't get to do nearly enough," she murmurs.

I stand still as she unfastens the button of my jeans, pulling down my zipper and tugging on my pants. She licks her lips while gazing at my cock straining behind my boxers before she slowly drags them down my legs.

She lifts her hooded eyes to meet my lust-filled gaze as she curls her fingers around my dick. I take a sharp inhale as she moves her hand up and down my shaft in unhurried, steady strokes. Pre-cum leaks from the tip, and she leans forward to lap it up with her tongue.

I groan. "Damn, Ev, you're fucking perfect."

I wind my fingers through her hair, urging her to take me in her mouth. She doesn't hesitate, sucking the crown like it's her favorite flavor of popsicle. Her mouth is heaven, and I tighten my grip, coaxing her to take me deeper. She hollows her cheeks until my head is at the back of her throat, and I let her set the pace while she adjusts, not wanting to hurt her.

I'm stunned when she abruptly stops, taking my dick out of her mouth.

"Do you like it when I suck your dick, husband?" She traces my shaft with her fingertip as it bobs inches from her mouth. "Be a good boy and beg me to finish you off," she orders, batting her eyelashes.

I shoot her a playful scowl. "You little minx."

She clicks her tongue in disappointment. "That's not how you beg, Stafford." She licks the crown of my cock in teasing strokes, her taunting gaze never leaving mine.

I am entirely at this woman's mercy—she owns me mind, body, and soul, leaving me utterly powerless. Every part of me belongs to her, and I'd surrender everything I have to guarantee she's mine forever.

"As pretty as you are on your knees for me, let me come so I can devour you." I tilt her head back to look at me.

"That wasn't very convincing. If you want to come, you have to do better than that," she says, clenching her thighs together. Clearly, this little game we're playing is making her even more aroused than she already is.

"I'm at your mercy, wife." I pull in a ragged breath when she presses a kiss to the tip of my cock. "Fuck, let me come, please let me come, Ev," I beg.

"Such a good hubby, begging so nicely," she croons. "You deserve a reward."

Everly wraps her hand around my cock, taking me back in her mouth. She cups my balls, squeezing gently as she sucks me off. I lose all sense of control, tugging her head forward. I fuck her mouth with abandon, and let out a low growl of approval. God, she holds all the power at this moment, owning me, and I fucking love it.

"Fuck, I'm coming," I warn as I stroke the column of her neck.

My cock jerks under her hand as my cum fills her mouth. I can't look away as she laps up every drop, licking me clean. When she's finished, my cock springs free from her mouth with a loud *pop*.

Her red lipstick is smeared across her mouth, and I thumb it off, sucking my finger into my mouth.

"Damn, Ev, that was hot as hell," I say with adoration, taking her hand to help her get up off the floor. "Now it's my turn to call the shots."

"Is that so?" She raises a brow.

"Only if you want to come." I press a kiss to her forehead. "Now be a good girl and lie on the bed for me."

She grins as she walks back to the bed and crawls in the middle, lying down like I instructed. My palms sweat, eagerly anticipating what I have planned. Everly peeks at me through her eyelashes, a seductive smile on her lips. She parts her legs, revealing that she's already dripping wet.

"Hold on to the headboard for me."

She puts her hands in place as I stride across the room, stripping out of my clothes as I go. I'm naked once I reach the bed.

"Can I blindfold you, Ev?" She gives me a weary glance as she tugs her lower lip into her mouth. "I've never played with anyone else like this before. Only you."

"I trust you," she says.

God, every time she utters those three words, it's a soothing balm to my heart, renewing our bond.

"Is that a yes?"

She nods. "Yes, please blindfold me."

"Hearing you say that means everything. Now close your eyes, beautiful," I whisper.

She does as I ask, and I open the bedside drawer, pulling out a couple of items, including a black silk blindfold still in its packaging. Once I've taken it out of the box, I set everything on the bed and hover over Everly.

"I'm going to put the blindfold on now," I explain.

She nods. "Okay."

I place the silk against her eyes and tie it behind her head.

"Keep your hand on the headboard," I remind her when her grip slips.

I move back to take in the vision of Everly splayed out before me. My gorgeous wife, laid out for the taking. During our time together, she has completely exposed me, stripping me of all my defenses, and it's only fair that I do the same to her.

The only sound in the room is Everly's labored breathing. As the seconds tick by, the tension in the air intensifies, and I commit every inch of her body to memory like a work of art.

I lean down to wrap my mouth around her nipple, gliding my tongue across the areola.

"I'll never get enough of these breasts," I say as I flick her nipple with my tongue.

"God, I love your mouth on me," she pants.

Her encouragement strokes my ego as I ravish her tits. I trail my hand down her chest until I get to her stomach, drawing patterns with the pad of my finger. Her breath hitches when I reach the apex of her thighs.

I lean over to grab the blue vibrator I took from the nightstand. It's one from Everly's private collection that I had brought on board ahead of time. Admittedly, I planned all of this in advance, and I'm not the least bit sorry.

When I turn the device on, a soft hum buzzes through the air.

"Hear that, Ev?" My voice remains steady, but my eyes burn with desire as I watch her lips part in recognition.

"It's a vibrator," she says.

"That's right. I thought it was about time we played together." I kiss her lips as I slowly push the device inside her, and she groans at the intrusion.

My gaze doesn't leave her pussy as I turn it up a notch, mesmerized as she writhes beneath me.

"Oh, fuck." Everly bucks her hips as she tightens her grip on the headboard when I increase the speed again. "It's too much," she whines, wriggling beneath me.

"You can take it. I know you can," I urge her.

I bite down on her breasts while plunging the vibrator inside her in rapid succession. She's quivering beneath me, hanging on by sheer determination, sweat dripping from her brow, when I turn the device to the max setting.

"Oh my god," she screams. "Stafford… I'm going to…"

"Be a good girl, and come for me, Ev."

I give her clit a pinch as her orgasm crashes over her like a tidal wave. My punishing onslaught with the vibrator doesn't stop until I've wrung every drop of desire from her body.

When she lets out a long sigh of contentment, I toss the device on the nightstand and remove Everly's blindfold. She blinks up at me.

"Are you alright?"

"We can play like that anytime you'd like," she says, a satisfied smile on her lips.

"Oh, we're not done yet. I haven't fucked that perfect pussy yet."

I line myself up at her entrance and guide myself inside. My gaze remains locked on her, pausing once I'm fully seated.

"You're mine, Ev," I say as I caress her cheek.

"And you're mine," she says in a breathless whisper as she places her hands on my shoulders.

Her declaration of ownership means everything to me, spurring me on to shower her with ecstasy. I move in a steady rhythm, and she meets me thrust for thrust.

"You're so fucking wet," I rasp. "Always so fucking wet for me."

She responds with a loud moan as I pick up my pace, moving in time with our matching heartbeats.

I abruptly pull out, causing her to whine in displeasure. "Flip over and get on your hands and knees."

Everly's eyes grow large before she scrambles to get in position. This part wasn't planned, but the first scene we read from the lumberjack romance was rather inspiring.

I grab two pillows and position them underneath her stomach to prop her up so her ass is in the air. Within seconds, I'm sliding back inside her cunt, taking her from behind.

From this angle, I'm able to go deeper, and she groans with every thrust. I move my hands to her front, one cupping her breast and the other rubbing her clit at the same feverish pace as I'm fucking her.

I drop my head against her shoulder, putting all my energy into driving home. She shudders beneath me, and I shout her name as we finish together.

"Such a good wife," I whisper, stroking her spine.

I shove the pillows out of the way and flip her so she's on her back. She looks up at me with her beautiful brown eyes, and I pull her into my embrace, neither of us ready to move.

"Are you okay?" I pepper kisses along her forehead. "Was that too much?"

"Let's do that every day," she says with a sated smile.

I kiss her, savoring the sweet taste. "Anything you wish, Ev."

I mean it. I'll do anything for her. All she has to do is ask.

28

EVERLY

CAN YOU ENVISION A LIFE without me? If the answer is yes, I'll let you go when the time comes. It will break me, but I'll do it for your happiness.

Since Cash uttered those words a few days ago, they've haunted me day and night. From the moment he stepped back into my life, he's made me his top priority. And how did I repay him when he laid all his cards on the table? By gaping at him like a fish out of water.

Cash is the kind of man every woman wishes she had. He would go to great lengths to protect me, is attentive to my every need, and has a gift for making me feel cherished and adored.

But that doesn't take away the shadow of doubt that this could all be an illusion. What if he wakes up one day and decides he doesn't want me anymore? Worst yet, what if I confess my feelings, only to discover later that our goals and aspirations don't align?

When things fell apart with Landon, I was left shattered and broken; losing Cash would devastate me beyond repair.

He hasn't brought up our conversation about the future again. I can only assume he's waiting for me to give him an answer when I'm ready.

What if I never am? Destined to be stuck in a perpetual state of unrest, too afraid to admit my love for the man I want to spend the rest of my life with.

There, I admit it.

I love Cash Stafford.

I'm jolted from my thoughts as we pull up to his parents' house.

Joining the mile-high club with Cash was hands down the most erotic sexual experience I've ever had. There was something exhilarating about being blind-folded and completely at his mercy.

Afterward, we cuddled in bed before returning to the cabin. I spent the rest of the flight working so that I can fully enjoy my weekend with Cash and his family.

Cash hands a hundred-dollar bill to the driver and retrieves our bags from the trunk. We're halfway up the driveway when the front door swings open.

"Mike, they've arrived," Johanna shouts as she runs across the porch to greet us. "Oh my goodness, I can't believe you're here." She throws her arms around me in a big hug, holding me close. "How are you, sweetie?"

"I'm good," I say with a smile.

"Is Cash treating you well? I won't hesitate to set him straight if he isn't."

Cash rolls his eyes. "Mom, I'm right here."

"That doesn't mean I can't—" She stops when she notices his short hair. "Oh, Cash, your hair. You look so handsome." She presses a kiss on his cheek.

"Thanks. Everly cut it," he says.

"You did a wonderful job," Johanna tells me, her voice catching.

I keep my eyes on Cash. "Thank you," I say, and we share a knowing look.

"Do you have to bring your mother to tears whenever you come home?" Mike asks Cash as he steps onto the porch to join us. "She was all smiles this afternoon, anticipating your arrival."

"These are happy tears," Johanna assures him. "I'm just so glad to have two of my kids home for the weekend."

My chest tightens with emotion when she calls me one of her own.

"We're glad we could come, Mom," Cash says.

"Why don't we all go inside and get something to eat," Johanna suggests. "I put a lasagna in the oven and made homemade garlic bread to go with it. I'm sure you must be starving."

"Good thinking about skipping the meal on the plane," I whisper to Cash.

He'd warned me that his mom would have a big spread planned for when we got here.

"Hey, Dad, is it alright if we go to the garage for a few minutes?" Cash asks Mike. "I wanted to check to make sure my Jeep's still running."

"Sure thing, son," Mike says.

"I'll be right back," Cash assures me.

Johanna drapes her arm around my shoulder. "She'll be fine, but don't take too long." "We won't, dear," Mike promises.

Cash and Mike head toward the garage, disappearing into the side door.

I follow Johanna inside the house, and the scent of sugar, spices, and warm butter welcomes me, making my stomach grumble.

"Good thing I made dinner," she says as she heads toward the kitchen. "I experimented with a recipe for cinnamon rolls, so you'll have to try one for dessert.

"Smells delicious," I say.

Halfway down the hall, I stop when I notice the new family photos hanging up in silver frames. There's a group shot with the whole family, everyone grinning from ear to ear. I laugh when I come to a photo of Lola running across the lawn with Waffles and the puppies gleefully chasing after her. Next are the couple photos, lined up in a row.

My eyes well up when I reach the last photograph—Cash and I sitting on the blanket, his arms around me and my hand covering his. I'm looking at the camera, and Cash gazes down at me with affection. His expression isn't manufactured. It's the real deal. I know because I've seen that same look hundreds of times since that day.

"They turned out beautifully, didn't they?" I spin around to find Johanna approaching, wiping her hands on a kitchen towel. She must have gone into the kitchen while I was distracted by the photos.

"Yeah, the photographer did an exceptional job," I agree.

"She really did," Johanna says proudly. "I've been wanting new family photos for years. I had hoped to wait until everyone settled down, but we can take new ones once Harrison finds his special someone." She flips the towel over her shoulder. "He's spent his adult life carrying the weight of the world on his shoulders, and I think he's forgotten what it's like to be happy."

"I'm sure he'll find his perfect match when the time is right," I say with a reassuring smile.

"Oh, I have no doubt, but I prefer not to leave things to chance." She steps closer to the wall of pictures. "This one is my favorite." She nods toward the photo of me and Cash.

"Yeah, mine too."

"It's the first picture where he's willingly showing his scar. Since the accident, his confidence hasn't been the same. He puts on a good front, but I'm his mother—I can tell when my kids are struggling." She rests her hand on her chest. "I couldn't believe it when the photographer sent me the photos, and I saw this one. My son proudly showing his scar, unconcerned about who might see it. It's all thanks to you, dear." She gently squeezes my arm.

"Me?"

She nods, wiping away a tear. "Being with you has helped him find the confidence he lost and to learn to be comfortable in his own skin again. I can't count how many times I've tried to get him to do more than trim his hair, and then you come along, and he does it willingly. To me, that's a miracle."

Another tear falls down her cheek. "You and Theo have been part of our family since you were kids, and it warms my heart that you and Cash found happiness in each other." Her voice breaks a bit, and she swipes her hands across her cheeks, drying them. "Oh goodness, even menopause can't keep my hormones in check." She laughs.

A lump forms in my throat, and if I'm not careful, I'll start crying, too. I used to dream about being part of the Stafford family, and hearing Johanna reaffirm that I am, means more than she'll ever know.

"I'm going to check on the lasagna," she says, as if she senses I need a moment to regain my composure. "As soon as Cash and his father come inside, we'll eat."

"I'll come help you in just a minute," I promise.

"Take your time, sweetie." She gives my arm another gentle squeeze before going to the kitchen.

I return my attention to the photo of Cash and me, tilting my head as I study it. This time, I focus on my features.

The day the picture was taken, I recall feeling nervous and disoriented. We'd only been married for less than twenty-four hours, and I had just found out about the acquisition.

Despite that, when I look at the image, my smile is genuine, and I'm holding Cash's hand like I never want him to let me go. Even when my whole world was turned upside down, my subconscious knew that I was safe in his arms, and no matter what, he would have my best interest at heart. My feelings for Cash have only grown stronger since that day, and I'm certain he would do anything for me, just as I would for him.

After dinner last night, Cash and I went straight to bed. This morning, we slept in and helped his parents with yard work. It's been nice to put my job on the back burner for once and focus on spending time with people that I care about.

Dylan, Marlow, and Lola got here a half hour ago to have lunch with us, and Cash went downstairs a few minutes ago after he made me come twice in the shower.

I step into the farmhouse-style open-concept kitchen featuring exposed ceiling beams, butcher-block countertops, and sage-green cabinets. On the opposite side of the room, a massive wooden dining table, with seating for ten, is also there. This was my inspiration for my dream kitchen, which I'll probably never see come to life, but it's always been the Staffords' generosity and kindness that's made the place feel so welcoming.

I hear giggling in the corner and look across the room to find Cash and Lola at a craft table near the bay windows overlooking the backyard. As I step closer, I see they're coloring pictures of rainbows. Lola's tongue is poking out in concentration as she tries to stay within the lines.

Cash is next to her, hunched over in a chair that is far too small. His hair falls to his ear, showing most of his scar, and it makes me smile to see how at ease he is.

He's an incredible uncle to Lola, and I can't help but envision him as a dad someday, holding a tiny bundle in his arms.

The idea of starting a family has never been a priority. Landon didn't want kids, and my career demands most of my attention, so I rarely think about it. Now, the image of a mini-Cash rushing into my arms and calling me "mama" is making me reconsider.

"Guess what, Uncle Cash?" Lola chirps.

"What's up, ladybug?" Cash pauses his drawing to give her his undivided attention.

She points out the window to the backyard where the dogs are chasing each other. "The puppies have names now."

"Oh yeah. What are they?"

"Muffin, Jellybean, and Cheez-It. I picked them out myself." She beams with pride.

Cash grins. "Those are some rad names, kiddo."

"I wanted to name one of them Unicorn, but Daddy said no," Lola pouts. She goes back to drawing briefly before scrunching up her nose. "Uncle Cash?"

"Yeah, ladybug?"

"What does rad mean?" she asks as Marlow returns from out back, where she and Dylan have been assisting Cash's parents with the BBQ.

"It means something is cool." Cash points at her picture. "Like your drawing."

"Oh." Lola's eyes light up with recognition. "I think you're rad, Uncle Cash."

"Back at ya, ladybug."

Marlow steps next to me, carrying a plate of grilled cheeseburgers covered in tinfoil. "That's going to be her new favorite word for the next month," she says. "Lola adores Cash."

"I can see that." Lola is now sitting in Cash's lap while he traces her hand on paper.

"How are you?" Marlow asks, transferring the plate to the oven to keep the cheeseburgers warm. "I hope you don't mind, but Dylan told me about you and Cash. Don't worry, he swore me to secrecy," she whispers. "I want you to know I gave him a piece of my mind for suggesting you stay married because of the acquisition. He and Harrison should never have put you in that position."

It means a lot that she's looking out for me, even though she's only met me once before today. Her genuine kindness and thoughtful nature put me at ease, and I could see us becoming good friends.

"I appreciate it, but there's no reason you should be upset with Dylan. He and Harrison made it clear they'd support us no matter what we decided." I grab a carton of strawberries from the fridge and empty them into the colander Johanna left on the counter. "My dad is the one who threatened to fire me if we got the marriage annulled."

"I'm sorry you're dealing with that." Marlow frowns. "I can relate to having difficult parents. I'm an only child, and having no contact with them has been hard, but in my case, it's for the best. The Staffords welcoming me with open arms has been such a blessing."

"Yeah, they've always been like this." I grab a knife and a cutting board from the drawer. "My brother, Theo, and I spent a lot of time here growing up, and it always felt like a second home."

It still does.

"I know what you mean. Johanna and Mike made me feel like family right from the start," Marlow says as I slice strawberries. She leans against the counter and says in a hushed tone, "It's none of my business, but I just want to say it's okay to be confused about your relationship with Cash."

Looking over, I find Cash and Lola still chattering away as they color, paying no attention to me and Marlow. "Were you? Confused, I mean?"

She lets out a humorless laugh. "Was I ever. I never stayed in one place for long until I moved to Aspen Grove, so it was a big adjustment. And I didn't know how my life would fit with Dylan and Lola's. It was just the two of them since Lola was a baby, and it took a while to find my place, but it was well worth it." A warm smile tugs at her mouth. "I'm in the process of adopting her and I can't wait for us to legally be a family."

"Did you know you wanted kids before Lola?"

Marlow shakes her head. "Before Dylan, it hadn't crossed my mind, but now that we're together, I love the idea of expanding our family. Although, that will have to wait a while until we get the puppies trained." She chuckles. "I hope I'm not overstepping by saying this, but watching Cash with Lola makes me think that he'd make a great dad someday. Don't you think?"

It's like she read my earlier thoughts.

I glance over at the pair again to see that they've moved on to finger painting. He holds his hand out while Lola applies a coat of pink paint to his palm, her eyebrows drawn together with intense focus.

Cash's easygoing nature makes him patient, and he seldom gets frustrated—ideal traits to have as a dad. Sensing my gaze, he looks up and winks, causing my cheeks to flush. His easy charm is infectious, and I smile back before returning my attention to Marlow.

"Yeah, Cash would make a wonderful father," I agree.

"Change can be scary, but it's much more manageable when you have the right person by your side to help guide you through unfamiliar territory," she says.

Marlow's right.

I think back to the last couple of months. Cash made moving in with him less daunting by getting me a coffee maker for my daily caffeine fix, having dinner on the table every night, and making sure I had access to the stairwell so I didn't have to ride the elevator. And those were only the things he did when I first arrived.

"Thanks for the advice, Marlow. I appreciate it," I say as I wipe my hands.

She smiles. "That's what family is for."

If she can take a leap of faith, especially with someone who has a child, why am I hesitating to take the next step with Cash?

Communication has a pivotal role in our pending relationship, and I realize the only way we can move forward is if we make sure our visions for the future align. Which means I have to ask Cash some important questions, starting with if he wants kids.

29

CASH

"WE'RE GOING ON A DATE." I lean over to pepper kisses along Everly's jawline and tilt her head to look up at me.

She's curled up on the bed with a copy of *Pride and Prejudice* that she found on my mom's bookshelf. It seems when she's reading alone, she prefers the classics over lumberjack romances.

After lunch with my family, I encouraged her to relax upstairs and take some much-needed time for herself while I ran an errand on the other side of town.

"A date?" Her eyes sparkle with excitement.

"Yeah, we better get a move on, or we'll be late." I nod toward the door.

"What should I wear?"

"It'll be just us, so whatever you want. But if I had to pick, I'd go with your red sundress. You look incredible in that one, and I like that it's easily accessible." I wink.

ANN EINERSON

Her cheeks flush as she climbs off the bed and changes, pairing her dress with the black open-toed heels she tried on at the boutique. They're now her favorites, and every time I see them, I'm reminded of how her face looks when she falls apart at my touch.

"Where are your parents tonight?" she asks as we head downstairs, noticing the quiet.

"They're meeting up with some friends."

Everly lets out a soft gasp when I take the blindfold I used on the plane from my pants pocket.

"What's that for?"

"Where we're going is a surprise."

"I thought you said I had to wait until the end of the trip for my surprise," she says with a hint of curiosity in her voice.

"It's not *the* surprise, but I would like to keep where I'm taking you a mystery until we get there if you don't mind." I motion for her to turn around.

She does as I ask, and I move her hair to the side before tying the blindfold in place, her breath quickening with anticipation.

As we step outside, a gentle, warm breeze greets us, and the scent of summer fills the air. I keep her close as we walk to my black Jeep parked in the driveway.

"I'm going to help you get in the car, okay?"

She gives me a small nod, and I guide her into the passenger side, careful to make sure she doesn't hit her head. Once she's settled, I shut the door and go around to the driver's side.

"It's a ten-minute ride," I say, adjusting the mirrors. "We'll be there soon."

"Sounds good," Everly replies.

My parents own a hundred acres of land offering incredible views, and I wanted to share one with Everly tonight. We used to play in this area as kids but never ventured to this particular spot.

I take her hand in mine, intertwining our fingers as we pull away from my parents' house. We drive in peaceful silence, and I rub my thumb along Everly's palm in reassurance.

She means everything to me. From the moment I wake up to the second I fall asleep, my thoughts are consumed by her, and every decision I make, big or small, revolves around how it will affect her. Everly's happiness is my priority, and I'll take every opportunity to show her that.

By the time we reach our destination, my stomach is in knots, hoping that she'll like what I have planned.

After bringing the Jeep to a stop, I exit and help her out of the vehicle, making sure she's steady on her feet. With a hand on the small of her back, I guide her forward with careful steps.

"Can I remove the blindfold yet?" Everly asks.

"Not yet. We're almost there," I assure her.

I lead her along the path to a transparent canopy tent and gently tug the blindfold off. Everly blinks rapidly, taking in the scene as the sun sets. We're standing on a hill crest that overlooks the lake on the edge of my parents' property. A rustic wooden table is set for two, adorned with flickering candles and fresh greenery. Two plush chairs are positioned next to each other. Nearby, there's a smaller table with a food warmer holding our meal and bottles of sparkling water.

"What is all this?" She gapes at me in disbelief. "How did you make this happen? We've been together most of the day."

I wanted to remind her of the magic of Aspen Grove. The last time she came here before we were married, she spent the holidays alone. Now, I want to make new, happier memories she can associate with our hometown.

Jack brought Presley to the same spot when they first got together, but it was on Christmas morning, complete with a horse-drawn carriage. It inspired me to create my own memorable moment here with Everly.

"I had some help," I admit. "I wanted to make sure everything was perfect."

My parents were more than happy to set things up earlier, and I reached out to the owner of Willow Creek Café, whose chef was thrilled to prepare a special meal for us.

"It absolutely is," Everly says with appreciation. "Thank you, Stafford." She winds her arms around my neck and tilts her head up to kiss me.

"My pleasure, Ev," I say with a warm smile. "Why don't we sit down and enjoy the beautiful view?" I gesture toward the lake.

I pull out a chair for her, and once she's seated, I get our dinner. Under the warmer are two plates of seared salmon with lemon dill sauce, roasted garlic mashed potatoes, and grilled asparagus.

"This looks divine," Everly says when I set her plate in front of her.

I take a seat next to her, and we dig into our food as we enjoy the breathtaking view, sharing memories of when we were kids and what we love most about Aspen Grove. The sun dips below the horizon, setting the sky ablaze with vibrant orange, red, and purple hues that cast a warm glow over the tranquil lake. Fireflies emerge, their tiny lights flickering like stars in the night sky. The distant sound of crickets fills the air. It's a serene setting, one that never gets old.

Once I clear our plates, I lean over to where the drinks are set up and retrieve the individual shots of tequila and whiskey I picked up at Main Street Market earlier.

Everly gives me an amused glance as I place them on the table, her lips curling into a playful grin at the sight of the shots.

"I figured this would be a harmless way to break our streak. Don't worry, it's just a single shot. It won't lead to any impulsive decisions, like marrying your brother's best friend during a work trip in Vegas." I smirk. "To our future." I hold out my shot of whiskey, bringing it close to the shot of tequila Everly has in her hand.

Her gaze meets mine. "To our future," she echoes, knocking back her tequila in one shot and slamming the bottle down on the table when she's finished. "Now that I've had the time to gather my thoughts, I have something I want to say." She smooths her dress and turns toward me. "I've spent a lot of time thinking about us, just like you asked me to. Honestly, it's all I've been able to think about."

"And?" I press when she doesn't elaborate further.

"We have amazing chemistry, and the sex is off the charts, but that's not what defines a relationship. It dawned on me earlier that we haven't talked about the important things. What if our life goals don't align? Or we think we're on the same page but find out later that we're not?"

Everly wasn't exaggerating when she said she's been thinking about this a lot.

I cross one foot over my knee and lean back in my chair, settling into a more comfortable position. "I don't see that happening."

"We won't know until we discuss it. I'd like to ask you some questions to start."

I feel like I'm about to be grilled in a job interview, but I don't mind.

"Ask anything you want."

"Do you want kids, and if so, how many?" she asks without blinking.

"Damn, Ev, I would have brought more shots if I knew we'd be getting straight to the hard questions," I tease.

"Cash, I'm serious," she warns.

I hold my hands up in defense. "You're right. I'll take this seriously."

"Thank you," she says, tapping her foot impatiently while she waits for my response.

"I want kids with *you*," I state. "And I like the idea of having at least two so they have a built-in friend, but I'm on board with however many kids you want to have."

Frankly, I never gave the idea of having a family much thought, but when it comes to building one with Everly? The thought of her pregnant, belly swollen with our baby, makes me feral.

She chews on her lower lip, mulling over my response before moving on to her next question.

"Once the Stafford Holdings London team is fully staffed and trained, are you planning to move back to the US?"

"This is an easy answer."

"If that's the case, are you going to answer it?" she sasses.

I lean forward in my chair, taking her hands in mine, my gaze locked on her brown eyes. "Wherever you go, I go. You love London, so if that's where you want to stay, I'll be there too. Next question."

She furrows her brow. "I don't understand. What about your career?"

"I love working in the London office. It's given me the chance to be taken more seriously and venture out of my usual comfort zone."

"But I thought you were just there temporarily to get the office set up?"

"The good thing about having my brother as my boss is that he's very accommodating and will no doubt let me stay if I tell him I want to," I assure her. "I've said it before, and I'll say it again—you are the most important thing in my life, and you will always come first. It's as simple as that." I lean forward to kiss her forehead. "Now, next question," I repeat.

"Aren't you worried about what Theo or your parents will say? What if they don't understand once we tell them the full truth?"

I shake my head. "No, I'm not. Our path to each other might not have been conventional, but it brought me to you, and I wouldn't trade it for anything, regardless of what anyone else thinks. Besides, they're our family." I chuckle. "They have to love us no matter what."

Everly gives me a ghost of a smile before moving on to her next question.

"Suppose I wanted a divorce and asked to date instead. What would that look like?"

"I would hope you'd be open to living together because I don't think I could go without you in my bed," I rib her playfully. "Aside from that, we'd go on lots of dates like we're doing now, and I'd woo you until you agreed to marry me again."

"What if it takes years?"

"Then the moment you agree to be mine will be even sweeter." I brush my thumb along her hand. "Let me make one thing clear, Ev. I will wait as long as it takes and will move heaven and earth for you if I have to. Just say the word, and I'll do it. I want you in my arms for the rest of my life."

Tears flow down her cheeks, and I gather her in my arms and settle her in my lap. I cup her cheeks with my hands, wiping away the moisture with my thumbs.

"You mean every word, don't you?" She hiccups as she tries to tamp down her emotions.

"Every single one," I state with absolute conviction.

She draws in a shaky breath as she wraps her arms around my neck, gazing into my eyes. "I want this, Cash. I want you."

Time seems to stand still, everything around me fading away when I hear those sweet words pass Everly's lips.

"Do *you* mean it? Because there's no going back after this. Once you're mine, I'm never letting you go."

She rests her hand against my cheek, caressing my scar with her fingertips. "Yes, Stafford," she says as she leans in closer. "I want to be yours forever, and I want you to belong to me too."

"Haven't you been listening, Ev?" I murmur. "I already do."

30

EVERLY

THERE'S NOTHING BETTER THAN WAKING up next to the man with whom I've agreed to spend the rest of my life. Although I admit, I was a little disappointed when Cash said he was going to the gym early and a long run after that and asked me to meet him at the park across from Main Street at nine.

After lying in bed for a while, I went downstairs to find Johanna and Mike had left the house, too. So, I walked to the local yoga studio and arrived in time for their morning session.

I've just finished my class and checked my watch to see that I still have an hour before I'm supposed to meet up with Cash. I head over to Brew Haven for some coffee to pass the time.

As I walk down the street, I notice Harrison coming from the opposite direction. His face is set in a stern expression as he types on his phone. He's dressed in jeans and a white T-shirt that looks to be covered in white and gray paint.

That's odd.

Cash didn't mention Harrison's plans to visit Aspen Grove this weekend, and he wasn't at the Staffords' house for lunch yesterday. As far as I know, he doesn't own property in town. And even if he did, the CEO of a multibillion-dollar real estate firm doesn't strike me as someone who would do their own painting or any manual labor.

"Hey, Harrison," I call out as he gets closer.

He glances up, and his expression softens when he notices me waving at him. "Hi, Everly. What are you doing up so early on a Sunday morning?"

"I could ask you the same thing," I say as he comes to a stop in front of me. "Cash didn't tell me you'd be in town this weekend."

He hesitates for a moment before saying, "Uh, yeah, I got here a couple of hours ago."

"How long are you here for?"

"My flight leaves this afternoon. I had to handle a few urgent matters here before heading to New York for an early meeting tomorrow."

I nod, refraining from asking about his peculiar appearance.

It is odd that he's only in town for a few hours, especially since he doesn't plan to see his family while he's here, as far as I know. I'm surprised Johanna doesn't insist he stay, but then again, maybe she doesn't know he's here. Regardless, I'm sure he has his reasons.

"Listen, do you have a few minutes?" he asks. "I'd like to talk with you if you don't mind." He nods toward Brew Haven.

"Sure, I was going to order a protein shake for Cash and a coffee for myself. He said he was going on a long run, so I have some time to kill until he gets here."

Harrison holds the door open for me, and we step inside. After placing our order, and picking up our drinks we grab a table near the front.

"So, what did you want to talk about?" I ask, tracing my finger around the edge of my coffee cup.

"How's work going?" he questions. "We might not be able to talk about the specifics of the pending acquisition, but overall, how do you like working at Townstead International?"

"Honestly, aside from the fact that I work for my dad, I love my job. Things have been challenging lately because he's been more irritable, probably because of the Stafford Holdings deal. He tends to take it out on me and my step-siblings," I explain as I sip coffee. "He hasn't been to London since the day he showed up at Cash's office, but that hasn't stopped him from inundating us with impossible amounts of work."

My dad's emails and phone calls have become more terse in the past week, and we've all been waiting for the inevitable fallout.

"How did Liam and August take the news about the acquisition?" Harrison asks.

"They have reservations about it," I tell him honestly. "For all they know, your team is planning to fire them or will micromanage every project they're working on like my dad does. But I assured them you weren't like that."

"I appreciate your confidence. All I can say for now is that big changes are coming to Townstead International. Positive changes," he adds, sensing my apprehension.

I give him a quizzical look. "How long until the deal is signed?"

"Off the record, we're looking at two weeks." He runs a hand through his hair. "We've had to speed up the timeline because of some unforeseen circumstances."

"I see." My gut tells me the fast-tracked timeline has something to do with my father.

At the same time, a wave of relief washes over me. The looming deadline has lost its significance. Yesterday, my marriage had an undisclosed expiration date. Now, it signifies the start of a new chapter in my life.

"Everly, I meant it when I said that Dylan and I will support you and Cash no matter what. You'll have a place at Townstead International as long as you want it. If I thought I could convince you to work at Stafford Holdings, I'd hire you to work directly for me."

I shake my head. "I would never leave Liam and August. We're a team, and I wouldn't want to work with anyone else."

"That's what I thought." He drums his finger on the tabletop as he glances at me, then back down at his coffee.

I'm surprised at how easy it is to confide in Harrison. He comes off as stern and reserved, but beneath that exterior, he's empathetic and caring.

"You don't have to worry about Cash and me," I say.

He raises a brow. "Oh, and why is that?"

"We've decided to stay together," I share with a beaming smile. "We're not pretending anymore."

He sighs in relief, and a pleased look spreads across his face. "Thank god it worked."

I tilt my head. "You were hoping we'd stay together?"

He nods. "I knew you and Cash would be in Vegas at the same time. During a call with our lawyers, your dad mentioned you were there for business."

"And?" I ask with a curious stare.

"I sent Cash to take my place at the board meeting, hoping he'd run into you. There was no guarantee he would, but I coordinated the time of the meeting based on your agenda that I got from Richard's assistant to ensure you'd both end your day at the same time and be at the same hotel."

"Why did you want us to meet up?"

"Because he's been hung up on you since high school. He's worn that bracelet for fourteen years, and his face lit up anytime anyone mentioned your name. I couldn't let the opportunity pass for the two of you to reconnect."

"Why not suggest a casual meetup in London like old friends?"

"Oh, don't worry. I had a contingency plan to bring you two together after the acquisition if the Vegas meetup didn't happen. I never expected you'd end up getting hitched and turn up to Aspen Grove as a married couple. I wasn't lying about the complications of getting an annulment in the middle of the acquisition, but we would have managed."

While I process his confession, he takes a drink of his latte before continuing. "My main priority was your and Cash's happiness. Even when you were bickering, there was an undeniable spark between you two. You just needed a nudge in the right direction."

"And encouraging us to stay married was considered a *nudge*?" I ask with a raised brow.

"In my world, yes."

I blink at him, stunned by this revelation. Harrison Stafford is the last person I'd have expected to play Cupid. Seems like, deep down, he's still the teddy bear big brother he was back in high school.

I recline in my chair. "Damn, Harrison, I never would have pegged you for a matchmaker."

"That title belongs to my mother," he grumbles.

"Whatever you say." I hide my knowing smile behind my cup. "You better watch out."

"For what?"

"Cash told me all about how Johanna has meddled in your siblings' relationships. Who's to say she won't have a hand in yours?"

"Who's to say she didn't have a hand in *yours?*" he challenges.

I point at him. "You just admitted that you practically orchestrated my run-in with Cash. Besides, she doesn't know our marriage isn't real."

Even though Cash and I have decided to stay together, I'm not looking forward to coming clean to Johanna and Mike that our marriage was fake from the start.

"Nothing gets past my mom. *Ever.*" Harrison rolls his coffee cup between his palms. "Just because I was involved, doesn't mean she didn't play a role in it."

I think back to Johanna's comment about not leaving things up to chance. There's no way she was talking about Cash and me. Is there?

I shake my head. "Regardless, you're next." I can't help but taunt him.

He smirks, folding his arms across his chest. "If she can find someone who can tolerate a man who spends twenty hours a day running a multibillion-dollar company and is hardly ever home, I give her props."

"Well, if we can't find you a wife, maybe we can find you a new personal chef. Cash mentioned that yours is quitting. I spoke to Fallon the other day, the private chef who's been cooking our meals, and she said she's interested in applying for the position. She's moving to New York, but I think she could be persuaded to travel between there and your penthouse at Stafford Holdings headquarters."

"Thanks." Harrison nods in appreciation. "Have Cash send her information to my assistant, and she'll set up a phone interview."

"Will do."

We spend the next hour talking about life growing up in a small town, and by the time I remember to check my phone I see that it's 9:05 a.m. "Oh, shoot, I'm late to meet Cash."

"No problem. I've got to get going anyway." Harrison stands and takes our empty drink containers to the trash.

On our way out we stop by the pickup station to grab Cash's protein shake that I had them wait to make.

When we step outside of Brew Haven, Main Street is bustling with residents enjoying a beautiful Sunday morning.

I spot Cash stretching at the park across the street, sweat dripping down his forehead. He's got on a baseball cap, black shorts, and running shoes, and predictably he's shirtless.

Harrison rolls his eyes. "He's such a show-off. In this town, going shirtless is bound to get people talking."

"Well then, I better go over there and give them something worthwhile to talk about," I say with a wink. "Did you want to come over and say hi to him?"

"Nah, there's one more errand I have to run before I take off."

"Okay, thanks for the chat, Harrison."

"Anytime, Everly. I'm really glad you're my sister-my-law."

"Me too."

He gives me a small wave before pulling out his phone and walking away, his expression turning serious again as he disappears around the corner.

I cross the street to join Cash, and he looks up as I approach, a megawatt smile on his face. He stands up straight and closes the gap between us, winding his arm around my waist and cradling my head with his hand.

"I missed you." He grabs my jaw, pressing his mouth to mine in an obscene kiss.

"Mmm," I moan softly. "You remember we're in a public place, right?" I glance around at several onlookers giving us the side-eye.

"They're going to gossip either way."

"I like your way of thinking, Stafford." I rise on my toes to give him another kiss. We're in our own private bubble, two souls ignited by a mutual love for one another, the outside world forgotten.

When Cash finally breaks away, I'm left breathless.

"What do you have there?" He motions to the drink in my hand. Thankfully, I didn't drop it during our impromptu make-out session.

"It's for you." I hand him the green protein shake.

"Thanks, Ev." He grins and ushers me over to a nearby park bench. "I saw you in front of the coffee shop with Harrison, but didn't want to interrupt."

"Did you know he was in town?"

He taps his fingers against his cup, avoiding my gaze.

"I know we said no more secrets, and I'll tell you this one. Tomorrow."

I narrow my eyes at him. "Is this a trick?"

He shakes his head. "No tricks." He leans in to kiss my temple. "It's part of your surprise. You'll see soon enough, I promise."

"I can't wait."

I'm looking forward to whatever *it* may be.

31

CASH

I'M ON CLOUD NINE. THIS trip to Aspen Grove has exceeded all my exceptions so far. As long as tomorrow goes well and Everly reacts the way I think she will when I show her what I've been working on.

After meeting her this morning, we stopped by my parents' house to change out of our workout clothes. Then spent the day browsing the shops in town, before catching a matinee showing of a new rom-com she's been wanting to see. After, we grabbed an early dinner at Willow Creek Café, we came back to my parents' house. They're at Dylan's, so we have the place to ourselves.

Just as I'm about to join Everly for a bath, my phone rings. I have every intention of ignoring it until I see that it's Harrison.

I poke my head in the bathroom. "Harrison is calling me. I should probably answer."

"Okay. You'll just have to make it up to me later." She winks.

"I'm going to take the call outside. I'll be right back."

I leave the room and head downstairs.

"Hey, Harrison," I say as I accept the call. "How was your flight to New York?" I step out the front door, closing it behind me.

"Good. I just landed," he responds.

I can hear the faint sound of typing in the background, which means he's likely catching up on emails he missed during the flight.

"I'm glad to hear it. Before we get to the reason you're calling, do you have anything you want to tell me?" I goad him.

He lets out a heavy sigh. "Let me guess, Everly told you about my part in getting you two together?"

"She did," I confirm.

Everly filled me on our way home earlier. It makes more sense that it was coordinated, considering Harrison rarely misses a board meeting and had never asked me to go in his place before.

"Was Dylan in on it too?"

"No, he wasn't." He leaves it at that. "You're welcome for me distracting her this morning. She probably found it strange that I was walking around town in paint-splattered clothes. Funny how you escaped without a single drop on you."

"I was meeting Everly after," I say defensively. "If I had been covered in paint, she definitely would've asked about it."

"Whatever you say." There's a hint of humor in his voice.

"Thanks again for flying in to help."

I ran into an issue with the surprise I'm working on for Everly, and my parents and brothers saved the day. We ran out of paint halfway through our project, and Harrison and I went to Brush & Palette for more. I wasn't expecting to see Everly in town that early, but thankfully, I spotted her before she saw us, allowing me to stay out of sight.

"No problem. I had another urgent matter to take care of in Aspen Grove, so it worked out that I was there today."

I'm intrigued by what this *urgent matter* is, but more curious about why he called.

"What did you want to talk about?" I ask, taking a seat on the porch swing.

"I know we agreed to keep you out of the acquisition as much as possible, but I wanted to loop you in." He pauses, and I hear a car door open and close. "After Dylan's team found those inconsistencies in the books, I hired a private investigator to dig into Richard's activities. It turns out the bastard has been manipulating his financial records and embezzling millions annually. I think that's why he handed the European division over to his stepsons and Everly—he kept his illegal activities stateside so he could operate without interference." Harrison's tone is sharp and biting. If there's one thing he hates, it's being lied to, followed closely by anyone who dares to mess with his family or business. Richard has done both.

"That son of a bitch," I scoff, clenching my fist at my side.

That explains his erratic behavior on the day he stopped by my office. He must have thought he could slip under the radar and panicked when our team wanted a closer look at his records.

"Dylan's department meticulously reviewed Townstead's financials again, and their US division is hemorrhaging money. The only thing keeping them afloat is the profitability of the European division, thanks to Everly, Liam, and August."

I fidget with my bracelet, thinking through the possible next steps Harrison might take. "What's the plan moving forward? The board won't let you buy the company once they find out about this."

"I'm not telling them. I paid the private investigator cash, operating under a pseudonym. He thinks I'm Richard's estranged son, digging up dirt on dear old dad." He lets out a low chuckle. "As far as the board is concerned, everything is on the up-and-up."

"Why would you do that? You could end up in serious trouble."

Harrison is a stickler for the rules, so I'm shocked by his uncharacteristic behavior, especially with millions of dollars on the line.

"Everly is family, and we protect our own," he states matter-of-factly. "I've seen firsthand the results of her work, and I will not risk her job because her dad's a criminal. She's not reporting to him any longer than necessary, especially when it risks dragging her down with him."

I let out a low whistle. "You're really embracing your role as protective big brother, huh?"

"You'd do the same for Presley or Marlow."

"Damn right, I would," I say. "So, what's the plan?"

"Like I told Everly this morning, we're accelerating the process. What I didn't tell her is that once the deal is inked, Richard's out. There's nothing in his contract that states we have to keep him on. If the board uncovers his shady dealings down the line, they can pursue legal action. For now, my priority is removing him from the company while there's still time to repair the damage he's done."

Given how Richard has treated her over the years, I doubt Everly will lose any sleep over it when he finally faces the consequences of his actions.

"What about Everly and her step-brothers?"

"They'll be in charge of the entire operation. Yes, they'll have to answer to Stafford Holdings, but the day-to-day oversight will be minimal. They've already proven they can do it, so I have full confidence in their abilities."

Everly will thrive on having more influence on shaping the overarching vision of the company alongside August and Liam, and I couldn't be happier for her. But then I remember my promise to her—not to keep secrets. There's no chance I can hold off on sharing this with her.

"How long until the closing meeting? I can't keep this from Everly," I explain.

"Two weeks, tops. Tell her there are details we can't disclose until everything is finalized. I'm confident she'll understand."

"I hope you're right," I mumble.

"I always am," he snarks. "I'm assuming this means you'll want to stay in London after this is all over?"

"I'm not leaving my wife." When I told Everly I'd follow her anywhere, I meant it. I had planned to have this conversation with Harrison later, but I guess now is as good a time as any.

"Good, because I need someone I can trust to oversee operations there. I've been impressed with your performance lately and have confidence that you can take this on. Our team in London holds you in high regard, so I'm sure they'll be thrilled about your decision to stay." I puff my chest out when hearing his compliment. "From a professional perspective, this is a fantastic opportunity, and as your brother, I couldn't be more proud of you. I'm glad you're so happy and that you and Everly finally got together."

"Thanks, man, I appreciate it. Now it's your turn," I tease.

It's hard to believe he's the last sibling standing without a partner. My brothers and I used to joke about never settling down, yet here we are. I have a hunch my mom is plotting how to change Harrison's relationship status as we speak.

"We'll see," he says, not fazed by my comment. "I have to go, but good luck tomorrow. You're going to need it," he teases in a playful tone.

"Bye, Harrison," I say, ending the call.

After our conversation, I'm looking forward to the future more than ever before. I'm married to the woman of my dreams, and can't wait to show her what it means to be mine for the rest of her life. And I'm fortunate to have a family that supports me unconditionally.

Now, all that's left for me to do is come clean to my parents and Theo about why Everly and I stayed married and propose to my wife. Although, not necessarily in that particular order.

I go up to the bedroom and find Everly sitting on the bed, working on her computer.

"Everything okay?" she asks. "Did Harrison get to New York safely?"

"Yeah, he's fine." I pause, considering my next words carefully. "He told me some things about the acquisition but asked me to hold off on sharing the details with you. He wants to meet with you, Liam, and August when he's ready to close the deal." I hold my breath, waiting for her response.

"Cash, it's okay. I can wait, but I appreciate you telling me." She offers me a reassuring smile. "And that's great news. It'll mean a lot to Liam and August to get the chance to speak with Harrison directly."

She looks back at her computer as she types away, and I observe her closer. She's wearing black shorts and a hot-pink tank top. Her dark hair cascades down her back in waves, and her brown eyes shimmer with happiness. She's become more carefree and vibrant over the past couple of months, and I'm lucky that she's comfortable sharing this side of herself with me.

It's still hard to believe that she told me she wants to be mine forever. Never in my wildest dreams did I think I'd be this lucky. There are three little words I've been waiting for the right moment to say, but I can't hold them in any longer.

"I love you, Ev." The admission falls effortlessly from my lips.

For a while I wasn't sure if that's what this emotion was, but as I look at her now, there's no doubt in my mind that I love her and would shout it from the rooftop if she asked me to.

Everly snaps her head up, her eyes wide in disbelief. "What did you say?" Her voice is barely above a whisper.

My heart pounds as I join her on the bed and take her laptop, setting it on the nightstand.

I gently lift her chin, meeting her mesmerizing brown gaze. "I'm in love with you," I say again, brushing a piece of hair from her face and tucking it behind her ear. "I love you so damn much, and I'm sorry it took me so long to tell you. You're my world, Ev, and there is no future without you in it."

She places her hand over mine as a single tear trickles down her face. "I love you, too, Stafford."

I heave a sigh of relief. "Thank god. I didn't have a contingency plan if you didn't say it back," I tease.

She smiles. "It's lucky I saved you from having to come up with one, then."

I lean in to press kisses along her collarbone. A soft moan passes her lips as I lick along her neck, rubbing my nose along her cheek and pausing when I get close to her mouth.

"Tell me you love me again," I coax her.

"I. Love. You." She enunciates each word as she sinks her slender fingers into my hair and tugs me closer.

I wrap my arm around her waist, tugging her onto my lap to straddle me and plunge my tongue past her lips, ravishing her mouth. I don't stop until she's a blazing inferno of blissful agony, pleading for more.

She belongs to me, and I plan to dote on her with love and affection for the rest of our lives.

I slip my hand inside her sleep shorts, teasing her entrance. "Fuck, Ev, you're drenched. Is this all for me?"

She lifts her hips as I shove two fingers inside her, the crude sound of her arousal filling the room. It's sexy as hell as she shamelessly grinds against the palm of my hand. She gasps when I plunge a third finger inside, increasing my pace.

"I need to come," she whimpers.

"Be a good girl and beg me for it," I taunt with a wicked grin.

"You're so infuriating." She groans as I tease her clit with my thumb.

"It's part of my charming personality," I quip. "Now beg me to come, wifey."

She gazes at me with hooded eyes. "Please make me come all over your fingers, Stafford." She plasters her body to mine, deliriously desperate to find a release that's just out of reach. "Pretty please," she asks as she bats her eyelashes.

"That's a start," I say, grabbing the bottom of her tank top and pulling it over her head to reveal her full breasts.

"Fuck, these are perfect."

I pinch one of her nipples, and it hardens beneath my fingertips. I eagerly suck it into my mouth, biting down on the soft flesh.

"Fuck," Everly cries out.

I switch to her other breast, giving it the same treatment. Her moans echo throughout the room as she welcomes the flash of pain I give with every bite to her sensitive nipples. She clings to me like I'm her anchor, and I revel in her closeness. Her arousal soaks my hand while I thrust my thick fingers in and out of her cunt. She's burning with need as I bring her to the edge again, pulling back just when she reaches the cusp of finding her release.

"Cash, I'm close," she pants.

"You want to come on my hand or my cock?"

"Your cock, always your cock," Her eyes flame with lust.

Damn, Everly is going to be the death of me.

And I don't mind one damn bit.

"Show me how much you want it, beautiful."

Her gaze never leaves mine as she lifts to take off her sleep shorts and panties, tossing them to the floor. When she settles back on my lap, she unfastens my pants. I let out a sharp hiss when she pulls out my shaft, guiding me to her entrance. She rubs the tip of my dick against her in teasing strokes.

"Fuck, Ev," I growl.

Unable to restrain myself a second longer, I grip her waist, shoving her down onto my cock, pushing to the hilt in a single thrust. Her pussy clenches around me at the intrusion and she grabs ahold of my shoulders, her nails digging into my skin as our intermingled groans fill the room.

"Holy shit. You feel incredible."

I hold her steady as she bounces on my dick, arching her back with every thrust. I'm bewitched, cherishing being hers in every sense.

"God, I feel so full," Everly cries out.

I slant my mouth across hers, kissing her fervently as I buck my hips in time with hers, picking up our pace. "You ready to come with me?"

"I've been ready forever," she cries.

I chuckle at her impatience before pinching her clit, sending her careening off the edge. I roar as ecstasy surges through me at the beautiful sight of Everly unraveling. I hold her tight as we ride out our orgasms together.

IF YOU GIVE A BILLIONAIRE A BRIDE

"Damn, you're such a good wife, coming on my cock like that." I nuzzle my nose into her neck, inhaling her scent.

I carefully lift her off me, not wanting to cause her pain.

We lie down, and she absentmindedly strokes my chest as she looks up at me.

"Stafford?"

"Yeah?"

"I'm really glad we got married."

"So am I."

"I think you're my soulmate," she murmurs so softly I almost miss it.

"You're mine too," I whisper.

I think back to the day we made our marriage pact in high school, and am struck by how my perspective has evolved. Back then, I believed I could only be Everly's court jester, tolerated only because of my sense of humor and carefree attitude. Now I understand that our paths were always destined to intertwine, brought together by fate despite the odds stacked against us. I'm determined to be her prince, her knight in shining armor, or anything else she wants me to be, just as long as I'm hers.

32

CASH

I WAKE UP TO PERSISTENT knocking. Sitting up, I see Everly is still asleep. The sound seems to be coming from downstairs. I throw on a pair of sweatpants and a T-shirt and go investigate, hoping to stop the noise before it wakes Everly and my parents.

When I open the front door, I'm stunned to find Theo standing on the front porch. I spoke to him on Friday to let him know I was taking Everly to Aspen Grove, and he said he was scheduled to visit one of his restaurants in New York this weekend.

"Hey, what are you doing he—"

"Where's Everly, I need to talk to her," he interrupts, pushing his way inside the house.

"Theo?" Everly's voice catches my attention.

She's standing at the top of the stairs, rubbing the sleep from her eyes. There's a faint smudge of mascara underneath them, and her hair is tousled. Thank god she put on a pair of gray sweats to go with my Linkin Park T-shirt before she came out of the bedroom.

"Can I talk to you in private?" Theo asks.

Everly comes down the stairs to join us. "What's wrong? I thought you were in New York."

"This is a conversation that we needed to have in person," Theo states, refusing to look at me.

What the hell is his problem?

Everly frowns. "Does it concern Cash?"

Theo nods. "Yeah."

"In that case, he's not leaving," Everly says, folding her arms across her chest.

I'm not particularly looking forward to being in the middle of their sibling showdown, but I like the idea of Everly wanting me here.

Theo runs his hands through his hair. "Richard called late last night and left me a five-minute voicemail. I thought it was a producer calling me back, and was surprised when I heard his voice. The last time we spoke was the day he walked out on Mom. I'm not even sure how he got my phone number."

"What did he want?" Everly asks.

"Between the shouting and colorful language, it was hard to follow his message. From what I did understand, he claims Cash married you because Stafford Holdings is acquiring Townstead International and is using your marriage as leverage for a better deal."

That fucking bastard.

Richard's erratic behavior makes it clear he's in a downward spiral. I wonder if he got wind of Harrison's private investigator, or at the very least, is worried that we're going to pull out of the deal because of the information his team was forced to hand over. It doesn't make sense that he would reach out to Theo after all these years. If anything, telling him would incentivize us *not* to do business with Richard. The problem is that he's not thinking rationally right now. He's in a panic and grasping at straws.

I'm counting down the days until he's out of Everly's life for good.

"Why didn't you call me?" she asks Theo.

"Like I said, this isn't something I wanted to talk about over the phone. I had to make sure you're okay," Theo explains, casting me a sideways glance.

"Is there something you want to say to me, Theo?" I interject.

It was only a matter of time until he found out about the acquisition and that it was the reason Everly and I stayed married in the beginning. Though I would have preferred Richard not be the catalyst and to have this conversation somewhere other than my parents' entryway.

"Did you lie to me about your feelings for Everly? Is it true you married her because of a business deal?" he mutters through gritted teeth.

"Everything I told you was true. Everly and I were tipsy and made an impulsive decision to get married in Vegas."

"Is Stafford Holdings buying out Townstead International?"

"Yes."

Theo's eyes darken, and he steps toward me. Before he can get too close, Everly steps between us, placing her hand on his chest.

"Cash and I planned on getting an annulment," she says calmly. "I found out about the acquisition the day after we got married. Harrison and Dylan warned us that the optics would look bad if we didn't stay together, and Dad threatened to fire me if I didn't wait until after the deal was finished to dissolve our marriage." Everly's voice softens toward the end.

Her recount of how things started between us makes me wince. It's painful to think our marriage started out as happenstance, followed by an unwanted arrangement. We've come a long way since then, and the notion of losing her sends a wave of panic through me.

Theo clenches his fists at his side, staring daggers at me. "So, Cash used you?" he questions warily.

Everly shakes her head vehemently. "No, he didn't. If anything, I used him. He was doing me a favor so Dad wouldn't fire me, and he's been nothing but supportive since," she states boldly. "What you saw when you visited our apartment was genuine," she adds. "I love Cash."

A rush of warmth crashes over me as her words sink in. This is the first time she's openly shared her feelings for me with someone else, and despite the circumstances, I'm elated to hear her heartfelt declaration.

Theo's eyebrows knit together, attempting to make sense of Everly's statement.

"Why didn't you tell me the truth?" he asks, his voice betraying his hurt.

"I was embarrassed about my impulsive decision to get married, and after finding out about the acquisition, I was worried you'd try to intervene if you found out."

"Damn right I would have." He sidesteps around her, shoving a finger in my chest. "How the hell could you let this happen? You were supposed to protect her."

"I did protect her. From your dad. That's one of the main reasons we decided against getting an annulment, so he wouldn't—"

"What is going on here?" a loud voice booms, cutting me off. "Theo, what are you doing here so early?"

We all look over to find my parents standing in the hallway. My dad is behind my mom, his hands resting on her shoulders, and she wears an unreadable expression. Based on their demeanor, it's obvious they overheard our conversation.

Fuck, this is not how I wanted them to find out.

Theo takes a step back, running his hand through his hair. "Maybe I should leave," he suggests.

My mom puts her hands on her hips. "Oh, I don't think so. From what we just heard, it sounds like you and Cash need to talk this out." She waves between Theo and me. "I won't stand by and watch your friendship fall apart because of a misunderstanding."

"I couldn't agree more," Everly chimes in. "The two of you should talk this out, and once you're done, we'll finish our conversation," she says to Theo.

"Well, you heard the women. Get moving," my dad orders when neither of us makes the first move.

It's like we're teenagers again as we shuffle down the hall toward the kitchen under my parents' watchful gaze. Everly lingers in the hallway, her expression impossible to decipher.

I settle into a chair at the island, drumming my fingers against the kitchen counter. Theo sits next to me, tapping his foot against the floor as he shoots me a disapproving glare.

"Why are you looking at me like that?" I mutter.

"I'm calculating how many punches I could throw before Everly and your parents intervene," he deadpans.

I turn my head so he can see the left side of my face. "Go ahead," I say, spurring him on.

He glares at me. "This isn't a game. You were my best friend, and you stabbed me in the back."

I roll my eyes. "I *am* your best friend."

"Newsflash—a friend doesn't marry your sister and keep important details about said marriage a secret."

I meet his hostile glare, swallowing hard. "Theo, I understand you're upset, but Everly specifically asked me not to tell you about the acquisition," I explain, my tone apologetic yet firm. "You're my best friend, but she's my wife. I couldn't betray her trust, even if it meant disappointing you. I hope you can understand where I'm coming from."

He narrows his eyes. "None of this would have happened if you had stayed away from Everly like I asked you to."

"That was over fifteen years ago. We're adults now, and a lot has changed since then. I'm sorry for hurting you, but I wouldn't change anything. She's the best thing to ever happen to me."

"Have either of you been with anyone else since you've been together?"

"Fuck no."

"What happens when the deal is finalized? Are you getting divorced?" His gaze bores into mine.

"No," I state.

"Why not?"

I take a deep breath as I feel my patience wear thin. Theo has every right to be angry, but it doesn't sit well that he's questioning my commitment to Everly.

"Because she is my entire world. This might have started out as an arrangement, but it's turned into the real deal. I love her, and by some stroke of luck, she loves me too."

Theo slumps back into his seat. "Damn, I never thought I'd see this possessive side of you."

"Everly's the only one who brings out this side of me. I'd do anything for her."

"Does this mean I flew in from New York for nothing?" Theo asks.

"It's a short flight. It would have been more impressive if you came from London," I retort. "Since you're here, I do have something important I want to ask you."

I glance toward the hallway to make sure Everly is out of earshot. "I'm going to ask Everly to marry me today. Since you're the most important person in her life, aside from me, of course."—I shoot him a smirk—"I want to get your blessing."

There's no chance in hell I would ever ask Richard. He doesn't deserve a say in his daughter's personal life, so it only seems fitting that I ask Theo instead.

"You're already married," he reminds me.

"I'm asking her properly this time."

"And what if she says no?"

"Then I'll keep asking until she says yes." I grin.

Although I have it on good authority that she won't. She told me she loves me and wants to spend the rest of her life with me. I'm hoping that means she's open to staying married, too. There's only one way to find out.

"I'm tempted to say no just to mess with you, but I think Everly would disown me if I did." Theo holds his hand up before I can reply. "But under no circumstances are you allowed to call me your brother," he warns.

I give him a sly smile. "Whatever you say, *brother*," I say, unable to help myself. "We're all made up now," I holler down the hall, not giving Theo a chance to respond.

In a matter of seconds, Everly rushes into the room, her eyes darting between Theo and me. My mom follows close behind, wearing a frown on her face, and my dad comes in last with an unreadable expression.

"I apologize for showing up to your house unannounced," Theo says to my parents. "And I'm sorry for worrying you, Everly." He gets up to give her a hug. "I just want to make sure that you're happy."

"I am," she says, smiling. "We should have been open with you from the start, and Cash and I have learned that withholding information from our families is never a good idea."

I couldn't have said it better myself. Ultimately, Everly and our families are what matter most. Secrets don't stay hidden forever, and honesty is the best policy moving forward.

"Mom, I'm sorry for not telling you and Dad sooner," I say, fixing my eyes on the floor between us. "When I saw how excited you were about me getting married, I couldn't bring myself to tell you that Everly and I were planning on getting an annulment. But then everything changed. Once we got back to London and spent more time together, our feelings for each other grew into something more."

Mom shakes her head. "Oh, sweetheart, did you honestly think you could deceive your mother? I knew your marriage was a sham on the day of family pictures."

My jaw drops open, and I stare at her in disbelief. "How is that even possible?"

"Let's just call it mother's intuition," Mom says, giving me a pat on the cheek.

"Did you forget your mother has a habit of leaving the windows open during the summer?" my dad interjects. "If you're in the living room and it's quiet enough, you can catch everything said out on the porch."

Unbelievable. She must have thought she was so clever, making Everly and me pose for photos even though she knew we weren't actually together at the time. This woman has no boundaries when it comes to meddling in her kids' love lives.

"I did no such thing," my mom scolds my dad.

"Sure, Mom, whatever you say," I add, rolling my eyes.

Between her and Harrison, Everly and I never stood a chance at getting out of this marriage, and I wouldn't change a thing.

Harrison is in serious trouble. As the last single sibling, Mom will definitely be on his case to find a wife. I can't wait to sit back with a bowl of popcorn and watch the drama unfold. His workaholic nature has always gotten in the way of his dating life, and whoever ends up with him will have her hands full.

"I don't want to be rude, especially since Theo flew in from New York, but Cash, don't you and Everly have plans this morning?" My mom taps her watch for emphasis.

"We do?" Everly asks, turning me for confirmation.

"Johanna's right," Theo agrees, shooting me a knowing glance. "You lovebirds should get moving. I have to be back to New York for an event this afternoon and need to leave now if I'm going to make it in time."

Everly gives him a puzzled look. "You flew all the way to Aspen Grove for a short conversation?"

"I would do anything for you, sis," Theo says, pulling her in for another hug and kissing her on the temple. "I love you. Once we're both back in London, come to the restaurant in London and I'll cook for you. Fallon might think she's better, but we both know the truth." He winks.

"What about me? Am I invited?" I tease.

"Depends on how the next hour goes."

"What is he talking about?" Everly asks, looking between us.

"You'll find out soon enough," Johanna interjects with a smile as she ushers us toward the front door.

Here goes nothing.

33

EVERLY

"WHERE ARE WE GOING?" I ask Cash, my curiosity getting the better of me.

"It's a surprise, remember?" Fortunately, I convinced Johanna that I couldn't leave the house in Cash's T-shirt and sweats, so I managed to get changed. I'm wearing a white summer dress and light blue open-toed heels.

Even though it didn't happen the way I wanted, it's a relief that Cash's parents and Theo know everything. It feels like a weight has been lifted off my shoulders, and it means so much to have their support as Cash and I move forward in this next chapter.

Cash drives to the outskirts of town, and my heart skips a beat when he pulls up to the old Miller property. Aside from the location, it's unrecognizable. A pang of sadness hits me when I realize someone must have bought the place and fixed it up, wishing it could have been me.

The previously overgrown yard, littered with debris, has undergone a remarkable transformation. Now, there's a neatly trimmed lawn and vibrant flower beds.

The house is painted white, with a black door and shutters, and the wraparound porch has been reconstructed with wooden beams and stained a rich mahogany. I'm speechless when I spot the white porch swing on the side of the house, just like I described to Cash.

"What are we doing here?" I gesture toward the house.

"Why don't we go inside and find out?"

Cash steps out of the car and walks around to my side. He opens the door and extends his hand to help me out. I let him lead me to the house, trembling with a mixture of nerves and excitement.

When he opens the front door, I gasp. The interior looks like it was lifted straight from the pages of *Architectural Digest*, with the perfect blend of farmhouse charm and modern elegance. The walls are freshly painted a light gray with white trim, complimenting the rustic wooden beams stretch across the ceiling.

The open-concept living room flows seamlessly into the kitchen, which has marble countertops and stainless-steel appliances. A sliding barn door opens into a pantry, and a farmhouse table in the corner, with a vase of daffodils in the middle. This place is better than anything I could have ever dreamed of.

"Why don't you go check out the upstairs?" Cash suggests.

"Okay." I smile, not waiting another second to explore the rest of the house.

The primary bedroom has hardwood flooring, walls painted robin blue, and crown molding on the ceiling. The en-suite has marble floors and a large soaking tub. There are twin vanity sinks with granite countertops. And the spacious walk-in closet has ample storage, including a full wall for shoes.

In addition to the primary suite, there are two more bedrooms with a Jack and Jill bathroom in between.

At the end of the hall, there is a small set of stairs leading to the loft. The door is ajar, and I gasp when I peek inside. It's been transformed into a cozy reading room, with built-in bookshelves lining the walls and a floor-to-ceiling window letting in natural light. Dozens of vases filled with daffodils decorate the room's perimeter.

I twirl around, taking it all in before looking through the window into the backyard. The grass is freshly cut, and a tire swing now hangs from the old oak tree at the edge of the property.

My attention is drawn to the two rows of vases, brimming with daffodils, that create a pathway leading to the center of the yard where Cash stands, in the same spot we made our marriage pact fourteen years ago. He looks up with a grin and motions for me to join him.

I hurry down the two flights of stairs as best I can in four-inch heels and exit through the back door of the kitchen. As I step outside, I can't help but feel a flutter of anticipation in my chest. The way he's looking at me with that familiar sparkle in his eyes, makes my heart race.

"What did you think of the rest of the house?" he asks when I reach his side.

"It's incredible. How did you manage to get it done while you've been in London?"

"I hired a contractor to expedite the remodel, and he had a large crew working on the place around the clock," he says.

"By chance did Harrison help you paint yesterday morning?"

"Yeah, he did." He smiles wryly. "The painter had a family emergency and couldn't finish the living room. We couldn't find a replacement in time, so my family stepped in to assist the crew."

Now it makes sense why Harrison was covered in paint when I ran into him and why he didn't offer an explanation.

"How long has this project been underway?"

"Since the day we got back to London," he admits.

I furrow my brow in confusion. "I don't understand."

"It's yours, Ev," Cash grins. "I ran past the place the morning after we took family photos and saw that it was for sale. It took me back to the day we made our marriage pact here, and I knew then that it belonged to you. When you told me about your plans for the place, we were able to make several modifications to match what you had in mind." He takes hold of my hands, and gives them a gentle squeeze. "We might not plan on living in Aspen Grove full time, but I want us to have a place to call our own when we visit. A retreat where we can relax and recharge away from the hustle and bustle of London."

"You bought me a house." My voice is barely above a whisper. "Not just any house, but the one I've dreamed of fixing up since I was a kid. I'm speechless," I admit, overwhelmed by the gravity of his gesture.

"Hold on, don't say anything yet." He nods to my ring. "I need to borrow that for a minute."

I give him a wary glance as I slip the ring off and place it in his waiting palm.

My breath hitches when he drops to one knee, taking my hands in his.

"Everly, I love you." His gaze meets mine, his hazel eyes brimming with devotion. "Most couples fall in love first before getting married, but we're the exception. We got married first, and the love part came later. Although a part of me has loved you since we were kids. I knew we were meant to be together the day we made that pact, but I never envisioned it would lead to this." He gestures around us.

"We're going to have it all—a house to call our own, or rather, houses." He chuckles as he gives my hands a reassuring squeeze. "Lazy weekends snuggled up on the couch, adventures traveling the world, and arguments followed by mind-blowing make-up sex. And every morning, I'll wake up with you in my arms, wondering how I got to be the luckiest man in the world."

Tears blur my vision as my heart overflows with love for him.

"Everly Stafford, will you do me the honor of marrying me… again," he asks, a nervous smile playing on his lips as he waits for my response.

I nod rapidly, unable to contain my excitement.

"Yes," I exclaim, throwing my arms around him in a tight embrace.

He slips my ring back onto my finger, his hand shaking slightly.

Cash has achieved the impossible. Just like he saw promise in the old Miller house, he recognized the same in me, by transforming my perspective, showing me how to cherish each moment, and to rediscover how to trust and love again.

"I love you, Ev," he says just before he kisses me.

"I love you too, Stafford."

There couldn't be a more perfect place for him to propose. The last time we were here together, we made a marriage pact, never believing we'd actually follow through. Now, fourteen years later, we're back, vowing to share our lives forever. My soulmate was right in front of me all along, and now that he's mine, I'm never letting him go.

34

CASH

TWO WEEKS LATER

EVERLY IS NEXT TO ME at the conference table, chewing on her lower lip, eyes fixed on the doorway.

I take her hand in mine and can't help but smile as I admire her ring. She's worn it since our Vegas wedding, but its significance means more now that she's said yes to my proposal.

It was meant to be when I saw the old Miller house for sale a couple of months ago. I purchased the property from an investor who was eager to sell. While remodeling a house in that timeframe is nearly impossible for most people, being a billionaire has its advantages. With access to expedited permits and fast-tracked labor, along with a network of connections through Stafford Holdings, I made it happen.

Luckily the contractor was able to revise the plans to adjust for how Everly described the place, allowing us to turn it into her dream home.

Once I saw the outcome, it felt like the right place to pop the question. Something tells me we'll spend a lot of time in Aspen Grove, so I'm glad we now have a house there to call our own.

"Don't worry," I whisper in Everly's ear. "Everything will be fine."

"I know it will." She squeezes my hand.

Harrison and Dylan occupy the seats on my right, with August and Liam on Everly's left. Today, the Stafford Holdings and Townstead International acquisition is being finalized. We all flew into New York because it was the most central location.

My phone buzzes, and I discreetly take it out of my pocket.

Mom's Favorites Group Chat

Mom: Is the deal finalized yet?

Presley: Yeah, it's so not fair that Harrison wouldn't let me be there.

Mom: Sweetheart, you don't work for Stafford Holdings.

Presley. I know. Last night I was seriously tempted to temporarily quit Sinclair Group and join the company for the day so Harrison couldn't deny my request.

Mom: That was a clever idea.

Presley: I know, right?

Cash: Are you two done? Richard will be here any minute and I can't be distracted.

Presley: Can't you give us a play-by-play?

Cash: No.

Mom: Your brothers didn't text me back this morning. Will you please tell them to reply?

Cash: Mom, we're literally about to finalize a major business deal.

Mom: I didn't mean right now. Just as soon as the meeting is over.

Presley: Just tell Mom you'll do it, or she'll never stop.

Everly looks over my shoulder at my phone, chuckling when she reads the text thread on the screen.

"How do I get added to that group chat?" she chuckles. "Your mom and Presley are so entertaining."

I blink at her in surprise. "You want to?"

She nods. "Yeah, I do. We should add Marlow too if she's interested."

"I'll have Presley add you both after the meeting," I promise.

Cash: Everly wants to join the group chat, and she said we should add Marlow, too.

Presley: This is the best news. Just wait, Cash, we're totally going to gang up on you.

Mom: Presley. Be nice.

Cash: I think it's time I follow Harrison and Dylan's lead and exit the chat.

Presley: No way! It wouldn't be fun without having you here to pick on.

Cash: I have to go.

Presley: Text us after the meeting!

Mom: Yes, and don't forget to remind your brothers to text me back.

I turn my ringer off and stash my phone in my pocket just as Richard opens the door. The atmosphere shifts when he steps inside the conference room and frowns when he sees everyone seated on one side of the table, clearly displeased that we're here first.

"What are you all doing here?" he barks at Everly, August, and Liam. "I wasn't told you'd be present. And where is my legal team? They were supposed to be here at nine." He checks his watch.

"I asked the Townstead and Stafford lawyers to come at ten so we could have a little chat first," Harrison states calmly.

That's a lie. They aren't coming. Assuming everything goes as planned, the paperwork will be sent to both teams and filed by the end of the day. No legal teams required... just one ruthless lawyer.

"You had no authority to do that," Richard hisses, his fists clenched in anger.

"Sit down, Richard," Harrison says in a tone that leaves no room for disobedience. "You're testing my patience."

Richard gapes at him, then sits on the other side of the table despite his reservations. He grits his teeth, visibly annoyed at being ordered around by someone twenty years his junior.

"Well, I'm here. What the hell do you want to talk about?" Richard snaps.

"This is Dawson Tate." Harrison gestures to the man seated at the head of the table, reclining in his chair with his hands folded on his lap. "He's my legal counsel."

"Why should I care?" Richard demands.

Last week, Dawson reached out to Harrison to confirm Landon's termination. Harrison saw it as an opportunity to get Dawson's advice on dealing with Richard. For a pretty penny, Dawson provided his guidance and devised a strategy to confront Richard.

Dawson is six foot four with a chiseled jawline, high cheekbones, and a straight, aristocratic nose. He's dressed in a custom-tailored suit with silver cufflinks and polished black leather shoes. His lips form a thin line, and his piercing blue eyes are cold and calculating as he observes Richard like a predator.

Harrison has a commanding presence, but Dawson's is meant to instill fear, and it's working.

He rises from his seat with a folder in his hand and strides toward Richard, perching on the table next to him.

"You might not know me, but I'm well acquainted with you," he states smoothly, holding the dossier up for Richard to see. "Someone's been a naughty boy." He clicks his tongue in mock disapproval, flipping through the documents.

"Embezzlement, tax evasion, kickbacks—should I go on?" he asks rhetorically.

"You hid it well, but the Stafford team is the best. You were desperate for this acquisition because you're hemorrhaging money." Dawson's tone turns icy. "You tried to deceive my client, which means you've made an enemy of me. And as you'll soon learn, my enemies don't fare well, Richard."

I swear I can hear Richard gulp in fear from here. Even I have a chill down my spine, and I'm not the one Dawson is confronting. I wish I could have been there when he fired Landon. I'm sure he gave an epic performance.

"My lawyers won't stand for this type of scare tactic," Richard declares, his voice wavering.

"Call your legal team. Be sure to tell them Dawson Tate sends his regards. I'm itching to make someone cry today." He smirks as he pulls out his phone.

"What are you doing?" Richard asks, sounding panicked.

Dawson shrugs. "I figured my friend at the FBI might be interested in hearing all about your extracurricular activities. Do you want to tell him yourself?" He holds out the phone.

"Hold on a minute," Richard says, turning red in the face. "There's no need for that. I'm sure we can talk this through."

"Now we're getting somewhere," Dawson says, his voice thick with sarcasm. "I'll let Harrison do the honors." He leans forward to straighten Richard's tie, tugging it tighter around his neck before returning to his seat.

Harrison pushes a hefty stack of papers across the table to Richard. "I'm cutting my offer for Townstead International by half," he says, with no sign of sympathy. "Given the extensive damage you've caused, it's a fair deal."

"That's outrageous," Richard blusters. "There's no way I'm selling it to you for that price."

"Does that mean Dawson should call his friend?" Harrison motions to Dawson, who sets his phone on the table in a silent challenge.

"This is extortion," Richard hisses.

It's remarkable how easily he can mistreat others, even stealing from his own family, but when he's confronted with his actions, he doesn't want to face the repercussions.

"Harrison's offer beats going to prison, wouldn't you say?" Dawson interrupts. "Trust me, I've been there. It's not all that it's cracked up to be."

I don't know if he's telling the truth, but it only adds to his intimidation factor. It's puzzling that he and Harrison are friends. I can't picture them letting loose at a bar and sharing jokes over a beer. I'm wondering if Dawson even knows how to smile.

Richard pushes up out of his seat and points at Everly. "This is all your fault. If you'd kept your feelings out of that marriage of yours, none of this would have happened." He's lost all sense of logic, only focused on causing the most damage on his way out.

Oh, fuck no.

As I rise from my chair, Everly catches my arm. "I got this," she says, her voice steady.

I nod, sitting back in my chair.

She stands up, placing her hands on the conference table, and locks eyes with her dad.

"Listen carefully, Richard. I'm only going to say this once." It's the first time I've heard her use his first name. "The only reason you're not being dragged out in handcuffs right now is because I will not allow Liam, August, or myself to pay for your mistakes. We've done everything you've asked, and you went behind our backs." Her gaze is cutting as she speaks. "Here's what's going to happen. You will sign on the dotted line and get the hell out of here. And if you *ever* contact me or anyone else that matters to me, Dawson will make sure you never see the light of day again."

Dawson has his arms folded across his chest, his lips curving into a sickly-sweet smile.

"You can't do this to me, I'm your father," Richard sputters with false bravado.

"No, you're nothing but a coward," Everly retorts. "A father protects and supports his family. He doesn't use them for his own financial gain. You lost the right to call yourself my dad a long time ago. It just took me a while to come to terms with it."

I blink rapidly, my heart swelling with pride, as I watch my determined wife stand up to the man who's mistreated her for years. The unyielding fire in her eyes is a testament to her inner strength and resolve to never let him intimidate her again.

Richard's eyes dart between Liam and August, looking for support that's not coming.

"Are you going to sit there and let this happen after everything I've done for you both?" he demands, his voice rising with each word.

Liam lets out a humorless laugh. "What have you ever done for us? You've overworked us while taking all the credit and have taken advantage of our mom since the day you got married. Give it up, Richard. It's over."

As it happens, Liam and August's mom filed for divorce last week after she caught him trying to withdraw a substantial sum from her bank account.

Dawson slides a stack of documents across the table toward Richard. "This is your only opportunity," he warns. "If you don't sign, the deal disappears, and I'll make sure law enforcement is here before you can walk out the front door."

We all watch with tense anticipation while Richard reads through and signs each document. With each passing minute, his face flushes crimson, betraying his growing agitation. When he finishes signing the last page, he throws the pen down in fury.

"I hope you're satisfied knowing you've robbed a man of his livelihood," he spits in anger.

Harrison clenches his jaw. "No, Richard, you did that to yourself. You're lucky I gave you anything at all. Now get out of here. You're no longer welcome at any Stafford or Townstead building."

Richard's expression hardens into a mask of resentment. "I hope you're happy," he snarls, his gaze pointed directed at Everly.

"I am. Now, get out," she states with finality as she points to the door.

Richard shoves his chair back, storming out and slamming the conference room door behind him.

"Damn, Everly, that was impressive." August gives her a round of applause. "Thank god that's finally over."

Everly sinks into her seat, sighing in relief.

I place my hand on her knee. "Are you okay?"

She nods. "Never been better," she assures me with a soft smile.

"That was hot as fuck," I whisper in her ear.

"I've been waiting for the right moment to confront him," Everly says. "It felt good to finally have the chance."

Harrison walks over to Dawson, offering him a terse nod. "Thanks for your help."

It's almost painful watching them interact. None of my friends are this formal, even when they're doing business. But then again, when they're both grumpy billionaire workaholics who don't know how to have any fun, or maybe they do?

Harrison pulls a white envelope from his suit pocket and hands it to Dawson.

"Your sister-in-law seemed to have everything under control at the end there." Dawson gestures toward Everly as he puts the envelope in his briefcase. "My paralegal will deliver these documents to the Townstead lawyers and file the paperwork by the end of the day."

On his way out, he glances back at Harrison. "Don't forget, you and your brothers owe me two favors—one for this and one for Landon."

Everly's brows knit together in confusion.

"I'll explain once we're alone," I promise her.

35

EVERLY

I STEP INSIDE THEO'S TEST kitchen in London, watching him whisk together eggs and parmesan cheese.

He glances up and smiles at me. "Hey there, you're just in time. I'm testing a carbonara sauce for our Italian menu and need a taste tester."

"Oh, thank god, I'm starving." I pull up a barstool as I watch him work.

Cash is meeting me here as soon as he finishes at the office. He had a call with Harrison and Dylan this afternoon that he couldn't miss.

"How does it feel to be Senior Vice President of Townstead International?" Theo asks with a proud smile as he sprinkles pepper into the mixture.

"It's fantastic," I say, grinning from ear to ear.

The week since the acquisition was finalized has been a whirlwind. My dad had to cut ties with the company, and I can't name a single person who felt sad to see him go. He let greed get the better of him, and it cost him everything.

The looming threat of jail will keep him out of my life, and I'm okay with that. The last shred of hope that he could shift his mindset died when he tried blaming me for his mistakes. In that moment, I realized he would never change. There was something cathartic about finally standing up to him after years of letting him beat me down. It felt liberating to put him in his place, knowing he'd face the consequences of his reckless choices alone.

While my dad's life is imploding, mine has never been better. When Cash and I got back from our visit to Aspen Grove, we returned to a fully furnished apartment, thanks to Marcus. My favorite part was the beautiful daffodil painting in our living room from Marlow's latest collection. She's a famous artist known for her floral pieces, and I'm honored to have her artwork in our home.

"I'm sorry you had to handle Richard and Mom by yourself all those years," Theo says, his eyes downcast. "I should never have ignored the situation the way I did."

I lean over to place my hand on his arm. "I was the one who chose not to tell you what was going on and should have confided in you instead."

Recently, I've learned that I don't have to face anything alone. Between Cash, Theo, and my found families, I have more love and support than I could ever ask for.

"Have you talked to Mom lately?" Theo asks while adding pancetta to a hot, oiled pan, the meat sizzling when it hits the surface.

"As far as I know, she's still in Miami. Hopefully it works out with Mark, the surgeon." I'm not interested in rekindling a relationship with her, but that doesn't mean I want her to be unhappy.

"Yeah, maybe," Theo says skeptically.

The day after the acquisition was complete, I came clean to him about supporting our mom all these years. The next morning, I woke up to a notification that her house and car were paid off. Then I received an email from Main Street Market in Aspen Grove saying she has a large credit there, allowing her to get groceries whenever she's in town.

Theo didn't want her to continue to be a constant burden on me. Cash would have done the same if I had asked, but he understood this was the one aspect of my life Theo and I needed to handle together.

"You've been my rock since we were kids, Theo. You're the best brother anyone could ask for."

"You mean the best older brother, right?" He smirks.

Here we go again.

"You were born two minutes before me," I remind him, holding up two fingers. "It doesn't count."

"It absolutely does." He grins as he mixes the sauce in with the pancetta, the rich aroma filling the air.

"What smells so good?" Cash asks from the doorway.

He's wearing slacks and a white button-down shirt with the top two buttons undone. With his tousled hair, he's utterly irresistible.

He has on the new bracelet I gave him when we got back to London. I found one online that looks similar to the one he's worn for the past fourteen years, which we're keeping in a box in the closet along with our marriage pact.

He comes over to stand behind me, wrapping his arms around my shoulders. I tilt my head and kiss him.

"I missed you," he murmurs against my lips.

"I missed you too," I say.

"Do you guys ever take a break from the PDA?" Theo teases from his spot at the stove.

"I'm afraid not," I say, unable to keep the smile off my face.

Thanks to Cash, I'm happier than I've ever been, and it's impossible to hide.

"Think you can keep your hands to yourselves for five minutes?" he quips as he plates the tagliatelle carbonara and garnishes it with parsley and pecorino Romano.

"Oh my god, this looks delicious," I gush when he places a dish in front of me.

"I'm glad you think so," Theo says as he serves himself some pasta. "How are the wedding plans coming along?"

"Johanna, Presley, and Marlow are handling most of the planning. All I told them is that I'd prefer something small and simple."

They called me the other day and offered to take care of everything. With my busy work schedule and wanting to spend my free time with Cash, I was glad to pass on a sizable portion of the planning to them. Since Cash and I are already legally married, the wedding is mainly for our families.

Cash scoffs.

"What?" I ask, casting him a sidelong glance.

"Ev, if you're wanting simplicity, involving my mom and Presley wasn't the best idea. It's the first wedding in the family, and I guarantee they'll go overboard on all fronts." He sits next to me and pulls his plate of pasta closer.

Now that I think about it, he may be right. When I suggested a dress shop in Aspen Grove, Presley texted me an hour later, informing me she had booked an appointment for early next month at an exclusive wedding boutique in New York. I don't need an expensive dress, but I'm looking forward to making memories with my new family.

"As long as you join me at the end of the aisle, I don't mind what the venue looks like," I say with conviction.

What matters most is being able to exchange our wedding vows surrounded by our loved ones.

For years, I dismissed the idea of a happily ever after. Love seemed like a fairy tale for those who didn't know better. Then Cash came along with his battle-worn armor and the scars from his past.

I think about the boy who brought me a milkshake and the man he's become. His kindness, patient heart, and sense of humor have shown me that true love does exist, and now I'm lucky enough to call him mine.

Getting a husband didn't turn out like I expected, but now I know what happens when a billionaire gets a bride...

She becomes the center of his universe, and he becomes the center of hers.

EPILOGUE

CASH

THE MONTH SINCE THE ACQUISITION was finalized has been a whirlwind.

Everly, August, and Liam have seamlessly transitioned into their new roles at Townstead International. They have weekly calls with Harrison to touch base but handle the daily operations.

I've been busy onboarding several new hires for the Stafford Holdings London branch, and I finally gave Marcus the go-ahead to decorate my office. When Everly visited me at lunch last week, she was pleasantly surprised to find the place fully furnished. Her favorite decoration was the photo of us in the pink Cadillac from our wedding night in Vegas, set in a vintage gold frame.

With Fallon in the process of moving to New York, Everly decided to enroll us in a couple's cooking class. However, after mixing up baking soda and baking powder when learning to make cookies and burning a lasagna in the third session—causing an evacuation of the entire building—we cut our losses. Instead, most evenings, I pick her up from work, and we grab a bite to eat on the way home.

I like the simplicity of our daily routine and am grateful for every moment spent with the woman I love.

However, tonight is the exception.

We're in Aspen Grove to celebrate our union. Everly and I agreed a vow renewal made the most sense, considering we're already legally married. We wanted to keep it simple, surrounded by the people we love. Thankfully we were able to convince my mom and Presley to go along with our plans for a small affair.

The sun dips below the horizon, casting a warm glow on my parents' backyard that has been transformed into a whimsical, romantic setting. A canopy of fairy lights glows above several rows of chairs, and lanterns line the path leading to a floral arch made of daffodils and hyacinth.

My parents are sitting in the front row, where my mom is already dabbing her eyes with a tissue, and my dad has his arm wrapped around her shoulder. They are the perfect example of true love. After thirty-six years, they still look at each other with unconditional adoration, and I feel so lucky to call them my parents.

Jack and Presley are seated next to my parents. Presley adjusts Jack's tie and when she's finished, he kisses her forehead. She leans against his shoulder, looking up at me with a smile full of pride and love.

Dylan and Marlow are in the second row holding hands. Waffles and the puppies are in the playroom in my parents' basement. Everly said she didn't mind if they were here, but I didn't want to chance them causing a mess. I wanted tonight to be perfect.

August and Liam are in the back row. Their love and support for Everly is the one silver lining in all she went through with Richard.

Despite the tension in their relationship, Everly extended an invitation to her mom. However, shortly after she replied with her regrets. She found out Mark was married with a family, and moved on to a dentist she met online, and they're traveling Asia together.

Everly was relieved she didn't have to worry about her mom on her special day. For now, she's content with minimal contact, but if she ever does decide she wants her mom more involved in her life, I'll support her.

I'm fidgeting with my bracelet when Harrison leans over to whisper in my ear. "Are you okay?" It was fitting to have him officiate our vow renewal ceremony since he was a key piece in bringing us together.

I grin. "I've never been better."

"Good, because here they come," he says, nodding toward the house.

Lola comes down the aisle first, dressed in a pink tutu dress that swishes with each step. She grins as she tosses handfuls of daffodil petals from her basket.

Everly and I decided against having a wedding party since we're only exchanging vows, but we couldn't tell Lola no when she asked to be our flower girl.

She waves at me with a big grin on her face, and I give her a thumbs up. When she gets to the end of the aisle she hands her basket to my mom before going to sit with Dylan and Marlow.

When I glance up, I'm left speechless when I see Everly and Theo walk toward us, her hand resting on his arm.

She's wearing a cream silk slip dress paired with a pair of open-toed heels. Her hair is loosely gathered into a bun with a few tendrils left out to frame her face.

She's perfect.

It's as if time stands still, and everything around us fades away—Everly's presence is all-consuming. She has captured my heart and soul, and they're hers to keep.

As they approach the front row, my patience dissolves, and I stride forward, closing the distance between us.

"I'll take it from here," I tell Theo.

He chuckles at my impatience before leaning over to kiss Everly on the cheek. "Take good care of her."

"I will, *brother.*" I wink.

My attention is back on my bride as I guide her to the floral arch.

"You sure you want to do this, wifey?" I whisper in her ear.

"This is just a formality, hubby. You're already mine," she sasses.

"Yes, I am."

Once we're in front of Harrison, he addresses our families. "Thank you for coming to celebrate Cash and Everly. They've each prepared vows and would like to share them with you now," he says.

Everly's eyes grow wide when I pull out a napkin from Willow Creek Café with my vows written on the back.

"I love you, Everly Stafford," I start with a smile. "Since we were kids, I've dreamed of making you mine, and now it's finally a reality. The last few months together have been the best of my life. You're my home. Every day spent together will be filled with learning, laughter, and love. I promise to cherish and protect you always, to support you in all your endeavors, and to love you unconditionally." I gently wipe away a tear trickling down Everly's cheek.

She looks at Harrison, who takes an envelope from his suit pocket and gives it to her.

"Thanks for holding onto this for me," she says.

"Sure thing," He replies with a smile.

A grin spreads across my face when Everly opens the envelope and takes out a napkin from Willow Creek Café with her wedding vows written on it.

"There's no one else I'd rather spend the rest of my life with. You're my safe haven. The one person who braves every morning with me before I've had my daily caffeine fix, and who also supports my shoe addiction." She reaches out to take my hand. "I pledge to be your partner in all things, and to be your unwavering support during your highs and lows. I love you, Stafford."

I tilt her chin so she's looking at me. "I love you so much, Ev, more than I'll ever be able to put into words."

After the vow renewal ceremony, we mingled with our family while waiting for dinner to be ready. Theo took charge of coordinating the catering and flew Fallon in, only trusting her to handle the food for Everly's special day.

Everly is inside changing into something more comfortable, and I'm with Harrison on the back deck, enjoying a plate full of appetizers while waiting for the main course.

"Have you met Fallon yet?" I ask.

He shakes his head. "No, but I'd like to. My secretary interviewed her last week, and says she'll be a good fit as my private chef."

"That's great news."

Fallon steps out of my parents' house carrying a charcuterie board, overflowing with artisan cheeses, cured meats, fresh fruits, and crackers. When she looks our way, I wave her over.

Harrison has his phone out and is busy typing when she approaches.

"Is everything okay?" she asks.

"Yeah, the food is fantastic. You really outdid yourself."

"Thank you."

"I wanted to officially introduce you to my brother, Harrison."

He looks up when he hears his name, and his mouth turns into a thin line when he sees Fallon. "It's *you*," he states coldly.

Fallon's eyes narrow, a smirk playing on her lips. "Cash, you forgot to mention your brother's charming ego."

Harrison scoffs. "Is sarcasm part of our standard approach with all of your potential clients? No wonder you had to move to another continent to start your new business."

My eyes widen in surprise. Despite his serious demeanor, he isn't usually this cutting or openly critical of anyone.

"At least I'm not the one suffering from a case of superiority complex," she quips.

My eyes dart between them, feeling the tension thick in the air. I'm confused since Harrison said he hadn't been introduced to Fallon yet.

"I take it you two have met before?"

"Yes," they say in unison, their heated stares remaining locked on each other.

Fallon breaks the silence first, clearing her throat. "Tell your assistant thank you for the interview, but you'll have to find another private chef, *Mr. Stafford*. I don't work for boorish narcissists," she states flatly. "Now, if you'll excuse me, I have to get back to work." She marches across the deck, her hands clenched at her side.

"What the hell was that?" I ask Harrison.

"Nothing," he mutters.

I raise a brow. "That was definitely something."

"It's nothing for you to worry about. You heard her. She doesn't want to work for me, so case closed."

"Uh, Harrison. I'm not so sure you'll have a choice in the matter."

He furrows his brow. "Why not?"

I nod toward the back door where our mom has cornered Fallon, shooting glances our way every few seconds with a mischievous smile on her face. "Because I think Mom is already scheming how to get you two down the aisle next," I taunt.

He rubs his temples. "Jesus Christ, she's relentless," he mutters. "She's wasting her time. Even if Fallon was the last woman on earth, I'd never date her, let alone marry her."

"Let's dial down the hostility, shall we? How did you two meet?"

Before he can respond, his phone rings.

"This is Harrison," he answers coldly. "Already? Fuck, you're serious." He pauses, running his hand through his hair. "Yeah, yeah, I know. My brothers and I will take care of it."

He abruptly ends the call and turns to face me. "That was Dawson. He's calling in his first favor."

Oh, this is just great. For all I know, he's asking for help to bury a body or something equally as terrifying.

I shrug. "Everly and I leave for a month-long honeymoon in the morning. So, you and Dylan will have to handle this one on your own."

"You're the reason we owe him in the first place," Harrison mutters.

I smirk. "You were the one who set me and Everly up, so technically, this is your fault."

"Fine, I'll handle this one, but you're helping with the second favor."

"Yeah, sure."

For the next month, my sole focus is lounging on a beach with my wife and indulging her every whim.

Want to see what happens during Cash & Everly's honeymoon when they get a surprise that will turn their lives upside down for the better? Type this link into your browser to read the extended epilogue for *If You Give a Billionaire a Bride*: https://bookhip.com/amcp6q14wz

Thank you for taking the time to read *If You Give a Billionaire a Bride*. If you enjoyed this book, please consider leaving a review on your preferred platform(s) of choice. It's the best compliment I can receive as an author, and it makes it easier for other readers to find my books.

Harrison's book is the most anticipated in the Aspen Grove series, and I need a little extra time to give his story the attention it deserves. His book will be released in January 2025.

In the meantime, *When You Give a Lawyer a Kiss*, a short standalone age-gap, workplace romance featuring Dawson, will be released in September 2024. Harrison and Fallon will make several cameos, giving you a sneak peek at their enemies-to-lovers romance. Thank you for loving the Stafford family just as much as I do!

ALSO BY ANN EINERSON

ASPEN GROVE SERIES

If You Give a Grump a Holiday Wishlist - Holiday Novella
If You Give a Single Dad a Nanny
Harrison & Fallon's Book – Coming January 2025

STANDALONE RELATED TO
THE ASPEN GROVE SERIES

When You Give a Lawyer a Kiss – Coming September 2024

STANDALONES

The Spotlight
Forgive or Forget Me

ACKNOWLEDGMENTS

THERE ARE SO MANY PEOPLE who made this book possible, and I can't thank you all enough for your love, kindness, and support. If You Give a Billionaire a Bride wouldn't have been possible without each and every one of you.

To my readers—For rooting for me from the very beginning and motivating me to keep writing even on the days I think this might be all for nothing. Your love for Cash & Everly means everything.

To my ARC team—Even before you saw the cover, read the book, or fell in love with Cash & Everly's love story, you gave If You Give a Billionaire a Bride a chance. Thank you for all your thoughtful messages, posts, stories, reviews, and comments. Your endless love and support never ceases to amaze me.

To Bryanna—For being the best co-worker and collaborator. You make the day-to-day of being a writer so much more fun and far less lonely, and am grateful for your friendship always.

To Autumn—I'm so lucky our paths crossed. Thanks for your blunt honesty when I need to hear it and your dedication to helping me achieve my goals. I couldn't do this without you.

To Tabitha and Kaity—Words cannot adequately express my gratitude for you. Thanks for putting up with my endless DMs, questions, and concerns. This story would never have made it down on paper without you cheering me on from the sidelines.

To Paula and Britt—I couldn't have asked for a better editing team. I'm grateful for your expertise and for pushing me to write a story worth reading.

To Jess, Kenz, and Madison—Thank you for helping to spread the word about If You Give a Billionaire a Bride and for your creative input. Your ability to bring my vision to life is invaluable, and I'm truly grateful.

To Sarah—For designing the most adorable cover for this book. It was love at first sight and it makes my heart so happy that my readers love it just as much as I do.

To Caroline, Wren, Lauren Brooke, Brenna, Meghan, Jessa Lynn and Hunter, Zae, Kat, Diana, Ada, Danie, Kelsey and Claire—Your honest, detailed, and candid feedback drove me to create the best possible version of this book. Thank you!

To Sandea, Roxan, and Randy—You taught me to believe in myself and to chase my dreams, no matter the cost. I love you always.

To Kyler—Thank you for supporting my insane work schedule while in the midst of moving across the world. Without you my dream of becoming a full-time author wouldn't have come true.

ABOUT THE AUTHOR

ANN EINERSON IS THE AUTHOR of imperfect contemporary love stories that will keep you invested until the very last page.

Ann writes dirty-mouthed heroes who love to spoil their women, often fall first, and enjoy going toe-to-toe with their fierce heroines. Each of Ann's books features a found family, an ode to her love of travel, and serves plenty of banter and spice. Her novels are inspired by the ample supply of sticky notes she always has on hand to jot down the stories that live rent-free in her mind.

When she's not writing, Ann enjoys spoiling her chatty pet chickens, listening to her dysfunctional playlists, and going for late-night treadmill runs. She lives in Michigan with her husband.

KEEP IN TOUCH WITH ANN EINERSON

Website: www.anneinerson.com

Newsletter: www.anneinerson.com/newsletter-signup

Instagram: www.instagram.com/authoranneinerson

TikTok: www.tiktok.com/@authoranneinerson

Amazon: www.amazon.com/author/anneinerson

Goodreads:
www.goodreads.com/author/show/29752171.Ann_Einerson

Printed in Great Britain
by Amazon